VICTIM OR THE CRIME:

THE DAY BEFORE JERRY DIED

A GRATEFUL DEAD THRILLER

By

Paul Sanders

Copyright 2022

BOOKS BY PAUL SANDERS

SECRET LIFE OF A JUROR: VOIR DIRE – THE DOMESTIC VIOLENCE QUERY

Copyright 2018

Awards:

BANQUET OF CONSEQUENCES: THE CARNATION MURDERS TRIAL OF MICHELE ANDERSON – A Juror's Plight

Copyright 2017

WHY NOT KILLER HER: THE JODI ARIAS DEATH PENALTY TRIAL – A Juror's Perspective

Copyright 2015

BRAIN DAMAGE: A JUROR'S TALE – The Hammer Killing Trial

Copyright 2014

Available as eBook, Paperback and AudioBook

And so I wrestle with the angel

To see who'll reap the seeds I sow

Am I the driver or the driven?

Will I be damned to the forgiven?

"Victim or the Crime" by The Grateful Dead

Dedicated to the memory

of

Shanna Hogan

With special acknowledgements to:

Grace Sanders

Larry Sanders

KC Wuraftic

Laura Rivers

Mary-Margaret Spallone

Gloria Norris

Mr. and Mrs. Clifton

Brad Palmer

Kelly Hemmerling

Gary Frizelle

Dan Healy

The Grateful Dead

David Gans

Robert Hunter

Cyndey Webster

Edward McClintock

Michelle F. Garamella

Michael Moore

Rebecca Madden-Sharpe

David Dieroff

Kevin Elde – Seattle Computers

Goran Tovilovic – bookclaw.com

Kerr Lordygan - Audible

CONTENTS

PROLOGUE

FRANKLIN'S TOWER

Fear is the harbinger of strength.

Dan let the words tumble over and over again softly in his brain as he paced in circles at the bottom of his parents' driveway. He wasn't worried that they would catch him because he was a good two hundred yards from the house. Further, it was late evening and he doubted that they would see him in the semi-darkness. If seen, his car was parked across the street and would allow him a fast and easy exit before they could figure out who this strange person was. Besides, what were the odds that they would recognize him?

This was the sixth time in six weeks that Dan found himself peering up at the mansion not being able to draw the strength to walk up that long, winding driveway. He knew that to a stranger he might have looked oddly curious as he occasionally kicked at the loose gravel bits below his feet, his hands tucked in his pockets and his collar turned up to brace himself against the slight chill in the air. Even though it was early August, Northern Michigan was always prone to a cool Artic snap. The weather report said a cold front was expected to move through the area later that evening bringing cooler temperatures and a brisk wind. The full moon was occasionally obscured by fast moving black clouds. Dan couldn't help but think that it was a sign of bad times to come. He tried to shake the thought as he risked smoking a quick cigarette.

For a brief moment, he played with the idea of hopping in his car and heading back to California. It would be easy to hit the open road, his head held high and his nose to the wind. That was exactly where he had been for the last fifteen years and, for a moment he felt that was exactly where he belonged. But, he had been seeing a local psychiatrist for the last six months in preparation for this moment and he wasn't sure how he would feel if he just walked away.

Fear is the harbinger of resilience then strength, he edited in his mind as he inhaled his cigarette deeply.

Dan thought it was strange that after fifteen years of not speaking to his family it was he who felt it necessary to go see them. After all, they were the ones who had asked his brother and him to leave when they were seventeen. He also felt a certain amount of resentment that he was the one who had to see a shrink and not they. He felt like a little kid at times, as if he were a problem child seeing a counselor for some sort of mental defect that he could not begin to comprehend.

Suddenly, Dan heard the loud hum of an electric garage door being opened. He almost jumped out of his skin. He flicked his cigarette to the street and dashed to his car. Before opening the door, he looked up the driveway to make sure he wasn't being seen. Noting that no one was in sight, he quickly opened the door to his Cougar and hopped in. Breath rushed out of him in short bursts as the adrenaline of fear coursed through his veins. Inside, he knew his fears were unfounded considering that he was too old now to be hit by his father or mother. But, unfounded or not, the deep set fears were still there just like a spider who clings to its web during a rainstorm.

He crouched down in the front seat and hoped the light from the single streetlamp behind him would not give away his presence. He peeked out the side window as he heard the sound of plastic wheels grinding on the pavement, slowly coming toward him. As the figure emerged in the dim light, he quickly deduced that it was trash night in the affluent neighborhood, many of the neighbors already having their cans standing out like soldiers guarding the street. Dan waited as he tried to figure out who was rolling the cans.

His stomach lurched at the sight of his mother, now fifteen years older.

Her hair was tied up in a characteristic bun and much grayer than it once was. She appeared to walk a lot slower than he remembered. He was also a little surprised that it wasn't his father wheeling the trash out as he always did every Thursday night for years. Although, he may not even have been home since his medical profession took him out of town quite often. Or, God forbid, he had passed away and Dan was none the wiser. He pushed the thought away as fast as it had come. There was no point in burying himself in irrational fears. He had enough fears without letting his imagination make the situation even scarier.

Dan watched his mother wrestle with the garbage can, feeling guilty that he could not step out of the car and give her a hand. It just wasn't the right moment to reappear in her life. Besides, he had no idea how she would react. Would she welcome him with open arms, or would she ask him to leave, threatening to call the police? He felt as if he were sixteen years old, afraid of being caught for some sort of heinous crime committed in high school.

Moments later, his mother tightened her house robe around her, looked up toward the threatening skies and made her slow ascent back up the driveway. Dan played with the thought of starting the car and taking off before her inevitable return with another trashcan. Unfortunately, he saw a dark Lincoln Town car bearing down on him from the opposite way. He could tell it was a Lincoln by the large grill and headlights. He knew his cars well since he had been collecting Hot Wheels for twenty years, a hobby that he and his brother, Mark, enjoyed immensely.

Instead of flying past him, the car slowed down when it hit 1050 Allouez, stopping for about thirty seconds. Then, the engine roaring, it took off and squealed around the bend behind him. Dan passed it off for kids playing around as they had done for years in that neighborhood, especially toward the Wilcox family. Not a moment later, his mother parked a second can in front. Dan ducked when she paused to look directly at him. He held his breath without having any clue what to say if she should approach his blatantly obvious car. His heart pounded in his chest as he tried to keep his panic at bay.

Dan waited.

After awhile, he summoned up the courage to take a look. All he saw was her backside as she walked up the driveway, apparently oblivious to his existence.

Dan moved fast, not wanting to risk her inquisition and started the car, pausing only to light up a cigarette shakily. He slammed the car in drive, and accelerated his way out of there, gravel spewing behind him. His heart thudded in his chest and he strained to get a hold of his breath.

Jesus, was he afraid she was going to beat the shit out of him? It was during moments like these that he thought he was throwing his money away on a therapist. It seemed to have served no other purpose than for him to become an oddball Peeping Tom spying on his house. Why couldn't he take that last step? Frustrated and shaking, he drove back to his rented home on Lakeshore Drive, bordering the dark blue waters of Lake Superior.

The moment he got into the house, he went directly to his bar and poured himself a Stoli and Tonic, heavy on the vodka. Within five minutes, he was pouring himself another, not even bothering to sit down. He was too wound up even to attempt to relax. It seemed better to let the alcohol numb his senses. Dan toyed with the thought of calling Diana, his psychiatrist, and then thought better of it. This was not a crisis that demanded her immediate attention. Instead, he decided it might be a good time to call Mark.

If there was one consolation that Dan had gotten out of his childhood, it was his brother. For a good number of years after he had graduated from college and Mark had graduated from the Air Force, they had traveled all over the country, working odd jobs and enjoying life. For sometime, it had been good until Mark decided that he was going to pursue a professional career in the sky. Both of them had wanted to see California, so they figured that was the best place to start. The next thing they knew, Mark had a private pilot's license, then a multi-engine rating, after which he became a flight instructor, followed by his being accepted in a commercial flight school. Eleven years later, Mark had reached the skies as a full-time pilot for Delta Airlines. He had done remarkably well, for his being two years younger than Dan.

Dan, on the other hand, liked the feel and freedom of the open road. So, while working a plethora of odd jobs, he found himself buried at a typewriter doing what he always loved best, telling stories. Eventually, he created a detective by the name of Rusty Wallace and a small paperback company in New York picked up his series. The income from his paperback books gave him enough money to travel as much as he wanted, within the limitations that thirty thousand dollars a year allowed. Dan found himself following the Grateful Dead for many months in a row before returning to Southern California.

The two brothers remained close in spite of their different careers and lifestyles. Dan exchanged Dead tapes, Hot Wheels and stories with Mark while Mark provided free airfare to Dan. Each brother was determined to preserve his limited family relationship while also obtaining the most enjoyment out of life.

The most important gift they'd received in life was that they were not ever going to live at home again.

Dan decided to brush his teeth and wash his hair before calling his brother. He looked at his face in the mirror. His brown hair was past shoulder length but well maintained. His face was clean shaven like his brother's and, if he had his hair tied back, the brothers looked almost like twins, with their high cheekbones and strong cheek lines, affording them a good amount of luck with the ladies, although neither was married. Dan found that staying with a woman was constricting and not conducive to his lifestyle on the open road while Mark preferred the solidity of living with a lady, one of whom he'd been with the last five years.

Feeling refreshed, Dan walked to the kitchen and picked up the cordless telephone. He was just about to dial the number when he had second thoughts. He would have to explain where he had been for the last few months, which meant telling his brother that he was back in their hometown. He did not think that his brother would understand why he was there in the first place. As far as Mark was concerned, he had his own opinion about his parents, and there was nothing further to discuss, end of conversation. Dan could understand his brother's sentiments but every time it had been brought up over the years, Mark would quickly end the issue by steering the conversation another direction or he would simply say that he did not want to talk about it, brushing it under the carpet like an annoying piece of dirt. Well, Dan thought, if Mark didn't want to hear about it then so be it but Dan knew he had to make an attempt and that's what was important. It was that kind of honesty that had kept the two close over the years in spite of their opposing directions.

Dan dropped a Duralog in the fireplace and lit it. He turned down the lights in his expansive living room and watched the multicolored flames lick at the log while taking a stiff drink of his cocktail. As he fired up another Camel Light 100, a long forgotten memory emerged. The year had been 1979 and the time of season was midsummer.

The two boys were working on Mackinac Island, a resort island located in Lake Huron between upper and lower Michigan, when they decided to spend an evening together, a difficult endeavor since they were working at two different hotels. It was also the first summer that they had spent away from home. Since they were underage, they got someone to buy them a twelve pack of beer at Doud's Mercantile, and bicycled their way to a secluded spot on the water where they could drink and bullshit without being bothered by tourists. The Stroh's went down easy while the sun approached the horizon, orange fingers beginning to stretch across the sky while the water softly lapped at the rocky shore. As another beer was finished, they would toss the can in the water and bomb the hell out of it with beach pellets until either it sank or floated off out of range to some unknown destination, banged and bruised.

They had just finished sinking a can, no sooner cracking open two more, when Mark suddenly fell silent.

"What's wrong?" Dan asked after awhile.

"Nothing in particular," Mark answered pensively. "Matter of fact, all things considered. I suppose everything should be pretty good." He paused as he took a swallow. "We're out of hell, aren't we?"

Dan knew that hell and home were the same thing and there was no arguing that he was happy to be out of there, also. "So, why the glum look?" Dan asked as he skipped a flat white rock across the water.

Mark thought about it for a moment as he carefully selected his words.

"I'm not glum, exactly, just a little nervous is all. I know, I should be grateful about this newfound freedom but it's not exactly what I expected. I just got to thinking about how many years we went through the shit and how we thought it would never end and, just like that, our dream came true and it's over just like that."

"So, what's the problem?" Dan asked as he watched a seagull arch its wings across the orange tinged sky.

"The problem is simple. Now what?"

Dan looked at Mark and could see that he was genuinely serious. They both drank their beers for a minute without saying a word. Dan suspected that this might be one of the last times that the two-year difference between brothers, the distinction between the older brother and younger brother, would make a difference. The older brother had been expected to give an answer as if he was the mentor, the protector. It was a responsibility that Dan had always taken seriously.

Dan approached the issue carefully but firmly. "What do you want to be?"

"You know what I want to be," Mark answered testily.

"Well, tell me."

"This is stupid," Mark said quietly. He took a drink of his Stroh's and pulled himself up from the rocks. He walked over to the edge of the water, framing himself against the setting sun. "I want the sky," he said with his hand upraised.

"You want to fly," Dan filled in.

"Hmmm. I do, more than anything. Do you remember standing at Dad's airport when we were five or six years old? I was pretending I was Charles Lindbergh and you were my co-pilot and we were going to conquer the Atlantic Ocean together? Do you remember that?"

Dan smiled, remembering a time when they were three and half feet shorter. "Yeah, you put me in charge of serving coffee and lunch as if I was a stewardess or something."

"You were my co-pilot in my mind. I didn't know what a stewardess was then," Mark corrected. "Anyway, I got to thinking how we're really on our own now. There's no going back but there's also no one to go to. And how am I going to afford this dream of mine? Flying's expensive and I have no idea where I'm going to come up with that kind of money. If we had a normal family, I could call up Dad and ask for a loan just like a normal kid might ask his dad for the car keys. We haven't got that choice, though. We're on the street and I'm scared a little bit, that's all. I know what you'll say; things will be fine but you can't blame me for being nervous. What if I don't make it? What then?"

Dan let the words fall into a sea of silence as he tried to figure out the true and proper answer. The last swallow of beer ran down his throat as he tossed the empty can in the water. Without hesitation, the two young men sank the can with a pelting of rocks in a matter of minutes. They cracked the last two beers as the sun touched the horizon.

"You know what I think?" Dan asked. He didn't wait for an answer. He took a deep breath and continued. "I think that I could be President of The United States of America. I truly do. I have no clue how that could be done but I know it can be and if I set my mind to it, it'll happen. If you look at Dad, he came from a family where they built cars all day long and look what he did. He became a doctor, a pilot, a...."

"... mean bastard," Mark finished.

Dan cringed. Maybe their father wasn't the best example to use. "Good point," Dan said. "Sorry. I'm figuring it this way. If we got out of the home situation, then becoming anything we want, such as a President of the United States or a pilot, should be a walk in the park. Do you know where I'm coming from?"

"I suppose," Mark said, not wholly convinced. "Let me ask you, are you serious about this president stuff?"

"I think so," Dan said, "I really think so."

For some reason, up to that conversation Dan had always felt the responsible one. But as years had gone by, their roles had changed. It was as if Dan had become the younger brother and Mark the older brother, thanks to the minor troubles that Dan found himself with.

Over the years, Mark bailed Dan out of many a hairy situation. There was an incident where Mark had to loan Dan a beater car for the better part of a year because Dan's car was repossessed. Another time, Dan was busted with a half a joint at a Soldier's Field Chicago Dead show and Mark had to wire a good amount of money for bail. Dan couldn't count the number of times that Mark had helped Dan move when he was trying to get out of one live-in relationship or another. It seemed that Dan was always in some sort of trouble or another and Mark was there with a bucket scooping water. Dan knew that the dream of being President was long gone, since his reputation could not stand up in front of his brother, much less the country. But, they were still brothers and many things were left unsaid because of the thread that had bonded them so many years before, a thread that was as powerful and sure as the arrival of a new day.

Those thoughts and many others ran through Dan's mind as he watched the burning log and played with the telephone. He had to call his brother in Santa Barbara and tell him what he was about to do. So, without another moment's hesitation, he finally dialed the number. Since there was a three hour time difference, Dan knew that Mark would still be up, if he was in town, of course.

"Sparky's! Can I pour you one?" Mark's familiar voice answered.

"Yeah, man," Dan, responded in a disguised voice, "You guys carry any Hot Wheels. I'm looking for red-liners."

"Dan?" Mark questioned. "What's it been, three or four months? You're not in jail or anything, are you?"

"No, I'm not in jail. Thanks for caring," Dan said as if he was hurt at such a question. "I was just hanging out and I thought I'd call my brother. Is that okay with you? How are you doing?"

"I suppose I could be better but I could be worse, too. Hey, guess what? I'm finally into the big-time," Mark said proudly. "I'm fully certified for a 757. Can you believe that?"

"No shit?" Dan said, surprised. "How does it feel?"

"Night flights are still the best!"

One of the few moments they loved, as kids were the night flights. They would never forget the moments when Mom, Dad, their sister, and the two brothers would be on approach to some distant airfield in their Dad's Twin Comanche, late at night. The red and blue lights on the tip tanks would sparkle in Mark's eyes while they flew over a sea of city lights, the flaps down, signaling their descent. Mark would jump in quiet excitement as he listened to the tower give Dad the proper coordinates, wind-speed and weather conditions for landing. It felt and looked oddly like Christmas at night. Dan and Mark would relive each of their landings, both good and bad, anytime they had their Hot Wheels and toy planes out.

"I'm proud of you," Dan said genuinely, hardly believing that Mark had gone so far.

"Thanks, Dan," Mark said. "It's good to hear from you. So what are you up to, and don't make a novel out of it because Carrie's about to serve dinner?" he said in reference to his girlfriend.

Dan paused, doubting again whether he should break the mood by bringing it up. If he was going to tell Mark, he knew he had better keep the story short and sweet before he either backed out or Mark got upset. So, he just dove in and told him about the Dead shows and how he got to thinking that there's a world of people out there who care about each other like the family they should have had. Further, Dan said he had learned that forgiveness should be universal and there was no reason that they couldn't strive for some forgiveness in their family, regardless of the past. Finally, he told Mark about his psychiatrist and how he saw their mother earlier in the evening. He didn't mention the other fruitless visits, though, attempting to shorten the story.

"Did you get to talk to her?" Mark asked. His voice significantly subdued.

"No, I figured it was best to talk to you first."

"You don't need my approval or permission," Mark said firmly.

"I was not asking for your permission. I wanted you to know what was going on."

"Well, you do what you have to do but my opinion still holds."

"Meaning what?" Dan asked, sensing that the conversation had changed tone.

"Meaning that, in my mind, they're still dead," Mark answered.

Dan paused, after hearing what he had half expected Mark to say. "All I'm trying to tell you is that..."

Mark cut him off, saying, "All this is well and good. I love you because you're my brother but this is something that we'll never agree upon. As far as they go, I see no point in opening up old wounds. I've gone through a lot of work to be happy and I'm not about to risk their taking it away from me. Do you know where I'm coming from?"

"Yeah," Dan answered, defeated.

"I'm sorry, Dan. I really am," Mark said. Signaling the end of their discussion, Mark changed his tone immediately, "Hey, thanks for the Red Rocks and Cornell shows. Great quality!"

Dan smiled. At least they had the ability to be straight with each other without their disagreement getting in the way of who they were to each other. They ended the conversation, promising to stay in touch.

It looked like Dan would have to take a go at his parents alone, a thought he did not relish but one that he accepted without resentment. Maybe this was an older brother thing to do.

The next day, Dan had his car washed and drove to 1050 Allouez for the seventh time in as many weeks. This time, he was determined to follow through. Butterflies twisted in his stomach while a bottle of Evian served to keep the dryness in his mouth at bay. He turned up the Grateful Dead's, Franklin's Tower, and checked his face in the rearview mirror. He knew that he probably should have had his hair cut but he couldn't book an appointment in time. Besides, a haircut would only have been another detour in procrastination and he was afraid that if he had put it off any longer, he would have been on the road back to California.

Dan hoped that his parents' reaction would not be like Mark's. Had they been telling their friends that he and Mark were dead? He hoped not.

Suddenly, the winding roads of Shiras hills were under the wheels of his Cougar. His stomach lurched while he inhaled deeply on his cigarette. He tried to ignore his shaking fingers. Before he knew it, he was banging a right on the familiar driveway that led up to his parents' mansion.

Dan pulled up the car and stopped. Just before he turned the engine off, he could not help thinking that he was almost ashamed that, in fifteen years, he had not become President of the United States of America. He stepped out of the car and shut the door, snubbing his cigarette out in the driveway.

The wind whispered through the trees that enveloped the English Tudor mansion. Dan took a deep breath and forced himself to walk up the steps, one by one. The double black, brass embossed doors loomed in front of him as if they were the gates to hell.

Dan raised his hand and pressed the lighted doorbell. He could hear it echo through the foyer behind the doors.

Just before the door opened, Dan had a fleeting thought. In all the years that he had been raised by them, he had never heard either one of his parents tell him that they loved him.

He should have known that things would not turn out like he had planned. He just should have known...

1

BALLAD OF A THIN MAN

A sharp stab of pain tore through Dan's neck like the drill of a dentist as it struck a nerve in an abscessed and decaying tooth, jarring Dan awake. He tried to open his eyes but couldn't, his contact lenses feeling like cornflakes stuck between his eyelids. The smoky tendrils of a quickly fading nightmare seemed to hinder his ability to think. What the hell were his contacts still doing in his eyes? To him, taking your contacts out of yours eyes at night was akin to zipping up your fly after taking a leak. It happened practically naturally.

His eyes itched terribly. He had to get to the bathroom to get them out or he would go absolutely crazy. His back squelched in pain as he swung his legs off the bed. He literally felt his way to the bathroom, tripping over a pair of shoes on the way. He cursed under his breath as he stubbed his toe on the bathroom door. He fumbled for the light switch, hitting the fan switch at the same time. It didn't matter. All that mattered was getting the foreign objects out of his eyes. He grimaced in pain as he forced his eyelids open with his fingers. He squeezed the dried bit of plastic out of the first eye, not even bothering to make sure it landed in the receptacle marked, "R". He did the same with the second although it took three tries to get the contact to peel its way off his eyeball. He quickly squeezed some refreshing fluid in each eye, ignoring the momentary sting that it induced. He put his glasses on, grateful that he still had sight.

In the bathroom mirror, the face of a stranger looked back at him. He almost didn't recognize himself. In front of him, there stood a man who looked like he had just come out of battle. His hair was disheveled as if it hadn't seen a brush or a wash in a week. His eyes were bloodshot and darkened as if of a heroin addict's, while a large welt rose out of the right side of his forehead. The outer edges were pink but turned dark purple toward the center of its peak. He reached up and touched the welt, causing dried and flaking pieces of blood to fall on the countertop. He grimaced at the pain of it.

Dan stepped back to look at the unshaven man in the mirror. He began trembling when he noticed his shirt and pants. A long tear ran down the right breast of his shirt. Drops of blood spattered across the pink oxford as if he had been sprayed with Hershey's syrup. His jeans carried the same spattering of blood, without the tear.

"Holy shit," he tried to say. It came out sounding like, "Hoiee Shii..." instead, his voice was cracked and dried as if he'd been in a desert without water for a week. This was no good. He fumbled with a mouthwash glass as he forced water down his throat. The liquid soothed the pain in his throat within moments, feeling almost as good as the contact solution had in his eyes. With the water still running, he washed his face furiously, avoiding the tender spot on his forehead. He opened the medicine cabinet and shook out two Advil, grabbed another glass of water and threw them down. Seconds later, he decided he had better have two more. His knees were trembling and his stomach was tight. For a moment, he just stood there and stared at himself in disbelief. For the life of him, he could not figure out why he was looking the way he was.

Dan had to stay calm. There was a rational explanation for this, he was sure but, at the moment, the explanation was doing a good job of avoiding him. Where had he been last night?

He turned the shower on until billows of steam unfurled over the top of the glass door while he tore his clothes off. He peeled his socks off and climbed in the shower, barely feeling the sting of the hot water. He washed his hair twice while trying to put the mysterious pieces together in his mind.

For the life of him, the only thing he could remember was knocking on the brass-embossed black doors of his parents' home. What the hell had happened next?

He climbed out of the shower and busied himself with the habitual manual exercises of drying his hair, brushing his teeth and shaving, all the while trying not to think too hard. It was as if he had gone out drinking last night and did not want to admit to himself that he had blacked out at some point the night before. Deep inside, he knew his current condition had nothing to do with drinking although he would have gladly accepted that explanation if it served to explain why he looked the way he did.

Dan wrapped a Polo towel around his waist and looked for his watch, a Marlboro edition Swiss Army watch that he had received from sending in Marlboro Miles coupons. It was nowhere to be found. Then, a rational explanation occurred to him. Was it possible that he had been robbed the night before?

A quick inventory of the basics in his bedroom turned up nothing to support his newfound theory. He quickly found his wallet in his pants and his car keys on the floor. Everything else appeared to be undisturbed, just as he had left it before visiting his parents.

Dan's fingers trembled as he rubbed his eyes and sat on the edge of the bed. He likened his current condition to an experience he had had years before. When he had been on Mackinac Island, working hotel jobs to pay for college, he had a bicycle accident. He had been working out for the annual bicycle race around the island. The length of the race was about nine miles on flat land and winning it required what amounted to a nine-mile sprint. He could remember his head tucked down toward the curl of the ten-speed handlebars, his eyes focused on the thin wheel rapidly spinning in front of him. At the last possible second, two tourists stepped in his way on the tree-lined road. In an attempt to avoid the two ladies, he had no choice but to hit the gravel on the shoulder, thereby losing control. He could feel the thin wheels swerve as they tried to obtain traction. He also knew, within those split seconds that he could not slam on the brakes or he would be a goner for sure. Instead, he tried to let inertia ebb its way out of his speed. It began working, too, as he gained better control of the bike. Just when he thought he could get back on the road, he hit the lip of the road between asphalt and shoulder of which there was a good two inches of height difference. The front wheel flipped right and he found himself flying over the handlebars. In slow motion, he could hear the bike diving into the brush while the pavement rushed toward his head. He squeezed his eyes closed as he waited to make contact with the unyielding road.

The next thing he remembered, he was stumbling downtown, miles from where he crashed, the memory of the accident vanquished from his mind like the writing off a chalkboard when a professor begins a new lesson. The more he tried to remember what had happened, the more elusive the incident became. "Amnesia", the doctors had told him. "Most of the time, the memory will come back. Other times, though, you just never know."

Six months after the accident, moments after waking from an afternoon nap, the memory of the accident surged back in vivid detail. Although it was frightening, the relief of having the memory back far outweighed not having a memory at all.

The situation he was currently in felt drastically similar to that bicycle accident of many years prior. There was only one problem.

Whose blood was all over his clothes?

Dan shakily got up and walked downstairs to the kitchen. Fog webs clouded his mind as the Advil strained to work. He methodically made a pot of coffee and sparked a cigarette while he waited for it to brew. Minutes later, he had a cup in hand, three scoops of sugar in it instead of two.

He walked into the living room and picked up a remote control. Without thinking about it, he turned on The Weather Channel and watched Dave Schwartz describe the latest hurricane, Bertha, that was threatening to hit Western Florida sometime tonight or early Friday morning. Dan's stomach tightened.

Friday morning? That meant that today was Thursday. Dan started to get a sense of how much time he was missing and he didn't like the sound of it.

A bicycle accident was one thing whereby he had lost a scant few hours. This case was entirely different as he was missing, by the best of his rough calculations, four days.

The thought was almost surreal in its magnitude. Four days?

Whenever Dan was nervous, he paced and this incident caused him to walk a good half-mile in his living room before he could calm down enough to obtain some sort of rationality back. There had to be an explanation, one that he could touch and feel. There had to be!

He checked his answering machine only to find nothing. That wasn't much of a surprise. Ever since he had come back to Marquette, he could go weeks without a message on his machine, except for an occasional call from his agent asking him when his next book would be ready. He had pretty much come to Marquette to resolve his problem with his parents and he had done that alone.

Dan hurried back upstairs into the bathroom to look at his clothes as if to confirm that the blood was really there. He picked up the ball of clothes and spread them on the bed. The blood was still there and the shirt was still torn. He smelled the clothes as if he knew what dried blood would smell like.

Upon closer observation of the shirt, it looked more like a cut than a tear.

Had he been in a fight with someone? Maybe. But whom? He hadn't been in a physical fight with anyone since he and Mark had kicked the shit out of a college asshole years before for accusing the brothers of being gay. The whole incident instigated by all parties being drunk. They had been a lot younger and a lot stupider. Prior to that fight, the only other fight was in pre-high school days, adolescence running amuck.

Dan balled up the clothes and stuffed them in the bottom of his hamper.

He didn't want to look at them. He walked over and collapsed in his easy chair that was situated below his wall of five hundred Grateful Dead tapes. If things were normal, he would have thrown a tape into the Nakamichi deck.

But, things were far from normal, like the time, for instance. The green digital display of his clock read 3:05 PM as if to make a mockery of his sanity. If he had been drinking the night before, the very latest that he would have waken up would have been 11:00. But, he hadn't been drinking, he was sure of it, making the mystery even deeper.

Dan had to do something and the best thing that he could think of was to retrace his steps from his parents' home. This was a thought he did not relish. He could see the look on either of his parent's faces as they stared at the obtrusive welt on his forehead. Had they welcomed him with open arms or had they slammed the door in his face? For the life of him, all he could remember were the two black doors as he had rung the doorbell. His stomach proceeded to knot itself up in dismay as he thought of going back home again.

Having no other recourse, Dan checked his face and appearance in the mirror and grabbed another pack of cigarettes from the freezer, where he liked to keep them fresh. At the last second, he grabbed a notepad and pen just in case a couple of clues came back to him.

Dan opened the door to the garage and was surprised to find the electric garage door closed. He rarely closed it during the summer. He walked around his car to see if there were any dents that might hint at a car accident that he might have been in. The car was as immaculate as it always was.

The drive to Shiras Hills was uneventful. A live Grateful Dead rendition of, *Ballad of a Thin Man*, sang out of the speakers, *"Because something is happening here, But you don't know what it is, do you Mr. Jones?"*, the lyrics mocked. Dan didn't hear a thing, as he was preoccupied with the thought of how he was going to re-approach his parents.

He flipped a cigarette out the window, as he turned right on his parents' driveway. Thus far, his memory of being here, in this identical spot days before was outstandingly clear. He hoped that the window to his memory would open before he had to knock on the door.

Unfortunately, as Dan stopped the car at the end of the cul-de-sac at the top of the driveway, no hints stepped forward. He turned off the engine and stepped out. He was greeted by the sounds of chirping birds and a whistling wind through the trees. Sunlight arched its way through the leaves, peaceful in its intensity.

He walked up the steps, each step becoming increasingly difficult to go up. Once again, the doors loomed in front of him. He paused and put his ear to the door as if to check on his progress. As he did so, he saw a white sheer drape blowing outside the adjacent bay window that marked where the living room was. That's strange, he thought. He didn't ever remember seeing that window open in all the years he had lived there. His curiosity having gotten the best of him, he decided to check it out before ringing the bell. As he stepped forward, he noticed broken glass shards spread out below the window. He thought of his torn shirt and shoved the thought quickly away.

He could not have had anything to do with this. It wasn't possible! But, the back of his mind screamed silently, "Or did you!"

The palms of his hands broke out in a cold sweat as the glass cracked under his feet. He grabbed the blowing drape and stuck his head in the broken window.

"Hello?" he called out. "Is anyone in there?"

He waited for an answer and was greeted by silence.

"Hello?" he called again, more adamantly this time.

Hearing no answer, he balled up the drape in his hand and used it as a punching glove to break out the dangerous points of glass that were hanging on the framework. He looked behind him, as if he was hoping for some moral support, and stepped into the living room.

Normally, his parents displayed their wealth in cabinets with curios from all over the world, each item carefully placed in their respective spots. The furniture would be religiously dusted once or twice a week depending upon the season. The carpet, of course, was impeccable. Instead, the living room was in a shambles, with virtually everything tipped over, knocked over or broken in little pieces. A black ebony table from Japan stood crookedly on three legs like a wounded war veteran. A six-foot high curio cabinet now ran six feet long across the living room floor, lying in a bed of broken items and shattered glass. Some pictures were on the wall while others lay destroyed on the embedded carpet. It took merely a matter of seconds for Dan to see the carnage that was once a wealthy shrine.

The next thing Dan noticed was the overwhelming sweet smell of death as it hung in the air, the heat only serving to accentuate its thickness. Dan turned around and stuck his head back outside the window, needing fresh air like a dog might need water on a hot summer day. He gulped breath in as he tried to come up with the strength to continue his investigation.

The back of his mind kept telling him to run as far away from here as humanly possible. The rational part of him told him he had to pursue this grisly task.

Dan unfurled the sleeve of his oxford shirt and used the other hand to hold the cuff over his nose and face. He forced himself back inside.

He carefully moved his way across the living room and into the two story high foyer where he could see the stairway to the bedrooms upstairs and the opposing stairway to downstairs where the family room and den were. Nothing seemed to have been spared from wreckage. To the right of him, he could see the sun streaked doorway to the kitchen. He went in that direction, artfully avoiding a smashed foyer mirror that used to hang over a bureau where his Dad kept the car keys. Even though it had been fifteen years, the layout of the house had obviously not been changed.

As soon as he stepped into the kitchen, his heart jumped at the droplets of blood that were spattered on the golden tiled floor, innocuously basking in the sun. His legs felt like lead as he walked past the kitchenette area toward the main heart of the kitchen, past the extended bar where the kids used to punctually eat their dinners at 4:30 every afternoon.

Time seemed to stretch toward eternity as he looked toward his feet.

Lying in front of him, feet and legs splayed out uncomfortably, was the lady he had watched taking out the trash only days ago. His reason for being in Marquette at that point in time had a knife sticking out of her purpled and bloodied neck. Her mouth hung open as if she was mid-scream when she died while her unclosed and deadened eyes were dull and blurred over in a mask of death.

Seconds passed as Dan looked at his living nightmare lying in front of him. His breath rushed in and out in short staccato bursts as his mind tried to grasp at what remained of his sanity. He felt a movement churn in his stomach. Whether it was the smell or the sight that triggered the explosion inside of him, he didn't know. All he knew was that he had made it to the sink just in time as the liquid bile burst out of him over and over again. His fingers fumbled for the handle of the window as he dry heaved the empty contents. A fierce blackness threatened to overtake his being. His knees went soft while his elbows locked him onto the sink. A massive sweat broke out on his forehead while his glasses slid down his nose.

Eventually, a cool breeze from the outside gradually brought him back to his senses. Strength returned slowly as a headache made its emergence. His eyesight cleared and his stomach mellowed out. He slowly stood up, allowing the air to kiss his face. If there had not been a dead body behind him, he might actually have enjoyed the nostalgic view of the sun as it sprayed filtered light over the tree-lined backyard. Birds chirped, unaware of the horrors in that kitchen on a Thursday afternoon.

Dan knew that things were out of his control. There was only one thing to do next and that was to call the police and let them deal with it. He wondered how long it would take him to deal with it in his mind.

He turned around, meaning to steadfastly proceed to a telephone. There was only one problem though, a problem he discerned in one infinitesimal second out of the comer of his eye.

A sunbeam seemed to playfully dance over an item that was lying askew below the molding under the stove. Dan had to look at it twice before he could believe what he was staring at. He absent-minded felt toward his left wrist, finding only a dusting of hair.

A Marlboro edition Swiss Army watch stared back at him in a reality-defying pose, mocking him.

This recent turn of events did nothing to trigger his memory. All it did was scare the living hell out of him.

This did not look good. No, it didn't look good at all.

2

WHARF RAT

Dan didn't like cops very much. As a matter of fact, he didn't like them at all. He knew it probably shouldn't have been that way. It was wrong to stereotype a profession just as it was wrong to stereotype a race. But, he had had enough experience with the men and women in blue suits to know that he could not trust them. The first experience had been when he was young. The next experience had happened in the late 1980's, long before Rodney King had become famous for getting the shit kicked out of him.

Dan and Mark were living in the San Fernando Valley. Mark had just moved in with Carrie, his current girl, while Dan had just struck up a relationship with Rita, an extremely attractive brunette with an addictive personality. She had soft brown eyes, long raven hair and legs that could stop an eighteen-wheeler in its tracks. Add on a witty yet dry sense of humor and Dan knew he was in love. She encouraged him to write more than he was turning out, while he encouraged her to seek a career that excited her.

They became wine connoisseurs, urged on by many candlelit dinners ending in a passion that seemed to be perpetual. They bicycled together in the northern reaches of California as much as they found themselves on the shores of the Pacific, basking in the sun, the conversations unlimited in their direction and dreams. In essence, they were in love.

Before long, they found a three-bedroom house and moved in together, thinking that marriage was not too far off in the distant future. A big screen television went up in the living room, an Irish setter made his home in the backyard while Dan found solace in using the third bedroom as a study.

Soon, Rita was talking about moving on from being a beautician to something more productive, something where she could actually contribute to society. There was many a time, especially during one of her brainstorms on a career idea, that Dan would voice his support in whatever career she chose.

There was talk of being a paralegal to being a paramedic. For a while she played with the thought of library science, given that she loved books so much, to being a 911 operator. At another point in time, she thought about going into computer science and that would change overnight when she would be talking about becoming a nurse with just as much enthusiasm. All the while, Dan listened and supported her just as a parent might support a daughter's ever changing ideas while she pursued college.

On a particularly cool morning, the day after Christmas, a post-sex cigarette still burning, Rita sat straight up in bed.

"I want to be a police officer!" she said with determination in her eyes.

Dan smiled, wondering how long that interest would be pursued.

Well, pursue it, she did. It took her three months just to get ready for the physical examination and another three months to pass it. Dan could not count the number of times he went on a five-mile run with her, or jumped a rubber tire obstacle course next to her and even fell off of six-foot high walls with her. Whatever she wanted to do, he was there.

But, one day, she found herself on the streets and the changes in her personality become more and more acute. He watched as she smiled less and raised her voice more. Words like "scum", "lowlife" and "dirty rotten son of a bitch" crept into her vocabulary, imperceptibly slow at first, until they became terms that were found in every other sentence. Dan was patient, qualifying these changes as things that were helping her become accustomed to her new environment.

To a great degree, Dan understood these changes because of the harrowing experiences she had on the street. He remembered one particular Christmas Eve when she had come home distraught and distracted. She avoided Dan's affections, saying she had other things on her mind. They exchanged a few gifts to take the edge off. Rita opened hers listlessly, as if she was merely opening an unwanted bill in the mail.

Dan looked at her point-blank, "Are you having an affair?"

Rita looked at him with such surprise that Dan knew he had missed the mark. She set her gift down and went to the kitchen and poured herself a Jack Daniels up. When she returned, she fingered and drank from her glass for a long time without speaking. Finally, she talked, the words forcing a blank stare to come out of her eyes. "It's Christmas Eve," she began slowly.

"They sent me out on patrol alone, Devonshire District area. I should know that there are no surprises in this job. But, for some reason, I kept thinking that it's Christmas and I was caught completely off-guard. Somebody had put a call in about a recently abandoned yet suspicious car that was parked off a Simi freeway exit. Maybe this call should have been a highway patrol call, I don't know."

She paused and took a drink. Tears welled in her eyes but she continued with as much strength as she could find. I pulled up behind this vehicle on a dark street. The nearest house was, maybe, a good mile away in each direction. There was virtually no traffic and no one to be seen in the area. I pulled out a notepad, wrote down the license plate number and then, as I pulled out my Mag-light, I approached the driver's side of the vehicle, a late sixties Mustang. I shone a light in the car and, I swear to God, I must have jumped back a foot."

"What did you see?" Dan asked quietly.

"There were two people in the front seat, both of them slumped over. In the back, Christmas presents were piled high. I opened the door and could feel heat coming out of the interior. It was as if the heater had just been turned off and there was still warmth inside.

The girl's head was lying in the driver's lap in his naked groin area with his pants to his knees. Obviously, they had stopped for a little sex, you know? Each had a dark hole in each of their heads. For Christ's sake, isn't Christmas sacred anymore? Can't we stop the killing, thievery and fighting? My God!" Rita said vehemently. "Then, an hour later, I get to announce the news to his parents, with my being the rookie and all. If you could have seen their faces as the shock settled over them. Turns out, the two lovebirds were on the way to the boy's parents to announce their Christmas engagement."

"I'm sorry," Dan said.

Since then, Rita had never been the same. As a matter of fact, she got steadily colder and meaner as time went by. The two of them saw less of each other and the silences between them grew greater.

Dan learned that living with one cop gave you a family of cops. He was also able to figure out that Rita was not the only one who had changed by joining the department. They all had experienced the same metamorphoses, going from normal decent human beings to hardened and cynical people bonded by the evils of the city.

The final straw was pulled when Dan was sitting home late at night, wondering why his girlfriend hadn't been home hours before. He turned on the police scanner only to hear jumbles of one voice after another, one car corresponding to the next. Words like "perpetrator", "black, no further" and "suspect" were used repetitively, in an excited yet formal bravado. Dan could not figure out what had happened, although, he did hear his girlfriend's voice a few times in the middle of it.

When she finally did come home, she was swearing up a storm and pacing non-stop. She couldn't stop saying, "fucking lowlifes!"

"What happened out there?" Dan asked as he followed her around the house.

"A car chase," she answered shortly.

"And..." Dan prodded.

"We had the pleasure of beating the living shit out of him and the scum is trying to threaten a lawsuit."

"What do you mean beat the shit out him?" Dan asked.

"A few cracks of the baton shut him up, alright? And, what business is it of yours? I don't tell you how to write, do I?"

It was the first time that Dan could say he had had enough. "What gives you the right?" he asked her directly.

"You'll never understand, will you?" she retorted defiantly.

And, no, Dan didn't understand.

The second time he said he had had enough was when he accidentally read about an affair, in a diary that she had errantly left out, with a very masculine sergeant who counterbalanced, in her opinion, what Dan was.

Weeks later, Mark was bailing him out of the house, a twenty-eight foot Ryder truck parked in front.

It took Dan quite a few months to recover from a relationship that left him scarred for life. It was also the first time that Dan found himself sitting in a psychiatrist's office, attempting to regain some semblance of balance. The surprising thing was that the psychiatrist had helped. After all, he had no family to go to, his brother was too busy flying and friends were few and far between, considering his only concomitants had been police. Over time, his psychiatrist had convinced him to create a new venue in his life. So, Dan had hit the road once again, a better man for it all.

There was just one problem, though. He still hated cops.

So, when he looked at that watch lying on the floor, he had picked it up and stuffed it in his pocket before calling the police. Yes, it was wrong. He knew that as well as he knew the sun would rise the next day. But he also knew that telling the cops he was there when she died would hurt him more than it would help him. Even further, he could just see the reaction of the police when he said he was there but didn't remember a thing. He was sure they would afford him some nice five by ten accommodations for a while, like for life.

Dan thought about his situation long and hard. If he were to find the murderer, he would have to leave his involvement out, until he had a better idea of what was going on.

While Dan waited for the police to arrive, he left a message for Mark to call him as soon as possible. Carrie could not pinpoint when he was coming back but she promised that she would notify him. Then, Dan called Diana, his current psychiatrist. He would have to see her; there was no question about it. Hell, if anything, she was the one who had convinced him to approach his mother to begin with. Wait'll she gets a load of this, he thought. He left a message with her answering service.

Dan was sitting on the porch when the first of eight cars came pulling up the driveway. He had not been able to take the smell in the house any longer. Nameless officer after officer hit him with a barrage of questions. Who was he? What was he doing there? What was his relationship to the decedent? When had he last seen her alive? Who were the other living relatives?

In the middle of the confusion, a detective pushed his way through the photographers, police and news people. The moment that Dan met him, he felt like a cat that had been rubbed the wrong way.

"Nice place," the detective said.

"Who are you?" Dan asked, irritable after two hours of interrogation.

"Robinson. Detective Robinson. You the one who found the body?"

Dan noticed a few things about him right away. First of all, the detective would not look him in the eyes as if he were some sort of nonperson. Second of all, Robinson talked at you and not with you and, finally, his shoes were spotless. One thing that Dan had learned from Rita was that spotless shoes meant you were an ass-kisser, always looking for a promotion and a person to step on to get there.

"I am," Dan said.

"Looks like you could stand a lot to inherit, judging from the size of the house and all."

"Is that supposed to mean something?" Dan asked with his guard up.

"Just making conversation, is all? Does that bother you?"

"If you want help in this case, I'm glad to give it to you. If you don't want help, we can talk through a lawyer. Which is your preference, Officer?"

"I prefer to be called, Detective. Do you mind?" Robinson said. Then, without giving Dan a chance to answer, he continued with his hand extended, "You must be Daniel Wilcox."

Dan reached for his hand, "Yes, I am."

"Pleased to meet you and I'm sorry about how we started out. Do you want to take a walk and get away from here for a minute so that I can get a statement from you?"

"Sure," Dan said.

"Give me a minute, then," Robinson said.

Dan waited while he watched Robinson orchestrate his crew of people giving commands to the coroner, photographers and the lot of other police running around in apparent confusion. Yellow police tape began going up virtually everywhere making his parents' home look like some sort of bizarre construction site. Dan half expected the Mayor to step out grinning, scissors in hand, at the groundbreaking ceremony.

Ten minutes later, they were walking down Allouez.

"Hell of a smell in the house," Robinson said. "I figured you'd have a clearer head out here. A real shame, about your mother and all."

"Yeah," Dan said.

"One of my officers tells me that you haven't talked to her in awhile. Is that true?"

The way that Robinson worded the question allowed Dan to speak truthfully. "Fifteen years, more or less."

"Hmmm. Any reason you care to let me in on?" Robinson queried.

"Would you believe me if I said that we didn't get along?"

"I had already gotten that idea," Robinson said. "Care to elaborate?"

"Not really," Dan said. "I don't see how it has anything to do with her murder."

"How about you start from the beginning. How you found the body, why you were here and maybe you can tell me a little bit about any enemies she might have had."

"I wish I could be more help but I'll tell you what I know," Dan said. He then told the detective about everything as he saw, except for the watch and the prior visits.

"Any other family?" Robinson asked as they turned around headed back.

"I've got a sister, Louise, whom I haven't seen or heard from in just as long an amount of time and then, there's my brother, Mark, who's in California."

"Where's your father?"

"I thought he was with my mother. I don't know," Dan said.

"You're not giving me a lot to go on, Mr. Wilcox."

"I'm sorry, but like I told you..."

"It's been fifteen years, I know," Robinson finished. "If you don't mind my saying, I'm sad for you."

Robinson pulled a cigar out of his pocket and carefully removed the cellophane. He bit off the end of it and spit the remnant toward the trees. He lit it and puffed before he started speaking again. "I consider myself lucky. I've got two kids in high school; daughter's a cheerleader and my son's All-American. My parents are still alive and you outta see the holidays. It's a real madhouse. I couldn't imagine my kids or my parents not talking to me, you know?"

Dan nodded, not knowing where this was leading.

"Then, I get on the streets and I see drugs, alcohol and crack and I realize that my family is in some sort of dinosaur era."

"This has nothing to do with crack or alcohol, Detective!" Dan said strongly. "I would prefer that we stay away from the innuendoes. Do you mind?"

"No offense, just an observation," Robinson answered. They had reached the bottom of the driveway.

If it hadn't been dark out, Robinson might have seen the color wash out of Dan's face as the detective leaned down to inspect an item on the ground. He whipped out a plastic bag and a pair of tweezers.

"Hold this," Robinson said as he handed Dan a flashlight.

Dan pointed the light toward the ground as Robinson dropped a cigarette butt into his plastic bag. He fought to keep the light from shaking.

"You never know," Robinson muttered under his breath.

Robinson released Dan from the scene moments later, promising to stay in touch. They exchanged numbers with Dan making a promise not to leave town.

A short time later, Dan was pulling into the driveway of his own home with only two thoughts in mind. The first was that he really hated cops and the second was that he was buried up to his eyeballs in deep shit. He knew how things looked on the surface. Lord knows this would make a great Rusty Wallace novel if he could ever get out of it alive.

Dan knew what he had to do the next day. It was time to get some help. He could wait on a lawyer; no charges had been filed against him. Besides, without a recollection of a very important four days, he had a feeling that a lawyer would do him no good except to get him locked up in an insane asylum.

The answer was buried in his head somewhere and there was only one person who could get it out.

It was time to see Diana Powers, his psychiatrist.

3

HE'S GONE

The next morning, Robinson called to give Dan the address of where he could find his father: 1400 Wright Street #104A. The conversation had been short and curt. The only other information that Robinson had given Dan was in regards to the expected release of his mother from the coroner.

"Four or five days, tops." Robinson said. "You got a decent funeral home?"

"Ah, no," Dan had said quietly. This was the first time that he had the responsibility of having anyone buried.

"You might want to try Swanson-Lindquist on the comer of Third and Park Street. Have them take care of the release forms. If you need anything, they'll take care of you right and proper," the detective said.

Right and proper, Dan thought bemusedly as he fingered the slip of paper with the address of his father on it. Nothing had been right and proper for close to a week now. As a matter of fact, he felt as if he had stepped right into a Stephen King novel, terrors hidden around every corner.

Dan booked an appointment with his psychiatrist for later that afternoon and put another message in for his brother. He stuffed the address in his pocket and headed out to Wright Street. Dan took Lakeshore Drive, bordering the crisp and cold waters of Lake Superior to Fair Street instead of cutting through the city. Even though Marquette had a small population of thirty thousand or so, it had enough streetlights and stop signs that the Lakeshore Drive route probably saved him twenty minutes of stop and go traffic.

He felt oddly foreign in this town now that his mother was gone. Further, he had gotten a glimpse of the headline on the Marquette Mining Journal, Brutal Murder Shiras Hills and in smaller writing, "Son Finds Body, Many Questions Unanswered." Dan felt like every person in that town knew who he was and could only begin to imagine what they were saying behind his back. To top things off, he knew he was not a Yooper, the term designated to those who inhabited the Upper Peninsula of Michigan. He wasn't a Troll, either, a term assigned to those who lived south of the five mile long Mackinac Bridge, the Lower Peninsula. By all rights, he considered himself a Californian, kind of like Charles Manson, people would say, he was sure.

He took a left on Fair and drove past the Marquette Medical Center; a building reserved for doctors with a private practice. Across the street was his old school, Marquette Senior High. Since no one had known where he was, he had missed his ten-year class reunion by a long shot. Northern Michigan University was just down the street. Moments later, he took a right on Presque Isle Drive until he found Wright Street. Gradually, the location became familiar to him.

The first thought that came to his mind was that Robinson was an asshole. All this time, Dan had expected his father to be at a house or, at worst, a retirement home. It had been fifteen years, hadn't it? God knows where his father was. As Dan pulled up beside the finely trimmed lawn with the wrought iron gate surrounding it, he smacked the steering wheel wishing it were Robinson's face.

"Son of a bitch!" he growled as he stepped out of the car.

The skies were gray, threatening rain. Dan grabbed his Ralph Lauren umbrella out of the trunk, obtained free with the purchase of a bottle of cologne, and used it much like an old man might use a cane, steadfastly poking the ground with it as he walked past the ironed gate. Moments later, he found #104A.

Dan slowly walked up and touched the smooth granite stone as if to confirm its existence. A funeral procession of six or eight cars drove by slowly, headlights beaming with little black and white flags perched upon each car marking their sad task. Dan wondered how many people had attended his father's funeral. He staved back a spark of anger as he thought of his recently deceased mother and how she could not even bother to give her sons a call. Had they been so bad as to deserve such an unforgiving act?

Dan read the simple and formal engraving almost void of all feeling,

"Doctor Daniel Dunham Wilcox 1932 - 1986 Loving Husband and Father"

Rain spit out of the sky in a mist rather than in droplets. Dan opened his umbrella and sat on the freshly trimmed grass and looked at the vacant lot next to him, to his right. He knew that inside a week he would be back here again, burying his mother and all the answers that she had had inside of her. He buried his head in his hands and tried to reach inside of himself for some tears. But try as he could, he felt remarkably devoid of any emotion. For all of the apologies he had over the years, he had to succumb to the knowledge that they would never be heard. He only hoped in his heart that he would be able to live with himself.

Dan watched as a young boy played with his dog, a game of hide and seek, behind the gravestones that dotted the lawn. He appeared to give the drizzle little notice, occasionally wiping it from his eyes while chasing after the Cocker Spaniel. The yelping of the dog was strangely out of place as the procession that had passed earlier pulled to a stop at some distant plot.

For the first time in a long time, Dan felt alone, isolated and quarantined. He tried to push the lines of the Garcia tune, *He's Gone*, out of his mind, "*Lost one round, but the prize wasn't anything, a knife in the back and more of the same, he's gone.*"

Dan breathed a quick and seemingly pointless prayer to the grave and picked himself up, wiping the damp grass from his pants. He took one final look and proceeded back to his car.

Twenty minutes later, Dan was searching for a parking spot on the comer of Front Street and Washington. He ended up parking about two blocks away near Thill's Fishery. He ejected the Avalon Ballroom tape out of the deck only to hear the end of a news clip on WDMJ, the local radio station. Dan slumped in the seat, not believing his ears.

Jerry Garcia was dead at fifty-three years of age.

This time, he was able to cry.

***

The moment that Daniel Wilcox stepped in her office, she knew that he was in trouble without his even saying one word. The dark circles under his eyes accentuated his unshaven face. His fingers trembled involuntarily while his stance suggested a man who had recently fallen off the wagon, an aura of guilt surrounding his person like the lingering fog of a hangover. Her first thought, as a matter of fact, was that he had started drinking again.

She couldn't have been further from the truth.

Diana understood the strength of first impressions. When Daniel had started seeing her a little over six months before, she had thought him to be a man who was solid in his success as a writer and just needed a little help to reconcile some differences with his parents. When she delved underneath, she found something much deeper. The first few months of therapy were spent dragging him away from alcohol so that he could clearly face what was lying underneath. But the more she looked, the more she discovered a very troubled man.

When he spoke of his murdered mother lying on the floor with a knife in her throat, his memory blocked, she was drawn even more because it was she who had convinced him to take that walk up the driveway. She knew the importance of facing your biggest fears.

There wasn't a day that had gone by that she hadn't thought of the trauma that had steered her life toward psychiatry.

Diana was raised as the only child of a farmer in Fort Wayne, Indiana. Her parents had been strict in her moral upbringing, consistent with the attitudes of the Midwest. One worked hard for what one had attained through strong family ties and a good education. She couldn't count the number of times that her parents had spoken of their parents emigrating from a famine-ravaged land in Ireland. This was the land of opportunity and, with a proper upbringing; any dream could be attained. Her parents were a living testament to that with a one hundred acre spread of land that eventually yielded a six-figure income. They never forgot where their roots were and how lucky they were to have a warm bed to sleep in with a solid roof over their heads.

She had been twelve years old when she was introduced to abuse, not from her parents but from an uncle who showered her with attention. As it turned out, it was not attention that any twelve year-old should experience. When she finally approached her parents on the issue, she received a slap on the face and was told to never bring up the issue again.

She didn't have to raise it again because she never saw her uncle again. It didn't mean that she would forget it, though.

She went on through high school excelling in both academics and physical education. She was able to attain a 3.96 GPA while also being captain of the swim team. She was crowned Summa Cum Laude while taking her fellow teammates to the national championships in Miami, Ohio. Her backstroke afforded her a second place finish in the country, which drew the attention of a swim team scout at the University of Michigan. Her eventual scholarship paid for the first four years of school. Nine years later, she had a doctorate to her name after graduating Valedictorian of her class.

If there was one thing she learned about herself right away, she saw that she was an idealist as opposed to a realist. She believed that with enough encouragement and faith, anybody could succeed.

Diana served her internship at St. Mary's Hospital in the heart of Detroit. She listened to hundreds of indigents, crack addicts and alcoholics only to discover the powerlessness of the system. Too many times, people in desperate need of help were turned away due to lack of insurance or the financial capability to complete psychiatric care. It frustrated her to no end. For all the times that she thought she was helping, she learned that she was merely a pawn in a system that was buried in bureaucratic red tape. Too many people were lost in a system where the problems were bigger than society wanted to admit.

That didn't stop her perseverance and drive. She became known as a maverick in the system. Most doctors were content when their patients came to their office, but she sometimes went to see patients when they missed an appointment. Her colleagues looked at her as if she was the one who needed psychiatric care. She couldn't count how many times that a coequal looked at her and asked, "What do you hope to change? Only they can change themselves and if they don't want to see you, move on to the next case. You can't change the world."

Diana didn't want to change the world. She wanted to help one person at a time to overcome his or her own personal barriers. Unfortunately, her idealistic attitude got her into hot water.

She had completed her internship about three months before. For two months, she had been seeing a black lady named Gertrude Gorman, or Gerry, as she liked to be called. She was on welfare and her visits to Diana were court mandated after she allegedly tried to kill her husband. She had been doing well, part of the reason being that she was off crack cocaine. It appeared that her life was straightening out. Then, she called in sick to one of her appointments. Two more appointments were missed before Diana became truly concerned. So, Diana did what she knew best and went to visit the lady.

It is one thing to see a patient in an office where you can control the environment. It is a completely different story going to a domicile in the worst part of Detroit where crime owns the city like a scab that won't go away.

When Diana knocked on the door, she knew there was trouble. She could hear the muffled screaming and crying of two children behind the door. She knocked on the door again only to be greeted by Gerry's husband, a sawed- off shotgun in his hand. He dragged her in and held a gun to her head while Gerry sat in the comer, her two children huddled around her. A glass pipe was lying on the coffee table; its end blackened from God knows how many rocks. Diana tried to mediate, pretending that the end of her life wasn't a trigger-pull away. Somehow, the situation imploded upon itself.

Diana watched in horror as Gerry's husband suddenly pulled the trigger again and again, ending the life of his wife, his two kids and finally of himself.

An investigation was mounted in the department of mental health. It was determined that Diana shouldn't have been at the Gorman's domicile, which left the State with a handful of potential liabilities in the event that someone chose to sue. She was given three months severance pay.

The loss of her job didn't haunt her as much as the loss of life. If only she had visited Gerry when she missed her first appointment. If only she had done a follow-up phone call. If only...

It was at that time that she met Clinton, a fellow psychiatrist who was close to retirement. From the moment that she met him, she trusted him. Maybe he reminded her of her now deceased father. She wasn't sure. But, he took her under his wing, helped her through her trauma and finally helped her start a practice in the northern reaches of Michigan, Marquette. They remained close for the next ten years and she was relieved to see that her services were helping a good number of people. Her only discouragement was that she rarely saw the results of her labors.

Daniel intrigued her and Diana wasn't sure why. The obvious reasons had to do with a murdered parent but there was something else. She saw a trait in him that was familiar to her when she had suffered through her ordeal of many years prior. She could see fear traced through his eyes. But this man was no crack addict. He was a man who was forced to face his past if he were to move ahead from his mother's violent death. He had been doing unbelievably well until this terrible event.

Diana sensed a man who was in grave trouble; trouble not only with the law, presumably, but within his mind. As he explained his recent memory loss and the chain of events that had brought him into her office, she could feel a new urgency in the air.

All she had to do was one simple thing; get his memory back. But, to get that memory back, she was going to have to take him into territory that he had previously avoided in prior visits with her. She explained that this was going to take time. She would do her best but she made no promises.

Daniel tried to convince her to hypnotize him.

Diana refused on the grounds that if the subconscious was not ready to give in, then the consequential results might be permanently devastating to him.

"Isn't there a truth serum or something you can give me?" he prodded.

Again, she refused on the account of addictiveness, which she was very familiar with.

Momentarily, the thing she found most interesting was that Daniel almost seemed more upset at the death of a musician than that of the demise of both of his parents.

"Mind if I smoke?" he asked.

Normally, she would have refused him but she found his predicament so interesting that she heeded preventing anything from getting in the way. "Feel free," she said.

He lit the first of what would be many cigarettes smoked in her office and stared out at Lake Superior. He seemed to be gathering images and anchoring them, readying himself for the painful task ahead. When he began to speak at last, she switched on the tape. She taped every session from then on with the feeling that she'd be listening to Daniel's story more than once.

An hour later, minutes after Daniel had left, Diana emptied the heaping ashtray and adjusted the blinds against the late afternoon glare. Daniel's presence lingered in the room so palpably she half expected to hear his soft voice continue the story for her.

All she had to do was press the "play" button and he would be with her again. Her tape recorder was like Pandora's Box, containing sorrow and mayhem; once she let it open there was no turning back and no forgetting.

The details Daniel had recounted, the pieces of his story that left him drained and almost peaceful when he'd finished, were captured here in a Sony tape recorder. There was no doubt in her mind that she must listen again immediately. Without his sad presence in her office, with only his voice to guide her, there would be nuances and signposts for her to follow.

She often stayed late in her office, listening to tapes and making notes, but tonight was different. She had rarely encountered a patient with so much to tell and so little grasp of how devastating his story was.

Diana's role had never felt so important because, deep inside, she could not believe that he was a killer. Only the Maxell XLII 90's could tell her for sure.

Daniel's case was the epitome of what she worked so hard to achieve.

From the very first moment, she believed that she could make a difference. Only this time, he wouldn't end up like Gerry and her family.

So, she pressed, "play", closed her eyes and heard the voice of a little boy, a little boy she would have to understand in order to help the man. She resisted the impulse to hear Daniel's words as part of a story. She was a psychiatrist, not a writer, and she had no idea how this story would end. She would take it as it came, measuring, sometimes playing the devil's advocate, and using her training and the words of Clinton to hear what sometimes remained unsaid.

Diana leaned back in her chair and opened the lid to the forbidden box...

4

DAYS BETWEEN

He was lying in bed, shaking. He was frightened, and only ten years old. None of his friends lived like this; he knew something was wrong. He didn't remember it always being like this. Not that it had been that good, either.

God, he was beginning to feel like an adult. The pressures seemed so great all of the time. Yes, he had heard the lectures from his father; he almost knew them by heart after hearing them so many times,

"You don't know what it's like," his father would say. "Every day, I go to the office and work my ass off for you ungrateful idiots. Do you have any idea what it's like? Do you? No, obviously you don't. Why can't you help your mother out? Do just a few chores to make the load a little bit easier. But no," he would bellow, "You can't do that, can you?"

And the answers were always the same; mumbled response, feeble attempt at trying to defend yourself. No answer was ever quite good enough. There was a lot of stress, being a kid.

At least in this family.

There was even more pressure being the oldest kid. He always had to set the example for the younger ones, like Caroline did for John Kennedy, Jr. after their father was murdered. Danny remembered many a time when his father would mention the Kennedy family because Danny was conceived when Kennedy became President. Mark and Louise, who were twins, were being born on the same day that Kennedy was shot. *"Profiles In Courage"* could always be found out on the coffee table, a grim reminder of their entrance into the world.

Danny always had to watch out for Mark. He and Mark got along well, though, almost better than best friends. It wasn't all that much easier being the older brother to Louise, either. He wasn't as close to Louise as he was to Mark. That was probably because Louise had her own room. With Mark, he had the nights to hold whatever conversations a ten-year-old and eight- year-old could have.   Alone in her room at night, Louise only had shadows and imaginary friends to confide in.

Danny always felt responsible for everything, too. He figured it was supposed to be that way. His father always said, "You're their big brother. How are they supposed to know how to behave if you don't set a good example for them?" Of course, Danny could never come up with the right answer. There was never a right answer for Daddy. But when one of them was about to be punished, Danny always felt like he had to be there, even if he hadn't caused the problem. When they were afraid, he had to listen, he had to try and comfort them.

They were afraid a lot more often lately.

Like tonight...

It was report card night. Danny had gotten an "okay" report card and Momma didn't seem too happy about it. She kept asking why he had "B minuses" and "C plusses" instead of "A's". He had answered that he was really sorry; he had really tried. He went without dessert as punishment. It didn't bother him too much. At least he wasn't going to get the belt. Mark was going to get the belt tonight. Danny knew it as well as Mark did.

And so, Danny sat in bed, shaking, afraid and sweating.

When Momma saw Mark's report card, she warned him that he was going to get it. There had been two "D's" on it. The teacher had also written on it that Mark "plays with toy airplanes" in school instead of doing his schoolwork.

Danny looked over at Mark, who was lying in the other bed. He had to sit up because there was a dresser between the two of them. He could see him lying there with his eyes open. The dim streetlight cast a snow -white glow over him, which made him look faintly like a ghost. Danny could see reflections of sweat on his forehead.

"Mark?" Danny whispered.

There was no answer.

"Mark?" he whispered a little louder.

"What?" Mark answered finally.

"You okay?"

"Yeah."

"Maybe Daddy will get home late tonight," Danny offered hopefully.

"Maybe."

"If he does, he'll probably be too tired," Danny whispered.

"Maybe."

They were silent for a while. Danny could hear Momma walking around downstairs in the kitchen. He heard the clatter of pans once in awhile and the opening and closing of the refrigerator door. Danny was just lying there, afraid to move. His stomach hurt and he had to go to the bathroom. It was always like this when one of them had to face the belt. Well, at least he wasn't going to get it.

Both boys waited in silence.

Outside, the first winter cold front was moving in. The leafless branches of the trees began knocking against the roof as the wind picked up. The snow (there were only flurries an hour earlier) pattered thickly against the window. Nobody had to be outside to know that the temperature had dropped; ice was spreading its crystalline fingers on the window panes.

"I'm scared," Mark said in the darkness.

"I know. So am I," Danny answered.

"Do you think I'll get it tonight?" Mark asked.

Danny didn't answer for a while. He listened but heard nothing but the increasing wind.

"Maybe," he answered finally.

"I wish it wasn't like this."

"So do I," Danny said in a whisper. The two of them were used to whispering softly. There had been many a time when they had been caught talking after eight o'clock. The light would snap on and then...

Suddenly, both of them heard the sound of the Blazer pulling up in the driveway. As the truck climbed and made traction, they waited for the lights to flash through their second story window. A moment later, they saw the lights and heard the sound of the electric garage door opening. Danny suddenly had to go to the bathroom very badly. He knew he was really scared because he had to go "number two" instead of "number one".

"He's home!" Mark said in a frantic whisper.

"Shhh!" Danny whispered back.

Danny hoped and prayed that Momma wouldn't say anything about their report cards. Maybe, just maybe...

Moments later, they heard the laundry room door slam downstairs. They knew Daddy would be unzipping his galoshes and placing them with the other three pair on the mat in the closet.

"Hi, honey," their mother said from downstairs.

Whenever their father would come home, he would come up to the middle level where the foyer was and drop his car keys in the bureau below the foyer mirror, open the closet door and hang his overcoat in it. They heard him walk over to Momma and give her a kiss on the cheek.

"How did it go?" Momma asked him

"I guess it went okay," he answered. "You know, it never ceases to amaze me."

"What's that?"

"Oh, the innumerable ways that people destroy their mouths." Daddy was an Oral Surgeon. "This kid, seventeen years old, drove his car straight into a telephone pole. It took me six-and-a-half hours to piece his jaw back together. Damn drunkards!"

"My goodness, you must be tired," Momma said.

"That I am."

Both boys cringed at his response. That was never a good sign for them.

"What's for dinner?" Daddy asked.

"Pork chops."

"Sounds good."

The two of them walked into the kitchen. Their voices turned to mumbles. Danny thought that if Daddy was too tired, it might be a good sign. Maybe he wouldn't worry about the report cards. He knew that Mark was in the other bed hoping the same thing.

Then they heard footsteps in the hallway.

"And how was your day?" he asked Momma while she was in the kitchen.

The boys were sweating more now.

"Fine," Momma answered. "By the way, today was report card day."

The boys' hearts jumped.

"I think you should take a look at them," she suggested.

As Daddy walked back into the kitchen, Danny knew what was going on. Report card day had always been a big deal, something Danny was very familiar with. He remembered hiding his very first report card in first grade because he had been afraid of their response, and he didn't even understand what his grades meant. As it had turned out, his grades had been excellent but he had received the belt for hiding them.

Momma handed Daddy the report cards. The chair slid back from the kitchen table, making a scraping sound on the linoleum floor. Danny could picture his father settling down to inspect them.

Silence followed, except for the sounds of Momma preparing Daddy's dinner. Danny heard a kitchen drawer sliding open and the sound of silverware being placed on the glass kitchen table.

"I better talk to him about these "C's"," Daddy said in reference to the oldest son.

Fear gripped Danny. Then he heard the rustle of another envelope being opened. He could almost feel the shivers running up Mark's spine. They both knew whose card he was looking at. Daddy never bothered much over Louise's.

"What the hell kind of grades are these?" they heard him ask in a much louder tone of voice.

"I don't know what's going on with him, honey. I was thinking of calling his teacher tomorrow," Momma answered.

"We damn well better speak with his teacher," he said. "Where is he?"

Both boys knew what would happen next.

"Upstairs. Asleep."

"I'm going to have a talk with him," he said firmly. The kitchen chair scraped the floor again as he stood up.

"Honey, please!" Momma implored. "Dinner's almost ready."

"Keep it warm. I will not stand for grades like these," he said. "Mark?" he hollered from the bottom of the stairs.

Mark didn't answer, pretending he was asleep. He was hoping that Daddy would go away.

"Mark! Get down here right now, or am I going to have to come up there and get you myself? "

"Yes, I'm coming," answered Mark as he threw the sheets back and scrambled out of bed.

Danny watched him hurriedly leave the room. He saw that the back of Mark's pajamas was wet.

"What is the meaning of this?" his father's voice bellowed as Mark reached the bottom of the stairs.

"I...I don't know," Mark answered in a fearful voice.

"I...I..." Daddy mimicked. "Well, Mark, grades like these will not be tolerated in my house! I think that it's time that you go down to the basement and drop your pants. Maybe then I can get an answer out of you!"

"No, Daddy, please!"

"I said get down there right now!"

"Honey, I wish you wouldn't," Momma interjected. "There's no need for this. Besides, you're tired."

"I'll only be a couple of minutes," Daddy responded. "Ten cracks with the belt and I'll have him back in bed."

"Okay. Only ten, though," Momma warned.

Danny heard his father come up the stairs and go past his room. He heard him rummage through the closet for his belt. Danny hoped, for Mark's sake, it would be the fat belt. The fat one hurt less than the skinny one, even though it left larger marks. Danny held his breath.

"And I'll talk to you tomorrow!" his father said to Danny, while passing his room on the way back downstairs.

He heard his father's footsteps go down the first set of carpeted stairs and then on to the tiled floor of the foyer and all the way down the next set of stairs to the basement. The sound of the basement door slamming was followed by the sound of a faint click. Danny wondered if his father had locked the door. He hoped not. He could picture what was happening next. Mark would be leaning over the tall box in the corner, where the kitty, Cookie, normally slept waiting for the belt.

Danny didn't know which was worse, the silence in the house now that the basement door was closed, or the noises he could imagine. Mark's whimpers, his futile pleas echoed upstairs. I don't want the belt, Daddy, please! The whimpers would turn into choked cries of pain as the belt cracked down, and after the fourth or fifth crack the cries would become screams. Danny knew. He'd been there, in the basement, trying to bite back the screams of pain and humiliation. It was a losing battle.

Danny lay rigid in bed, his hands balled into fists. He tried to calculate how much time had passed, counting off the cracks, the screams, until he was sure that Mark had received the promised ten. The silence was terrifying, because he had no way of knowing what was happening.

Suddenly he heard his Momma's heels clattering down the steps to the basement, then her fists thudding on the thick door.

"Honey!" she called. "Stop it."

His father must have opened the door, because now he could hear Mark shrieking.

"He's had enough," Momma yelled. There was panic in her voice.

"He'll get what he deserves. He's got to learn." Now Danny could hear the crack of the belt as it continued its' assault beyond the promised ten and he flinched each time as if it were flaying him, too. Mark's screams were thin and hopeless now, as if he didn't have the strength to protest anymore. It frightened Danny more than any other sound, and he began to cry.

It stopped as suddenly as it started. "That'll teach you to play in school when you're supposed to be studying!" his father said in a disgusted voice. "Now pull up your pants and get out of my sight. Now!"

Danny heard the sound of Mark's feet running up the stairs, and then he was collapsing at the door to their room. He crawled to his bed, whimpering.

"Jesus, honey, didn't you get a little carried away? " Danny heard Momma ask.

"It was a long day," Daddy answered. "I lost my temper. I'm sorry."

The wind and snow beat furiously against the window muffling out the sound of Mark's fading whimpers.

It was a long time before Danny fell asleep.

* * *

Diana pressed "stop" on the Sony cassette player and let the silence settle over her before she pulled out Daniel's file. Although the file was thick, she knew it would soon be thicker since they were going to meet three times a week instead of once a week.

She scribbled notes in the Observations section: "The subject was cooperative and lucid throughout much of the interview, although he exhibited sporadic fits of anger. Speech and activity showed some signs of abnormality. His intelligence is well above average."

Diana folded the file closed and placed it in the file cabinet and locked it.

She locked up the office, thinking of the last patient who had walked out, feeling drained yet hopeful. She got into her car and turned the ignition switch. The radio blared a tribute to Jerry Garcia. She turned down the volume, only to catch a phrase from a tune that the DJ called, *St. Stephen*, *"Fortune comes a crawlin', calliope woman spinning that curious sense of your own. Can you answer? Yes, I can. But what would be the answer to the answer man?"*

Two days later, Daniel was back in her office, looking worse for the wear. He mumbled something that she didn't quite catch at first.

"What did you say?" she asked.

"I said, I don't think I could take it if I found out my sister was dead, too."

"You have no idea where she is?"

"No," he answered softly. "But, I can't shake this feeling that wherever she is, it isn't good." He lit a cigarette and appeared to pick at something on his jeans. He looked up slowly. "Is it possible that I can't remember what happened because I really killed her?"

"It is," Diana answered truthfully.

"That's what I thought. I'm thinking that I had every reason in the world to do it."

He smoked his cigarette and stared out the window as an iron ore boat gracefully slid its massive structure into an ore dock. His eyes were glazed as he slipped back into his frightful rhetoric.

5

CHILDREN'S LAMENT

"Emergency! Emergency!" Slide down the chute!"

"He's got a snow bomb, hurry!"

Robbie and Danny looked behind them, as they were running toward the hole in the snowbank. A bundled-up figure chased them with a snowball the size of a basketball. It looked like an Abominable Snowman, with its oversized parka, black and white ski mask and frosted fur-lined face, as it ran through the snow toward them.

They jumped in a hole and disappeared. The figure chasing them tripped and fell as the snow bomb went flying. It picked itself up and dove in after them. They slid down fifty yards of the ice-packed tunnel into the gulley. They had spent weeks building the snow fort. The three of them landed in a heap in the "Control Room".

"Wow!" Danny screamed.

"That was cool!" Robbie added.

"I almost peed my pants!" giggled Mark.

The three of them watched each other's breath whistle in and out, as their heartbeats settled. The "Control Room" was the vortex of their huge underground fort. Five tunnels lead to the outside world somewhere...

"Shoot," Danny said.

"What's wrong?" asked Robbie.

"We need wood. Whose turn is it?"

Mark and Robbie looked at each other. "Not ours," they said at the same time.

"No way," Danny said. "I got it last time."

Mark and Robbie both tugged a glove off.

"Ready?" Robbie asked. "On the count of three." Both of them extended their fists.

"One, two, three, GO!"

Robbie won by extending two fingers, while Mark extended a flattened palm.

"Ha, ha, scissors cuts paper. I win," Robbie announced triumphantly.

Mark admitted defeat by crawling out a tunnel to fetch wood for the fire pit in the center of the fort.

While waiting, Danny and Robbie talked about subjects that fascinated ten- year-olds, like combat soldiers in the far-off Vietnam war, the latest Hot Wheels (which happened to be the release of The Heavyweights) and the airplane that Daddy had just bought, a single-engine Beechcraft Debonair.

Danny had met Robbie about three years before after seeing him sledding outside his bedroom window at about nine o'clock at night. That normally wouldn't have caused any comment, except he was sledding down Daddy's driveway and Daddy didn't like strangers on his property. Mark and Danny had already been in bed for a half hour, but Robbie had to be warned by Danny rather than by Daddy...it would be too dangerous if Daddy caught him. Danny sneaked downstairs, threw on his winter coat over his pajamas and put his boots on. Well, imagine Daddy's surprise when he saw two boys sledding down his driveway an hour later. It was a friendship sealed in snow.

Mark re-appeared with the wood at Mach II, the wood flying everywhere as he careened into a frozen wall. The boys hurriedly made a fire.

"I think we're gonna move," Mark said, out of the blue.

Robbie looked up surprised, "Huh?"

"You're making up stories again," Danny said to Mark.

"Uh-uh, no way," Mark answered. "I heard Momma and Daddy talking the other night and they want to go back where they came from, now that Daddy has so much money."

"Where'd they come from?" Robbie asked.

"Detroit," Mark said dejectedly.

"I never heard that," Danny said. "I know he doesn't like it up here all that much, though. He calls everybody Yoopers."

"So what," Robbie commented. "You're gonna be Trolls now."

They bickered about five minutes over it and it was forgotten until spring when the rumor became reality.

Daddy closed his practice in Marquette, called up Allied Van Lines and, the next thing they knew, they were eating their last pasty in the Upper Peninsula and driving southward over the Mackinac Bridge to their new home in the suburbs of Detroit.

Daddy had been very successful in Marquette. He was the only oral surgeon in all of the four-hundred square mile area of the Upper Peninsula. When they moved to Detroit, though, Daddy had a lot of added pressure. There were many oral surgeons and he couldn't quite seem to find enough business. "I don't have enough patients," Daddy would say. He had a new three story house to pay for and there wasn't near enough money coming in. So, Daddy was working twelve and fourteen hours a day. After awhile, the pressures became too great. He was getting upset at the simplest of things.

Momma noticed, too. She decided to make sure that the kids were fed before Daddy got home from work. She told them that Daddy was tired and wouldn't want to put up with any of their shenanigans. Danny, Mark and Louise were learning to stay away from him when he was irritable and grouchy. They would greet him with a perfunctory "Hello, Daddy" when he got home from work and then they would dash to the safety and seclusion of their rooms. They were learning that it was best to hide from him and to say as little as possible.

Although Danny knew things were changing, there was one particular incident that served as the beginning of a number of events that would mold Danny into the protector. In Marquette, he had just been Danny. In Detroit, he learned to become something else. The only friend he had in Detroit was Mark. The years of whispering in bed made them very close and Detroit made them even closer. He still wasn't particularly close to his sister, Louise. Only sissies hung around with girls too much.

One Sunday afternoon, he and Mark were playing with their gliders in the driveway. That was one thing that Daddy approved of. Since Daddy now owned a Twin Comanche airplane, he thought it would be a good idea if the boys took an interest in flying. So, Danny and Mark used to figure out all sorts of ways to warp the balsa wood into real aircraft which would perform high flying stunts, loop-the-loops and crash landings. For hours at a time the two boys could make their gliders go on the longest flights, the smoothest flights or the coolest flights. There was always the danger and the end of the fun when one of the planes would sail into the street where it would get crushed by a passing car.

Playing with the gliders came with every detail imaginable. You had to have a landing strip complete with hangars, control towers and parking lots. Hot Wheels were the perfect complement to their simulated airport. Every car imaginable could be seen scattered about in a plethora of Spectra-flame colors. They had the Twinmill, the Splittin' Image, the Paddy Wagon, Red Baron, Whip Creamer (with the really cool fan in it that produced a whirring sound when you blew on it) finished out by the "real" looking cars like the TNT-Bird, Rolls Royce, Custom Corvette, Custom Cougar, Heavy Chevy and a classic Light-My-Firebird. The two boys could milk hours of time in a fantasy world of cars and planes.

On this particular Sunday, they came home from St. Anthony's church itching to be outside playing in the sun. They always went to ten o'clock mass on Sunday and then they were free to stay outside for the remainder of the day.

"You wanna try a take-off?" Mark asked Danny.

"How do you do that?"

"Wind up the propeller, put it on the ground and let it go," Mark answered.

"Okay."

Each boy wound up their Sleek Streaks and placed the wheels on the ground. It didn't work on the first few tries. The planes would race forward simultaneously only to flip over sideways or crash into each other. So they'd pick up the planes and put them back together. Then they would warp the wings with their saliva in hopes that it would do the trick. They produced some impressive crash landings but they could never manage a successful take-off.

"Okay, you ready?" Mark asked in anticipation of another try.

"Just a second. Let me wind it up a few more times," Danny said while twisting the little red propeller another turn or two. Finally, he squatted down next to Mark and placed his airplane about a foot away from Mark's airplane.

"Okay, tower," Mark said, lowering his voice. "Ready for take-off."

"You ready?" Danny asked Mark in his adult voice as if they were at a real airport. Whenever Daddy would go to the airport, Danny and Mark could be seen standing at the end of the runway watching their father practicing "touch and go's". They'd pretend they were the ones in the plane instead of their father while Mark would be the pilot and Danny would get stuck being the copilot. Little did Mark know that the seed had been planted for what would turn out to be a lifelong dream.

"Just a second, let me taxi forward a little bit," Mark said while making a whirring sound with his lips. "Ready for take-off!"

The two boys let their planes go simultaneously. The buzzing sound of the propellers increased as the planes picked up speed, the little red wheels scraping the asphalt. And, to their surprise, both planes lifted into the air. Neither boy said a thing. It was too important a moment for words. They stared in awe as the planes caught the breeze and lifted higher and higher. They couldn't believe it! They had done it! They had mastered the perfect flight!

"Get in here right now!" Momma screamed from the garage. Danny and Mark looked at each other for a moment, tom between watching the rest of their perfect flight or running in to Momma.

"Yes, Momma," they answered in unison.

"Who did this?!" she yelled accusingly. Neither boy knew what she was talking about.

"Did what?" Danny asked.

"This," she said, suddenly grabbing him by the back of the head and yanking him into the laundry room from the adjoining garage. Danny vaguely heard splashing sounds when his feet hit the laundry room floor. Mark was standing bent over, peering questioningly, while Danny was staring at the water, dumbfounded. Momma grabbed Mark by the hair and pulled him into the house and threw him against the opposite wall of the laundry room.

"Who is responsible for this?!" Momma asked them again.

"I don't know!" Danny answered, worried that Daddy might appear at any second, wondering what the commotion was about.

"Mark...?" Momma questioned.

"I don't know, either," Mark answered in a quivery voice.

"Well, somebody's lying here and I expect a truthful answer right now!"

And then Daddy appeared. When he saw the quarter-inch high water, both boys saw the angry look cross his face like the shadow of a cloud on a sunny day. They had seen the rage before, usually reserved for when one of them was receiving the belt. His lower jaw jutted forward and the muscle in his face suddenly became defined. His hands clenched into fists at his sides, the knuckles accentuated by a white tightness.

"What the hell happened here?" he shouted.

"One of the little brats left a sponge in the sink!"

Danny looked over to the sink which was actually a wash basin next to the washer. It was then that Danny realized what had happened. Mark had left the sponge in the sink when he washed his hands and the washer had been running. When the water from the washer emptied into the sink, it caused the sponge to plug up the drain, causing a minor flood.

"How many times have you been warned to never leave the sponge in the sink?" Daddy asked Danny accusingly.

"I didn't do it!" Danny answered defensively.

"Oh, you didn't?" he said, looking at Mark now. Suddenly, he reached over and grabbed Mark by the hair. "Come here, you little bastard! Do you see this? Do you?"

"Yes," Mark answered, yelping with pain.

"I don't think you do!" Daddy yelled. Danny watched in shock as his father yanked Mark off of his feet and shoved the nine-year-old boy's face into the overflowing water. Then he yanked him up just as quickly. Mark was sputtering, choking and crying.

"You don't ever learn, do you?" he said. His clenched fist backhanded Mark across the room, while Danny watched, cowering in the comer.

"I did it!" Danny blurted out. His assumed role as the protector had been born without his even realizing it.

"What?" his father asked. Mark stared at Danny, his eyes uncomprehending.

"I said that I did it. I left the sponge in the sink!"

"Are you telling me that you lied to me?" Daddy asked with a tightened face and a building rage in his eyes.

"Well, I..."

"Wasn't that a lie?"

"I, well, yes, it was," Danny answered in a high-pitched voice.

"How dare you watch your brother take the punishment that you should be getting?"

His father backhanded Danny just like he had Mark. Danny slammed into the wall, dazed. It didn't actually hurt him as much as it had shocked him. What was happening to Daddy?

"Mark, get the hell out of here! I think Danny and I have some cleaning up to do," Daddy said. Momma took the hint and left with Mark. Danny and his father were left alone.

"Get up," he commanded. "Now!"

Danny stood in front of his father, trembling. If he had known what he was in for, he might never have jumped in defense of his brother. He felt himself wet his pants out of fright. His father apparently didn't notice, as Danny was already wet from the laundry room floor. Daddy struck Danny much harder.

"This will teach you not to watch your brother get punished for something you've done. Now, my boy, let's clean this up, shall we?" His wing-tipped shoes drove into Danny's shins with an unbelievable force. "That'll teach you to be dishonest with me!"

He kicked Danny again. Pain seemed to sear his legs as he fell to the wet floor. And Danny was kicked again and again. He was sure he could feel blood oozing from his legs but was afraid to look. All the while, he could hear his father's voice booming but he couldn't understand what he was saying. He was too busy trying to defend himself, warding off kicks and blows.

"I said clean it up, you sorry excuse for a son!" His father grabbed Danny by the hair and shoved his face into the floor.

Danny could feel his father putting a sponge in Danny's hand and then squeezing his hand so hard that he thought it was going to break. He had never seen his father like this and it kept on for what felt like forever, the hitting, kicking and smacking.

Then it was over just as suddenly as it started. Somehow, they had gotten the laundry room clean. Danny had been beaten all the way through the task, but it was finally done. His father sent him to his room.

For a long time, Danny sat on his bed, crying and sniveling. Every bone and muscle in his body throbbed and ached. His back, legs, arms and, most of all, his scalp hurt where his father had yanked his hair so many times. Danny eventually sneaked down the hallway to the bathroom. He looked in the mirror and was stunned by the sight. Bruises were beginning to show up on his face. One eye was red and Danny knew it was destined to become black. He lifted up his shirt and looked at his back. It, too, was scratched and red. After seeing it, it seemed to hurt even more. For a moment, Danny wondered again why he had tried to cover for his brother. Had it really been worth it? Danny wondered. He hurried back to his room.

"Danny! I'm really sorry," Mark whispered when he walked back into the bedroom.

"It's okay. Really," Danny said.

"You shouldn't have done that."

"I don't mind," Danny said, trying to make himself believe it.

"Danny! Mark! Louise!" Momma's voice commanded. "Get downstairs and eat your dinner right now!"

The three of them hurried downstairs. Danny tried to ignore the pain as he followed his way down the steps. He walked into the kitchen and carefully pulled himself up on a stool, where the kids always ate. Momma dropped a plate of macaroni and cheese with a slice of bologna on it in front of him.

"You had better..." she said, stopping in mid-sentence. "Oh my God," she whispered.

Daddy walked into the kitchen.

"Look at him," Momma said.

Daddy looked at Danny's face and turned away. "Jesus Christ," he muttered. It grew silent in the kitchen. Daddy looked at Momma and then back at Danny. "Did I do that? No, I couldn't have done that," he reasoned, transfixed with Danny's face. He reached over to inspect the bruises. He felt around his cheekbone and chin. "Well, nothing seems to be broken. It's just a little bruising. There's nothing to worry about."

Momma looked at Daddy accusingly.

"Dammit," he said, returning her stare, "if I could earn just a little more money...things would be better." He turned and walked out of the kitchen, running his fingers through his hair.

For the next couple of weeks, Danny's parents kept him out of school. Louise and Mark were told not to tell anyone what had happened. Neither one said a thing especially with Momma's provocation, "You can understand how difficult it is for parents, can't you"? Momma called Danny's teacher and told her he was sick with a bout of mononucleosis, he'd be out of school for awhile. The teacher was very understanding and sent Danny's homework home with Mark.

During those weeks, Danny was treated very nice. His parents bought him books, gliders, models and all the Hot Wheels that he wanted. Danny loved his parents again. He knew they were sorry and that things would get better. He enjoyed life again. The only thing that he didn't particularly relish was the daily ritual of having makeup being put on his face, neck and his legs every morning.

When he finally did go back to school, he was given a note to take to his gym teacher, saying that he should be excused because of his recent illness. Danny knew it was because the bruises and marks on his legs hadn't gone away, yet. He didn't mind, though. Danny didn't care much for gym class anyway. Besides, his parents said it was one of those fluke things and they were really sorry for what had happened.

Danny remembered the strangest thing about that incident. Particularly, it was about the two gliders that had taken off so majestically on that Sunday afternoon. Danny was depressed when Mark found the two gliders the next day, crushed in the street by a passing car. They were never able to get two gliders to take off the way those two had.

6

SAINT OF CIRCUMSTANCES

Diana slowly pressed the door closed after Daniel finished his session with her. She walked over to the window and looked out over the sunlit waters of Lake Superior for a long while before returning to her desk. She was becoming more disturbed about Daniel's mental condition. She was all too familiar with his situation. The mind remembers only what it wants to remember and she had sat in shoes like his not far in the past.

She forced herself to open Daniel's file and pulled out a pen to make a summary in the "Observations" area. The blank page returned her stare for a long time before her pen began scribbling the necessary notations:

"The subject was uneasy and restless throughout the interview today. One striking difference was that Daniel was more rational. Despite a haggard appearance and sunken eyes, he stated that he had a good night's sleep the night before. As he relates these stories of his childhood, he appears to be releasing some of his blocks.

Although he is somewhat paranoid, he appears to have a firm grasp on reality. I see signs of a narcissistic personality disorder typical of adults who were abused as children. When I made a comment about his success as a novelist, he brushed it off with a laugh, saying that his books were merely trash books. As a child he was constantly made to feel inadequate and worthless; as an adult, he constantly punishes himself. He can take, and expects criticism, because he relates to what he knows best: punishment.

Guilt covers his being like a blanket.

This punitive environment has also led him to combined feelings of rage and fear. It is the combination of these two things that makes him most dangerous to himself. It also increases the possibility that he may have had something to do with his mother's death. He is genuinely frightened at that thought.

"What bothers me most," he said at one point, "is that I know the answer is inside my head somewhere. Every time I sit in your office, I'm pleased with what I remember. I mean, some of this stuff, I haven't thought about for years. I've gone through a lot of work to try and forget it. Then, I tell you a story and everything gets all disturbed again. These are areas that I no longer want to delve into, you know? Much of it, I really feel that I've forgotten. My brother and I have done this many times over the years. He'll tell me a story where I was there and I won't remember a thing about it. And I know I was there. It frustrates the hell out of me because if there's that much that I've blocked, what chance do I have of remembering what happened when she was murdered?"

He continued, "I know I'm fighting it. But am I fighting it because I did it and don't want to admit it?"

"Are you?" I asked him.

"I really hope and pray that that's not true," he said dejectedly.

The patient is definitely suffering from PTSD (Post Traumatic Stress Disorder) more commonly known as the "flashback syndrome". Mostly, I've seen it in the treatment of Vietnam veterans. The horrors that these people faced were suppressed for many years; without warning, the flashbacks occur, sometimes many years later. The subconscious begins releasing tiny bits of information to the conscious mind so that the victim can begin dealing with it. Many times, these people will re-experience everything about what they felt at the time of the trauma first, before remembering the trauma itself.

Daniel seems to be reliving the feeling of fear and paranoia but is at a loss as to what actually happened. The point of having him relive the childhood memories is to eventually build to that fateful day.

He is rushing his memory yet, simultaneously, is fighting it.

I will continue at the same pace."

Diana closed the book and sat at her desk and stared at the skeleton for a long time, as if the skeleton would be able to give her some answers.

She remembered the help that Clinton had given her during her terrifying ordeal and was grateful to him for it, even though the memory was one of the worst experiences she had ever had.

She hoped she could do the same for Daniel. The problem was, as he had stated, that time was running out for him. She did not want to be in his shoes and felt for his situation.

He was expected to meet with the police tomorrow and she could tell that he was scared as hell. Repeatedly, he begged her for hypnosis but she couldn't do it.

If he had murdered his mother, and she drew it out of him that way, he might never recover.

Recovery was the name of the game, wasn't it?

7

BOX OF RAIN

Dan was standing in the office of Detective Robinson. He wiped his hands on his pants repeatedly. He couldn't seem to shake the cold and clammy sweat on his palms. He did his best to look at Robinson straight in the eyes. He had nothing to be afraid of, did he?

"I appreciate you coming down here," Robinson said formally. "Can I get you a cup of coffee or anything?"

"No, I'm fine," Dan said as he took a seat on a swivel chair in front of the detective's desk.

Robinson had closed the door, blocking out the busy sounds of the Marquette Police Department. Dan was surprised at the number of phones ringing and their corresponding staff of such a small town. It appeared that crime did not take much of a holiday, regardless of the city. The station looked nothing like he had remembered it from years before, technology being the biggest difference with computer terminals everywhere.

"So, I brought you down here for some questions," Robinson said as he sidled into his seat. His pale blue shirt was open at the collar while his sleeves were rolled up, giving him the appearance of a man just sitting down to have a chat, as if they were going to discuss how the Detroit Tigers were faring this season. His language was casual. "There are just some formalities that I'd like to clear up. If you want a lawyer present, we can delay this. But, you should know that this is not a formal questioning. I just need to tidy up the paperwork before we release the body to you. Are you okay with that?"

"Sure," Dan said. "Would you mind giving me a quick rundown on what you think happened?"

"There's not a whole lot we know right now," Robinson said as he leaned forward on his desk. He delved into a pile of paperwork in front of him. "We know that she died of penetration trauma, the knife is being analyzed in Lansing for prints. One of her wrists was broken and she suffered numerous bruises and contusions on her body although it appears that none were contributing causes of death. The knife itself severed her Carotid artery which probably accounted for a quick death."

Dan listened to Robinson's rhetoric as best he could. He felt as if he was in someone else's nightmare.

"The autopsy report states that she had minor arteriosclerosis which wasn't life threatening. She had a trace amount of alcohol in her system and no drugs in her system except for an antihistamine. I'm still waiting on a complete toxicology report," he said with a formal tone in his voice. "I'm concerned, though."

"How so?" Dan asked while shifting in his seat, ever so slightly.

"First of all, remember how the house was ransacked?"

"How could I forget?" Dan said.

"Well, we first went on the assumption that we had a burglary. Unfortunately, I can't see what was taken. Her purse had about three hundred dollars in it and her jewelry box was full. There was an untouched diamond ring on her hand and a gold necklace around her neck. I'm sure a burglar would have taken these things. As far as the house being ransacked, I can't tell if this was "pre" or "post" death. Somebody went through a lot of work to destroy what was there. Whether the intent was anger or to confuse the investigation, we don't know at this point in time. Let me ask you again, why weren't the two of you talking?"

"Suffice it say that my brother and I were kicked out of the house fifteen years ago, after graduation from high school. Neither of our parents showed any interest in reuniting, so we didn't reunite," Dan explained.

"Did this make you angry?"

"Of course, it did," Dan said. "But not enough to murder her, if that's what you're asking."

"I'm wondering what kind of enemies she had because I believe that this murder was committed out of vengeance. It looks strikingly like a hate crime without the blood on the walls. The strange things is, after interviewing the neighbors, I can't find that she had any friends, much less enemies. It's as if she was totally cut off from the world."

"It could be that she didn't have any friends," Dan said. "My parents kept to themselves outside of professional contacts."

"Hmmm," Robinson said. "Can you tell me where you were the night of the murder?"

"At home," Dan said, his palms breaking into a sweat.

"Do you have any witnesses who can support that?"

"Uh, no. I wish I did, though. Am I a suspect?" Dan asked.

"Anyone who knew your mother is a suspect. By the way, where was your brother the night she died."

"A million miles from here," Dan defended. His brother didn't even know she was dead, yet. "He was in California."

"Can he prove that?"

"Of course, he can!" Dan said vehemently.

"I may have to get a statement from him." Robinson said matter-of-factly while he jotted a note down. "Where's your sister, Louise?"

"Again, Detective, I don't know. I've had no contact with my family."

Robinson rubbed the area above his eyes, obviously disturbed by the lack of information he was getting. He opened a drawer in his desk and pulled out a bottle of Excedrin. He shook out three and dropped them in his mouth and started chewing.

"We need to find her," he said. "I've put out a nationwide A.P.B. for her. I need anything I can get on this and it appears that we've got to start with the family, her direct source of enemies."

"I wouldn't classify us as enemies," Dan defended, "we just didn't talk to her, that's all."

"There's no need to get uptight, Mr. Wilcox."

"Call me Dan."

"Alright, Dan. All I'm trying to say to you is that we need some help. The best things that I've got right now are some latent prints on the knife and three fibers that we found in her neck. The fibers aren't consistent with her clothes or to the environment around her. I think they came from her killer's clothes," he stated.

Dan tried not to think about his torn shirt.

"Looks like you got a nasty bump on your head," the detective said. "How'd that happen, if you don't mind my asking?"

Dan could feel himself turning four shades of white. "I smacked it while working on my car."

The detective jotted another note down and took a deep breath, "You're not leaving town any time soon, are you?" the detective asked.

"No," Dan assured him. "I'll call you if I do, though."

"Here's my card if you should think of anything that might help us. Feel free to call anytime. Oh," the detective said as an afterthought, "sign this release form and you can pick up the remains."

Dan signed it, took a copy and left the detective's office. He resisted the urge to go directly to a bar. He had to think clearly so he took a drive to Presque Isle, a nature wonderland at the north end of town.

Dan could honestly say that he was scared. He was scared of the things he didn't know, like specifically, the missing four days and the watch that he had found at the scene. He also knew that his lack of an alibi did not help him in the least. A tight knot twisted in his stomach. Son of a bitch, he thought. If only Diana could hypnotize him. It was a hell of a lot better than not knowing at all. He tried to calm himself down by turning up the tape in the deck. The driving words of, Truckin', assailed him with the lines, "Your typical city involved in your typical daydream, hang it up and see what tomorrow brings."

Dan made his way home, lost in paranoid thoughts. The moment he got in, he checked the machine for messages. His brother had finally returned his call, apologizing for being out of town. He hurriedly picked up the phone and called him.

"Murdered?" Mark said.

"Yeah, I found her with a knife sticking out of her neck."

"Wow," Mark said without hiding his surprise.

"The detective asked if you had an alibi I said you did," Dan explained. "You do, don't you?"

"Of course, I do," Mark answered. "I'll just pull a manifest from the airlines."

"Good," Dan said. "There's something else. Dad's dead, too."

Dan could hear Mark breathing on the other end, the silence heavy and thick. Finally, he started talking, "I never wanted to make contact with them again. I really didn't. Now, I kind of wish I did. I kept expecting them to call one of us, you know? Like in the back of your mind, you played with the thought that they would somehow realize that what they did was wrong. But, I guess that's not going to happen, is it?"

"I'm afraid not," Dan said quietly.

"I just can't get over it. Do they have any suspects?"

"Yeah, us."

"We didn't kill her," Mark said. "What do we have to do with this?"

"Well, I don't think the detective understands why we didn't talk to them. He's got a perfect family and he doesn't relate. There's something else, too," Dan added.

"Yeah? I'm afraid to ask. Whenever you get that tone in your voice, I get the feeling that you're in trouble."

"I think I am but I'm not sure. You see, I don't remember a thing for four days," Dan said. He then told Mark about his complete memory loss from the beginning to the end.

"You think the psychiatrist's going to be any help?"

"It's all I've got," Dan answered.

"Shit. This is bad. Do you think there's a chance that you lost it and things got out of control?"

"No way. I don't think it's in me, no matter how angry I might have been with them," Dan said.

They stayed on the phone for another ten minutes discussing what they would do about a funeral. Mark agreed to get a week off from work, promising to fly out in the next day or so.

"Do you mind if I tell you something without you getting upset?" Mark asked.

"What?"

"Let's just say you find out that you did kill her..."

"I didn't!" Dan interjected.

"I believe you, Dan. I do. But, let's say we did find out the worst. I'm behind you in whatever way I can be."

"Thanks, Mark. But I had nothing to do with it."

"Well, if you did, I can tell you this," Mark said.

Dan clenched his teeth in frustration, upset that Mark was pursuing the issue. He continued, "I wouldn't blame you a bit."

Dan let the sentence hang in the air, knowing he would have said the same thing to his brother. Both of them had a motive but would they go that far? Maybe...

8

LOOSE LUCY

"Do you want to be a doctor like your father?" Daddy would ask.

"Yes, Daddy," Danny would answer.

"Then, you're going to have to study hard."

Danny did study, a lot. It had started as far back as he could remember. Just before kindergarten, he had taken an I.Q. test. Evidently, he had done well on it, a little too well. For, while all the other kids were out playing Frisbee, baseball and all the other games that kept kids entertained, Danny was forced to sit in his room and study flashcards of arithmetic, books on penmanship and novels that Daddy deemed necessary reading for an intelligent boy. He could remember reading *Black Beauty*, *Little Women*, *Tom Sawyer* and a lot of Charles Dickens. He liked the reading the best as it transformed him into a world that was very much unlike his undesirable world. Even reading *Oliver Twist* out loud to his brother and sister, every evening at 6:30, brought some welcome relief to a family that was becoming strained and tense.

Huckleberry Finn quickly became a favorite of Danny's. He must have read it cover to cover ten times.

In Daddy's eyes, education was a continuing process. Every waking hour of the day seemed dedicated to learning with all the kids but especially with Danny. If Danny was going to be a doctor like his father, he had a long way to go and his father was the relentless mentor. But, learning was not always fun. It could be pure hell if you wanted to really get down to it.

Just before they moved to Detroit, Daddy rented a Winnebago Brave, a motor home that was probably a little too small for a family of five. It was Daddy's intent to drive all the way through Canada to see Quebec, New Brunswick, Prince Edward Island and finish off the trip by seeing the largest rodeo in the world in Winnipeg, Ontario. If they had a normal family, the trip might have been fun. Unfortunately, it was the trip from hell. The better part of the days was spent driving over the great expanse of Canada in an effort to make it to the rodeo. When they would stop at night, each child was ordered to complete a "journey book" or a diary of everything they had seen and learned.

Daddy would read each of their entries in the diary aloud and then critique it. This was usually a two-hour event that ended in hair-pulling, finger-smashing and a good bout of hollering. When words weren't spelled right or sentences were worded wrong, Daddy would be sure to point them out, belittling each child as much as possible, all in the name of education. "Without education, you're going to end up a goddamn garbage collector! Is that what you want?" Daddy would say.

The cramped quarters and the two hour lectures eventually split up the family for part of the trip. Momma got upset when

Daddy kicked Danny in the shins while they were making a campfire one night.

"Sweetheart, there was no need for that," Momma said in defense of the oldest son.

Daddy stopped what he was doing and grilled her with his eyes, "You will not teach me how to discipline our son!"

"All I'm trying to say," she said, "is that we're on vacation and we don't have to do that. Leave him alone, can't you?"

Daddy was pissed. So, he said the hell with it and ignored Danny and Momma for a good two days while the flat landscape of Eastern Canada rolled under their wheels. The kids could not talk to each other if Momma and Daddy weren't talking. So, Daddy took sides with Louise and Mark while Danny stood alone with Momma. The hitting stopped, though, a blessing in disguise.

Then, while they were eating a lobster dinner on Prince Edward Island, Danny watched Momma lean over to their father and apologize for what she had done.

"All I want you to remember," Daddy said, "is that I am head of this household. Now, let's enjoy ourselves, okay?"

It was the only time that Danny had ever seen them fight. Momma knew where she stood and Daddy was happy for it.

"I love you very much," Momma said to Daddy, ending the issue once and for all.

They returned home vowing to never go to Canada again. "A waste of money," Daddy had said many times over again.

In Detroit, the incidences of punishment remained sporadic. They seemed to happen at the most unexpected times but now they were happening closer together. Of course, Danny knew that was because the family wasn't financially on its feet yet. Daddy even had to lay off his receptionist.

Momma replaced her while the kids helped lick and stamp envelopes for bills for the few patients that Daddy did have.

Danny could see his father trying to control himself. Sometimes, when Danny thought he was in for it, his father would suddenly hold back and send him to bed. Unfortunately, it made Danny more nervous because he felt that a time would come when his father might not be able to hold back.

One day, Danny left his glasses at school. He was midway through sixth grade and had worn glasses only a short while. He hated them because all the other kids made fun of him, calling him things like "four eyes" and such. So, he tried not to wear them as soon as he was out of sight from his parents.

"Where are your glasses, Danny?" Momma calmly asked him while she was fixing dinner.

Danny saw his father look up from the kitchen table. Daddy was home early because he had no patients that day. Danny also knew he was very tired. He was reading the newspaper with a sour look on his face.

"Answer your mother," his father said sternly.

"Well, I don't know," Danny answered while frantically trying to remember where he had left them.

"You don't know?" Daddy said with a sigh. "We spend forty dollars on new glasses so that our idiot son can see what he's doing and he doesn't know what he did with them?"

Danny stood there, not knowing what to do. It was like a test in school: the harder you tried to remember, the harder it was to think. Danny stayed silent.

"Maybe you'd like some help remembering," Daddy offered.

"No, I'll remember," Danny answered quickly. He had an idea as to what kind of help Daddy would give, especially when he was this tired. Danny's breathing speeded up a little while he wrung his fingers desperately behind his back.

"Where did you leave them, Danny?" Momma piped in again.

"Ummm..." he struggled. If he knew where he left them, they wouldn't be lost. There was no point in giving Momma and Daddy a smart-aleck answer like that. So, he did his best to stall for time.

"Danny?" Daddy asked, laying more pressure on him.

Did Daddy's jaw just jut forward a little bit? He had to remember...he just had

to.

"I'm thinking," Danny said with his eyebrows furrowed in thought. He needed just a few more seconds. Unfortunately, the more the pressure was on, the less he could remember anything save for his impending doom.

His father suddenly had enough. He stood up and took three strides toward Danny. "Maybe this will help you to remember!" Danny backed up to the wall, as his father started poking him in the chest with his index finger. He was taunting the boy and poking him harder and harder.

"Do you remember, yet?"

"I...I..." Danny stuttered. He tried to sidestep Daddy's prodding finger. He was thinking more about avoiding the pain than he was about the location of his stupid glasses. Danny's foot hooked on the molding, causing him to fall to the floor.

Daddy reached down and grabbed him by the ankles and yanked him up in the air by his feet. Naturally, Danny started crying and screaming. There was no way he could remember now!

"Maybe you left them in your pockets, huh?"

He started shaking the boy up and down by his ankles. Danny's head was hitting the floor over and over again! He was feeling dizzy, while at the same time, he could hear his comb, pennies, gum and two Hot Wheels, the Snake and the Mongoose, dropping on the floor from his pockets. And then, finally, he remembered.

"At the library! At the library!" he screamed between sobs.

Daddy dropped him back on the floor. "Very good, you little brat! How about you get your skinny little ass back to school and get them before somebody steals them!"

Danny didn't need to be told twice. He quickly picked up his stuff from the floor, scrambled to his feet and ran out the front door, grabbing his sneakers along the way. He heard his mother holler after him, "You had better be back here with those glasses or don't ever plan on coming back here at all!"

"I will," Danny answered, running down the driveway.

When he got to the street, and far enough out of sight from their house, he started walking with his hands shoved deep in his pockets. Tears were streaming down his face. He wished he never had to go back there.

A light drizzle was falling and the air was cold in the late afternoon. The remnants of winter were still around and the rain didn't make his trip any more pleasant. Danny didn't care; he was relieved to be out of the house. The rain beaded on his face, masking his tears.

For some reason, he started thinking about Huckleberry Finn and how that kid didn't have a worry in the world. Wouldn't it be cool, Danny thought, if you could just become someone else? If you got tired of your life, you'd turn your life in for someone else's like the way you change clothes for church on Sunday. Even though Huck's father was a drunk, Danny thought that he would be better than the one he had. Besides, it didn't matter to Huck Finn what kind of father he had because he just ran away.

Quite out of the blue, it hit Danny: if Huck could run away, why couldn't he? The more that Danny let the fantasy roll around in his mind, the better he liked it. Food couldn't be all that hard to find. It would be spring soon which meant that the woods would be alive with apples, berries and whatever else he could find. In the meantime, he would steal food from school or something like that. Any life had to be better than the one he was living. Boy, when they found out that he was gone, they'd be sorry. They might not even holler at Mark or Louise anymore if they were afraid that they'd run away too.

In spite of the drizzle, Danny began walking a little bit taller. The more he played with the thought, the more reasonable it became. Slowly but surely,

Danny came to the decision that he was never going home again.

When Danny got to the school, Harry, the old, grizzly janitor let him in.

"What 'cho want, boy?" he asked.

"I left my glasses in the library. Can I get them, Harry?" Danny asked.

"Kids ain't 'sposed to be here after hours, don't you know that?"

"Please?" Danny begged.

Harry stared at him a moment, the relented. "Get a move on, boy! Don't say nothin' to no one!"

"Thanks, Harry!" Danny said as he ran down the hallway of the vacant school. He heard the plop of a wet mop as Harry continued about his work.

He ran into the library and went right over to the area where the new books were stacked. He found them in the Hardy Boys section. The school felt odd with only Harry and him there.

He was about to leave the library from where he came in when he got the idea of going out the other door toward where the cafeteria was. Quickly, he pushed his way through the double doors and ran down the hall, his shoes squeaking on the floor. He looked around twice and ran in the cafeteria. The first thing he saw was someone's windbreaker sitting over the back of a chair.

He picked it up and sized it. It might be big but it would fit, giving him some protection from the rain outside. "Empire Gas" was emblazed in white lettering on the back with a catchy phrase written underneath: "Where To Buy It". It reminded Danny of the cafe out by the airport with the red neon sign that said, "Good Eats". No matter, Danny thought, it would work as a satchel, too.

He went into the back door of the cafeteria and found everything locked except for a cabinet with a bag of Lay's Potato Chips in it and a jar of Goober Peanut Butter, with the stripe of grape jelly running through it. Without hesitation, he took them both. At the last second, he grabbed a box of wooden matches.

He wrapped the coat around them and went back into the hall. He could hear Harry whistling as he mopped the floor but he couldn't see him. Danny picked the closest door and dashed out of the school, unseen.

The drizzle had stopped, which perked up Danny considerably. He shoved the peanut butter in a coat pocket, put the coat on and tucked the chips under his arm so that he wouldn't look like a kid on the run. To any casual observer, he was just a kid walking home from school. He knew that daylight was only good for about an hour or so, so he had to think of where he was going to spend his first night alone. He was actually anticipating his adventure much more than he realized.

Danny thought of the pond down by the entrance to Woodcreek Hills. He and Mark spent many Saturdays there sailing their hand-made boats and digging up duck eggs, much to the consternation of the neighboring residents. He figured that it would be a great place to hide out temporarily since one side of it was bordered by trees. In case his parents came looking for him, he didn't want to be seen from the street. Danny shivered, not from the cold, but rather from remembering Momma's warning when he left. She had practically given him the idea to begin with, he thought bemusedly.

When he reached the pond, he looked up into the weeping willow trees. Although the branches hugged the ground, offering a good hiding place, they also looked eerie and dark blowing in the slight breeze. He was scared for a moment and then regained strength at the thought that it was better than going home. He dug the Mongoose Hot Wheels out of his pocket and rolled the wheels absentmindedly with his fingers while walking into the trees. The hill sloped downward toward the pond.

As he walked up the hill, pushing the wispy branches of the trees out of his way, he thought he could hear the slow grumble of a car every once in awhile. It made his head hurt as he imagined his parents angrily realizing what their son had done. Too late now, he thought. He had made a decision and he had to stick to it. The only other sound he could hear was the matted crunch of deadened leaves and pine needles as he trampled on nature's carpet.

Ahead, in the murkiness of the trees, he saw what looked like a doghouse. Danny warily approached it, thinking that it was probably a good place for a wolf to hide. He carefully set the bag of chips down by a tree, cringing at the light crackle of cellophane. He then proceeded to tip-toe up to the structure and cautiously peered inside. It was empty, except for a piece of old carpet that covered the floor. It smelled rank, but Danny figured that it would have to do until he found something better. The roof was covered in muddy clear plastic; at least he would be safe from the rain.

Danny crawled inside the house after he retrieved his chips from the tree. He lit a match to double check that he was the only occupant. A bug scurried out of sight. He maneuvered his body around so that his head was at the opening and cracked open the bag of chips, unscrewed the peanut butter and jelly and began dipping. Half an hour later, he had both Hot Wheels out, pretending that he and Mark were on a really cool adventure in their cars. He pushed away the thought that he was going to miss his brother. An hour later, the darkness falling, he fell asleep, the Snake and the Mongoose guarding the entrance to his new home.

When he awoke, he couldn't tell what time it was. All he could see was darkness except for the twinkling of the neighborhood lights off in the distance, past the pond. He rubbed his eyes and tried to get his bearings. Moments later, he realized what had awaken him. The coat did little to break the chill that was seeping in his bones. He thought about making a fire but discarded the idea because of the neighbors across the way. He would be too easily seen.

He wondered what his sister and brother were doing as he fought off a tinge of jealousy when he thought of them sleeping in warm beds. Then, he realized that he was lonely and couldn't help wondering if they had even noticed he was gone. Maybe they wanted him to stay away forever. Maybe his parents didn't want him anyway.

Danny started crying. When Huck Finn ran away, it sounded like a whole lot of fun, like an adventure. This wasn't fun at all. As a matter of fact, it was downright scary, Danny thought. Danny hated to admit it, but he actually thought that he missed his home. Maybe it wasn't the best place in the world, but it was sure better than being crammed in a cold and damp doghouse. At home, he had a warm bed and food to eat. He also had a brother and sister that seemed pretty far away.

He stopped crying when an idea occurred to him. Maybe he could go back. But he couldn't go back without trying to tell his parents what was wrong. Danny crawled out of the dog house and tore a piece of plastic off the roof. He took a wooden match out of the box. He leaned toward the dim glow of the streetlights and started punching holes in the plastic with the opposite end of the match. It took the better part of an hour to painstakingly make the note. It was like connect-the-dot without having the lines to connect. Each dot was close enough that you could read the note if you held it up to the light. When he was finished, he double checked his spelling. It read:

"Dear Momma and Dad, please don't hit and holler at us anymore. Danny."

It looked readable to him, so he decided to run home and drop it off. It seemed perfectly reasonable that he could leave the note on the front porch and then, the next night, his parents would leave him a note agreeing not to hit or holler at him, so that he would come home.

Danny walked back home, hiding whenever a car would come by.

Though his shivering stopped with walking, he was still cold right down to the bone. It didn't help when he had to hide, because the grass and weeds always got him even wetter.

It took him about forty-five minutes before he finally saw his house looming in the distance. All the lights were on, as if his parents had been waiting for him. Danny knew it would be difficult to run up the front steps, leave the note on the doormat, ring the doorbell and then take off before they saw him. But there was no other way. They would never see it on the back porch which would mean he'd freeze to death before they ever saw it. Once he started shivering again, he found the courage to make the twenty-five yard dash.

He dashed across the street and ran up the driveway, trying to avoid the blinding glare of the lights. He was aiming straight for the front porch steps when he saw his mother standing at the living room window. She had seen him! He felt like a raccoon trapped in front of Daddy's headlights, frozen in fear. It was too late for Danny to turn around. For some reason, he lost his courage and shoved the note in the bushes as he ran up the front steps.

"Danny! Danny!" His mother cried when she opened the front door.

"I'm sorry," he said as he ran into her arms.

"Where have you been?" she asked with tears running down her face. "We were so worried about you."

"I was..." Danny started to say.

"Oh, never mind," Momma said as she squeezed him close to her. "What counts is that you're okay!"

Momma got him some clean clothes and threw some hot dogs in the oven. The next thing he knew, he was eating food that tasted like manna from the gods. All the while, Daddy stayed silent.

"Why did you run away?" Daddy asked him when he had finished eating.

"I don't know," Danny answered hesitantly.

"Don't worry," his father said calmly. "Just tell us why."

Danny thought about it and then got up his nerve. "I was afraid," he said.

"Afraid of what?"

"Well, ever since we moved to Detroit, you get mad a lot. It seems like we get hollered at a lot and...Uh," Danny said, losing his courage.

"And what?"

"We get hit a lot."

Daddy looked at him, as if he was surprised. He looked down and started picking at his fingers. The kitchen settled in silence as Daddy thought about the words he had just heard. Then, he started talking very quietly, without looking at him.

"Danny, there are some things that you won't understand until you're an adult. As a parent, I have a lot of responsibilities. I have to work very hard every day to provide this family with a good home, food on the table and a decent education, something I always didn't have. It gets very difficult sometimes, especially when you kids misbehave. But," he said with an upraised finger, "we have to discipline you so that you'll learn the right way to behave. We don't do this because we dislike you; we do it so you'll learn. We want the best for you. Do you understand?"

"A little," Danny answered.

"We'll try to be more patient. Is that a deal?"

"Yes, Daddy. It's a deal."

"Good, champ. Why don't you go to bed and get some sleep? It's been a long day."

Danny went to bed, his spirits uplifted. It was the last time he'd ever be glad that he came home.

9

REUBEN AND CHERISE

Diana pressed stop on the tape recorder and proceeded to scribble her observations in the margins. She had no sooner finished writing her notes when she casually glanced at her watch.

"Damn!" she said out loud to herself. She was supposed to have dinner with her husband that evening. Time had slipped away from her and she had a mere half hour to get from her office on Front and Washington to the Northwood Restaurant on U.S. 41, ten miles away. She grabbed her briefcase and threw Daniel's file in it along with a few other case studies. Diana ran into the bathroom, straightened her hair and threw on a touch of make-up finishing it off with some fresh lipstick.

Diana ran down the stairs instead of taking the elevator. She knew that she was going to be late. Adam, her husband, was not going to be happy since he was a stickler for punctuality. Well, she thought, he was going to have to be as understanding about her career as he was about his. She couldn't count the number of times he showed up late for an engagement with her, yet when she was late...

Her black BMW 535i strained effortlessly with her increased acceleration. She narrowly missed an accident at Washington and Lincoln Boulevard as a station wagon, loaded with kids staring wild-eyed, slammed on its brakes to avoid her. She slowed down, thinking that it was not worth the risk.

She and Adam had been married for almost five years. They had both met at a medical conference that was held at the University of Michigan. From the moment that she had met him, she had felt comfortable and safe. He didn't believe in drinking (except for an occasional bottle of wine with dinner), as opposed to her first husband, which was a plus in itself. If she never saw a drink again, she would willingly trade it for a husband who believed in a mutual respect for each other. Both of them, being in the professional arena, did suffer for the demands. She couldn't count how many evenings that each of their pagers interrupted. She was only one of three psychiatrists in town while he was headed for chief cardiologist at Marquette General.

Lately though, it seemed that the strains of their careers were showing. They made love less often and when they did, it was short-termed, with Adam falling asleep only moments afterwards. Further, it seemed as if they were both getting more irritable with each other. Maybe this was a trade-off of the comforts of marriage for successful careers. Sadly, she suspected that these minor rifts were running deeper than she had suspected.

The turn for the Northwood showed up on her left just as the sun had reached the horizon. She glanced at her watch to see that she was only five minutes late. That was better than she had anticipated. She quickly parked her car and dashed into the restaurant. The hostess directed her to her table where her husband was waiting. He glanced at his watch, a slightly irritated look on his face.

"You're late," he said.

"I'm sorry, Adam. The traffic," she said offhandedly.

"Hmmm. Good to see you." He stood up and gave her a quick peck on the cheek and pulled out a chair for her.

"I hope you don't mind but I took the liberty to order a bottle of Cakebread Chardonnay. Does that sound alright with you?"

"I'll have a glass. Thank you."

Moments later, the waiter showed up with a bottle and opened it. Diana couldn't help but notice that her husband seemed distracted and fidgety, the silences growing greater while the sentences remained short.

They began their meal with a smoked Whitefish appetizer followed by a light Caesar salad with two anchovies over the top. Adam had the Filet Mignon, rare, while she elected to have the roast duck finished with a red wine black currant sauce. Diana couldn't help thinking that they talked more at home than they were talking here.

"Is there something on your mind?" she asked after a sip of Chardonnay.

"Just work," he answered perfunctorily.

Diana picked at her food, moving it around the plate. "How does the promotion look?"

"Oh, you know, politics," he answered while stuffing a rare piece of beef in his mouth. "There are arguments over tenure, education and the like."

"Do you still have a shot at it?"

"I wouldn't be here if I didn't feel it was possible. I'll get it," he said. "I'm sure of it."

They settled into the sounds of the restaurant with people talking happily while crazed waiters ran around trying to fill the needs of their exclusive clientele. Diana recognized at least ten affluent doctors and their wives along with a few lawyers, a judge and his wife and even two interns that she had seen at Social Services.

A pager went off, providing welcome relief to each other's presence.

Adam glanced at the digital display, wiped his mouth and excused himself with an apology saying that it was the hospital calling.

He pulled himself up from the table and left in search of the telephone. Diana wiped her mouth and quickly put on some fresh lipstick while he was gone. The next time the waiter came by; she told him that she was headed to the ladies room.

"Don't worry," he said. "I know you'll pay your check."

Diana walked past the hostess stand toward the ladies room. She saw her husband standing by one of the payphones talking anxiously. Her first thought was that she wished that he wasn't on call twenty-four hours a day. She was able to use Clinton as a back-up when she needed an evening off and why couldn't he afford himself the same back-up plan? Surely, there were surgeons who could split the responsibility. Then, for some reason, she stopped by the bathroom door and strained to hear his conversation from five feet away.

The first thing she noticed was that he was talking in a rushed tone. The second thing that she observed was that he appeared to be keeping his voice inordinately low, as if he were hiding something. Five years was a long enough amount of time to detect nuances in conversational tone and this sounded like a man who was buried in something that was heavily personal. She leaned forward to hear.

"Candice," he pleaded, "I'm going to tell her. That's why I brought her to dinner to begin with."

Diana tried to tell herself that she didn't hear what she thought she heard.

"I mean it, Peaches. Have a little understanding...of course, I love you..." he whispered. "...She'll take it fine...I know I've said this before but this time I mean it..."

A gray haired lady, in a sequin outfit that would have looked better on a person twenty-five years younger, almost tripped over Diana as she made her way into the bathroom. They both returned cold stares.

"...Yes, sweetheart, I have every intent of telling her tonight...I love you, I really do..."

Diana didn't want to hear anymore. She pushed into the bathroom, steaming. How could he do that to her? Had she ever done it to him? Where did he get the right to treat her like that? Son of a bitch, she thought. She turned and stormed her way out of the bathroom back to their table. Adam was sitting there with a small grin on his face.

"I thought you had left," he said as he stood up to pull her chair out.

"I am leaving," she said. "Enjoy the rest of your sorry dinner."

"Diana, wait. What's wrong?"

"Try the peach cobbler here. I hear it's wonderful!" she said, seething.

She then grabbed her full glass of Cakebread and threw it in his face. She grabbed her coat and forced her way through the patrons to the door. Diana vaguely heard him call out after her. Surprised looks emanated from everywhere but she couldn't see anyone through her rage.

She got in her car and roared the engine to life. She slammed it into drive and squealed out of the lot in a way that would have made Starsky and Hutch jealous. She had no sooner hit U.S. 41 when she decided that she needed a vacation desperately, by herself. In the background, she vaguely heard the sounds of Gilbert O'Sullivan's, Alone Again, Naturally. She wasn't amused at the coincidence and flipped the radio off.

The moment that she walked into their home, she ran upstairs and hurriedly packed a suitcase. She had already been through a bitter divorce and she knew what the road ahead would entail. This time, though, she wasn't the one who was going to walk out. It would be him who would not be allowed in. She had her rights and she knew what they were. She walked into the bathroom and literally threw his shaver, toothbrush and his half of "His" towels into his suitcase. "Son of a bitch," she muttered furiously.

She walked out to the front porch and reeled his suitcase into the driveway. It bounced and scraped on the asphalt without opening. Moments later, she heard the engine of his

Mercedes come screaming up the road. She changed the code to the security system, locked all the doors and closed the curtains.

Diana heard him run up the steps. Moments later, he started pounding on the door.

"Please, sweetheart," he yelled behind the barricade of the oak doors, "it's not what you think!"

"Stay away!" she screamed back.

"You don't understand," he retorted.

"You have to the count of three or I'm calling the police!" she answered as serious as she had ever been.

After five minutes of a stalemate, she watched as he walked down the steps, threw his suitcase in the car and left.

Diana walked around the house, not believing how fast her world had turned upside down. She should have seen it coming, she really should have. There was no sense in believing in anyone because people couldn't be trusted and she had seen that all her life. Her fingers trembled in anger. If she ever wanted to kill anyone, this was one of those moments.

Just then, slow in its approach, a vision crossed her mind. It was that of a hand on the inside of her thigh, warm and firm, but moving steadily forward. The smell of Old Spice seemed to bury her in its thickness. She felt as if she was a young girl and she was terrified. A blackness slowly moved across her senses as she fell back on a couch. Just as suddenly as it had appeared, it disappeared, leaving Diana feeling powerless and weak. She had the vision before but was it from a nightmare? She was familiar with it but couldn't quite place her finger on it. It was not an experience from either of her husbands but rather from...

But, she couldn't grasp it. It felt like it was on the edge of her memory like when one can't quite remember the name of a famous star from a famous movie when you damn well know the answer. It had something to do with Old Spice but she didn't know anyone who wore it, including her father. It was...it was...

Diana made her way over to the telephone. She prayed that Clinton would be there. Thankfully, he answered the phone on the third ring. She quickly told him what had happened with Adam. "It's as if I knew it was going to happen," she said sadly.

"You probably did," Clinton said reassuringly. "We do have those things happen that we don't want to believe."

"It seems like I just got out of the Tony mess, you know. Then, to be kicked in the face again like this, I don't know if I can handle it."

"But you will handle it, Doctor," Clinton said firmly. "What have I always said? You must learn to control it and not let it control you."

"But, Clinton, it's as if everything has repeated itself all over again. What am I doing wrong?"

"What do you feel you're doing wrong?"

Diana was at a loss for words. Clinton waited patiently for her response. "Maybe career women shouldn't be married," she said.

"That's horseshit, and you know it," he rebutted. "How do you feel right now?"

"I'm angry," she said quickly. "But beyond that, I'm not sure. I can easily say that I'm ashamed, afraid and I feel..."

"Feel what?"

"I feel used up inside. It's as if I'm empty. I have no room for any feelings, anymore. I'm almost afraid to tell you that I just want to move away and start over somewhere else. I look at my home and it looks like a fortress to a lie. I can't live like this," she said, an exasperated yet drained tone in her voice.

"Is that what you really want?" he asked her.

"Yes," she said, "I believe so."

"What of your patients, Diana?"

"I'll turn over the files to someone else. If anything, I need a vacation to get my head together."

"You can't do that."

"Clinton, I must do it."

"No, my dear, and here's why," Clinton said. She could hear him light up a cigar and puff thoughtfully. "You have a fiduciary responsibility to each one of your patients to follow through on a promise you made to them when you took them on as a client. You promised to help them through their problems until the very end. If you want to fade yourself out, you can. It will take awhile if you're serious about leaving. You cannot walk away and leave them in limbo. Each one of them has their own individual problems where they expect and demand that you're there. If you were to walk away, God knows what the ramifications would be. I could lighten the load for you," he said, "but I won't allow you to dump them. You know better than that."

"I understand, Clinton, but how do you expect me to take care of them if I'm not taking care of myself?"

"I have a suggestion that you may not like," he offered.

"Which is?"

"You bury yourself in what you enjoy doing the most, your work. Over time, with each minor success, the better you'll feel about yourself and the stronger you'll be in the face of adversity. Life happens, Diana. I know you're talented and bright or I'd be suggesting that you walk away. Instead, take your career by the horns and help people. You'll learn a lot about yourself."

"Thank you, Clinton," she said genuinely. "I'm almost ashamed that I called you to begin with."

"Don't talk that way," he said. "Doctor's orders. Make yourself a glass of warm milk and go to bed. Things are always better in the morning."

"I hate warm milk," she answered. "I'll relax, though, if that'll make you happy."

"It'll make me happy. Now get yourself some sleep and remember that I'm here if you need me."

Diana smiled and hung up the phone. She felt better but not by a whole lot. After a time, she got up the energy to take a long bath. All the while, she thought of all the things that made her life worth living. She realized that it was truly her patients. She had a gift for listening, similar to Clinton's ability that had helped heal her.

After she dried herself off from her bath, she lazily made her way into the living room, picking up her purse along the way. She turned on the television and absentmindedly watched a re-run of L.A. Law. Meanwhile, she fingered the lid to a bottle of Valium.

Her stomach was still in knots. Although she was against drugs, she dropped one of them down her throat. She had to calm down.

Just before she dozed off, she thought about a little boy named Danny and the world of problems he had had. At the same time, she pushed away an image...

There was a hand on her leg, calloused, large and warm. It moved upwards ever so slightly....

She didn't sleep well at all that night

10

SWEET LITTLE WHEELS

The spade full of dirt made a resounding thump as it hit the gunmetal gray casket. Dan stepped back and handed the shovel to his brother, Mark. Both men remained silent as Mark followed suit. Father McKevitt looked on as a throng of gawkers and reporters strained to watch their every movement. A warm breeze softly whisked their hair on the summer day.

"May she rest in peace with the Lord," the priest said somberly.

"Amen," the brothers said simultaneously.

The crowd was surprisingly quiet as they observed the burial of Marquette's first murder victim in eleven years. Their faces were dark and curious as they stared at the two brothers. It was as if they expected either one of the men to jump up and say, "We did it! We did it!" But that didn't happen. Instead, they saw two men who looked genuinely sad at their loss. Tears did not spill forward, though. The brothers stood there, stoic and firm in their stance, silent in their strength.

Mark reached over and squeezed Dan by the shoulder. Dan returned his arm over Mark's shoulder. In their eyes, they marveled at what a long strange trip it had been. Mary Wilcox, mother and dedicated wife, was laid to rest next to her partner of almost twenty-five years. All that could be said wasn't said and all that should have been said was left in the summer wind.

Father McKevitt, his services done, reached over and shook each of their hands quickly, as if he was relieved to be done with the matter. He acted as if it was not his business to ask questions and each brother could see it in his eyes: he was wondering what had brought them to this space in Holy Cross Cemetery. He averted his eyes as he stepped away from the plot. Dan and Mark didn't need a billboard to tell them what everyone was wondering. The press had not been good to their past, citing problems with truancy and drug abuse. Did they have a murderer in their midst on that summer day?

Dan looked toward the grave and said a final prayer to each of his two deceased parents. Inside, he was as genuine as he could be but he felt as if his prayers were as empty as the words of a blessing before a meal. This was not how he had wanted things to end and, in the back of his mind, he couldn't shake his fear wondering what hand he had in his mother's demise. It was one thing not speaking to his parents in fifteen years. It was quite another for his mother's life to end in murder. The gunmetal gray casket reflected the rays of the sun, the finality of it marked by the two spadefuls of dirt. As he closed his prayers, he fervently made one final wish: that it wasn't he who had plunged the knife into his mother.

Dan stepped back and looked Mark, who was preoccupied with picking at some loose threads on his suitcoat. "Well, shall we?" Dan asked, motioning that they exit.

"Yeah," Mark said, a faraway look in his eyes.

They turned and walked toward the car, the crowd splitting in half to let them through. A gutsy reporter from the Mining Journal called out to them, "How do you feel, now that you're a primary suspect in the murder of your mother? "

Dan ignored the outburst with a wave of his hand as if to say he had better things to do than answer questions from an ignorant reporter who didn't know his ass from a hole in the ground. They quickened their steps and hopped in the car. Neither one said a word as Dan started the car and pulled down Wright Street, each lost in their thoughts.

They found their way to U.S. 41 and headed toward Ishpeming. A few miles shy of it, Dan turned right at the airport. They parked in the parking lot that was meant for those who were departing on private aircraft. It was a spot that both were familiar with. It was where they always parked when their Dad used to go flying. They got out of the car and walked toward the end of the runway where Mark's dreams had been born so many years before. Charles Lindbergh was a memory that was still preserved in their heads, flying without a care in the world except to be in the air above everything else.

"Weird, isn't it?" Mark said more as a comment than a question.

"Yeah," Dan said as a Cessna 152 prepared for take-off. The engine increased in intensity as the pilot pushed the throttle.

They watched it creep forward, gaining speed with every foot. Finally, the plane bounced once, twice and then caught the wind as it lifted in the air, looking very much like their Sleek Streeks of years before.

"Remember that day?" Dan said.

Mark knew exactly what Dan was referring to. "Never saw another pair of gliders pull that off. How many times did we try to do it again?"

"No shit," Dan said. "Fifty or a hundred times?"

They watched a Beechcraft King-Air arc its way around for an approach, the sound of the propellers increasing in sound. They watched the flaps drop while the landing gear released. As it got lower and lower, they saw the nose raise itself ever so slightly as it approached the runway. It seemed to glide its way in, only inches above the runway. It made a familiar "chirp" as the wheels squeaked on the pavement, signifying a perfect landing.

"It was bad, wasn't it?"

"No, that was perfect," Mark said.

"No, I mean living at home."

"Yeah, it was," Mark answered.

"I don't think that any of this has hit me, you know? Then, you hear this guy trying to say that I'm the number one suspect. This is scaring the crap out me."

"Has the psychiatrist helped?" Mark asked.

"I guess so. As far as remembering those four days, though, I'm no closer than I was before. She keeps saying that it's going to take time. My concern is that I'm running out of time."

"Is there anything I can do?"

"Yeah," Dan said. "Tell me who killed her and help me find the rest of the family."

"It's a cold trail," Mark said. "I barely remember the family as it is."

"Where do you think Louise is?"

"Good question. The last I remember of her is in 1981. There are a lot of places you could disappear to in that amount of time." Mark reached into his pocket and pulled out a folded sheet of paper. "When you first told me about Mom's death, I wrote these people to let them know what happened. I didn't have any phone numbers and 411 was no help. There are grandparents on both sides, two cousins, one niece and an uncle on this list," Mark said as he handed Dan the sheet of paper.

Dan looked at it while the Beechcraft taxied past them to park with the privately owned airplanes. After it had passed them, Dan looked at Mark. "This is pathetic."

"What do you mean?"

"How can a whole family just disappear? Didn't they wonder what happened to us?" Dan asked no one in particular. "All those years and we didn't receive one Christmas card, birthday card or even a phone call. It doesn't seem fair."

"It stinks," Mark said. "I get this feeling that they knew what was going on and they didn't want to get their hands dirty. Like, it was none of their business what Mom and Dad did to us. So, they let us go like a bad dream."

" Thanks for coming all the way out here, Mark. I mean, from California."

"That's what brothers are for," Mark said as he put his arm around Dan's shoulder.

The two of them watched the airplanes for another hour without saying very much. They were lost in the nostalgia of being a kid again, without a worry in the world. They couldn't help but think of the rougher times but they remembered the times when they were left alone. One of those moments was always when Dad went flying and he left them to watch and dream at the end of the very runway at which they were standing.

"Is she dead?" Mark asked in reference to his twin sister.

"No," Dan said. "I don't think so. I've checked the records in every state. Louise isn't listed on a death certificate that corresponds with your birthday. She was one of the first that I tried to find after calling you. I've come up empty."

Mark thought about it for a moment. "What could have happened to her?"

"Do you miss her?" Dan asked, temporarily ignoring his question.

"I don't know anything about her except the way she was when we left. If

I remember then, she was practically a basket case."

"Weren't we all," Dan said, mused softly.

"I have an idea," Mark said. "Do you want to go to the house?"

"Not really. Why?"

"I left something there. I don't know if it's still there but it's worth a shot."

"What are you talking about?"

"Well, remember when we used to hide stuff from our parents?"

Mark was referring to the hiding of their toys such as Hot Wheels, model airplanes and the like. They hid some of their favorite things to keep them safe from their father's rages.

Punishment oftentimes included the smashing of their toys which usually hurt more than the bruises because the wounds went away but the toy treasures were never replaced. They still recalled GI Joe sets and favorite cars that they never saw again. As a preventive measure, they hid toys outside, in the basement and behind shelving in the garage so they wouldn't get destroyed.

"I remember," Dan said. "What's still hidden?"

"It'll be a surprise."

So, the two of them drove to the Villa Capri, an inexpensive Italian restaurant across from the mall, and had dinner. It was Mark's idea to wait until after dark. They had a cheese pizza and split a pitcher of beer. After dinner, they stopped at K-Mart to check the latest releases of Hot Wheels. They were elated to find two Flip-outs, spring loaded cars that would flip upon contact with each other.

An hour later, they parked the Cougar a block from the house.

"I don't know if we should do this," Dan said.

"The police aren't going to let us in. It's our house now, anyway," Mark answered confidently.

They grabbed a flashlight out of the trunk and headed up the long and winding driveway, careful not to be seen by anyone. The house looked eerie and large without any lights on, framed against a moonlit sky. Every once in awhile, small animals rustled in the leaves: causing their hair to stand up on the back of their necks.

"Watch out for the police ribbon," Dan whispered. "And don't touch anything!" he warned.

"I know," Mark whispered back. They felt like two boys again, on a childhood adventure.

They crept up to the porch and walked toward the living room window which was taped over with cardboard. They slowly unsealed it and crawled through.

"It stinks in here," Mark said quietly.

"You should have smelled it when I found her body."

Dan followed Mark to the winding stairs that lead to the basement. They pushed the door open, their flashlights on. Being inside, they were a lot calmer as they knew that no one could see them from the street but still avoided hitting the windows with the beam of their light.

"What are we looking for?" Dan asked.

"You'll see."

Mark went to the room where their father's workbench was. He climbed up on the table and removed a ceiling tile, handing it to Dan. He pointed his light into the rafters and strained to reach in. Dan's heart was beating a mile- a-minute, partly out of fear and partly out of excitement.

"Shh!" Dan said sharply.

"What?" Mark whispered back.

"Don't move! I think I heard something!"

Both of them remained frozen as they waited for another sound. All Dan kept thinking was that if they got caught, they were going to be in a world of trouble.

"I guess it's nothing," Dan finally said.

"You scared the crap out of me!"

"Sorry."

Mark reached back into the rafter and finally began tugging on something. Finally, he pulled out a two-foot long board. A moment later, he retrieved something else.

"I got it!" Mark said excitedly. He jumped down from the table with his prizes in hand. He sat on the floor and assembled their find. Dan pointed the light at it and was surprised to see a gas-powered toy Stuka airplane.

"Remember this?" Mark asked excitedly.

Dan did remember it but it had been twenty years since he had last seen it. Mark had hidden it to be safe from destruction and to see it again was like a trip to a long and distant memory.

"Wow!" Dan whispered.

Mark snapped the wing to the fuselage and held it up. They admired it with awe. It was two feet long with a two-and-half-foot wingspan. Twenty years of dust had accumulated on it but it looked shiny and new to them.

They were children again in that one infinitesimal moment.

Then, Mark asked for Dan's Flip-out. He put it with his and crawled back up on the table and stuffed them in the rafters. "This way, we'll always be part of this house."

They put the tile back up and left the basement.

"You found her in the kitchen?" Mark asked, leading the way.

Their flashlights beamed across the floor until they reached the blood- spots. Each spot was marked with a number on a piece of masking tape.

They came around the kitchen counter to see the taped outline of the body. A darkened area of blood surrounded it.

"You must have shit!" Mark said.

"Actually, I threw up," Dan responded.

Suddenly, a vision crossed Dan's mind. It was a brief second but it was enough to jolt him back to reality. If he were to describe the feeling, he would liken it to the fading feeling of a nightmare moments after one is awakened.

Mark must have sensed that something had happened. "What is it?" he asked.

Carefully, Dan spoke, unsure if he was correct in his analysis. "I just remembered something," he whispered excitedly.

"What?"

"Somebody was here with me," he said, struggling to prod the brief memory. Dan's eyes became furrowed in thought as he tried to reach deep in his mind for a picture. He raised his finger as if to grasp the thought like one reaches up to a cabinet to get a glass. "I remember getting hit," he said slowly.

"By who?"

"That's just it, I don't know. But I remember the blinding white flash and reaching back to catch myself. I don't think that I knew who it was," Dan said.

"Could it have been a burglar?"

Dan struggled but couldn't get anymore out of his mind. He looked at the grisly scene carefully, searching for a clue. "Maybe. Dammit!"

"Calm down," Mark said. "You know you didn't do it, though. Right?"

"Yeah," Dan said. "Now I'm almost sure I didn't kill her. If only I could remember more."

"This is giving me the creeps. You want to get out of here?"

"Let's go," Dan said.

The two of them carefully walked through the carnage that was once their home and made their way out the living room window, their flashlight turned off. Dan pressed the cardboard back over the window.

As soon as they got home, Dan cracked open a couple of Icehouse beers. They settled in the living room and reminisced over their airplane find. Dan threw in a 1969 Marin County show without paying attention to it. Minutes later, they were having another beer.

Mark took a swallow of beer. "Where are the clothes you said you were wearing?"

"In the bedroom," Dan answered offhandedly.

"Can I see them?"

"Sure."

Dan went back to his bedroom and reached into the hamper. Moments later, he walked out of the room, his face pale. "They're not there."

"What?"

"Just what I said, they're not there." Dan started pacing and thinking. "There's no place else that I would put them. I'm sure that I balled them up and put them in the hamper. I know it!"

"Who would take them?"

Dan pondered his situation for a long time, rechecking the hamper three times. He then looked under the bed, in his drawers, the bathroom and back to the hamper one more time. He walked back into the living room. "I know that this is going to sound preposterous but do you remember my telling you about the detective and how he treated me?"

"Yeah," Mark said. "You said that you thought he suspected you right off."

"Uh-huh. Are you ready for this?"

"What's that?"

"The reporter this morning. Remember when he asked how I felt being a suspect?" Dan was thinking quickly, assembling pieces in his mind. "How do you think that happened?"

"Nobody's arrested you so they may not have much," Mark offered.

"Yeah, but what if they have the clothes?"

Mark thought about it for a minute. "That doesn't prove anything."

"Except for one thing," Dan said. "If the fibers of the clothes are the same material that they found in her neck..." His voice trailed off.

Mark finished the thought out loud. "Then you're in deep shit."

"I don't like this at all," Dan said. Suddenly, he left the room and busied himself in the bedroom. Mark watched as Dan kept carrying things to the car.

"What are you doing?" he finally asked.

Dan was tossing his Marlboro camping gear in the trunk including a sleeping bag, tent, portable grill and a backpack loaded with his basic essentials. If Mark doubted his seriousness, his doubts were dashed when he saw Dan load his most prized possessions in the car, his Grateful Dead concert tapes. He slammed the trunk closed and looked at Mark.

"I can't go to jail," he said adamantly. "I can't! Not until I know what the hell happened in those four days."

A concerned look crossed Mark's face. "You're not telling me that you'd run from the law, are you?"

"You're damn right I am," Dan said. "I've done the jail thing before and I'm never doing it again. I mean it! This isn't California, Mark. This is the land of the Yoopers versus the Trolls. Do you know what I mean?"

"I can't get what you're driving at," Mark answered honestly.

"This is a town that hasn't changed one bit since we left. In other words, in a small town like this, there's not a chance that people would believe me.

They believe what they hear and what they don't want to hear, they shove it under the rug. I'm not going to be an unwilling victim again. I refuse to be!" Dan said with a fervency that almost scared Mark.

"You can't be serious, Dan."

"I'm as serious as a goddamned heart attack! This will not happen to me twice. If this cop wants to play Mark Fuhrman, then so be it. But those clothes went somewhere and I wouldn't put it past him or the city."

"Think about what you're doing," Mark warned.

"I might be paranoid, Mark. I'll give you that. That doesn't change the fact that those clothes are gone. If I have to, I'll run until I can find out what the hell happened to me. Either you're going to be there for me or you're not."

Mark walked over to the window and looked out over the front porch into the midst of the moonlight washed trees. He could see the shimmering reflections of the waters of Lake Superior. Slowly, he turned around. "Are you absolutely sure that you had nothing to do with her murder?"

"Yes," Dan answered, a solid tone in his voice.

"Then, like always, I'm there."

"Thank you," Dan said. "I'm going to continue going through this therapy because it's the only chance I've got at getting my memory back. But, I know that I'll do whatever it takes until then."

Mark picked at the label on his beer. "I'm scared," he said quietly.

"Me, too," Dan said. "I've got to think, though. All I'm thinking is, just in case."

"I hope it doesn't come to that."

"Just in case," Dan said. Under his breath, barely audible to Mark, "Who the hell was there? Who hit me on the day she was murdered?"

The next day, Dan went to his psychiatrist while Mark waited at the house for him to return.

That's when the whole shithouse went up in flames, as Jim Morrison of The Doors once said.

11

TOUCH OF DARKNESS

Danny's alarm clock went off at 6:30 a.m.; it was a school morning. The sun beamed through the bedroom window telling him that it was going to be a beautiful day. At least it was a school day, Danny thought. After his running away, he didn't relish the thought of being in the house more than was necessary. As was becoming the usual fare, he woke up with nervous butterflies bouncing around in his stomach.

The kids had about forty-five minutes to be out of the house if they didn't want to run into their parents. They would rather hang out at the bus stop early than be in the house when they awoke. The trick was, Danny had to wake up Mark and Louise as quietly as possible. All they had to do was get dressed and eat. They weren't allowed to take showers in the morning because it woke Daddy up. He was usually not very happy if disturbed by the kids prior to when he awoke. Danny learned to ignore the other kids when they made fun of him for not taking a shower before school. Actually, he wasn't sure how they could tell, either. It wasn't as if it was something he announced. Momma allowed them to take showers twice a week after school. Danny and Mark shared a three minute shower because Momma and

Daddy didn't think it worth the money to waste water on a bunch of ungrateful kids.

As the kids got dressed, they were careful not to make even the tiniest of sounds. If you had to say something to someone, you whispered so softly that it was almost to the point of reading lips. If you walked down the hallway past Momma and Daddy's door, you tiptoed very slowly so that the floor wouldn't creak. Further, you tiptoed across the tile floor so that the thumping sounds wouldn't rouse the parents. All this had begun when they moved to Detroit. There were many times when one of them would bump into a closet door, sneeze, cough or, at the worst, giggle and then Daddy would come stomping out of the bedroom, clad in only underwear, yelling, "You just had to wake me up, didn't you? I work my ass off to keep a roof over our heads and you can't even afford your father a decent night's sleep!" Then, the kids would feel like garbage and the whole day would be ruined. It was worth it to read lips than to risk his anger.

After the kids were dressed, they'd creep downstairs to the kitchen. They were allowed one of three breakfasts: Corn Flakes, Cheerio's or puffed wheat cereal. One bowl, no more and no less, complemented with a half a teaspoon of sugar, although Danny was known to dispense more. With the cereal, the kids were allowed one glass of their milk but not Daddy's milk. Daddy drank the expensive real milk while they were only allowed powdered milk because, the white emblazoned lettering read: one box MAKES TWENTY QUARTS! Once in awhile, if Momma were in a good mood, she'd flavor the milk with a grape or Cherry Kool-Aid, masking the chalky taste. If Daddy thought his milk was too old, he'd allow the kids to have it. Unfortunately, sometimes it was too old, greeting the back of your throat with chunks that, needless to say, would make you instantly want to throw up. If Momma noticed that, she'd be nice and throw it away where the grape flavored milk became a welcome relief. The point was: Momma and Daddy didn't want to be put in the poorhouse trying to feed the kids.

In Danny's opinion, powdered milk ranked right up there with Momma's substitute for potatoes, "Potato Buds". Sometimes Momma wouldn't stir them quite enough, or she'd add a little bit too much salt making them inedible.

The one time that Danny complained about their culinary choices was the last time he complained.

After they consumed their breakfast, they took their pre-prepared lunches out of the pantry. They, too, had a ritual set in stone behind them. It was primarily why Mark started begging for food, although that's a later story.

They could expect one of four types of sandwiches, depending upon Momma's mood and the budget that week. Plain peanut butter (creamy style, no butter or jelly), bologna, pickle-pimento loaf or peanut butter with bologna (if she was in a good mood the day before). On Mondays, they always could expect peanut butter sandwiches because they were made on Fridays and were the only sandwiches that wouldn't spoil from sitting in the pantry all weekend. They had learned never to mention that the bread went stale and the peanut butter became a dark brown, the consistency of a soft rubber. The one sandwich a piece was served with three animal crackers, or Vanilla Wafers, if they were on sale that week, and an apple. The thermos was filled with Kool-Aid, though, affording them an enjoyable drink.

It was no wonder that Momma bragged that she could feed three kids on sixty-eight cents a day.

When they left the house, without a confrontation with either parent, their sense of relief was incomparable. On the other hand...

Danny liked school for the most part. If anything, it was a welcome reprieve from his home life, as he didn't have to worry about teachers hitting and hollering at him. He felt free and relaxed for those eight hours away from home. Mondays were the best, after a long weekend at home, while Fridays were the worst because of the anticipation of a long weekend at home coming up. All day, he could expect an increasing amount of jitters to settle in before the final school bell would ring. If weekend nervousness was bad, then Christmas vacation would be worse with the thought of spending two weeks at home with Momma and Daddy. The final day before summer vacation topped them all because, well, three months at home could be almost unbearable. Danny could have sworn, at times, that he was going to get an ulcer worrying that much. He wasn't sure if kids could get one but there were times that his stomach got so knotted up that he thought he was going to die. It was hard to understand why all the other kids would scream with glee at the final summer vacation bell.

School gave Danny a chance to daydream and to read. Momma and Daddy told him that there was no reason why he couldn't be a straight "A" student. Unfortunately, that was not always the case because Danny loved to read. He always got a seat in the back of the class, a luxury bestowed upon him because his last name began with a "W". In the back of the class, he could read books held under his desk, propped so that the teachers couldn't see what he was doing. He had already learned everything that was being taught way back in kindergarten. So, to alleviate the boredom, books were his perfect escape. He read everything he could get his hands on, in part out of defiance, but mostly to escape.

The Hardy Boys were his favorite because he imagined his being a part of that family. Their dad was really nice and allowed Frank and Joe to go on any adventure they wanted to. If the boys did something wrong, their dad showed understanding about it. The best part about The Hardy Boys was that there were so many books about them. Just as soon as he thought he had finished them all, he would discover three more mysteries.

Another one of his favorite authors was Edgar Allen Poe. He could get lost for weeks at a time in his stories, imagining the worlds of terror that were bestowed upon people. At times, he could picture the characters being members of his family. In, *The Pit and The Pendulum*, for example, he imagined his father being the man who was trapped on the table, the arc of the ax coming closer and closer until it would slice him in half.

His favorite book, though, was, *Death Be Not Proud*, by John Gunther, the story of his son dying of cancer. Danny tried to imagine what his parents would think if he suddenly got cancer. He bet they'd be sorry for some of the things they had done. He could see himself in the final scene, reaching toward his father and mother and telling them not to worry. Then, the ravages of the disease would overtake him and he would expel his final breath, with all the theatrics that came with death. Danny wished there was a way that he could get cancer but, unfortunately, he couldn't get so lucky. He must have read that book fifty times; it was great meat for daydreams.

There was one problem with reading that much. Without his realizing it, it began affecting his grades. The worse his home life got, the more that he could be found buried in a book. Momma and Daddy started noticing how much Danny was reading so they took all of his books away, forcing him to work on his studies. Danny found that he couldn't concentrate after awhile so he increased his reading at school, out of the watchful eyes of his parents. He needed that world of fantasy desperately and he wasn't going to let them take away that one simple enjoyment.

There came a fateful day when he became a victim of his voraciousness. It was near the middle of the semester when all the teachers handed out "Progress Reports", a sort of update on how the students were doing. He did fairly well in all of his classes except for his English Class with Mrs. Hamilton. He had this feeling that she didn't like him very much. He stayed away from her because he likened her to an old gray witch with her stringy hair and crackly voice. Wrinkles criss-crossed her face like a roadmap to a big city while her black mascara made her eyes look dark and mean. On top of that, she had a big mole on her chin with six black hairs protruding from it.

He knew he was in trouble the moment that she called his name. He walked up to get his report and she paused before giving it to him.

"Tsk, tsk, tsk...Danny, Danny, Danny," she commented, her dark eyes staring into his. She handed him the report, nodding her head disdainfully.

Danny walked back to his desk. He could pretty well tell that he wasn't going to open the card and receive an "A" like in all his other classes. His fingers trembled as he fingered the envelope. He was worried. If he got a "C" again, he was in trouble and he knew it. He crossed his fingers, took a deep breath and held it as he pulled the green slip out of the envelope. He peeked at it out of the comer of his eye. It was at that moment that he felt his bowels sink.

Danny asked for permission to go to the bathroom and darted out of the room, his report stuffed in his back pocket. Once he got to the boys' room, he pulled it out and looked at it as if to confirm what he had really seen. A blaring "D+" stood out as if it had a neon sign attached to it. To make matters worse, she had scribbled a note on the bottom: "Danny doesn't pay attention. Danny has to be pushed!"

Nobody needed to tell him that he could look forward to the belt when he got home after Daddy saw the report. His pacing footsteps echoed off the tiled walls as he tried to figure out what he was going to do. He couldn't shake the queasy feeling in his stomach as he re-read the report over and over again.

The rest of the day, Danny did not read because he was too pre-occupied with his problem. Further, he didn't pay attention to any of his teachers as he had bigger things on his mind, like how sore he was going to be.

It wasn't until his last class, social studies with Mr. Peters, did he fall upon an idea. What if he never showed his parents at all? He started thinking that he could get away with it if he was really careful. The only hard part entailed affixing his father's signature on the bottom and he doubted that Mrs. Hamilton would ever notice the difference. She had never seen his father's signature, had she? If it spared him a whipping, Danny thought it was worth the risk. The best part of the plan was that Danny was the only one in middle school with the other kids being in grade school. Momma and Daddy would never have to know that they had given out progress reports. Lord knows, if he had known he was going to get a progress report, he never would have let his grade slip that far. On top of that, Danny knew that he could raise his grade by the end of the semester and nobody would be any the wiser that he had done so poorly.

If only it had been a "C-" he wished over and over again.

Danny's heart sunk when he saw his father's Blazer in the garage, parked next to Momma's Cadillac, when he got home from school. He nervously walked into the house, his report hidden inside the book jacket of one of his schoolbooks.

Daddy was sitting on the couch in the family room, reading a Flying magazine, with a Police Woman episode on the television. Daddy liked to relax by reading with the television playing softly in the background. He'd look up once in awhile, get the gist of the show, and go back to reading. It was hard to understand how he did it.

When Danny walked in, Daddy looked up at him over the rim of his reading glasses.

The very first thing his father said to him was, "Well, let's take a look at your progress report."

Danny couldn't believe his father asked him that. How did he know? "We didn't get one," Danny lied, his voice as confident as he could muster up at that moment.

"Oh really?" he said. His glasses slid a notch down on his nose, exposing his eyes more clearly. He waited for Danny to respond.

Danny wasn't sure what to say, so he buried himself a little deeper by saying, "We don't get them anymore." He almost wished that he had altered the letter "D+" into a "B+", instead. It was too late now.

"You wouldn't lie to me, would you?" he asked calmly.

"Oh, no, Daddy. I'm not lying," Danny answered with a false bravado.

"You can call the teacher if you want to." He figured that there was no chance that Daddy would risk embarrassment by calling his bluff. Of course,

Danny would have died if his father went right to the phone.

Instead, Daddy looked at his son very carefully, his face expressionless but his words were slow and firm, "You had better not be lying to me or there won't be a piece of skin left on your hide after I finish with you. Is that clear?"

"Of course, Daddy," Danny answered quickly, a shiver cascading up his spine. He figured that he may as well run away forever if his scheme didn't work.

Daddy returned to his reading and television, which Danny took as his intimation to leave the room. As soon as he got to his room, he exhaled quietly as if he had held his breath the whole time. He noticed that his hands wouldn't stop shaking.

The next day, on the school bus, he pulled out his report and set it on his math book. He waited for the bus to stop at a traffic light before he affixed his father's signature to the bottom line. The light turned green just as he was in the middle of his father's last name. The pen scrawled erratically as Danny cursed his luck. He scrutinized it carefully and eventually accepted it as authentic.

The first thing that Mrs. Hamilton did was to pick up the progress reports. At each desk, like a sergeant on inspection of his troops, she stopped and looked at the corresponding student's reports. The room was quiet, with each kid wishing they were someplace else. As she got closer to Danny's desk, he broke out in a cold sweat, his palms reaping the rewards. His stomach felt like it had a knot in it the size of a basketball. She'll know! Danny thought. With every step closer, Danny regretted his scheme a little more.

When she finally took a stand next to him, Danny couldn't find the guts to look up at her as he handed her his report. He felt like her eyes were drilling into him and that she seemed to be standing there inordinately long. He kept thinking, *Go away! Go away!*

Instead of going away, he heard her ask him if his parents had seen the report. She hadn't asked any of the other kids that! He couldn't believe his luck.

"Yes, Mrs. Hamilton," he said in his most polite and angelic voice. His eyes averted hers.

"Is this your father's signature?" she asked, inspecting the report carefully.

Danny could feel his classmates staring at him as if he had just walked in from another planet. "Yes," he answered quietly, frightened beyond comprehension. Please, he prayed, go away!

Mrs. Hamilton fingered the report card envelope. He could hear it ticking as her fingernail played with it.

"You're not very good at this," she said sternly.

"What do you mean?" Danny asked, feigning honesty.

"Since it appears that you want to continue this charade, young man, why don't you accompany me to the principal's office?"

"No, please, Mrs. Hamilton!"

She pulled Danny to his feet by the back of his collar. "Class?!" she said to all the attentive eyes of the other students,

"Get to your studies. I'll be back in a few minutes to resolve this little problem. And if anyone wants to misbehave, they can sit with Danny in the principal's office. Is that understood?"

"Yes, Mrs. Hamilton," they all answered in unison. They knew who the chief was of that tribe.

To the embarrassment of Danny, he was paraded out of the class by his shoulder. As soon as they got to the principal's office, she lead him to an adjoining room where bookshelves adorned the walls and file cabinets stood by a desk that was clear except for a rotary black telephone.

"Sit down," she commanded. She picked up the receiver of the telephone.   "What's your telephone number?" she asked.

"It's eight-two-four-five-six-zero-zero-one," Danny stuttered.

"You must think we were all born yesterday. Well, this is what God invented telephone books for," she said as she reached into a drawer.

Danny knew that he had given a fake phone number. A moment later, it occurred to him that he had given one too many numbers. He wrung his hands in consternation and dread. He also had to go to the bathroom terribly bad as soon as she found the number that she was looking for.

"Mrs. Wilcox?" she said.

Pause. To Danny's furthering dismay, Momma was home.

"I was calling to find out if you had seen your son's progress report?"

Pause. Danny could have sworn that he was going to wet his pants. He picked at the green vinyl of the chair he was sitting in, avoiding any eye contact. His goose was cooked, as Grandma would say. He waited out Momma's response.

"Yes, Mrs. Wilcox, I'm Mrs. Hamilton from Calgary Middle School. It's in reference to your son, Danny. I don't believe I know Mark, yet."

Danny could picture Momma on the other end, assuming that the phone call would have been about his brother. He could imagine her surprise.

"As I was saying," Mrs. Hamilton continued, "Danny returned his progress report today and I just needed to confirm that you and your husband saw it."

Pause. Danny stared at the twitching hairs coming out of Mrs. Hamilton's mole, trying not to think about his father's warning the night before.

"Hmmm. That's what I thought. The signature did look pretty phony to me. I've been teaching for a lot of years and I'm used to their tricks. I'll be quite frank in saying that I didn't expect this out of Danny." She gave him a sneering look that didn't make Danny feel any better about his situation. "Although, most children choose to alter their grades. I've seen very few of them actually have the audacity to forge."

Danny looked down to the white tiled floor as Mrs. Hamilton informed his mother of his true grades. Then, she ended the conversation as quickly as she had started it and hung up the phone. She looked at Danny with accusation and disgust in her eyes.

"What is wrong with you?" she asked.

"Nothing," Danny answered meekly.

"Do you understand that what you have done is despicable and underhanded? Not only did you lie to your parents, you've lied to me. I don't like lying. Do you understand that?"

Danny didn't say anything. What was there to say?

She leaned on the desk and looked at her student. "If your father wasn't a doctor, I'd march you into the principal's office and ask for a suspension if not an expulsion. I don't feel that you understand the seriousness of what you've done. If you were an adult, a forgery conviction means that you'll go to prison. Imagine how your parents must feel. As far as I'm concerned, you can count yourself lucky that you're not my son or you'd get a tanning of your hide that you could tell your grandchildren about," she said with a warning from her index figure. "As a matter of fact, if you were my son, I would tell you that you are a lousy son!" She stood up abruptly, her words of admonishment complete.

Danny felt like he had been slapped in the face. For a moment, he wanted to tell her the real reason he had done it. He knew that she'd probably pick up the phone and call Momma again. If only he could tell her that he didn't realize what he'd done. He'd only been trying to protect himself. As he stood up, he realized that other kids suffered like he did, considering what she had said about tanning his hide.

He deserved to be punished, didn't he? He asked himself.

He hung his head all the way back to class as he followed her marching heels going click-clack all the way down the hallway. When they got back in the classroom, he could feel the eyes of all the other kids boring down on him like he was the bearded lady at the carnival or something. They couldn't care less as to what he'd done and why he'd done it, and Danny knew that. The fact that he was humiliated in front of everyone by going to the principal's office was almost worse than the prospect of getting the belt.

Almost, but not quite.

For the second day in a row, he sat there lost in another world. Would it be the skinny belt or the fat belt? Needless to say, he didn't pay attention to any of his teachers and he found no respite in, The Hardy Boys, nor any other piece of literature. All he could do was contemplate his demise and how severe it would be.

When Danny got home from school that afternoon, things didn't happen exactly as he thought they would. Momma made him nervous by giving him the silent treatment. He could imagine what inmates on death row felt like: doomed. Just before Daddy got home, she fed him a tasteless dinner. Danny felt like it was going to be his last meal on earth. As she threw the plate in front of him, she commanded tersely, "Eat. You're going to need it!"

Danny ate alone because Momma said the other kids weren't allowed to be near him, as if forgery was contagious. Danny forced the food down only because he didn't want to be sitting there like a trapped animal when his father walked in. Here and there, he tried to swallow the biggest chunks of food that he could in the hope that he might choke to death, a fate better than dealing with Daddy. It was to no avail.

"Go to your room!" Momma said curtly when he had finished.

As he was walking up the steps, he heard the sound of his father's truck pulling into the driveway. He quickened his steps to his bedroom. As soon as he got there, he dropped to his knees by his bed, did the sign of the cross and started praying as hard as he could. In school, they said that if you prayed hard enough, and God was listening, he would grant anything you wanted. All Danny wanted was to make it through the evening unscathed.

He prayed hard, too, apologizing for his forging and begging not to get the belt. When he ran out of pleas, he moved into as many "Hail Mary's" and "Our Father's" as he could say. He was probably into his second or third rosary's worth of prayers when he heard his father walk into the foyer.

"And how was your day?" Momma asked, like always.

"Another lousy one," he answered tiredly. "I saw all of two patients today and I'll be damned if we think we're going to manage like that!"

"We'll manage," Momma said. "We always do."

"At this rate, I'm starting to think that we had it a hell of a lot easier in Marquette," he said, as Danny heard his car keys drop into the foyer bureau drawer.

Danny quit praying because he couldn't concentrate anymore. He completed the sign of the cross and sat on the edge of his bed, wringing his hands in nervous frustration.

"I've got some news for you," Momma said.

Danny's stomach lurched on cue.

"Oh, what's that?"

"We've got a busy little boy named Danny."

"Oh?"

"I got a call today from Danny's teacher, Mrs. Hamilton."

"Have we met her?"

"No," Momma answered. "She sounds like a very nice lady, though."

"What did she have to say?"

"Well, she asked if we had seen Danny's progress report and..."

"I thought he didn't get one," Daddy interrupted.

"Oh, it gets even better than that," Momma said, as if she enjoyed telling the story. "Not only did he get a progress report, he returned it with a signature on it. You won't believe whose signature it was."

"Don't tell me," Daddy answered as if he already knew. "Whose signature?"

Danny was wringing his hands so hard that he thought his knuckles were going to break.

"Yours," Momma answered. "Oh, one more thing. Wait till you see the grade that he got in his English class. Here, take a look at this."

Danny could hear Daddy opening the envelope. There were a few interminable moments of anticipation.

"Danny?" his father called from downstairs.

"Yes, Daddy?"

"I think you had better march your ass down these stairs right now!"

Danny wiped his sweaty hands on his pants, looked up toward the ceiling where God was and said a final, fervent plea. He then hurried down the stairs and faced his father.

"Do you have an explanation for this?" Daddy asked.

"I'm sorry!" Danny blurted out prematurely.

"What?"

"I didn't mean to do it," Danny confessed, his voice cracking.

Daddy leaned against the kitchen counter and looked at him. "You're sorry for what?"

"Yes, Danny," Momma said with her hands on her hips, "Why don't you tell your father what you're sorry for?"

From the way everything looked, Danny knew that he was cornered. So, rather than beat around the bush, he figured it best to come clean on everything. "I got a "D" in English and I was afraid to tell you about it. And then, I lied last night when you asked me about it and I wrote your name on the report. I'm sorry," Danny said in a high-pitched voice.

"You did what?!"

"I got a "D" in English and..."

"No, Danny," his father said, stopping him, "Let me hear that again about my name on a progress report."

"I accidentally put your signature on it."

Daddy stared at his son with an incredulous look on his face, as if he couldn't believe what he had heard. He looked at Momma and she nodded her head in the affirmative. He looked back at Danny. "You little son of a bitch."

"I'm sorry," Danny said. "I didn't mean to do it!"

"Do you know what you've done? Do you?"

Danny took two steps back.

Daddy slammed his fist on the kitchen counter causing everything to jump, including Danny. "Not only have you gone against my wishes by getting poor grades, you have lied to me. As if that isn't enough, you forged my name! Are you a doctor?

Have you earned that right to use that title? Did you go to school for fourteen years to become a doctor?"

"No," Danny said.

"You're damned right, you didn't! And with these kinds of grades, you never will!" Daddy yelled, white foam coming out of the comer of his mouth.

Danny watched the usual begin happening. He braced himself as Daddy's jaw jutted forward and his fists clenched. Danny waited for it, expected it, and watched the first blow backhand him into the wall.

"Now, Why don't you tell me what you did again."

"I...please don't!"

Daddy reached down and pulled Danny up with a handful of hair.

Danny's scalp screamed, as it felt like a hundred-thousand needles were piercing his head.

"That's enough, honey!" Momma suddenly interjected.

Daddy let go of Danny's head, glaring at him.

"Remember what it says in the book, I'm OK, You're OK? We're learning to have patience, remember? You're tired and he's not worth it," Momma said.

Danny felt like he was going to wet his pants. He could see his father thinking about what his mother had said. He was contemplating, letting reasoning sink in. He never broke the stare from Danny's eyes, his face red with anger, as he asked Momma, "Tell me why I shouldn't punish him."

"Don't get me wrong, he should be punished."

"Tell me why I shouldn't beat him to a pulp."

"Honey, look at me," Momma said.

Daddy looked at Danny for a few seconds, as if to say, "I'll get back to you later!" He turned toward Momma.

Now that she had his attention, she continued, "First of all, I don't want to be putting make-up on him for the next two weeks. Second of all, if we do that, we're running the risk of having to explain it to his teachers. We just went through this not too long ago. Finally, if you want my opinion, I think our son is very screwed up in the head. I don't hear about other kids running away from home and forging their father's signature. Do you?"

"So, what do you suggest?"

"I think he should be grounded and then we should follow the advice of that book and take him in for some counseling."

Daddy turned and looked at his cowering son.

Although Danny could tell that he didn't like the thought of it, he could also tell that Daddy was backing down to Momma's logic.

"Besides," Momma said, still trying to convince him, "you've had a hard day. We've discussed this and you promised that you wouldn't touch the kids if you were exhausted."

He turned back toward Danny and looked at him. "You make me sick to my stomach!"

Danny felt the droplets of spit hit his face, the froth dancing at the corners of his father's mouth.

"Forgery! That is my name, not yours! Mine!" his father reiterated.

"I'm sorry!" Danny said, feeling as lucky as a kid who had found change on the street.

"Get the hell out of my sight before I change my mind!" Daddy said with an upraised backhanded stance. "And consider yourself lucky. Next time, I won't be as nice!"

Danny didn't need to be told twice. He ducked out of his father's way and ran upstairs to his room.

Later that evening, Danny was called downstairs to the family room. His mother was sitting on one of the designer couches, Cookie in her lap, watching Hawaii-Five-0 while Daddy was stretched out, completing his Flying magazine. He could hear Mark and Louise playing quietly in the basement. He stood in front of his parents, his hands wringing behind his back. This felt like it was going to be a lecture session on what a terrible kid he was.

"So, have you learned anything?" Daddy asked, peering over his glasses like a far-sighted professor.

"Yes," Danny answered meekly.

"And what have you learned?"

"I learned that I shouldn't forge and lie."

"Something you weren't aware of before today?" Daddy questioned sarcastically.

"Well, I was."

"Well, sport, your mother seems to think that you have a problem. I've given this a great deal of thought and I've decided that I agree with her. So, here's what we're going to do," Daddy said, laying his magazine down.

"We're going to take you to see Father Andolini. Maybe he can straighten you out. Wouldn't you like to be straightened out?"

"I..." Danny faltered.

Daddy mimicked an answer for his son. "Yes, Daddy, I would like to be straightened out. I would like to see Father Andolini so that I can learn how NOT to forge, lie or run away. Isn't that true?"

"Well..." Danny said, not quite wanting to belittle himself some more.

"Don't you agree, Danny? You don't want to make me upset again, do you?"

"No, Daddy."

"Well?" Daddy prodded.

"Yes, I would like to see Father Andolini so that I can get my head on straight," Danny answered, said the way he thought his father would want to hear it.

"Good. I bet you feel better already," a mocking smile gracing his face.

"Yes, Daddy. I feel better."

When Daddy picked up his magazine again, Danny knew it was his cue to leave as the discussion was over. As he was walking upstairs toward his bedroom, he heard his father mutter, "Time and time again, you get slapped in the face. Now, we're wondering if we have a mental case on our hands. Christ!"

"He's just a confused little boy," Momma commented.

Danny undressed himself quietly and headed toward his bed. He thought that what Daddy had said hurt him more than what his teacher had said earlier. He was twelve years old and he might be a mental case.

When he crawled under the sheets, he remembered to say a little prayer and thank God for what he had prevented. Who knows? Danny thought, maybe Father Andolini was God's way of talking to him. He hoped so.

Danny stared at the ceiling, as tears trickled down the side of his face and made the pillow damp.

Nobody heard him cry.

12

WOMEN ARE SMARTER

Diana turned the tape recorder off and let the silence fill the air. Outside, she could hear the muffled tones of the five o'clock rush hour on the corner of Front and Washington. She dumped Daniel's ashtray and squirted some air freshener around the room. She turned around and looked at her desk.

Papers and tests were scattered about in piles, scribbled notes embellishing the margins: scraps of people's lives that she was supposed to make sense of. Fragments, like pieces of a shattered mirror, stared back at her.

There was the Minnesota Multiphasic Personality Index, completed by a patient suffering through a recent miscarriage. Then, the Thematic Apperception Test (her observations attached to it) completed by a divorcee trying to get back on his feet. Diana tried not to think of her current marital status. Piled near the gold embossed ebony lamp, was the Shipley Intelligence Test, used for a teenage girl whose grades had mysteriously slipped from superior to failing. Diana suspected the onset of drug abuse.

The blotches of a Rorschach test suggested images of chaos, a mirror of Daniel Wilcox's predicament.

Standing in the corner, the bones of a skeleton hung, a permanent grin on its face, parodying the atmosphere of her office.

She sighed heavily as she straightened her office. She didn't look forward to going home. Besides, she couldn't get Daniel off her mind. They were no closer to a breakthrough in his memory than when they had first started.

Diana jumped at the light taps on her door. She assumed everyone had gone for the day and she expected no more patients.

She opened it to reveal a gentleman around the age of forty-five, gray hair playing on his temples. He looked distinguished with a square-cut jawline and firmly defined cheekbones. He was dressed in an oxford shirt with a casual tan sweater hanging loosely over his shoulders. His chino pants ended with mirror polished wing-tipped shoes.

"I hope I'm not intruding," he said, politely.

"No," she answered, "I was just finishing up for the day. If you'd like to book an appointment..."

"No, thank you," he said with a wave of his hand. "I'm trying to quit."

Diana was not amused at this feeble attempt at humor. She was tired and had too many things on her mind.

"Sorry," he said. He extended his hand. "I'm Detective Robinson, Marquette Police Department," he said as if it was a question rather than a statement. "Dr. Powers, I presume?"

"You presume correctly," she answered, shaking his hand. "What can I do for you?"

He looked out the door behind him, seeing no one, he pushed it closed. "Can I have a moment of your time?"

"Sure. Have a seat," Diana said, directing him to a seat in front of her desk. "How can I help you?"

Robinson slid back in the chair and rested his arms on the armrests. "Let me ask you, are you seeing a patient by the name of Daniel James Wilcox?"

"Detective, that's privileged information. If you'd care to..."

He cut her off by tossing a Mining Journal on her desk, the headline stating blaringly, Son Named Suspect In Shiras Hills Murder!

"Take a moment and read it," he said. "Please."

Diana quickly scanned the article. "What's this got to do with me? If you've got so much evidence, why aren't you arresting him?"

Robinson shifted in his seat, uncomfortably. "The damn press jumped the gun. We're waiting on lab results from Lansing. Look, I'm here to tell you that your life may be in grave danger. I believe that we may have evidence coming in that will pin Daniel Wilcox as the murderer of his mother. Now," he said, lowering his tone of voice as if they were very old friends, "I'm here off the record, so to speak. I felt it necessary to tell you because, well, this is a small town and if I didn't tell you, you'd probably be upset."

"I appreciate the city's interest but I can handle it myself," she said confidently, suspecting a ruse in Robinson's motives.

"I'm sure you can, Dr. Powers. Look, would you care to give me some insight on his personality or his mental stability? If we're going to arrest him, I'd like to know what we're dealing with. The last thing we'd like to get into is a row with some sort of psychotic. Does he have violent tendencies? Is he in cohorts with anyone? Where does he...?"

"Detective, I'm afraid that I can give you no information, whatsoever. Now, if you wouldn't mind leaving my office?"

Robinson started chuckling. "I'm afraid you've got me all wrong. Both of us know that his arrest is imminent. Instead of going through subpoenas and the usual bullshit, how about we work together? I don't believe anyone wants to see a killer loose on the street. If you can give me something, anything, we can have this guy taken off the street this evening, before he kills someone else." He leaned forward in his chair. "Come on, Doctor. This guy's a menace to society. You know it and I know it."

Diana couldn't believe what she was hearing. In a city like Detroit, she didn't think such behavior would have been tolerated or accepted, although there had been some borderline incidents recently. She spoke calmly and self-assuredly, in the type of language that she had learned to use in a profession that was predominantly male, "Detective, I'm going to ask you one more time to leave my office or I will call your superiors. If you are, in fact, here off the record, then I think it would heed you to listen to my warning. You are receiving no information about a patient that I am currently seeing or one that I've seen in the past without a court order. Is that clear?"

"So, that's it?"

Diana stood up, motioning the detective to stand at the same time. "Yes, Detective."

"Well, then, I guess we'll be seeing each other in court," he said. He turned and walked to the door. Before turning the handle, in a style reminiscent of Columbo, he turned around and faced her. "I'm willing to post an officer or two with you, just to keep you safe. You never know what this guy's gonna do next."

"That won't be necessary," Diana said. "Have a good evening."

The detective smiled and walked out.

Diana exhaled, wondering what the visit was about. She was visibly shaken although she wasn't exactly sure why.

She picked up the phone and called her mentor, Clinton. They arranged to have dinner nearby at The Office Supper Club, located just down the street on Washington Boulevard. Clinton was happy to get out of the house and they agreed to meet at around seven-thirty.

Two hours later, Diana was eating a Shrimp Scampi dish, complemented with tomato-infused angel hair pasta while Clinton sliced into his usual fare, a New York strip steak, cooked black and blue with a baked potato, extra sour cream and chives, hold the butter.

Diana had told him about her recent predicament with her soon -to-be ex- husband. Clinton was the ever present listening ear, offering advice that helped ease some of her guilt.

He took a sip of wine and set his fork and knife down. "So, what's the real reason you're here?"

She smiled at his perceptiveness. "How do you always know things like that?"

"Was I a psychiatrist or a psychic in a former life? How long have I known you? Besides, you knew it was coming. We've talked about him before and I told you to be careful before you married him, didn't I?"

"Well, why didn't you stand up when the priest asked if there were any objections?" Diana asked bemusedly.

"Because Mildred," Clinton's wife, "wouldn't let me!"

They stopped talking while the waiter refilled their water glasses and removed some excess dishes. When he walked away, Diana related the visit from Detective Robinson.

Clinton chewed thoughtfully on a piece of steak. "So, you are seeing the guy suspected of the murder in Shiras Hills?"

"I've been seeing him for seven months now."

"What's your assessment of the man's character? Is there any validity to the cop's notion that he's a threat to you?"

Diana sipped her wine. "He's not a threat to anyone except possibly himself, if more pressure comes down. I know that I'm dealing with a Post Traumatic Stress Disorder complicated by a Narcissistic Personality Disorder. Further, I believe he has partial amnesia to complicate the situation."

"It could be a dangerous combination," Clinton said.

"It could be but I don't think he's a murderer."

"What do you base that assumption on?"

"Intuition," Diana said.

Clinton laughed. "Just like a woman.'"

Diana wasn't amused. "I'm serious, Clinton. You're not talking to an intern, anymore. Listen to me. If he gets locked up, it'll break everything that I've worked for. Judging from the past that he's had..."

"You can't step in the way of the law. If you want to request to the court that he be put on suicide watch, twenty-four-seven, then I'm sure that it'll be done. I doubt a judge would have a problem with that."

Diana set her water glass down, exasperated. "Listen to me. Why did the detective walk into my office? What was the point? Aren't I protected by doctor-patient confidentiality?"

Clinton thought for a moment. "Yes, everything that your patient says is protected. As for this detective walking into your office, he was fishing.

"Hey," Clinton said with a raise of his wine glass, "you're a woman and he thought you'd be an easy target for information. He doesn't know you like I know you. You can be a pretty determined lady, at times. It's a small town with small minds. This isn't Detroit."

Diana picked her food for awhile.

"What's going on in that mind of yours?"

"Let's just say that he's innocent of murder. Let's also say that I think he knows who the murderer is. Now, if the police toss him in jail, I'll have no chance of helping him release that memory. The stress of jail, it's a small town and then, read the papers and tell me what kind of chance that he's got. He's not O.J. Simpson, you know."

"That's not your concern," Clinton said, seriously. "Just do the best you can with him. Don't interfere where you're not supposed to. That's where things went wrong with you in Detroit."

Diana was stung by the reference to her deceased client, Gerry. "I understand that it's not my concern but then I have to ask you, whose concern is it?"

"Diana?" Clinton said, as if he was reading her mind. "We've been this road before. I'm not sure what kind of scheme you have in your mind but discard it right now. If he has to be arrested, then let it be. Justice always rings true in the end."

"Does it?" Diana asked.

"Think of it this way. Maybe the cop has nothing. If that's the case, let this patient continue his therapy with you. Hopefully, he'll remember what he needs to remember before it gets out of control."

"And if he doesn't?"

Clinton sighed, pushing his plate in front of him, finished with his meal. "What have I always told you? Don't let life control you, you control life."

Diana set her utensils down, her appetite greatly diminished. "There's a line from a movie, I believe it's called, Somewhere In Time, where W.F. Robinson looks at his student actress, Ms. Elise McKenna, and he says "Excess within control"."

"Meaning?"

"I'm not exactly sure," Diana answered honestly. "It just seems like a good rebuttal to what you're saying."

Clinton smiled. "Please, we don't need anything in excess around here. Isn't that why we left Detroit?"

"That's what I thought," Diana said pensively.

After dinner, Clinton walked her to her car. He opened the door for her. "You've got a classic case, Doctor. Let me know what happens."

"I will," Diana said, greatly calmed down compared to when they had started the meal. "I should have married you."

"Yeah," Clinton said with a laugh, "Too bad Mildred already got me." Diana smiled and promised to call him.

The next day, as Daniel sidled into his seat, Diana did her best to heed the advice of Clinton. It was easier said than done.

13

CRY DOWN THE YEARS

"Bless me, Father, for I have sinned."

"Speak up, son."

"Yes, Father," he said a little louder.

"I am ready to hear your confession."

"Yes, Father," Danny said. He tried to organize what he was going to say.

Evidently, the priest sensed that the boy needed a little prodding. "When was your last confession?"

"The last time that I went to confession was, uh, two weeks ago."

"Yes?" Father Andolini responded from the darkened screen in the confessional.

Danny could see the silhouette of the side of the priest's head, tufts of hair and a rounded crown finished off with a large nose that curved dramatically out, it's size appearing enormous. "I wasn't very good," Danny hesitantly admitted.

"Don't worry, son. If you say your confession, the Lord will forgive you. Please continue."

Danny waited a minute before he started. He always felt uncomfortable saying his confession even though his parents forced them to go at least twice a month, with extra times during holidays. Danny wondered why his parents didn't feel it necessary for they themselves to go. Not that he thought his parents committed sins. They surely didn't lie or steal, or stuff like that. He figured it was probably the kids who committed all the sins.

He maneuvered himself uncomfortably in the tiny, musty room, his knees becoming cramped. He wondered what kind of horrendous crimes had been confessed over the years in that little space. He could picture murderers, thieves and a lot of little kids baring their souls to nameless clergymen. The good thing about that little room was that everything you told, remained with the priest. So, if there was something you did that Momma and Daddy didn't catch you at, at least you could clean your slate and never have to worry about their finding out. Only God and the priest knew those deep and dark secrets.

He could tell the priest anything and it would be a secret.

"Son?" Father Andolini prodded.

"In the last two weeks, I wasn't very good," Danny started. "I disobeyed my parents, I ran away from home, I lied about six times and I forged my father's name on a progress report," Danny repeated from memory. He had had to rehearse this scenario twenty times in front of his parents ahead of time so it probably sounded like he was a criminal in the making. He tried to ignore how ashamed he was inside.

"Hmmm," the priest answered after a moment, "is there anything else that the Lord should know?"

"I think that's all," Danny responded.

"Let's start at the beginning, son. Why did you disobey your parents?"

"I don't know, exactly," Danny answered. "I wasn't thinking, is all."

"Are you aware of the Ten Commandments where it says, Honor thy mother and thy father?"

"Yes."

"Hmm. Why did you run away from home?"

"I was afraid." He wondered, should I tell him?

"Afraid of what?"

Danny debated the question. He wondered if he should just go ahead and tell the priest everything. He had to tell him! Surely, a priest would protect him. He could imagine the priest, after hearing what was going on, getting somebody to watch his parents so that they'd be caught in the act. The priest would make sure that they wouldn't get hit anymore. There'd be no more pain!

He faltered, "Well...because...I was..."

"Was what?"

Why couldn't he just say it?!

"Ummm..." Danny started again, a war going on in his head.

Say it! Say it!

"What?" the priest queried.

"I was afraid that I'd get punished. When my Dad gets mad, he gets carried away and..." Danny said, stopping.

"And what, son. This is the house of the Lord. You can speak to me," the priest said. He was leaning closer to the screen, looking larger than life.

"What do you mean when you say, carried away?"

Despite the close confines of the confessional and the implied confidentiality, Danny lost his nerve. "I didn't mean anything," Danny blurted out.

"Are you sure, son?"

"Yes, Father, I'm sure. I was just afraid of being punished."

"Well, son, your parents punish you because they want you to be the best person that you can be in God's eyes. Do you understand that?"

"Yes."

"You must try and be good for them. But, I want you to remember something," the priest said, leaning forward and lowering his tone of voice.

"If you should need anything, the House of the Lord is always open. You can see me or any priest anytime you like. We're all part of a greater family."

"I'll remember that," Danny said meekly. He felt like dirt for almost telling the priest about his parents. What was he thinking? It wasn't like they had cast him out on the street. He was sure that they loved him, wasn't he?

"Son, try to be helpful and understanding of your parents. They carry a large burden on their shoulders, much like Jesus did when he was crucified. You may not see their cross but it is very heavy. Now," the priest said, closing the matter, "I want you to say a complete rosary in repentance for your sins. Can you do that?"

"Yes, Father."

The priest ended the confession with a closing blessing and a shadowy wave of the cross.

Danny pulled the red velvet curtain aside and knelt in a pew. He made the sign of the cross and pulled out his light green, glow-in-the-dark rosary. He began belting off prayers as fast as he could.

Out of the comer of his eye, he saw Father Andolini quietly step out of the center of the confessional, genuflect and make his way toward the back of the church, where Danny's parents were standing and waiting impatiently. Danny listened until his echoing footsteps disappeared. He heard the increased crescendo of muffled voices in the back vestibule of the church.

He looked toward the crucifix at the front of the church and admired the life-sized victim hanging from it, colors of blood dripping from the feet, hands and abdomen. He looked at the thorns that gashed the skull and the magnificent size of the nails. Danny couldn't help thinking that his problems were small compared to what happened to Jesus Christ. He finished his prayers and made his way to the back of the church.

"So, don't you feel better now?" Daddy asked him.

"Yes, Daddy."

"Why don't we all go back to the rectory where we can sit down and have a little chat?" Father Andolini suggested.

Danny and his parents followed the priest outside to a small building that was adjacent to the church, the priest's living quarters. Father Andolini directed them to the sitting room while he went back to the kitchen to get Danny's parents some coffee. Danny had politely refused an offer of hot chocolate because Daddy always said that they didn't need handouts from strangers.

Moments later, the priest returned with a service set of coffee. "So, where would we like to start?" he asked, when everyone had served themselves.

Danny remained in a straight backed chair while his parents settled into a comfortable looking couch that one might expect in Grandma's house. The priest stretched back in a reclining chair, stretching to get the blood going.

The priest was a large man with jowls that seemed to overflow from his face. Danny thought he reminded him of a friendly Alfred Hitchcock with his balding head and errant strands of hair that were tucked behind his ears.

Danny had always liked this priest. He was like an overfriendly grandfather who had an ear for a good laugh and a bellow to match. On the other hand, he was also the man who taught Danny everything he needed to know when he received his Confirmation.

Momma volunteered first. "I think we need to start with our son, Danny." She pointed Danny out, as if the priest wasn't sure which person the name belonged to.

"Explain."

"We're at our wits end with him. He's acting very poorly, lately. We've tried very hard to raise him well, in the eyes of the Lord, but he seems to be getting worse. He's run away from home, he's lied to us, he's..."

Daddy interrupted, "Now he's taken to forging my signature on school documents. We're at a loss here. I work very hard to provide for this family but Danny insists on behaving in a manner that just, well, it's come to the point where I'm almost embarrassed."

Danny's eyes fell to the floor, ashamed.

"We don't know what to do," Momma said, her hands folded in her lap. She threw Danny a glance, as if to enunciate that he was the insurmountable problem. Danny averted his eyes. "As his parents, we've decided that he needs some religious counseling. He needs the fear of God put in him. Maybe then, he'll understand the consequences of what he's doing to himself and to this family."

Father Andolini looked over at Danny. "Let's hear from you, son. What do you think?"

"I don't know what to say," Danny said with a squirm in his seat. "I try."

"Danny," Daddy said, "If that's trying, I'd be amused to see what you'd be like when you're not trying," a sarcastic tone in his voice. "What are we expected to do with you? We provide you with everything that a growing boy could want. We..."

"Let Danny talk," the priest interjected.

"I'm sorry for what I've done," Danny said sullenly. "I won't let it happen again."

The priest leaned forward. "Listen, Danny. We're here to help you. You must tell me what's on your mind. Why have you been behaving this way?" Father Andolini prodded. "Don't worry. Just tell us what's on your mind?"

"Nothing's on my mind," Danny said. He couldn't bring himself to talk in front of his parents. He knew if he said something that they didn't approve of, the priest wouldn't be there to help him when he got home.

"Is it drugs?"

Momma looked up, shocked. "Our son would never do drugs. We're a God-fearing family! How dare you insinuate..."

"Mrs. Wilcox," the priest said, raising his hand like a referee at a baseball game. "If we're to get to the bottom of this, we have to let your son speak for himself. Let him tell us what the problem is. That's why we're here, aren't we? To get to the root of his problem?"

"The problem, Father, lies in the fact that this boy is ungrateful for the good family that he's been given," Daddy said.

"Dr. Wilcox. Will you please let the boy speak," irritation crossing the priest's face. "Now, son, is it drugs?"

"No!" Danny answered vehemently.

"Then, what is it?"

Danny looked around at the three sets of eyes that were waiting for his answer. He shifted in his chair. Looking down at the carpet, he said quietly, "Uh, I'm afraid."

"Of what, Danny?" the priest asked softly.

"Of getting punished."

"Why are you afraid of getting punished?" the priest asked, obviously looking for a particular response.

"Because they get so mad that I get hit a lot," Danny said.

At that moment, one could have heard a pin drop. Danny was surprised that he finally said it in front of someone while Momma and Daddy couldn't believe their ears.

"Oh my God," Daddy said, shock in his voice. Now, do you see what I mean about lying, Father? We have never laid a hand on the boy. He does it time and time again. He makes up one story after another!"

"Yes, Father," Momma piped in, "it's all a fabrication!" A flushed look was on her face.

"Hold on, folks! Let's all calm down," Father Andolini said. He stood up and walked toward the window, his bushy eyebrows crested in concentration.

Danny opened his mouth to retract his damning statement when his eyes caught that of his father's. His father didn't have to say anything, the eyes spoke, piercing with anger:

You dare say anything more and you'll get a beating like you've never had before, you ungrateful son of a bitch! Just try me! You'll be the sorriest looking boy on the face of this earth!

All was quiet as the priest began talking slowly and confidently, turning around to face them, "I detect a problem here that may be getting out of hand. The boy is obviously frightened of the repercussions of his statement. We're not here to fight things out but rather we're here to get to the root of the problem. I've got this feeling that the problem lies in how we discipline our children. There's a fine line between discipline and, shall we say, damage? If you have to correct your son, do you use a switch or an open hand?"

Daddy shot his son a dirty look and then looked back toward the priest.

"In the most severe of cases, and it's rare, we might use the belt."

"I would suggest the use of an open hand, in the most severe of cases," the priest modified. "But, the open hand should be used more as shock value than as a weapon of punishment..."

"Wait a minute, Father," Daddy interrupted.

"Allow me to finish, Doctor. I would also suggest watching your tongue around your children. I'm not sure what is happening here except that I see fear in your son. He shouldn't be afraid of you nor should he be afraid of God. The two of you should be supporting Danny in whatever endeavors he might be going after. Sit down and talk with him. If you're upset with him, talk about it after you have calmed down. If you're not careful, this could develop into something that you may, one day, regret."

Daddy was furious. "I'm not sure what you're saying, Father, but I don't like the insinuations. Danny is the problem here, not us! Danny!" Daddy directed his attention toward him. "Tell the priest about your problem with lying. Now!"

"I lied, Father," Danny said, obediently.

"Danny, you don't have to say that. If we're to get to the bottom of this, we're..."

"I believe that we've had enough counseling for one day," Daddy interjected. "Put your coat on, Danny. Father, I'm afraid that this isn't going to work out. What our son needs is some professional help. I don't like having these problems focused on how we discipline our child. We appreciate your efforts, but we can't do anything about his lying. If it's okay with you, I believe that the matter is settled." Daddy stood up, making it clear that the conversation was finished.

"If that's the way you feel, Dr. Wilcox, I can't say anything else. I just wanted to offer my help."

"We know you tried," Daddy said, extending his hand toward the priest's hand. "Let's go, honey," he said to Momma.

The three of them walked out of the rectory, said their good-byes and piled into the Cadillac, Daddy at the steering wheel. Danny looked out the window at Father Andolini, who was leaning against the rectory door with a troubled look on his face. Danny felt sorry for the priest and the attempt that he had made. It was no use. Nobody could help this family. Nobody, except maybe Danny.

Daddy waited a moment before turning the key in the ignition. He just sat there while Danny squirmed, uncomfortable and claustrophobic. His father looked in the rear-view mirror at his son. "What is your problem?" he asked.

"I don't know," Danny said.

"Is that all you can say?"

"No."

"Then, why don't you explain to your father what the meaning was in that stunt you pulled in there?"

"I have a problem with lying," Danny answered, in the words he thought his father wanted to hear.

"You're damn right you have a problem with lying! You're the sorriest excuse for a son that a father could ask for!"

"Honey, please!" Momma said. "The priest is watching us!"

"Please! Jesus Christ! He's making us crazy!"

"He needs professional counseling, honey."

Daddy twisted the key in the ignition and pulled out in the road, out of the sight of the priest. "Professional counseling, hah! I'm not throwing away one more dime than I have to on that brat. Besides, we'd be the laughing stock of this town and he's embarrassed us enough! We'll take care of our problems our own way, thank you!"

"That's enough, sweetheart," Momma said again.

"Won't we?" Daddy asked with a look in the rear-view mirror.

"Yes," Danny answered.

"You're damn right, we will!"

Later that night, while Danny was lying in bed, staring at the ceiling, he listened to the windows rattle as a storm front moved over the land.

14

DIRE WOLF

When Daniel was finished, he smoked his cigarette thoughtfully. It was as if he was trying to phrase something in his mind but couldn't quite piece it together. He slowly stood up and walked over to the skeleton. He ran his fingers across the clavicle, the sternum and then to the skull.

Diana waited patiently, carefully watching him, allowing him to associate.

"Interesting," Daniel said.

"What is?"

"The skeleton. Why do you have this here?" he asked.

"Why do you think?"

"I think it gets people talking. And, if it doesn't get them talking, it gets them thinking. Is that why you have it here?"

"Partly," Diana answered.

"Ah," Daniel said with a smile. "So there's more. Well, let me guess." He lit a cigarette and looked at it, as if it would speak to him at any moment. "It represents something, a symbol, if you will. I use things like this in writing a lot. It brings depth to the story and character, although my symbols rarely have anything to do with the plot. In this case, however, it has everything to do with the plot. You are looking at the psychological skeleton, so to speak. On the surface, everything is complete. It represents structure and foundation. Without foundation, the human body is not complete. And, the human mind isn't complete without every piece. So, what am I missing, doctor?"

"Very perceptive, Daniel. What do you think you're missing?"

Daniel turned to look at Diana and walked over to her desk and rested his knuckles on it, looking into her eyes. "You know, I wish we could get past this psychiatric bullshit and talk like two people. Games people play. That's what this feels like at times, just another game and just another dollar in your pocket. Do you think you're really helping me? Because, I swear to God, this has done nothing toward helping me recall anything except for a bunch of things that I want to forget. Yet, I find there to be a terrible irony in that the thing I want to remember most, eludes me like the smoke off a cigarette. It's disappeared, gone in the wind."

"These things can take time."

"Time is something I don't have, doctor. Don't you realize that?"

"I do."

"Shit," he said softly, with smoke coming out of his nose like the entrails of a jet. "I feel like a goddamned mental case."

"Daniel, the time's up for today. We'll reschedule for Friday. Is that alright?"

"Certainly," he said with a wave of his hand.

Just then, the telephone rang. Diana picked it up, speaking in a low tone of voice. "I've told you not to interrupt a session, Cindy. Now, I'll get back to you in just a min..." she stopped talking, listening to her receptionist. "Fine, fine. Hold on one second." Diana held her hand over the mouthpiece. "It's for you. I think it's your brother."

Daniel looked at her, question marks in his eyes. He took the receiver from her, saying, "That's strange. Sorry about this."

Sensing that something was wrong, Diana decided to leave Daniel to the phone while she left to use the restroom.

When she returned five minutes later, she found Daniel sitting on the couch, his head in his hands. The atmosphere in her office felt remarkably different, as if a dark cloud made its ominous and oppressive presence.

"What is it?" she asked.

He looked up at her, pausing before he spoke. "I had to tell my brother to leave."

"Why?"

"It would seem that Detective Robinson has received some of the lab results from Lansing, confirming a high probability that the blood found on my clothes contains that of myself and the decedent. He had evidence, apparently, to get an order for my arrest. Further, he tried to pressure Mark into turning State's evidence. He refused," said Daniel, a paled look on his face.

"Meaning?"

"Do you know how long he's worked to get where he is? He knows what I would do if this happened. I'm on my own. He's going back to California." He shakily lit a cigarette and looked at Diana, resolution in his eyes. "I've got to go."

"The police are after you," she stated.

"Yes, they're after me. Look I'm cancelling Friday. As a matter of fact, I've got to cancel us, in general. I'm sorry." He picked up his coat and turned and walked out the door.

And there comes a time in everyone's life when they find themselves at a crossroads and that's what Diana was looking at right then. She had half expected the police to go after him earlier than they had. There had also been a point at which she thought he had been guilty. Now, she wasn't so sure.

In a matter of seconds, a hundred thoughts went through her head. One of those thoughts was a failed marriage. Two failed marriages were hanging over head, at that. She felt that she was a huge reason that those marriages had failed. Somewhere deep inside, she was afraid of commitment, even though she had signed pieces of paper to show she was obligated. Her heart had never truly been committed. It was as if she had followed through the motions but knew both ventures were doomed from the first moment. She couldn't commit to anything. Why? She thought.

Without realizing it, she grabbed Daniel's file and her appointment book and ran out the door. This is crazy, she thought: absolutely, certifiably crazy. She wasn't sure what she was doing except following by her gut instinct. She thought of all the cases that she had never seen the ending to and she thought of Clinton's words of encouragement. She had a fiduciary responsibility to...

She thought of warm hand on her leg, sliding upward, ever so slowly, many years ago.

When she got to the street, she looked in both directions quickly. She saw the back of Daniel's coat walking toward Thill's fishery. She ran after him, files gripped in her hand.

"Daniel!" she called out.

He turned around, looked at her and started running. He got to his car and fumbled for his keys. He had just opened the door when she reached the passenger's side.

"Daniel, please!"

"I've fired you, doctor. Now get out of my way!" He jumped in the car.

Diana pulled the passenger door and was surprised to find it unlocked. She jumped in just as he was slamming his car into reverse. He jammed on the brakes when he saw her next to him.

"Get out of my car," he said sternly.

"No, listen to me," Diana said, still out of breath. "You can't do this! You can turn yourself in. I can explain to the court..."

"Explain it to the court? Now what are you going to explain to the court? Maybe you're going to say that I was temporarily insane. Oh, sure," he said sarcastically, "are you aware of how many cases are won by pleading temporary insanity? Do you want to take a guess? I'll answer for you. Less than two percent are won on those grounds. No, it isn't going to happen!"

"Daniel," she pleaded, "you'll make things worse for yourself. Don't do this!"

Daniel gripped the steering wheel until his fingers were white. He took a deep breath. "I've been to court before. I know what it's like and I can't do it again. I truly can't. The answer is inside of me somewhere. I believe that. There's a line from the Grateful Dead that goes, "*half of my life, I've spent doing time for some other fucker's crime*." I've spent that kind of time. I know how the system works. I'm sorry," he said. "Now please, get out of my car." He looked forward and waited for Diana to open the door.

Diana put her hand on the handle and looked toward him. "I believe that you're innocent."

"Innocent of what?" he asked. Before she could answer, he spoke. "Am I innocent of murder or was I temporarily insane when I killed her?"

"I believe that you're innocent of murder."

"Really," he said. "Why? What do you think happened?"

"If you want to know the truth, I think you're afraid to admit what you saw. You mentioned remembering someone else there. I don't think you're making it up or you would have run a long time ago. Considering that I've been seeing you for almost seven months, I don't think you had the capability."

"I appreciate that, but the police's evidence seems to point toward me or they wouldn't be trying to arrest me."

"But they haven't heard my evidence. Do you want to know what I think happened?"

Daniel looked at his watch, irritated.

"You got to the house and went to the door. You've been afraid to see them for years. They scared you as much as they scared you when you were a child. You were under an incredible amount of stress, hoping for their acceptance. If they didn't accept you..."

Daniel sighed, "I'm running out of time."

Diana spoke faster, "The doors opened and, either you saw something you didn't want to see or you saw something you didn't expect. It could have been the murderer or your mother told you that you weren't welcome. Your mind couldn't accept that. You experienced a syndrome called post-traumatic stress disorder, a blocking of the memory. Then, you were knocked out, further complicating the block. I think you know who the murderer is!"

"That might be a good analysis. I don't believe a court of law is going to buy it, though," he answered. "That's why I'm not turning myself in until I know what happened. But I can't find out what happened if I'm in jail for murder one. Do you understand?"

It wasn't until that moment that Diana became sure of what she was going to do. She was sure of her decision more than she had ever been in her life. It was why she went into psychiatry to begin with. She was there to prevent what happened to her from happening to anyone else. She looked steadfastly ahead, anchored in her seat.

"I'm going with you," she said, firmly.

"This is ridiculous. You've got a practice, a life. There's no need for this.

I can't let you do it."

"Listen to me, Daniel. This is my life and I'm offering my help. I know very well what I'm doing and this is the right thing. Let somebody in. Let somebody help," she implored.

Daniel was looking in the rear-view mirror when he saw a MPD police car head in the direction of the psychiatrist's office. "Get out," he said, reaching over and disengaging her door.

"No," Diana said, pulling the door closed.

"Damn it to hell!" He hit the accelerator and pulled out onto Lakeshore drive. He then took a right on Baraga and a left on Front Street, which eventually turned into U.S. 41.

Neither one of them said a thing as Daniel, with sweat dripping down his face, watched his rear and side view mirrors. There were no police to be seen. He tensed as they drove up the hill, with Shiras Hills on their right. He didn't relax until they were well down the other side, with Lake Superior's Marquette Bay on their left. Ten minutes later, Daniel pulled into a gas station in Harvey, a small suburb of Marquette.

"Can I make a phone call?" Diana asked.

Daniel looked over at her before he got out of the car. "I really wish that you'd reconsider."

"Don't leave," she said. "Please."

"I must be nuts."

"Two minutes, I promise."

Daniel agreed but he obviously wasn't pleased with the turn of events. He gassed the car while Diana ran to a pay phone. She called the only person she knew to call: Clinton.

Fortunately, he was home enjoying his retirement. She quickly updated him on what was happening.

"Do you realize what you're doing?" Clinton asked.

"Yes, I do."

"You could lose your license for this."

"I know," Diana said. "But what did you tell me? You told me to take a stronger interest in my patients. Isn't that what we got into the head business for? I thought we were here to help people. I know what I believe and I think I'm the only one who can unlock what's inside. I have nothing left but my profession and he needs me. No one was there when I needed it."

"I've always been there for you, Diana," Clinton said, as if he was defending himself.

"Yes, you have, for the last eleven years since I've known you. I am referring   to something that goes further back. Something that happened to me."

"Listen to me, Diana. I told you to take a professional interest in your clientele. This is a personal thing that you have going on. You're running the risk of things like counter-transference which, as you were taught in school, can be devastating for your patient. You're going too far. Listen to yourself," he said, sounding more like a father than a mentor.

"Please, Clinton," Diana pleaded, "I'm not asking for your permission or your advice. I'm asking for help from a friend. Call my patients. There aren't a lot of them. Let them know that I'm sick or something. I'll leave the appointment book here at the station. I'm so close to a breakthrough that I can't let this go now. This man's life is at stake!"

"I am whole-heartedly against this."

"I understand."

"It's dangerous," he said. "You don't know anything about this man."

"What I know is that he's innocent. Listen, what kind of good are we if we don't go out on a limb once in awhile. This is the biggest limb that I've ever gone out on. I'll never be able to live with myself if I don't do this."

"...harboring of a fugitive."

"Somebody else was there."

"If he's murdered once..."

"He's not capable of it."

"Your life will be in danger...

"Not if I'm careful," Diana answered. She could feel Clinton mulling the issue over in his mind.

"Think of what happened in Detroit. You weren't able to change that scenario. Do you remember what happened after that?"

"Clinton, of course I remember. There's not a day I've lived since that I haven't thought of it," Diana answered quickly. "But, if I had done something earlier, if I had seen the signs, I truly believe that I could have prevented that tragedy. Maybe this is crazy, I know. I also know what my intuition tells me and if I don't do something..." her voice trailed off.

"You're going far beyond your responsibilities."

"Please, Clinton. Even you, yourself, said that this case is classic. Don't let this man fall through the cracks like so many others. He deserves a chance and I'm the only one who can do something. It'll only be for a few days or so. Please?"

"Where's the appointment book?" he asked, relenting.

She quickly gave him the name of the station and told him the book would be with the manager. "Thank you, Clinton. I'll stay in touch with you, I promise."

"If you need anything..."

"I'll call you."

"I still don't approve. But, I know you and if you get a craw up your ass, I guess there's little I can do to change it."

"Thank you, Clinton. I mean it. I've got to go. I'll call," she said, as she hurriedly hung up the phone.

She dropped the book off to a garage manager named Steve.

"When's he going to pick this up, eh?" he asked with a typical Yooper accent.

She tipped him five dollars for his efforts and ran back to the car. Daniel was waiting impatiently, his fingers drumming on the steering wheel. She got in the car.

"Before we go anywhere, you have to make a promise," Daniel said, the engine idling quietly.

"It depends."

"If all this should go sour, and I get busted, you are to say that I kidnapped you. Is that clear?" Daniel asked firmly.

"No, I..."

"Listen, Doctor. I mean it. I'm not going to live with the destruction of your life, also. Make me that promise or we're going nowhere. If I have to drag you out of this car, screaming, then..."

"I promise," Diana said.

Without another word, Daniel pulled out and headed south on U.S. 41. A few miles later, he took a left on M-28 and began putting miles under the wheels of the Cougar.

"Where are we going?" Diana asked an hour later.

"It's time to find some family," Daniel answered stoically.

"I thought you had no idea where they are?"

"I don't, yet. But I will," he said. "For now, we need to hole up for a day or so and come up with a plan." He turned and looked at her. "I sound like Jesse James, don't I?"

"There're people out there who are going to think that I've lost my mind," Diana answered.

For a long time, each one stared out the window at the scenery of the Upper Peninsula. The Grateful Dead's version of, *GDTRFB (Goin' Down The Road Feelin' Bad)* played in the background, although neither one was listening to the words.

It wasn't until they hit the Simi stretch, a 27 mile straight-as-an-arrow, road did Daniel finally speak. "Why are you doing this?" he asked, never removing his eyes from the road ahead of him.

"Because I care," Diana answered.

Dan smiled lightly. "You'd make a good Deadhead."

Moments later, they both tensed at the sight of flashing red and blue lights behind them. Daniel broke into a sweat.

As he pulled over, Daniel looked at Diana, "Remember, I kidnapped you."

Diana looked at the frightened man beside her, not believing how terribly unlucky he had been.

The wheels of the car had just hit the shoulder when the police cruiser blew by, leaving them in the wake of his wind. They exhaled a sigh of relief.

"We got lucky, this time," Daniel said quietly.

"We did, didn't we?"

Moments later, they were back on the road while both of them wondered how long their luck would last.

Five minutes after they had driven through the city of Simi, Daniel began talking slowly and carefully. Diana pulled out her notebook and began making notes. His story pulled them far away from where they were and what they were doing. Because, somewhere in that story there laid the answer to what Daniel had forgotten.

Both of them did their best to ignore the thought that they were on the run.

15

TRUCKIN'

"You son of a bitch! I want to kill you, you bastards! Do you hear me, you bastards? Fuck you!" he screamed. "Fuck you! Fuck you! Goddammit! I hate you! I've had it! Do you hear me?! I swear to God that I'm gonna kill you...!"

Then, Danny was awakened by a sharp jabbing in his ribs. He awoke, startled to see an angry father standing above him. He was confused and disoriented. All he could see was light shining in his room. Out of the comer of his eye, he saw Mark sleeping in a fetal position in the other bed. What had he done to deserve this? He felt uncomfortable with the vague memory of a dream that he couldn't quite grasp, that he couldn't quite remember. It had something to do with gasoline. His ribs hurt as he struggled to a sitting position.

"What the hell is your problem? What were you yelling about?" his father demanded to know, as he leaned over the bed.

Danny rubbed his eyes in confusion. "I don't know," he answered, dumbfounded.

"Yes, you do! Now, what's going on?"

Danny squirmed. "I don't know what you're talking about!"

"You little bastard! Stand up!" Daddy yelled. He yanked Danny out of his bed by his hair.

"I'm sorry," Danny answered, still in the cobwebs of confusion and sleep, having no idea what he was apologizing for.

"You're damn right, you're sorry! You're the sorriest thing I've seen all day! Now, what was the meaning of that?!"

As Danny struggled for a response, he saw the frightened eyes of Mark quickly look at him and close again, only pretending to be asleep. Momma appeared behind Daddy, clad in a bathrobe, looking at Danny with uncomprehending pity. For a second, Danny thought he was dreaming.

"Where did you learn that kind of language? "

Danny knew he was in trouble, but for the life of him, he couldn't figure out what for. He had been sleeping and then, suddenly, his father was yelling at him in the middle of the night. "What language? " Danny asked in a high- pitched tone of voice.

"Fine, play dumb with me!" Daddy said.

He reached over and grabbed Danny by the ear and dragged him down the hallway to the bathroom. He grabbed a bar of Cameo soap and held Danny by the back of the neck. He forced it into his mouth as Danny gagged on the bitter taste. His screams were muffled by the soap as Daddy kept yanking his head back and forth, trying to force the soap in between Danny's clenching teeth. Danny coughed and suddenly felt like he was choking to death, the soap, spit and suds forcing him to gag uncontrollably. He bent over to gag, only to have his father yank his head back, the soap bar flying out of his mouth. Danny's eyes stung from the pain.

"Honey! Stop it! " Momma said, harshly. "We're doing it again. We said we'd stop this!"

"Fine!" he answered, letting go of Danny's head.

Danny stood there, weeping and coughing; the soap leaving a rank taste in his mouth.

In a much quieter tone, Daddy asked Danny again, "Where did you learn that kind of language?"

"I don't know what you're talking about," Danny repeated, wanting to spit but knowing better. For the moment, he felt safe with Momma's presence.

"Okay, stupid, I'll bite. You woke everybody up by yelling and screaming your brat head off. Now," he said with his face about two inches from Danny's, "Where have we learned words like fuck, goddamn and bastard? "

When Daddy said those words, which he rarely said, they seemed dirty and filthy, although Daddy had said all of them except for the F-word, when he was upset.

Danny couldn't believe he had said all of those words in his sleep. Sure, at school, with the other kids around, it was cool to say those kinds of words. They seemed strong and resolute, giving him a way to fit in, although he really wasn't sure what they meant. He never intended his parents to know about them, though.

"I learned them on the bus!" Danny blurted out, his safest avenue of escape. It seemed like a good answer. If anything, it was better than the alternative of saying that he had learned them from Daddy. "Jesus Christ! The bus? I'll tell you one thing, if I ever, ever hear that language come out of your mouth again, you'll be so sorry that you'll wish you were dead! Do you understand me?"

"Yes, Daddy," he answered, still whole-heartedly confused.

"Get your little ass in bed," Daddy said, pointing toward the bedroom.

Danny hustled back to his bedroom, turned off the light and jumped into bed. He, like Mark, closed his eyes and pretended to go to sleep.

Shortly thereafter, he could hear Momma and Daddy getting ready to go to bed. They were both abnormally quiet for what seemed like the longest time. Danny could hear drawers being opened and shut, water going at the vanity as Momma took her make-up off, and even the sound of Daddy as he took the decorative pillows off of their bed and tossed them on the floor with a muted thump.

"Damn it," Daddy said furiously.

"What is it, honey?"

"I can't believe we live like this. On the bus? It's those lowlifes he's got for friends."

Danny winced from the other room. He liked his friends, although he only had a couple, and Daddy didn't have a right to say that. He didn't even know who his friends were.

"We're in Detroit, what do you expect?" Momma volunteered.

"It's not just that. It's everything. I wanted to make the best for this family. This move to Detroit was supposed to be better for us. I thought I'd be able to give the kids everything that I didn't have the luxury of getting as a kid, myself. Is it too much to ask? A nice car, a nice house and a good education shouldn't be too much to want." He yawned, and then continued. "I feel like it's all falling apart."

"If you want to know my opinion," Momma said, "I think we've taken too much upon ourselves."

"Well, what other choice have we got?" Daddy asked.

Daddy had been forced to re-start his practice in Marquette by flying up there for five days a week and then flying back to Detroit for the weekend to be with the family. Unfortunately, the stress of trying to make ends meet was getting greater instead of easier.

"You knew that this would be a risk when we decided to move down here.

I would've been happy staying in Marquette," Momma said.

"What? Are you telling me that you would've been happy living with a bunch of uneducated Yoopers? You call that a life? Besides," Daddy said, "didn't we move here so that we could be closer to your family?"

"Don't blame this on me. Your family lives down here, too."

"Yeah, well my family is not an issue here," Daddy retorted.

"Of course, they're not. I can't help it if you haven't talked to them in ten years."

"Are you trying to start an argument?"

"No, honey," Momma said, condescendingly. "All I'm trying to say is that we had a better life in Marquette, regardless of the reasons we moved down here. You're gone five days a week up north, while we're struggling to keep a house that we can't afford, anymore. You come home and the kids..."

"The kids what?" Daddy asked accusingly.

"They seem to upset you. You never used to get that angry at them. You lose your temper."

Danny heard Daddy sigh heavily. He was hoping that this wouldn't develop into a fight like it had in the motor home. He crossed his fingers.

"Yes, I lose my temper. Do you know why? Because I get home and all you can tell me about are all the bad things that they have done while I've been gone."

"That's not true," Momma defended.

"Oh, come on. Wasn't it you who told me about the kids scavenging from the neighbor's cherry tree? How about when you heard about them digging in the school dumpster? Or was it some other wife who told me that?"

"There's no need to get sarcastic with me," Momma said.

Danny cringed when he heard where the conversation was headed.

Momma had told Daddy about the cherry tree and the dumpster. Danny had been embarrassed when the neighbor came over one afternoon and told Momma about their ravaging the tree for fresh cherries. It had been a combination of playing and foraging for food. As far as diving into the school dumpster, well, it was true. Danny, Mark and Louise had been dumpster diving for a good two months before somebody called Momma.

When pressed for a reason why they had done it, Danny had said they were just playing. The truth was that they had been happy to dig through old lunch bags thrown away the day before, in hopes of scoring a left-over sandwich or whatever the bags might yield. Danny was afraid to tell Momma that the fact of the matter was that they were hungry. It was half the reason that they had scoured the Randolph's cherry tree.

Of course, when Momma told Daddy about it, Daddy was tired after being gone for five days, sleeping in his office in a recovery room. When Daddy confronted the kids about it, the usual fare in punishment happened again...

"I'm not being sarcastic," Daddy said, "I'm telling you what kind of impression you're giving me when I come home. As far as it looks to me, they lie, they steal and they disobey. They do everything they can to make us crazy. Can't they see how hard I'm working? Do other kids treat their parents the way that they treat us?"

"They don't understand, honey. Sometimes I don't understand what's happening to us. I would be glad to trade the pursuit of wealth for having a normal family back. They want it like it used to be. I want it like it used to be," Momma said, a determination in her voice. "We never take trips anymore and we rarely get to spend time together as a family. Did it ever occur to you that the reason that they're doing these things is because they're looking for attention? Don't you miss having a family?"

"Of course I miss it. Are you trying to say that it's my fault?"

"No, I'm not."

"You're damned right it's not my fault. It's the people down here; they don't accept us. It's the company that the kids keep. They're taking everything for granted without even attempting to understand what I'm going through."

Momma sighed. "Come to bed, sweetheart. Things will be okay. I love you," she said.

A teardrop slid out of Danny's eye. He felt an overwhelming sense of grief for his father and mother. Maybe they were bad kids, after all.

For some reason, Danny's dream came back to him, the one he had had before he had gone into a swearing tirade. It was about a little boy who was sneaking his brother and sister out of the house at 3:00 in the morning. His parents had been asleep. He remembered the feel of the cool, hard tin of a gas can, as he spilled liquid throughout the house, screaming obscenities as if he wasn't afraid of waking them. He remembered the glee he had felt as he sparked a match to the liquid and the resonant whoosh as it sparked a seemingly innocuous flame in the night. He remembered their screams of terror and his feeling of elation...

"It has to stop," Danny heard his father say. "There's no getting around it. We have to do something."

"I'm right beside you," Momma said, supportively.

Danny finally fell asleep, not hearing the rest.

Two weeks later, the family found themselves eating at an expensive restaurant called Machus Red Fox. It was a restaurant that had been in the news recently. Some famous mob or union boss had disappeared there. Daddy said the guy was probably part of a Quarter Pounder at McDonald's or something now. From the moment that Daddy had announced that they were going out to eat, he knew something was up. It wasn't anyone's birthday and it wasn't a special occasion that he could think of. As it turned out, Daddy had good news.

"We're moving," Daddy announced after they had finished their salads, while waiting on entrees.

Danny took a sip of his strawberry soda. "Really?"

"Where to?" Louise asked excitedly.

"Back to Marquette."

"Why are we moving?" Mark asked as he fiddled with the little umbrella that came in his soda.

"For a number of reasons, Mark," Daddy answered elusively.

"What reasons?" Danny asked.

"Reasons that you don't need to be concerned with," Momma said. "Now fix your napkin on your neck. I don't want to see food on your new sweater."

The rest of the dinner was spent in virtual silence, nobody discussing the issue again. Danny felt like he was the reason that they were moving, though. He was getting older and he wasn't deaf. He remembered their late night conversation and knew, as the oldest brother, that he had set a bad example. But, he knew not to inquire further because his parent's business was not his business, unless they chose to involve him.

As far as Danny could tell, money was the only other reason that they were moving. With an oral surgeon on every block, it was only a matter of time before Daddy had to admit that he had no chance of getting established in Detroit whereas in Marquette, he had been the only oral surgeon in all of the Upper Peninsula. Daddy had received many a letter from patients that he had worked on, begging him to come back. This was further supported by fellow dentists who needed his services up there. They all said that his presence was invaluable. He had been well respected there, and had made a decent living. There were times that Danny had heard his father complain that, "the only reason they want me back is because nobody else would be stupid enough to live in such God-forsaken territory." Danny knew that his father didn't relish the thought of going back to live with a bunch of Finlanders, Yoopers and Hicks. But, they were the ones who paid the bills and he surely needed to get them paid.

Danny also had a sneaking suspicion that Father Andolini had somehow had an effect on their decision to move. He knew that his parents were feeling guilty about hitting their kids so much. He also knew that his parents loved each other but he couldn't help wondering whether they still loved their kids. When they had lived in Marquette, it seemed like a wonderful world that was far away. Detroit, though, had been a nightmare in itself because when the bills were in trouble, it followed suit that the kids would be in trouble. Their parents couldn't take their frustrations out on each other, nor could they take it out on the collectors and nor could they take them out on a priest named Father Andolini. So, it was easiest to take it out on the kids. Sadly, the kids couldn't help noticing.

Because of all those reasons, Danny was optimistic about their move. With his father re-establishing a practice, there was no reason that things weren't meant to improve. Once the bills were paid, they would have no pressure on them. Danny hoped they would have a real family again. He felt that they were moving just in time, too. Otherwise, if he didn't kill himself, he was sure that the dreams of killing his parents might come true. That was scary.

For the next few months, the family made preparations to move. A "For Sale" sign went up in front of the house. Danny heard Daddy mention that he was selling it for just over a million dollars, a figure that surprised Danny given that they were eating on a budget of sixty-eight cents a day. Twice a month, Daddy flew his family up to Marquette in the Twin Comanche so that they could see the progress that the builders were making on their new house, an identical replica of the one they had had in Detroit. The five of them would stay in a nearby motel on U.S. 41 while Daddy would go supervise the construction workers, making sure every detail was completed in the manner that he had wanted.

Daddy had decided to build their house in Shiras Hills again, only this time, they had a plot on the exclusive street called Allouez, or "Doctor's Row", as all his old friends had called it. He also picked an area where he could have a lot of land. Danny remembered a workman asking why they had wanted so much property. Momma had answered that it was because the woods were so pretty and she didn't want to see the trees cut down.

Then Daddy added that he didn't want neighbors moving in next to them, creating an eyesore. The workman had laughed and said something like, "Must be nice, eh? You don't want any neighbors, so you buy up all of the land. I wish I had that kind of money."

Daddy gave him a strange look, muttering, "Damned Yooper," under his breath. Then, Daddy came out and said, laughing with a bite of sarcasm,

"Yeah, well, this way, when the kids are real brats, we can take care of it and not worry about the neighbors. Know what I mean?"

The workman forced a laugh and walked away. Danny could have sworn that he had heard the man say, "Damned doctors, eh?" or something to that effect.

The comment had made Danny a little sick to his stomach. He wasn't in the mood for jokes like that, wondering if maybe Daddy had been serious. If he was, their moving was going to be a real letdown considering that the kids could get the shit kicked out of them and there wouldn't be a neighbor in the world that could help. It worried Danny a lot, affecting his dreams at night, mostly. He started having horribly vivid dreams about his sister bleeding, him dying and his brother running away all of the time. He kept picturing his father, grinning, bragging about his forty acres and the solitude that they were afforded.

Well, destiny was running its course with a neurosurgeon purchasing their house in Detroit for a million dollars even, much to Daddy's elation. The bills were paid, good-byes were said to Momma's family and their family was off to a better life. Momma and Daddy no longer were pressured by bills, which meant that the kids didn't have to be their whipping posts to vent their anger.

That's what the children were hoping for, anyway.

So, three Allied Van Line trucks pulled up, their orange and black lettering sticking out like signposts: they were really moving. In a span of three days, the trucks were loaded and the cars were packed. The following three days were spent driving the long journey northward. Although Daddy complained about moving back with the Yoopers, Danny could tell that his father was optimistic about seeing an end to all their financial problems. He could even be called cheery; he acted like a normal father, the one they previously had, long ago in Marquette. He told the kids that he would teach them how to fish.

Danny and Mark could get on a baseball team and they could look forward to picnics every Sunday.

On the trip, Danny rode with his father in the Blazer. Momma and the other kids followed in the Cadillac. Danny got to know his father a little better and found out that he actually liked him, he didn't seem afraid of him.

Danny had never really talked with his father before, well, not the way that he and Mark talked. It had always seemed like a quiz session between father and son where Daddy would ask a question and Danny was forced to come up with the right answer. Danny never answered what he wanted to answer but was less distant as they got closer to the Upper Peninsula. They both admired the bridge without saying a word. Before they knew it, they hit the incline of the structure. Danny looked, in awe, at the deep blue waters below.

"Look over there," Daddy said.

Danny looked where Daddy was pointing, seeing a piece of land out in the water.

"That's Mackinac Island. We'll go visit it one day. A fight between the British and the French was fought there in the 1700's. Would you like to visit it, someday?"

"Sure," Danny answered.

"By the way," Daddy said as an afterthought. "You do want to go to college, don't you?"

"Yes, Daddy."

"Do you know what you want to be?"

Danny didn't have to think about it. The last few days had felt more like a real family than it had in a long time. He was in a great mood and enjoyed his father's company immensely. So, he answered right off the top of his head.

"I want be just like you, Daddy. I want to be a doctor."

Daddy looked at his son proudly.

The family settled into their new home without a problem. The kids were registered at their new schools and, in the fall, Danny would be entering high school, while Mark and Louise were entering middle school at Bothwell.

Sadly, not three days or three weeks could change, overnight, what had occurred over the previous three years. Sure, at that point in time, things could have been straightened out, but the fact is, they weren't. The sudden and erratic outbursts that had begun on a fairly infrequent basis, now turned into something that happened regularly. What was once a freak accident had turned into habit. Unfortunately, an apology wasn't going to make the family normal.

It was far too late for that.

But it didn't stop the kids from dreaming...

16

DEAL

During the time that Daniel was talking, they drove through such towns as Blaney Park, Engadine, Naubinway and Epoufette. Most of these cities were one stoplight cities with a convenience store, gas station and, of course, a bar. If one was blinking, the town would be missed altogether. The good thing was, they didn't see a cop the whole way, giving them some sort of respite from their dilemma.

Just outside of a tiny roadside stop, Brevort, they stopped to enjoy a pasty, a pastry wrapped meat and potato pie. The orange rays of the descending sun cascaded off of the waters of Lake Michigan, marking the end of an extremely unusual day for the both of them. For most of the meal, Dan and Diana found little to say with the fears of the future weighing heavily on their minds.

"How much time do we need to buy?" Dan asked toward the end of their meal.

"It's hard to tell," Diana answered. "If you're asking when your memory is going to come back, I can't say. It could happen in an hour, it could take weeks. The worst case scenario is that you won't remember at all."

"Failure is not an option," Dan said, lighting a cigarette. "I don't take defeat very well. So, here's what we're going to do." He reached into his back pocket and pulled out a crumpled and folded sheet of paper. He pushed it toward Diana. "I got this list from my brother. It's all I have left for family. There are two possible sets of grandparents, two cousins, a niece and an uncle." Diana looked it over for a minute. "This isn't a lot to work with."

"I know," Dan said quietly. "But, as far as I can see, it's all we've got. The way I look at it, every day that we can buy time with, we use. We're going to have to be extremely careful, though. That means that from now on, we make no phone calls. As far as these people go, they haven't seen me in fifteen or twenty years. Our best bet is going to be in the use of the surprise factor. In other words, we just show up and get whatever information we can."

"How do you know who's alive and who's not?"

"I don't," Dan said. "We run the gauntlet and hope for the best." He pulled deeply off of his cigarette. "I think that every police agency in the country is going to be after us. In that, we leave no paper trails. That means that if we stay in a hotel, we have to use an alias and we pay with cash, only. We have to assume that they're one step ahead of us at all times. I think a disguise might be in order, also."

"It's hard to believe that we're doing this."

"Are you having second thoughts?" Dan asked.

"Of course I am," Diana said. "It's too late to do anything now."

"You can always walk away."

"I know. I'm not ready to give up, yet. Don't worry."

Dan ran his fingers through his hair as he snubbed his cigarette out. "Here's the plan for the moment. We're going to stay on Mackinac Island for a few days. It'll be easy for us to blend in as tourists. There're no cars allowed on the island which'll greatly reduce our chances of being caught. I've been thinking about the car, too. I'm sure the police will be looking for it. So, it either means that we get it painted or we get ahold of another vehicle. We'll see which way it plays itself out."

They paid their check, in cash, and went back out on U.S. 2. The rest of the way to the Mackinac Bridge, they read the signs that advertised various businesses on the island. There were signs for Shepler's Ferry, announcing the fastest hydro-plane ride to the island. Signs for The Grand Hotel hinted that by staying there, one would be staying with a part of history.

Periodically, there were billboards for various fudge shops that must be visited when staying on the island, such as Ryba's Fudge, Murray's Fudge and May's Fudge. Each one, of course, said it was the best fudge in the world.

The only thing that Diana could think about was that she had no clothes. Wouldn't they look odd checking into a hotel with no luggage?

Forty-five minutes later, they drove into a small town by the name of St. Ignace. Dan looked at his watch. They had about two hours before the last ferry was to leave to the island. He reached into his glove compartment and pulled out a small address book. They pulled into a Holiday Station upon seeing a pay phone. Without saying a word, Dan hopped out and ran to the phone. Five minutes later, he jumped back into the car.

"I think I've bought us a few days," Dan said.

"How's that?"

"An old friend of mine lives here. We met while on the road, seeing the Grateful Dead. His name's Derry. He runs a little auto body shop down near Arnold's Ferry. I'm thinking that he might help us out with the car. Let's go," said Dan, his spirits high.

Five minutes later, they pulled into Main Street. On one side of the road, hourly ferries were departing for the island while on the other side; tourist traps dotted the road with fudge shops, Indian craft shops and small local taverns. "Derry's Auto Body" was tacked behind the town's only theater.

A small white framed house had a three-car garage attached to it. Cars were scattered about. Dan could see a '49 DeSoto that looked like it hadn't been worked in years, looking like an abandoned corpse. Two shells of '67 Mustangs sat, their engine compartments raped of every possible piece. A '55 Nomad stood like a primed soldier, ready for a paint job. A lone, red Honda Civic was raised on a platform in the garage, pieces of hose and wiring hanging out of it like the intestines of a dismembered robot.

In front of the house, in apparent working order, was a blaring green '69 or '70 VW Bus, a throwback from the days of Haight-Asbury, with its flower- power stickers and Grateful Dead Memorabilia stuck in every conceivable place.

The front door opened. A man, looking very much like a modern day Jesus Christ, stepped out, grinning from ear to ear. He was tall and thin, framed by long and brown, curly hair that came midway to his back. He wore a brushed leather jacket over a Steal-Your-Face concert T-shirt that had seen better days. He walked up to Dan with open arms.

"Dude," he said as they hugged. "How's it hangin'? Long time no see? Where'd I last see you?"

Dan felt like it had been months since he had last smiled. Seeing this face from the past made it hard for him to believe that they were on the run. "It seems to me that the last time I saw you was in May. Vegas, am I right?"

"Yeah, I think it was Vegas," Derry said, a smile still adhered to his face. "Was that in May?"

"It sure was."

"Is that your old-lady?" Derry asked in reference to Diana.

"Diana, meet Derry Palmer, the world's most renowned Deadhead. Derry, meet Diana, a very good friend of mine."

Diana cautiously shook Derry's hand. "Pleasure to meet you."

"Pleasure's all mine, ma'am. Why don't you two come on in?" Derry said. "The place ain't much, but it's dry."

Once they got into the house, Derry served them a couple of iced teas and proceeded to show them his place. In every conceivable comer, there stood one memento or another from his travels with the Grateful Dead. His claim to fame was meeting Jerry in a hotel lobby in Dallas. Since then, he had seen another three or four hundred shows, literally following them for seven years. He led them back to his studio where all four walls were lined with three or four thousand tapes, each in alphabetical order, with a twenty-five page list in chronological order. Dan's tapes looked like a mere pittance compared to what Derry had.

Derry proceeded to drop in one of the last shows ever performed by the Dead, July 8, 1995. The quality, with audience, was clear and crisp which Dan guessed correctly to be a DAT. "It was sad about Jerry," he said, settling down in one of the four beanbag chairs, *China/Rider* playing softly.

"Yeah," Dan answered. "I still can't believe it."

"I like to come in here and get wired on the good ol' days. There was nothin' like it. Bam, it's over just like that. Thirty years they stuck together," he said, a light sadness to his voice.

Diana looked at her watch, prompting Dan to get on with business.

"Derry, I've got a problem and I need your help," Dan began. "You see, we're in a bit of trouble with the law."

"What kind of trouble?" Derry asked.

"Would you be insulted if I said, the less you know, the better off you are?"

Derry thought about it for a moment. "I've seen some trouble in my days," he said. "There was a time, up in Oakland, I had a sheet on me. Someone ratted on me and then the police..."

"Listen to me, Derry," Dan said, cutting him off. "We're headed over to Mackinac for couple of days. We need to get my car painted. I'm not particularly concerned as to what color. All that matters is that it's not easily recognizable. Can you paint it?"

"Hmmm," Derry said. "I can paint it, alright. Is it hot?"

"You know me better than that," Dan said. "I don't steal. The thing is, if it stays in its current color, I'm afraid we'll get picked up before we have a chance to do what we need to do."

"How's it running?"

"It's in perfect condition," Dan said. "Why?"

"I'm thinking that all you need to do is to get a parking ticket and you're dead. The cops will get the I.D. number off of the dash. Why don't you sell the car?"

Dan looked over to Diana and shrugged his shoulders. "I hadn't really thought about it. Also, we haven't had time to take care of it. Are you saying you don't want to paint it?"

Derry stood up and motioned Dan and Diana to follow him. They went back out on the front lawn. "I'll trade you," he said, pointing toward the VW bus.

Diana started laughing. "We're not going around in that thing, are we? I mean, you're not taking this seriously, are you?"

Dan looked at Diana and then looked at Derry. "Might not be a bad idea," he said.

"You must be kidding. We'll stick out like a sore thumb!"

"Actually, I don't think we'll stick out at all," Dan said.

He and Derry walked around the vehicle while Derry showed him all of the working amenities, including a sink, a commode and a microwave oven.

"I wouldn't call this roughing it," Derry said. "Her name's Blossom. I bought it from an ex-girlfriend who dropped off the face of the earth after she found the funny white stuff. You know what I mean?"

Dan did, as cocaine had taken one or two of his friends out of circulation.

"This little baby's been through Canada, the Rockies and from one coast to the other. You do her right by checking the oil, water and tire pressure and she'll do you fine in return. I know it ain't what you're looking for but I'll bet they'll never expect you in this."

"No," Diana said, "I doubt anyone would expect us in this." The syrup of sarcasm dripped from her voice.

"Think about it, Diana. It's only temporary. We've got nothing to lose and everything to gain. Namely, we can disappear under the ruse of being a Deadhead. We wouldn't have to stay in hotels, we can hide in the darkness of campgrounds and, most importantly, we'd be recognizable to other Deadheads."

"I am not a Deadhead! I'm a professional psychiatrist..."

"We're on the run, remember?" Dan reminded her. "Unless, you'd like to hop off the boat right now."

"You'd be surprised, lady," Derry piped in. "Ain't nothin' like the feel of the open road while you're in her. Let me tell you, she's been around. You could drive her with your eyes closed and she'd find a concert for you to see. No sweat, man. She's got new tires, a new engine and the tape player works fine. Even got her rigged with some Jensen coaxial's in back." Derry smiled proudly. "Always watch her temperature, though," he added.

Diana looked to the ground and then put her hands on her hips. "Make up your mind. If you want it, then let's get on with it." Obviously, she wasn't thrilled at the thought.

"It's a deal, then?" Derry said.

"Yeah, it's a deal," Dan said as he extended his hand for a handshake.

"I'm gonna hate to see her go," Derry said. "Anything for a friend in need and I know it'll come back to me when I'm in a bind."

The three of them talked for a while longer before parting ways. Derry agreed to tune it up and stock it with some supplies in trade for ten Grateful Dead shows that he didn't have in his collection. They agreed to meet inside a week or so.

Dan and Diana walked across the street to the Arnold Line Ferry in spite of Derry's offer to stay with him. Dan felt it would be better to hide out on the island than risk compromising his old friend.

That night, they registered under the name of Mr. and Mrs. West at a resort on the far western side of the island, the Mackinac Hotel. They left a credit card number as a deposit and paid in cash. The front desk employee promised that he wouldn't run the card. No one seemed to give them a second look even though they had virtually no luggage with them. They got a room with twin beds.

The next day, Diana walked downtown while Dan was asleep. Not only did she not want to wake him but she also wanted to go shopping before he got up. She found plenty of clothing stores and finished off getting her bare make-up essentials at Doud's Drug Store. She also picked up a tape-recorder and a manicuring set which included scissors. She knew that Dan would have to cut his hair. At the last second, she got two sets of Clairol Hair Dye.

"Cash or Credit, ma'am," the cashier asked her.

She reached into her purse for cash and found that she had almost none left. Because there was a line of eight people behind her, she opted for her American Express Gold Card.

That night, they had dinner on the porch of Stonecliffe, a restaurant located in the center of the island with a magnificent view of Lake Huron, Lake Michigan and the Straits of Mackinac.

It also provided a sense of security in its location by being away from the heart of downtown, where they didn't need to risk being recognized by anyone.

While they waited on appetizers, Diana looked at Dan, who seemed to be lost in a world of his own. "You haven't told me anything about Louise," she commented.

"It's a long story," Dan said.

"It appears that we have the time," Diana commented.

Dan took a deep breath. He was tired and weary but he knew that they had to pursue what lay hidden in the webs of his memory. It was an area that he didn't want to visit, yet, he knew he had to. Every minute of everyday counted and their freedom might be up at any moment. There was no time to waste and Dan knew it as sure as he knew the sun would rise the next day.

Neither one of them knew how short their time was on the island.

Unfortunately, there were some credit card slips that were going to get in the wrong hands.

When Dan started talking, he became oblivious to everything in the world except where he had been a long time ago, a time when things were worse than they were now.

He went back to a time when he didn't want to go home.

17

FIRE ON THE MOUNTAIN

See, it happened some more. Things had not gotten better, as Danny had hoped. They got worse and worse and worse. Not in degrees, but by leaps and bounds. Danny was growing up, which meant that he was establishing a mind of his own. He was also obtaining feelings that he didn't understand, given that he was bordering his teen years. Though he tried to make sense of those conflicting feelings, it was to no avail.

It was only a few weeks after their settling in, that the problems began again. This time, they began with Mark's twin, Louise. She had a problem. Even though she was a twin, she had not been graced with the same intelligence level as Mark.

When the kids were registered at their new schools, they were given a test to determine their proper placement into their proper grade levels. Mark and Danny fit where they were supposed to but Louise didn't. Both parents were called into the guidance counselor's office to discuss her problem. She had been diagnosed as having a learning disability. Although she was said to have been a slow learner, she was not mentally retarded by any stretch of the imagination. To teach her, the counselors said, it would take some additional work on the part of the parents. They would have to be very patient with her.

Well, Daddy was pretty upset about the whole situation. He immediately registered all of the kids into summer school, even though Louise was the only one who had a problem. Daddy said that he was determined not to raise a bunch of ignorant, good-for-nothing, idiot kids. So, every night, when the kids got home from school, Daddy would supervise study sessions. It might have been productive except that Daddy lacked a virtue called patience. For Mark and Danny, they learned to be happy with the extra schooling as it kept them away from home during the dreaded summer months. They ignored the other kids who made fun of them because they assumed that Mark and Danny had failed their previous grade. The two boys ignored the comments that implied that the Wilcox kids were stupid.

Louise didn't mind what the other kids said. She had a naturally sweet quality about her that Daddy interpreted as signs of being a simpleton. She would smile and laugh with the other kids, having no idea of what they were saying behind her back. She just did her best to fit in and tried to learn what was requested of her.

Every night, the same routine was replayed over and over again, like that of a favorite Beatle's album. The kids would eat at 4:30 and at 4:55, they were finishing up before Daddy walked in the door. Momma would pull out the three minute egg timer, at which time, all three kids had to brush their teeth until every particle of sand had fallen through the timer. If Momma knew that Daddy was going to be late, she would test their tooth brushing skills by giving them a pill that would show how much plaque they had missed, requiring them to turn over the timer again until they got it right. If they had to brush their teeth for a half hour before Momma would release them, then so be it. Usually, they were done by the second or third try.

Then, they were expected to go to their rooms until Daddy came home and ate. There were many times that the children's mouths would salivate at the smell of pork chops, steak or fried chicken that Momma would make especially for their father. They, of course, were subjected to the same potato buds, canned peas and slice of sandwich meat. Daddy would finish eating by six-thirty, at which time, study hour began with each child lined up at the kitchen counter, books open and pencils out. When each child said they were finished, Daddy would subsequently quiz them until their answers met to his satisfaction. Usually, Mark and Danny fared well. Louise, on the other hand, was unfailingly subjected to a battle.

"Read it out loud, Louise," Daddy would order her.

"Okay," she'd answer, a Nancy Drew book propped in her hands. "Nancy walked over to the...the...g...grok..." she'd stutter.

"What's that?"

"I don't know this word," she'd answer.

"Yes, you do. It's right in front of you. Read it!"

"...Groker...ah...gr..."

"Read it!" Daddy would repeat firmly.

It always started the same way. The harder she tried, the more that Daddy would get upset and that would only proceed to slow her down even more.

"I don't know the word," she'd say, almost in tears. "I can't get it!"

"Well, hold the book open and maybe you can see what you're doing," Daddy would say. He'd reach over her shoulders and roughly press her frail hands against the bottom of the pages. "Now, read it!"

"It's...um..." struggling to comprehend what the word might be. "Um...groker..."

"Does that make sense?" Daddy would ask sarcastically. "You idiot! Do you think that makes sense?!"

"No?" she'd answer in the tone of a question.

"What are you looking at me for? The words are in the book, not in my face!" He'd then take his fist and slam it down on Louise' small hand. She'd yell in pain while the book would inevitably fly away from her. She'd bend over, wincing, waiting for the next blow.

"Dammit!"

Daddy would pick up the book from the floor and roughly force it into her hands. Then, he'd grab her by the back of the head and force it into the pages of the book. "Now, can you see what you're reading?!"

Louise would answer in a mumbled scream of fright while Danny and Mark would look down at their studies, pretending that their sister wasn't getting the bejesus kicked out of her, if they were unlucky enough to still be sitting there.

"You're not reading!"

"I will! I will! I will!" she'd scream, not wanting to get hit, anymore.

Danny and Mark would be as scared as she was.

"Well? I don't hear anything!" Daddy's voice would roar.

Sometimes, if she was really lucky, the word would come to her as she'd belt it out, "Grocery."

"Now, that wasn't so hard, was it?" Daddy would ask, his voice thick with sarcasm. Then, she'd do well until the next word and the whole scene would repeat itself.

Every night that occurred, with one subject after another. Daddy would land one blow after another, assuming that the more he hit, the more that she might be able to retain. He also liked pinching under the arms as an effective learning technique, of which all the kids had the experience of going through.

It was handy in that it caused a lot of pain but left a bare minimum of physical marks. No bruises could be seen and accidents were prevented from a fist landing in the wrong spot. The opinion was that the more pain, the better, just don't leave any marks.

Because of those study sessions, Danny saw it wasn't going to get any better. Little by little, Danny was growing to hate his father so much that he thought murder might actually be a plausible solution. Danny felt each blow to Louise as if he were receiving them himself. He'd get so frustrated, at times, that he'd go upstairs, in the privacy of his own room, and proceed to pull his own hair or slap himself as many times as he could, for lack of anything else to do. His frustrations were no longer released exclusively in his dreams, but on himself. Louise didn't understand, and it wasn't fair.

Maybe Daddy didn't understand why Louise was afflicted with her learning disability. Maybe he didn't understand that pain didn't help but rather, worsened an already regrettable situation. Maybe, he thought he could get some results.

One day, the results would be seen, results that almost killed her. But, Danny wouldn't see those results for a few years yet.

Danny felt like he was going to explode. He despised the life that he, his brother and sister were leading. It was inevitable that he would crack. And, one day, he did, in fact, explode.

This time, the incident centered on Mark. Mark was in seventh grade, for his summer school session. Mark hated Momma's food, just as much as Danny did. He also felt, like Danny, that he never got enough to eat. So, he devised a little system with the food. Since one bowl of corn flakes hardly satisfied the needs of a growing boy, he would eat his lunch on the way to school. When lunchtime came, though, he was up a creek. The children were not allowed to have money on them and that posed a problem. He resorted to begging for food from other kids. He would wait until they finished eating, and then he would come up and ask for any leftovers. It was a success if he got a partially eaten sandwich or some fruit. Regardless of the other kids poking fun at him, he continued his begging. All that mattered was a full stomach and that took precedence over pride. It usually tasted better than Momma's food, anyway. Mark tried to convince Danny to do it, but Danny had devised his own system.

Danny would steal food out of the kitchen pantry late at night, after everyone was asleep. He would sneak downstairs very quietly, head toward the kitchen and steal whatever he could without Momma's noticing. It might be a couple of pieces of bread, some crackers or some cookies. He would stuff the food in his underwear and creep down to the lower bathroom, where he could gorge himself with whatever morsels of food he'd stolen. Fortunately, he was never caught at it.

Mark didn't experience the same good fortune that Danny did. All the kids at school commented on Mark's behavior, and one of the kids told his own parents about it. One night, Momma and Daddy got a phone call, while the kids were eating their dinner.

"Yes, this is Dr. Wilcox," Daddy said, after a moment on the phone.

Pause.

"Do I feed my kids?" he questioned in an insulted tone of voice. "What kind of question is that?"

Mark's eyes lit up, intuitively knowing what the question was in reference

to.

"Mark does what?"

Mark turned a few shades whiter.

"Look, I'm very sorry about this," Daddy said to the person on the other end.   "Don't you worry. I'll get to the bottom of this and when I do, the problem will be solved. Our children are well-fed and there's no reason for that kind of behavior."

Pause.

Mark's fork was shaking involuntarily in his hand. He knew that he was in for it.

"Yes, we'll take care of it. Thank you for calling," Daddy said. The phone hit the cradle in a resounding crash. Although each child was afraid to look, they could feel their father's presence behind them.

"Guess who that was?" he asked, directing his attention toward Momma, who was preparing the parents' dinner.

"Who?"

"The mother of one of Mark's school friends," he said calmly.

"And...?"

"It seems that we have a brat kid who is begging for food from the other kids. Now, who would do that?" Daddy asked, focusing in on the guilty party.

Mark did not turn around. Daddy grabbed him by the back of the head and threw him out of the stool. Louise and Danny flinched when the stool went crashing into the kitchen table.

"What the hell is the meaning of that?!" he screamed furiously at Mark.

Mark tried to scurry away as Daddy chased him, Daddy's jaw jutted forward in anger. He caught up to Mark and tried to backhand him, but Mark ducked while Daddy's hand crashed into the wall.

"Dammit! Come here, you little bastard!" he yelled, his frustration increased because of his throbbing hand. He grabbed Mark by the ears and literally lifted him off of the ground and threw him to the floor. He started driving his wing-tipped shoes into Mark's body. All the while, he was screaming at his flailing son, "I'll teach you to beg! You wanna beg? Come on and beg like you do with the other kids!"

Mark only screamed in response to Daddy's anger.

"I said beg! " His foot went crashing into Mark's stomach.

Mark screamed louder.

Danny thought that he was going to die from frustration as he sat at the counter and pretended that the mayhem wasn't going on around him. He was powerless to do anything but sit there and sweat, knowing that his father would beat the shit out of him if he tried to interfere.

At the same time, Danny noticed that Momma wasn't intervening like she used to do. Ironically, that made Danny almost madder at Momma than at Daddy. It was as if she approved of what was going on. On the other hand, it was possible that she knew that it would be to no avail so; she stuck by her husband's side, no matter what the confrontation was about.

Danny stared at his food, now cold and dry, the muscles tightening in his face. He held his breath as long as he could, hoping to pass out. His brother's cries got to the point where Danny thought he'd rather get the punishment than sit there and listen to it. He felt crummy and dirty in his powerlessness. Once again, he wished he was in the solitude of his own room. If he had been, he knew he'd be hitting himself. He looked over at Louise and saw tears streaming silently down her face, her attention focused on the plate that she hadn't touched in five minutes. It was obvious that she didn't understand what was happening except that she hurt like Danny did.

"You want to make a mockery of our family in school? Then, why don't you show me how you beg"?

About the only begging that Mark could do, came in the form of, "Please don't! Please don't!"

"That doesn't sound like begging!" Daddy hollered, his toe ramming into Mark's shin.

Mark took the cue as best he could, "Please, can I have some food?" he asked, screaming.

"You want food?" Daddy asked.

"Yes," Mark answered like he thought he was supposed to.

Daddy yanked him off the floor by the ear and pulled him to the kitchen counter where the two other kids were sitting, but no longer eating. He took Mark's dinner and slammed the plate in front of the frightened boy. Louise and Danny kept their eyes focused downward, afraid to watch. Then, Daddy grabbed handfuls of potato buds and crammed them into Mark's mouth. One handful after another was shoved in. As he kept shoving, food fell all over the front of Mark, on the kitchen counter and on the floor. Mark was gagging and choking. Daddy pulled the hair on the back of Mark's head and tried ramming more food down Mark's unyielding throat. Mark suddenly bucked and began throwing up. Daddy let him go, watching Mark fall to the floor, retching.

"Fine, you little bastard! Go ahead and throw up all over!" he yelled at him.

Momma watched, a momentary look of concern crossing her face. Still, she remained silent, while Mark retched on the floor, sliding in his own vomit.

Daddy proceeded to kick him again, "Now, clean it up!"

Mark was unable to move. Daddy prepared to kick him again.

What it was that snapped in Danny, he would never know. Deep inside, anger welled like it never had before.

"Stop it! Stop it!" he screamed at his father.

His father looked at Danny with a stunned look on his face. Danny would have thought that he had just kicked him in the groin. Daddy couldn't believe the gall of his oldest son. Not to be talked back to, he backhanded Danny from across the counter. Danny flew backwards, chair and all. His head slammed into the glass table where Mark's chair had just hit, minutes before. Danny's head flashed in white-hot pain.

"Don't you ever talk back to me!" said Daddy, walking steadfastly toward Danny. Danny scurried to his feet, knowing what was next. As Daddy came toward him, a grimace of anger sealed on his face, Danny dodged out of the way. He didn't stop dodging, either. He ran out of the kitchen, into the hallway and straight out the front door. He continued running, despite his father yelling after him, "You little son of a bitch! Get back here right now, before I show you what a real beating is!"

Danny kept running as hard as he could. He ran past the forty acres of land that Daddy was so proud of, past his neighbor's houses, and on and on and on. Before his parents could find him in the street with the Blazer, Danny cut through a trail in the woods, behind the Leadgarten's house. He hoped that Lucy didn't see him cut through there; he wouldn't want to explain anything to the girl that he secretly had a crush on, dismissing the thought that his schoolmates called her, "Loose Lucy." Then Danny thought again of his father...if he was caught. Danny cut through the trees even faster.

Suddenly, he broke into an open area called Farmer's Field. He collapsed in the long, brown grass, his heart beating uncontrollably while his legs felt like leaden posts. As Danny looked around, he realized that he had found a haven where his father would never think to look.

Although the neighborhood kids called it Farmer's Field, there was no land being tilled and no crops being harvested. Instead, it was a grassy field which was intercut with motorcycle trails and dotted with apple trees. It was a great place for kids to play, without any adults around to ruin any childhood fantasies that might come into action.

Danny's whole body shook for twenty minutes as his lungs gasped for oxygen. Sweat dripped into his eyes. Whether it was from the trauma of witnessing what happened at home, or whether it was from the sudden rush of adrenaline that coursed through his body, Danny didn't know. All he knew was that his running was the only solution to a situation that was far beyond his control. He had run for Mark and Louise, as well as himself. The Lord only knew how long his father might have continued his assault. Danny honestly believed, that if he hadn't intervened, Mark would have been killed. His role as the protector had come into play once again. He knew that, by now, his father was too pre-occupied with finding Danny, rather than beating up on Mark. At least he was sufficiently distracting Daddy's attention, or so he hoped.

Danny picked himself up from the grass and began traversing the rutted motorcycle trails. As he made his way through the field, he became more determined to never step into that house again. Never! Furthermore, he never wanted to see his parents again. He left the trail and cut through the weeds to a grove of scraggly apple trees. As he reached up and plucked a green apple off the tree, he realized that he felt good, he was free from their vengeance.

He found himself a shady place to sit under a tree and bit into his apple, chewing thoughtfully, thinking about a future away from his parents. The first thing that he'd have to do was to get out of Marquette altogether. He wasn't exactly sure how he was going to arrange that. He figured that he could try hitch-hiking but that might be risky, especially with his parents looking for him. He played with the thought of stealing a bicycle and making his way south, like Detroit, and finding a job. He would claim that his parents were dead and he was an orphan, supporting himself.

Though he'd be alone, it was a better fate than going back home to try and survive through more hell.

After Danny's optimism was renewed, he decided to stay where he was for the night. The sun was dimmed considerably with a sheet of white clouds moving overhead. He piled a bunch of leaves under a tree to make a modest bed. He lay back on the crunchy leaves and stared up at the line of clouds moving overhead.

In spite of Danny's renewed outlook, the sky stared grimly back at him.

The clouds had the strange appearance of looking like an ocean that was frozen in motion, the ripples of darkness looking like the heart of waves cresting to an ominous white. They seemed oddly strange and forbidding, as if it represented a sign of times to come. Not a sound was in the air as the evening grew, save for an occasional cricket screaming in the distant field.

That night, it was deathly quiet.

The heavy silence in the air made Danny feel alone and isolated. Not that he missed his parents, which was for sure. But he missed the company of Mark and Louise. He wondered what was going to happen to them now that he was gone. Would his parents continue their charade? Would they be punished for what Danny had done? He had a feeling that the answers to those questions would be in the affirmative. How long would it take before one of them died?

He reached into his pocket and pulled out two Hot Wheels, a Bugeye and a Peeping Bomb. He rolled them back and forth, thinking about Mark. He remembered the last time that he had run away and realized that nothing had changed. Deep inside, he didn't think that he could leave Mark and Louise alone to fend for themselves. He started to cry. Tears streamed down his face, making soft pattering sounds when they hit the leaves. Somebody had to know what was happening! Things didn't seem right in his family. All families couldn't be like his family. If that were the case, parents wouldn't have to support kids because they would have all run away. Robbie wasn't afraid of his mother and father.

Danny decided that when he did talk to somebody, that person would have to make sure that Danny wasn't brought back. If he had a choice, he wanted to live in a foster home with his brother and sister. Danny was the protector and the others had to be saved. If one of them died because of his parents and Danny could have prevented it, well, he couldn't live with that.

He racked his brain for an adult that he could trust. Nobody came to mind except for Father Andolini, who was in Detroit. What about another priest? Sure, Danny thought, why not? If one priest understood then there had to be others who would feel the same way. Danny remembered the haunting look in the eyes of Father Andolini as they drove away that afternoon. He was sure that the priest would have done something about their situation if Daddy hadn't gotten so upset. This time, though, Danny would not back down. He'd stick to his guns until the priest got them safely out of there.

He wiped the tears off of his faces and lay back on the bed of leaves. The sky didn't look so insolent.

As the clouds rushed silently over the sky, Danny fell asleep. Hours later, he was awakened by large raindrops splashing on his face. The tree provided almost no protection from it. He saw flashes of lightning in the distance and realized that he had to find shelter quickly. Judging by the darkness, Danny guessed that it was very late. It looks like rain, he thought, and a lot of it.

As the patter of raindrops increased so did the ferocity of the thunder. He counted the seconds after the flash of lightning to determine how far away the approaching storm was.

"One chimpanzee...two chimpanzee...three chimpanzee...four..." BOOM! He nearly jumped out of his skin as the sound reverberated across the land. There was only one thing to do and that was to run like your pants were on fire and that's what Danny did. Since he had to see a priest, he headed for St. Peter's Cathedral, about four miles away. He ran across Farmer's Field and then had to turn around and run back because he had forgotten his two Hot Wheels. He cursed his stupidity as he retraced his steps back into the woods. Then, the rain fell with unrelenting force. Lightning traced the sky like an Etch-A-Sketch gone wild. Thunder followed, sounding as if it was shaking the ends of the earth. Water cascaded into Danny's eyes as he stumbled blindly through the wet foliage.

The thunder and lightning became so intense that Danny knew that he had to find shelter immediately, or he was going to be a goner. He knew that he'd never make the distance to the church without getting struck by fifty thousand volts of electricity or whatever voltage lightning had. He broke from the trees and found himself in someone's backyard.

He looked around, attempting to get his bearings. He wiped the rain from his eyes and pushed the hair back from his forehead. As the lightning flashed, he saw that a six-man tent was propped up in the back yard, its characteristic dome looking like a mosque in the periodic flashes of white light. It was probably out there to be used to camp out during the hot summer.

Danny ran toward it and unzipped the front door and dove in. Although the floor was hard, it was dry. He looked around and realized that he couldn't have asked for a better place to hide. It had flapped windows all the way around, which would allow Danny to see if anyone was coming. The doorway faced the woods, affording an easy escape route. Powerful lightning bolts tore across the sky while thunder echoed an immediate response. As the rain hammered the canvas, Danny said a fleeting thank you to the man upstairs...it was dry.

Up until that night, Danny had loved the excitement of thunderstorms.

Yet, as nature ravaged the land with her fury, Danny was frightened to the point that he almost considered running back to the safe haven of his home.

He dismissed the thought as quickly as it had come, knowing it would have made his running away an exercise in futility. He decided that it was best to ride the storm out so he laid down in the spacious tent and tried to get some sleep, even though the noise outside was deafening. He started to shiver, his wet clothes only making it worse. Not being able to bear it any longer, he stood up and walked over to the screen door to get a look outside.

Suddenly, a shower of orange sparks showered him, as lightning kissed a cable that was evidently hanging overhead. Intense heat followed, as Danny's body was lifted into the air, to the other side of the six-man tent. He landed on his back, pain smarting up from the hardened ground. His ears were buzzing' while the smell of ozone hung thick in the air. It scared the hell out of him. For a moment, he was awash with disorientation as panic rushed through his body.

He jumped to his feet, claustrophobia burying him in its weight. He hurriedly unzipped the door and ran headlong into the storm, oblivious of its fury. At first, he was going to run right up to the neighbor's house, the ones who owned the tent. He quickly dismissed that idea, being too close to home. Instead, he decided on completing his run to the church. Even though the church was a few miles away, Danny figured it worth the risk. There was no way that he would've lasted a moment longer in the tent.

He didn't know how he made the forty-five minute run to St. Peter's Cathedral without getting hit by lightning, but he made it, the steeples looming in front of him against the lightning scarred sky. He dashed up the cement steps to the large oak doors and pulled. Thankfully, they were unlocked, ready for any potential parishioner who needed the solace of the church. The doors swung closed behind him, shutting out nature's rage.

An eerie flicker cascaded the church walls from the small candles near the altar. His tennis shoes made squishing sounds as he made his way down the center aisle toward the front of the church. He found himself a pew and slid in, not forgetting to genuflect. And, for a long time, Danny sat there lost in thought. Eventually, the distant booming sounds faded, the storm passing. He lay back in the pew and was instantly asleep.

He had no idea how much time had passed when he was awakened by someone pushing on his shoulders.

"Who are you?"

"Huh," Danny said, trying to shake the comfortable sleep from his eyes.

"I said, who are you?" he asked again.

He looked up and saw that it was a priest, evidently preparing for morning mass. If took Danny a moment to figure out where he was. Judging from the diffused light coming out of the windows, it was not only morning, it was cloudy out. He told the young priest his name.

"Have you been here all night?"

"Ah, no," Danny answered. Then, he reconsidered his answer. "Actually, yes."

"What are you doing here?"

"I got lost," Danny lied.

"Well, then, let's get you home."

"No!" Danny answered emphatically.

Questions of confusion were written all over the priest's face. "What?"

Danny sat up in the pew and, as much as he tried to avoid it, he cried. The priest sat down next to him and placed a comforting arm around Danny's shoulders. Danny cried and babbled for fifteen or twenty minutes, before he finally calmed down. He felt like a wimp, it seemed like he was always crying.

"Have you eaten?" the priest asked, after his sobbing had subsided.

"No."

"Well then," the priest said with an uplifting tone in his voice, "you come with me and we'll take care of that."

Danny followed the priest into the adjoining rectory. He was offered a seat in the kitchen while the priest busily cooked a breakfast of bacon and scrambled eggs, humming softly. He watched the priest in silence. He didn't look at all like Father Andolini. This priest was young, with a full head of dark black hair. He was also dressed in normal street clothes, giving him a more youthful look without his collar. If anyone had passed the priest on the street, they probably would never have guessed that he was a priest at all.

He laid the food in front of him and Danny ate it ravenously. It sure wasn't a lousy bowl of corn flakes. The only time he ever saw bacon and eggs was when Momma cooked them for Daddy. Danny readily accepted the glass of orange juice that was offered to him, quickly drank it, and was offered another of which Danny didn't refuse. Orange juice was a perk they never enjoyed at home, either. When he was finished, he sighed with adult-like contentment.

"It was pretty good, huh?"

"Sure was, Father."

"I'm Father Regan. Can I ask why you were here this morning?"

"I was lost," Danny repeated.

"Danny, please..."

Danny didn't know what to say or how to say it as he had lost the nerve he had had the night before. He was also having second thoughts about the plan he had devised. Why was this priest going to be different from Father Andolini? The priest patiently waited for a response. Danny finally told him that he ran away.

"Why?"

"Because...well, because..."

"Because why?"

Very hesitantly, his eyes downcast, "Because me, my brother and sister get beat up all of the time," Danny said.

"Tell me about it," Father Regan prodded gently.

And so, Danny spilled his guts. He told Father Regan about the belt and his father's temper. He told him about the day with the gliders. He dove in about Mark and Louise, emphasizing that they were just as scared as he was. Finally, he told him about how Daddy had made Mark throw up and still continued to kick him. All this was said between tears and anger. Danny even told him that he was so scared that he never wanted to go back. Never! After he was through with his account, Father Regan pondered Danny's predicament.

"I have to call your parents and let them know that you're safe," the priest said.

"No, please don't!"

"Everything will be fine."

"You're not going to make me go back, are you?" Danny asked, the fright obvious in his eyes.

"Not if I don't have to. Now, what's your phone number?"

"You don't believe me, do you?"

"I believe you."

"Really?"

"Trust me, Danny," Father Regan said.

He told the priest his phone number and watched, as he dialed it.

"Hello, Mrs. Wilcox?"

Pause. Danny crossed his fingers.

"My name is Father Regan and I'm calling about Danny."

Pause. Danny looked to the floor, imagining her response.

"Yes, he's fine. We're both here at St. Peter's."

Pause.

"No, that won't be necessary," Father Regan said. "Actually, I'm wondering if we might come by in a little while and talk."

Danny's heart lurched at the apparent deception.

After the priest hung up the phone, Danny started to cry again. "Please don't make me go back," he implored.

"Don't worry, Danny," the priest said, squeezing Danny's shoulder. "These things take some time to straighten out. I'm trying to look out for the best of all those concerned. We just have to talk to your mother. If I'm to help you, your brother and sister, we have to get to the bottom of this."

"Do I have to stay?"

"No, you don't. You can stay with me here at the church," the priest answered.

For the first time, Danny felt that he had real hope. The priest believed him and everything would be alright. Danny was filled with confidence upon the realization that it looked like his plan was working. All he'd have to do is stand tall...

Danny and the priest drove out to the house. On the way, Simon and Garfunkle's, *Bridge Over Troubled Water*, played on the radio. Danny's stomach was a wreck because of nervous anticipation. Hopefully, they wouldn't be there any longer than they had to be. As the car made its way up the long and winding driveway, Father Regan commented on the beauty of the house.

"Not really," Danny answered dryly. A beautiful house didn't necessarily mean it was a beautiful family.

As soon as they stopped the car in front of the garage, Momma came running out of the house.

"Danny, I've missed you so much! We were all so worried," she said, as she hugged him. "Thank you, Father!"

"He's fine, Mrs. Wilcox."

Momma tousled Danny's hair. "He looks wonderful!"

Danny never remembered having his hair tousled by his mother.

"Why don't you come in and have some coffee?"

"That sounds good," the priest said. "Maybe we can talk."

The three of them walked in. Momma left Danny in the kitchen while she showed the house off to the priest. The priest kept commenting on the beauty of it. Then, he saw the bird feeders in the backyard and said that his mother used to do the same thing. For the next fifteen minutes, they talked of their common interest in birds.

"Wait a minute," Father Regan suddenly said. "Dr. Wilcox is an oral surgeon! Your husband?"

"Yes, he is," Momma said, resplendently.

"Well, I'll be. He pulled my wisdom teeth a few years back. He did a great job, too. I haven't had a problem since."

Big deal, Danny thought. He wasn't too thrilled with seeing Momma and Father Regan getting along as well as they were. When was he going to tell Momma that Danny and the kids weren't staying?

"Anyway," he said, "I came into the church this morning, only to find Danny sleeping in one of the pews."

"My goodness!"

"We got to talking for a long while over breakfast."

"What did he have to say?"

Danny braced himself for the inevitable.

"Well, I'm sure you know kids, they can have pretty vivid imaginations" said Father Regan. "With his being at the border of his teenage years, they always think that the world is falling apart around him."

A look of confusion crossed Danny's face.

"How do you mean?" Momma asked, with a sidelong look at Danny.

"Oh, there's nothing to worry about. What counts is that we were able to talk and come to an understanding between us. All kids, his age, go through some sort of trauma or another. They tend to get confused about a lot of things and there's a tendency to blame it on their parents. He's at a stage where he doesn't feel loved and the only solution to that would be taking extra care to give him some attention."

"We can give him more attention," Momma said, with another look toward Danny. "His problem is that he reads too much. It gives him all sorts of crazy ideas. I'm not sure what kind of story he concocted for you, but I can bet that it was a real doozy," she said, reaching over and patting Danny's head.

She never did that, either.

Father Regan directed his attention toward Danny. "You should realize how lucky you are. There are a lot of kids around the country who are homeless. You can bet that any of them would be glad to trade places with you, considering the beautiful home that you live in. Every day, I deal with orphans, children with alcoholic parents, and even children who are born with a drug addiction. You can't know how lucky you are until you sit in their shoes."

Danny looked down at his tennis shoes, as if he was ashamed. He wasn't ashamed. He was angry and he felt betrayed.

He knew, though, that if he looked into their eyes, they would see it on his face. At that moment, he hated the priest, just as he hated the teacher. With this nice house, the birds in the backyard and Daddy's profession, who would believe the horrors that happened behind closed doors?

He had failed.

The two of them finished their conversation. Momma walked the priest to the front door. He stood in the open doorway and looked at Danny.

"Are you going to be okay?" he asked.

"You promised..." Danny said.

"Tch...tch...tch..." Father Regan answered. He smiled and walked out.

The moment that the door shut, Momma looked at Danny, admonishment in her eyes and tone of voice, "Wait'll your father gets home."

No, everything was not going to be okay.

18

WHEN I PAINT MY MASTERPIECE

The waiter set their check down. Instead of leaving right away, he appeared to falter uncomfortably.

"Is something the matter?" Dan asked.

"Well, if you don't mind my asking, are you Dan Wilcox, the writer of the Rusty Wallace books?"

Dan looked at Diana, as if he was looking for help. She shrugged her shoulders.

"You must have me confused with someone else," Dan said.

"I don't know," the waiter answered. "I've got every one of his books and you sure look like him. I could swear that..."

Dan interrupted him. "Well, I'm not. If you don't mind we'll take care of the check in just a minute."

The waiter stood there a moment. "Excuse me, sir." He turned on his heel and stormed off.

"You didn't have to be snotty about it," Diana commented.

"I wasn't being snotty. I don't think I need to wear a billboard establishing who I am, that's all." He picked up the check, slid some cash in it and stood up.

A half hour later, they were in a taxi headed back to The Mackinac Hotel. The clip-clop of the two horses that were pulling the taxi lulled Dan and Diana into silence. Unfortunately, the serenity of the island was lost with both of them. If they were two different people, the charm of the island would not have been wasted. But, as it was, their situation hadn't changed. Dan felt like he was looking over his shoulder constantly while Diana questioned her motives in trying to help.

"I'm sorry," Dan said quietly.

"For what?"

"For the way I behaved back there. There was a time when I'd be happy to sign autographs. Now, I'm terrified of being recognized."

"It's understandable," Diana answered. "The trick here is to remain calm. The more stress that we put ourselves under, the harder it will be to remember what needs to be remembered."

"I don't see how we can be under much more stress than we are right now. Do you know what I mean?"

"I know."

The rest of the drive, they remained silent, lost in their own worlds.

Finally, they pulled up to the cul-de-sac in front of the hotel. Dan paid the driver and they both got out. The driver waved a fleeting good-night and pulled away.

Dan remained where he was. In the streetlight, Diana thought that he looked unusually pale.

"What's wrong?" she asked.

Dan whipped out a cigarette and lit it, pondering. "I think I just remembered something."

"What?"

"A woman," Daniel said. "Maybe it's because we were talking about Louise, I'm not sure," he said.

"Are you referring to the murder?"

"Yes, I am. There was a woman there, but..." he faltered.

"What do you remember about her?" Diana asked.

"Not a damn thing," he said, a frustrated tone in his voice. "All I remember is that there was a woman at the house. I don't think that I recognized her. She had long dark hair and she was thin. What she was doing there, I have no clue. I can't quite pick it up," He inhaled off his cigarette. "Dammit! I feel like a radio station whose signal is too weak. It's like I get a little bit at a time, but none of it makes any sense. I couldn't tell you if she was responsible for the murder."

"Try and relax. Don't push it," Diana said.

"This is good, isn't it?"

"I would say it is. It means that your memory isn't lost forever. The one thing you're not going to get back is everything that happened after you were hit. Anything before that, though, I have full confidence that it'll return. Just give it some more time," she said. She reached over and squeezed Dan's shoulder. "We're tired. Let's go get some sleep and we'll get back at it in the morning."

The moment that they stepped into the hotel lobby, Dan sensed that something was wrong. Two cops were standing by the front desk, chatting with a desk clerk. Neither one of them noticed Dan and Diana. Dan dropped his head and led Diana down the hallway toward their room.

Their room was located on the first floor of an L-shaped wing, past one turn. Just before they got to the turn, Dan pulled Diana aside.

"Shhh!" he whispered.

"What is it?"

"I've got a bad feeling about this," he whispered. "Remember the cops in the lobby?"

"Yeah?"

"Wait here," he commanded. He walked down the hall as close to the wall as he could. When he got to the comer, he looked around it and then shot his head back. He leaned against the wall, sweat breaking out on his face. Suddenly, he hurried back toward Diana.

"There are two cops waiting at the door. Shit!" he said furiously. "We've got to get out of here!"

"What about our things?" Diana asked. She knew it was a stupid question the moment she asked about it.

"Well, they're gone now. Let's go, now!"

He led the way out of the hotel. Instead of going down the front entrance, where the cul-de-sac was, he chose to cut through a sidewalk that lead to a side-street. It was a fortunate move, to say the least.

Moments later, as they were rounding the bend to St. Anne's church, Dan grabbed Diana and pulled her into the trees. Two cyclists raced by, dressed in uniforms, cop's uniforms. Dan was sure that he recognized the rider of the cyclist on the inside track.

It was none other than Detective Robinson.

The psychiatrist and the suspected murderer weren't going to get much sleep that night. They were like two hens that had been rousted from their nests, ready to meet the butcher's ax.

They were on the run again, their time running out, as surely as the last particle of sand would drop out of an inverted three-minute egg timer.

Dan realized that the situation was surprisingly similar to that of when he had run away as a kid. Only this time, he was into the big-time.

19

BELIEVE IT OR NOT

All day, Danny thought about Momma's menacing warning, "Wait'll your father gets home." His stomach was twisted in a cobweb of knots. Momma gave him a huge pile of chores to keep him busy. First, he had to clean the garage. The workbenches were washed down completely. Momma's car was then washed by hand, both inside and out. The tips of Danny's fingers were reddened by scrubbing down the huge chrome bumpers with Bon Ami, every speck of rust disappearing with his efforts. Momma scrutinized every detail wordlessly. Inspection was done silently and, if the job was done right, she would curtly hand him another chore. If it wasn't done right, she'd hand him the bucket, point and walk away, a stem look embracing her face. Danny knew it was in his best interest to do each job to perfection. If anything, she might pity him enough to go easy on the story with Daddy. He knew that the chances were slim but it was worth the effort.

Although Danny worked tirelessly, he found that the best way to keep his fears quelled was to pretend that he wasn't there at all. Instead, while he was scrubbing away furiously on the bumpers, he pretended that he wasn't working on a car but rather he was busily preparing a large submarine for battle. He was not a boy in a garage on an overcast day in Northern Michigan; he was really out in California as a member of the navy. He was a strong man ready to take on the world in what would surely be a perilous fight against a foreign enemy. In his mind, he knew that he may very well lose his life underwater in some distant ocean but he was not afraid. He had seen the movie, Gray Lady Down, and knew that the idea of sinking could be very real. Would he be strong enough to survive?

Scenarios of fear, death and torture flew threw his imagination like a plethora of colors intermingling like the twisting of a kaleidoscope. He found that it passed the time and it kept his mind off of the prospect of his father coming home, a thought that he did not relish. Also, it seemed like a much better thing to do than wasting his time with praying. All God ever did was to let him down. Besides, this was a lot more fun.

Hours later, after raking the pounds of used sunflower seeds under Momma's birdfeeders in the backyard, he found himself picking at the reddened blisters that had formed on his hands. He looked up, only to see his father standing in the bay window of the kitchen looking back at Danny, his hands on his hips. Danny just about wet his pants with the corresponding heat flash. Danny quickly looked down, grabbed the rake and continued raking at a highly accelerated rate. His heart thudded in his chest while his forehead broke out in a cold sweat. This wasn't the movie, Gray Lady Down, this was home and it was much more frightening than the prospect of drowning in some unknown waters. He quickly found, that while his father was staring at him, his mind was totally incapable of jumping into that safe fantasy world.

Two hours later, Danny was surprised that neither his father nor his mother came out to get him. He was in a sort of stalemate with them, as if to say that he would rather work his fingers to the bone than go in and face them while they were testing him to see how long it would take Danny before he gave up and went into the house. Before he knew it, the driveway was swept, the two porches were cleaned immaculately and the shrubs were weeded. Then, it was dark.

Danny reluctantly took his shoes off and went into the laundry room. He kept wiping his hands on his pants but the annoying dampness clung to his palms. He listened upstairs for a sound, any sound, so that he could surmise what kind of punishment he would be receiving. The only sound that was heard was that of the central air conditioning kicking in. He walked slowly to the bottom of the landing where the foyer was, wondering if his parents were in the kitchen off to the left. Hearing nothing, he could only assume that they were upstairs in the master bedroom. He took a couple of deep breaths and tip-toed his way upstairs to the bedroom, careful not to let any creaking sounds disturb the resonant silence that seemed to hang in the air. He exhaled when he stepped into the confines of his room.

Mark was in the corner, busily putting the finishing touches on a control tower that he had assembled out of their Lego's. Small airplanes were lined up at forty-five degree angles, the completion of the airport almost done. Hot Wheels and Johnny Lightning's were parked in neat rows in the parking lots. A heavy-duty dump truck was filled with small rocks. He looked up upon seeing Danny.

"I didn't even hear you come in," Mark said.

"As long as Momma and Daddy didn't hear me," Danny whispered back. "What's going on? Am I in trouble or what?"

"I don't think so. I heard Momma and Daddy talking about two hours ago and Momma told the whole story about Father Regan. I was waiting for Daddy to run outside and grab you but he didn't."

"I wonder how come," Danny said softly. He didn't like the sound of the way things were turning out. He almost wished that they would do what they needed to do rather than keeping him in anticipation.

"I think you got lucky, real lucky. I know he was pissed at you but something happened at work."

"Like what?"

"Well, like I think somebody's suing Daddy big-time. I heard him say that they were going after seven figures which I think that Daddy thinks it's a lot of money. He pulled somebody's wisdom teeth and then they got infected later. He performed some big operation but it didn't go well." Mark attached a beacon on the tower and pushed the dump truck away as if to say that the airport was complete. "What do you think? Is this cool or what?"

"Yeah, this is a great airport" Danny said casually. "So, what's going to happen to me?"

"Oh, Daddy went into his lecture about what a bunch of rotten kids we are and then said that he's giving up on us. All he looks forward to is the day that we all move out. He told Momma that you're gone the very day that you turn eighteen. He'd even buy you a set of luggage for your graduation from high school. He said that that was the end of the matter and you could rot in hell as far as he was concerned. See, you're out of trouble," Mark said with a grin.

Danny sat on the edge of Mark's bed. "So, that's it? I'm not getting the tar kicked out me."

"Guess not" Mark said, ending the issue.

For the rest of the night neither one of the boys heard from their parents. It was as if everyone had shut themselves off from each other. To Mark and Danny, they couldn't have been more pleased.

For the next few weeks, the tenseness remained at home. Conversations were short and curt with everyone doing their chores and maintaining a silent stability. School was welcome for the three children and the fear of weekends were most intense as the three o'clock school bell rang each Friday. But, the weekends flew by in a stony silence. Daddy was pre-occupied with his lawsuit while Momma was doing her best to be with him. The kids were virtually transparent in their existence, making sure that chores were done ahead of time and to perfection. At least it was better than the other world that they were becoming unwillingly accustomed to.

During that period, Danny and Mark got even closer than they had ever been before. They were young, curious and destined to find their own breed of trouble. For the most part, they had avoided detection. And, fortunately, Momma and Daddy didn't find out about the things that could have turned out really bad.

For instance, both Mark and Danny had been fascinated with fire for a time. It was a passion that began slowly. They'd sneak out to Farmer's Field and take wooden fruit boxes out of the trash. Daddy liked blueberries on his cereal. The boys would see a container get emptied and they'd save them up until they had a few of them. On any given Saturday, once their chores were done, Momma would send them outside so that she and Daddy could get a little peace and quiet. No sooner were the boys out the door, they'd be dashing up the trail, magnifying glass in one hand, the boxes in the other. Of course, they'd dash off on Louise because they knew that Louise would probably tell on them. They'd play hide and seek and when it was her turn to hide, they'd be gone. For the next hour or so, the boys would be gleeful at watching their pretend buildings being consumed by flames. Surrounding the burning building, they'd have Hot Wheels' ambulances and fire trucks around it while they'd be pretending they were adults trying to contain this imminent emergency. Then, they'd reappear at home with a bewildered Louise wondering where they were.

"We were looking for you, Louise," they'd answer innocently.

Just as quickly, Louise would respond, "No, you weren't. You were tricking me again."

"We're sorry," the two boys would say, their secret fires intact.

But, they always made sure to spend at least a little time with her in retribution.

One afternoon, in the front of the house, Mark and Danny took their secret trail to the woods leading to their miniature cabin. The cabin was made out of twigs, much like a badly deformed Lincoln Log house. It had the main body of the house and a small attached overhang to it where they parked a few small cars. It was Danny's idea to get ahold of some gasoline from the tank that Daddy kept in the garage for the boat. They half-filled a coffee can, carried it to the site of the house.

"You ever done this before?" Mark asked.

"Of course," Danny lied.

"Just burn the house part," Mark said. "Should I take the cars out of the garage?"

"Oh no, don't worry about it. They'll be fine," Danny said as he pulled the lid off the can. He poured most of the can on the house.

Mark looked nervously around, making sure that nobody would see them. "You want to light it?"

Danny handed Mark the matches. "Naw, it's your turn."

Mark looked at Danny and then at the matches. He carefully pulled one out and struck it. He waited a moment and then dropped it on their cabin.

WHOOOSH!

The fire blew to twice their height, kissing the underbrush and small trees around them. Both boys were thrown back on their butts with the force of the blast.

Within a time period of two minutes, with a lot of running and a lot of panicking, they had the fire out. Both of them knew how close they had come to getting into trouble. If Momma or Daddy had seen it...

Mark wasn't pleased about the melted blobs that were once their cars.

Another time, Mark and Danny found that plastic bags were really cool to burn. One could twist the bags around upper branches of trees, place Hot Wheels or model airplanes underneath as targets, and light the bags. Not only did the damage to the toys look really neat, the sound of the ZIPP, ZIPP, ZIPP of the melted plastic dripping added to the intensity of playing with fire. It wasn't until a drip dripped late, when they found out the pain of having it land on the back of Mark's hand, did they decide that burning plastic wasn't too much fun.

One afternoon, they met Robbie in Farmer's Field and he showed them both Cherry Bombs and firecrackers. Mark couldn't build models fast enough to watch them explode into a million tiny fragments. And then, there was the time that they blew up a B-25 Mitchell and Danny could have lost an eye. Fortunately, his wearing glasses saved his life as a tail smacked against his lens. To explain the scratch to Momma, he said his glasses had fallen off while he was riding his bike. It didn't look like Momma believed him when she took him into the optometrist to get new ones. Danny didn't much like fireworks after that.

For the most part, they didn't get caught. But, there were the times they did.

Danny liked to tease Mark. Just little things, nothing that should have been life threatening. There was the time that Danny had had a flat blue elephant shaped eraser with small glue-on eyes and the jiggling eyeball. One morning, for lack of anything to do with this ugly eraser, he decided that it would be hilarious if he slipped it into Mark's peanut butter sandwich. So, he waited until everyone was asleep when he did the deed. Unfortunately, at lunchtime, the next day, Sister Theophane happened to be standing behind Mark when he happened to bite directly into the eraser. Momma got a phone call within a moment after he spit it out in disgust.

When Danny got home that night, Momma walked him out to the backyard without saying a word. It was the silence and then her ripping a branch from a fir tree that he first began to get nervous. She stripped the needles off with a swipe of her bare hand. The feeling of getting whipped by it was surprisingly similar to that of being hit by the thin belt, except that it stung a little more. He knew he deserved it.

So, he didn't put erasers in his brother's sandwiches anymore. When he pulled up his pants, tears stinging his eyes and his underwear stinging the fresh wounds, Momma looked at him directly in the eyes,

"We will not be mentioning a word of this to your father. Do you understand me?"

"Yes, Momma," Danny answered.

"He's going through enough without your shenanigans making it worse. Just because he won't discipline you now doesn't mean that I won't. Is that clear?"

Danny had a few extra chores that night. He also had no dessert and went to bed early. Mark gave him dirty looks for days.

Mark did his share of things without getting caught also. On the other hand, there was the time that Mark took an over-extensive interest in bugs. In particular, he liked June Bugs because they were very sedate when placed in his pencil box that he took to school every day. The June bug is a large insect, much like a Beetle or Palmetto Bug. No sooner would he get to school, he'd stash the three or four bugs in his desk. He'd let them out of his pencil box so that they could roam freely in his desk. In darkness, they tend to remain fairly sedate. One afternoon, though, he opened his desk and they flew free.

Sister Cora was none too pleased about the ensuing ruckus that developed.

And, Mark was clearly busted.

The strange thing was, Momma repeated her performance with the fir tree branch ending with the admonition that Daddy was not to be told.

The next morning, Mark showed Danny the profuse amount welts on his backside and Danny could have sworn that they were much worse than what he had gone through.

Otherwise, Daddy remained aloof of the children. They could see that things were weighing heavily on his mind and knew that it was best to steer clear of him.

For the most part, Danny enjoyed being a freshman. He had a renewed sense of responsibility and enjoyed the challenges that it sometimes presented. In particular, he liked his English Class. Not only could he read as much as he wanted, under the ruse that it was for school, he discovered that he enjoyed writing. His teacher, Mrs. Iverson, took a particular interest in his writing. So, she pushed him. One day, Danny sat down and wrote a story called, "Steel and Magnets", the story of a little boy who runs away from home because he accidentally put a baseball through his parents' front window. When he runs away, a thunderstorm passes through and scares the boy so much that, in the dark of the night, the rain furiously pounding, he runs back home into the welcome arms of his parents. The story bemusedly ends with the little boy pondering that going back to your parents is just like steel coming to a magnet, it's only natural.

Mrs. Iverson graded it with an "A+" and had Danny read it in front of the class. He was as proud as he had ever been. She showered him with the attention that he deserved.

He did not plan on her calling his parents to congratulate them on her son's achievement. Daddy picked up a copy on the way home from work. The problem was that Danny had written about a taboo subject. Further, he had written things that he knew might be a little risqué in the eyes of his parents. But, it had been intended to be graded and his parents would never know any better if he destroyed it.

When he walked in the door, his father was sitting in the living room reading it.

"Danny, before you go upstairs," Daddy said, the story in hand, "wait a minute. I think we have something to discuss."

Danny stood nervously in front of his father. He slowly realized what Daddy was reading, while subconsciously wringing his hands behind his back. Even though the fireplace wasn't lit, it felt very warm in there suddenly. He tried to detect the reaction on his father's face but drew nothing out of it.

He knew that he was in trouble but could not surmise the extent of it. Nothing ever turned out like he had planned. He didn't plan on the "A+\ nor had he planned on the teacher's reaction. For a time, Danny thought that maybe, just maybe, his father might do as Mrs. Iverson did. Maybe he would congratulate him on his spelling, grammar and sentence structure. Or, would he be happy that his son was able to construct a theme? Mrs. Iverson did say that he might strongly consider becoming a writer. It was good, wasn't it?

And, for the first time in his life, he was able to say what he was feeling and be congratulated for it.

Only his parents were not supposed to find out about it.

And he knew very well that the story was not all fiction like everybody thought. It came pretty damn close to the truth without the bad parts.

Daddy slowly set the paper down on the coffee table. He removed his glasses and stared at Danny.

Danny didn't know what to say. He could read something on his father's face and he didn't think it was about a warm congratulations. He squeezed his hands behind his back a little more vigorously, as Daddy stared him down.

"What the hell is the meaning of this?!"

Danny nearly jumped. "I wrote it for school and got an "A+" on it," he answered, quickly yet defensively.

"I don't give a damn if you wrote it for the goddamned President of the United States of America! I'm not dumb. Is this some kind of joke?"

"Well, no," Danny answered meekly. What was the harm of it? He hadn't told the real story.

"Well, no," Daddy mimicked. "You want to know about sex? You want to use words like, "damn" and "screwing around"? I didn't raise you to talk like that. Swearing is forbidden in this family, in case you need to be reminded. We believe in God in this family. Do you remember who God is?"

"Yes."

"I sure hope you do. Because if you write like this again, God will make sure that you burn in hell. Is that what you want?"

"No."

"I hope not. Don't say that I didn't warn you. Now, get your ass to bed. There'll be no dinner on the dinner table for you, champ."

"Goodnight," Danny said, turning to hustle upstairs to his room.

"Oh, Danny?"

Danny turned back around.

Very slowly and methodically, Daddy picked up his glasses and put them on. Then, he picked up Danny's story and held it toward him. Danny was reaching for it when Daddy pulled back and tore it in half. He then tore it in half again. And again three more times. He tossed them toward Danny, the pieces slowly scattering on the soft-pile carpet.

"If you think running away is cute, then how about next time making sure that it's for good?"

Danny hurriedly picked up the pieces without saying a word, his sight blurry, but determined not to let a tear fall. He dropped the pieces in the bathroom trashcan and went to bed. For a long time, he stared at the ceiling.

He had a feeling that he had won a battle, in spite of how angry his father had been. His father hadn't raised a finger to him. How could he? It was an "A+" and you couldn't argue that, could you? Maybe his father was afraid now that he knew that Danny could think. Even better, Danny felt like he had hit his father harder than his father had ever hit him.

Just think what Danny could have written. Did it make Daddy think twice?

The only thing that really bothered him before he went to sleep was Father Regan. He had let the priest trick him. Well, just like Daddy had warned, next time, Danny wouldn't come back. Next time...it would be the last time.

For then, he had been like steel coming to a magnet. That didn't feel like victory at all.

20

THE OTHER ONE

Dan and Diana kept their heads down as they walked past the Bennett House, La Chance Cottage, the Inn on Mackinac and the Island House. On their right, beneath the dimly lit colonial streetlights, Marquette Park stood out like a welcome refuge. Dan grabbed Diana's hand.

"Come on. There's a pay phone on the other side."

"Who are we calling?"

"Derry. We've got to figure out how to get off the island."

They traversed the park in the matter of two minutes, staving off the urge to run to the phone. Even though they were on the run, they couldn't show it. Fortunately, they hadn't seen another cop since they had seen Robinson.

Dan dropped a quarter in the phone. Relief washed over his face when Derry answered. He quickly and calmly explained that he and Diana were going to try and get to his place later that night. Of course, he apologized for the hour of the night.

"No sweat, man," Derry said. "But what's up? Why not take a ferry in the morning?"

"Let me put it this way. We've had some unwelcome visitors. If we could leave in the morning, we would. But, I think we'll all be better off if we can get off this rock tonight. You know, the cover of darkness and all?"

"Have you put any thought into how you're going to pull this off?" Derry asked.

"I'm working on it," Dan said, nervously looking toward Diana. "I'm thinking of making our way to the center of the island, where the airport is."

"You're wasting your time, man. I'm sure you know that it's a private airport. Your last shot at scoring a charter was about six hours ago. You know anybody with a boat?"

Dan kicked at the loose gravel beneath his feet. "It's been years since I've known anyone on this island much less knowing anyone with a boat. Dammit!" Dan said, not bothering to hide the exasperation in his voice.

"Calm down," Derry said. "Let me think a minute. I believe I know someone who might be able to help you. What time you got?"

"A little after twelve."

"Shit," Derry said.

"What?"

"The fella I'm thinkin' of is probably damn close to bein' three sheets to the wind. He does a lot a private chartering after hours. Thing is, there usually ain't much need for him after ten or so. So, this fella hangs in the bar 'til closin' time, goes home and passes out. If you want to catch him, you better hurry or he ain't gonna be no good to you. You'd take more of a risk with his drinkin'. 'Bout an hour from now, he'll be lucky to find his way home much less crossin' the straits to find St. Ignace."

"Well, let's not keep this a secret," Dan said. "What's his name?"

"He calls himself Cap'n Jones. I can about guarantee that you'll find him out with the locals at one of three places. Check the bar at the Chippewa Hotel first. It's called the Pink Pony. If he ain't there, hit Horn's Bar, just down the road about two blocks. Your last shot will be at The Lamplighter Lounge. It's in The Murray Hotel. If you have no luck by then, he's already crashed."

Dan was familiar with all the places. "What's he looking like?"

"Just like a boat captain. He's always wearing a hat. Usually, it's a yacht club hat. He's about fifty, greying hair. Also, he sports a short beard, bigger guy and kinda scraggly."

"Thanks, Derry. If we can't find a way off, we'll call you. If you don't hear from us, assume we're on the way. Is that cool with you?"

"Like I said, no sweat, man. Oh," Derry said as an afterthought, "make sure you bring some cash. He isn't gonna be too pleased about havin' his saloonin' interrupted, if you catch my drift. And, another thing, the guy's kinda ornery, so watch your step."

"Thanks again, Derry," Dan said, hanging up the phone.

"So, what's up?" Diana asked.

"Well, we might have a shot at getting out of here but we have to move quickly. The first thing that we have to do is go the bank. There's an ATM about two blocks away up on Market

Street. There's a Captain Jones out there who might be able to help us. But, money talks. Then, we're going bar hopping."

"This is crazy," Diana commented.

"You're telling me!"

Minutes later, they were at the bank. Diana pulled her credit cards out and dropped a Visa in for a cash advance. While she was waiting on the machine, Dan looked at her.

"You shouldn't be using a credit card."

"We're leaving anyway, aren't we?"

"Good point," Dan said. He had his card in hand already.

"Besides, where do you think I got my clothes this morning?"

"What?"

"Don't you remember? I left with virtually nothing on me yesterday. I had to have some basics!"

"That explains it," Dan said. "Remember how we said we weren't going to use credit cards? How do you think they found us so quickly?"

Before Diana had a chance to answer, the ATM spat out a slip of paper. Diana read it and crumpled it up. "That son of a bitch!"

As far as Dan was concerned, it was the first time that he had ever heard Diana swear. If their situation had been different, he might have been amused at seeing her display some human characteristics. "What is it?" Dan asked.

"My credit has been denied and the ATM is keeping the card. There's only one person who could have done this. It's a long story having to do with my husband. Or should I say my ex-husband?" She was surprised at how long it had been since she had last had a thought about him.

Not wanting to waste any more time, Dan dropped his card in and took out his maximum allowable advance of a thousand dollars. "Whew, you had me worried that I wouldn't get anything."

The two of them backtracked and made their way to The Pink Pony, the small bar attached to the Chippewa Hotel. A guy by the name of Beans was sitting up on the small stage, jamming on a guitar while intermittently jumping into a harmonica solo. The Jimmy Buffet tune gave it a Floridian flair. Neither of them noticed as they scanned the bar stools for Captain Jones. Within a minute, they found the door to the way out. Nobody even nearly fit the description.

Next, they pushed their way through the throngs of drunken cyclists and pedestrians to Horn's Bar. For five minutes, they anxiously waited in line as a bouncer checked I.D.'s. It looked more like a college crowd than the type of place where they could find a local seaman. As soon as they got in the door, they were greeted by a band doing a loud rendition of a Ramone's tune. They weren't doing it well, either, but the crowd didn't seem to mind. A lot of beer was being swilled and a lot of yelling was done as people bounced quarters on tables to see who was designated to drink next. A quick search of the bar revealed nobody in a hat.

Moments later, they found themselves back on the street, their ears ringing. They backtracked about a block and a half to find The Murray. There was no line at the door. They walked in to the sounds of an older gentleman doing, *Little Red Rooster*, on a baby Grand. Dan's heart dropped when he saw only about ten people sitting around the bar in a quiet solitude. And then, in the furthest corner, he saw who must have surely been their Captain Jones. Dan pointed him out to Diana.

They sidled up next to him. Dan ordered himself a beer and looked at Diana to order. She looked back at him while the bartender popped the cap off his beer.

"I thought you weren't drinking, anymore," she said to him.

Dan sighed, running his fingers through his hair. "Can we talk about that later? I don't think that now is the right time," he said softly.

She ordered herself a Kurant and tonic.

Dan lit a cigarette and sipped off his beer, attempting to get a feel for the man he suspected of being Captain Jones. The man raised his hand and pushed his empty beer glass forward. The bartender, taking note, refilled his beer.

"I've got this one," Dan said. He extended his hand. "My name's Rusty Wallace. Yours?"

"Jones. Casey Jones," he said, returning the handshake. "Thanks for the cold one. It's been a long day."

Dan's hand was enveloped in Captain Jones' large hand. He also noticed the leathery feel of his hand matched his tanned and weatherworn face. "Pleased to meet you. We have a mutual friend who's told me a lot about you. I hear that you've got a charter business."

"That I do," Captain Jones said as he raised his beer to his lips. Been on this God-forsaken rock for fifteen or sixteen years. I'm startin' to lose track of the years. You a fisherman?"

"I've done my share."

"Who's the pretty lady?" Ross asked.

"Oh, I'm sorry," Dan said. "This here's my..." he faltered, "sister. Her name is, uh, Katie. Katie Mae."

Diana extended her hand, hiding the questioning look on her face. Fortunately, the bar was significantly darker than the others they had visited. "It's nice to meet you, Mr. Jones."

"You, too, little lady. You married?" Jones asked, not letting her hand go.

"As a matter of fact, I am," she answered, pulling her hand away.

"Sorry to hear that, Katie Mae. Mighty fine name you got there. I was getting the feeling your brother here almost forgot it, eh?"

Dan forced a smile out. "No, actually, it's been one hell of a day."

"Lookin' for a charter in the morning?" Jones asked as he leaned his elbows on the bar.

Dan threw Diana a glance. He looked back at Jones. "Well, if you want to know the truth, we're looking for one tonight."

"You ain't gonna find one on this island. You gotta wait 'til morning."

Dan reached into his pocket and pulled out two C-notes. He slid them toward the seaman.

Jones looked toward the money and raised his glass to his lips. "Like I said..."

Dan deftly slipped another one over.

Jones set his glass down. "Must be awfully important."

"It is," Dan said. "We have to make our way to Detroit, tonight. Our mother's awfully sick. They're saying she might not last the night. What do you say?"

Jones fingered the bills, folded them and slipped them into his jacket pocket. "When do you want to leave?"

Dan looked at Diana, and then looked back at Jones with a shrug of his shoulders. "Now would be nice."

"Alright, folks. Which side you headed to? Maniac City or St. Ignorance?" Jones said in reference to Mackinac City and St. Ignace.

"The car's parked in St. Ignace."

"You got a lotta luggage?"

"Believe it or not, Captain Jones, we don't have any that we need to worry about. I mean, we're thinking of leaving it here. We'll come back and get it. What you see is what you get."

Jones ordered another beer and drank it just as quickly. "Let's head out, folks."

Five minutes later, they were crawling onto a thirty-foot Bayliner complete with poles, life-jackets and a cabin underneath. Although the air was cool, Dan and Diana preferred to sit up top behind Jones' captain's chair. He busied himself with warming up the engine and turning on the radio. Dan grabbed the ropes and unleashed the boat. They eased their way out into the open waters. Jones didn't pull the throttle back until they had crossed the breakwall. A beacon and a lighthouse danced their red, green and white lights across the waters. The great expanse of the Grand Hotel could be seen framed against the island off to their right.

The wind chill increased significantly, chilling Dan and Diana to the bone. Finally, Diana hollered to Dan that she wanted to use a restroom. Dan made his way to Jones and asked if he had one on board. Jones pointed downward toward the cabin. Dan motioned Diana forward. They both stepped into the warm refuge of the room underneath.

Dan sat on the bed while he waited for her. Suddenly, something made him get up and walk back toward the door. He could have sworn that he had heard voices. He put his ear to the door.

"...a Roger, sheriff. I'm thinking that they've gotta be those two fugitives that you're all lookin' for, over?" Static followed.

"Lost Sailor? Listen to me," the radio crackled back. "Consider them armed and dangerous. Proceed with caution. Buy some time until we can get the Coast Guard out there. Do you read me? Over?"

"That's a Roger, Sheriff. Say, uh, these guys got any money on their heads, over?"

"Ten grand, Lost Sailor. What's your twenty? Over?"

Diana stepped out of the bathroom, smacking her head on the doorframe when they hit a particularly nasty wave.

"That son of a bitch!" Dan said. He quickly pulled Diana close and told her everything that he had just heard. "We're trapped!"

Diana thought about it, concern all over her face. "Can you swim?" she asked him.

"Sure," Dan said. "Thing is, you don't know how cold these waters are. I'm guessing the temperature is sitting around forty-five degrees. Hypothermia is an extreme possibility."

"So," Diana said thoughtfully, "we make him bring the boat in as close to shore as possible. Didn't the sheriff say we were considered armed and dangerous?"

"Well, yeah, but..."

"So, we become armed and dangerous. Let's start looking!"

The two of them, quietly began opening cabinets under the bed and over the sink, quickly.

Diana discovered two flares and held them up for Dan to see. "Well, come on. We don't have much time."

They each stuffed a flare in their shirts and made their way back up on deck. Jones was chewing on a cigar as he neared the boat parallel to the town of St. Ignace. They could both see that it was about a mile and a half away, black and cold waters being their only obstacle to freedom.

"Isn't that the harbor right there?" Dan hollered in the wind to Ross.

"That there's a private harbor," Jones answered. "We gotta head up a couple of nautical miles to where I can let you off."

Dan knew he was full of it. There was only one harbor in all of St. Ignace, it accessed on the side they were on. Besides, they could have been dropped off at either of three ferry docks. He turned back and looked at Diana for support. "Jones. How about you take us straight in, right now! Help us out!"

"Like I said," Jones hollered in the wind, "I can't..."

Dan whipped out the flair and rammed it in the sailor's back. "Now, before we kill you and take the boat in ourselves!"

Jones didn't need to be told twice. He steered the boat aft, toward the harbor lights.

"Faster!" Dan said. He knew the clock was ticking.

The boat caressed the waves powerfully as the lights grew nearer. Jones turned around to look at the two.

Dan rammed the stick harder into his ribs. "There's no need to look at us unless you want to give us this boat!"

"Hey," Jones said, definitely irritated, "Lighten up with the gun. I know what side my bread's buttered on!"

"No bullshit and I'll lighten up! Deal? "

"Yeah, don't get crazy now."

Dan slowly relaxed the pressure until the flare was no longer in his back. Diana motioned Dan toward the back of the boat.

"What is it?" Dan asked her, never taking his eyes off of Jones.

"Think we can swim from here?" she asked.

Dan surmised the distance and decided they'd give it another hundred yards. He looked at Diana, not believing what they were about to do. But, the way things had turned; there was no other way out. Both of them slipped off their shoes and climbed up on the back. Jones never turned around. The lights loomed closer. They had about three hundred yards to go. In the dark, Dan raised his fingers arid counted back from five.

The two of them slipped off the side into the wake of the water.

And, it was as cold as hell in the wintertime. It felt like a vice had grabbed their lungs and was squeezing the hell out of them. Both of them jumped up in the wake, gasping for breath.

Suddenly, they heard a sharp retort. And, then another. And another followed after that. It wasn't until a bullet whisked by

Dan's head and hit the water, sounding like a small torpedo, did they both realize what was happening.

Jones was shooting at them.

Dan felt Diana grab his hand as they dove under water.

Another bullet pierced the water between them and Dan wondered what death would be like in those frigid and black waters.

21

STELLA BLUE

Things twisted significantly downward the day that Daddy found out that the patient who was suing him, died. Never mind the fact that she didn't take the antibiotics that were prescribed to her, Daddy would comment furiously. Or, what of the basic hygienic regimen that he laid out for her after the operation? It was the bloodsucking lawyers looking for a fast million bucks out of his pocket. Compound that with the fact that both the American Medical Association and The American Dental Association had opened an investigation into his private practice. He voiced his opinion all too clearly about the prospect of both financial and professional ruin, something he had worked to build all of his life.

It didn't take too long for it to affect an unstable family that was already walking on needles and hanging on by the barest of threads.

Mark reacted by going out and finding himself a paper route. He could not have cared less about earning money. What mattered was that it afforded him a few more extra hours out the house. Every morning, he was out the door by 5:30 a.m., delivering a meager twenty papers in the neighborhood. He enjoyed delivering papers in the morning and in the afternoon while also taking care of collections door to door on Saturday afternoons. Besides, it gave him a few extra bucks to grab a few new Hot Wheels and some model airplanes. The more time away from Daddy during those times, the better.

Only, it wasn't just Daddy, anymore. Momma was starting to change, too.

One Sunday morning, he got a little overly zealous as he bombed down the driveway on his ten-speed Western Flyer. He had twenty Milwaukee Journal newspapers rigged on the back of his bike. They must have weighed a good fifty pounds. Well, he rounded the corner at the bottom of the driveway with just a hair too much lean and a little bit too much speed. The next thing he knew, all the newspapers that he had spent the last hour assembling and rigging to the back of his bike, were airborne, fluttering all over the street. A stiff breeze was blowing, complicating his already harrowing near-death accident. Before he knew it, he was on his feet, scrambling for sports sections, comics and T.V. guides.

Fortunately, the neighbor across the street, Dr. Pugh, a respected gynecologist, came out to assist. Both of them were fighting the breeze and grabbing every scrap of newspaper that they could find. Mark knew that he shouldn't have gotten the neighbor involved but the neighbor volunteered and as much as Mark wanted to do it himself, the neighbor would have it no other way. Soon, they had a huge pile of mixed up papers stacked in the driveway across the street.

Daddy had to work early that morning. He came out to the garage and decided to amble down the driveway, wondering why the garage door was open. Mark's face turned eight sheets of white when he saw Daddy. Mark looked at the neighbor who was busily helping him, as if to say, "You better go in the house."

It was too late. "Hey, Doctor Wilcox. Your boy had a little accident here."

Daddy stared at Dr. Pugh and then at Mark. "There's no need for you to help. Mark is learning the meaning of responsibility. What happened Mark?"

"I skidded on my bike and fell," he said quietly, nervously.

"I can see that."

"You know boys, Doctor. Accidents happen," Dr. Pugh volunteered.

"Not to my boys, they don't. Why don't you let us work on this? It's pretty chilly out here. There's no need for you to step into our affairs," Daddy said, a stern tone to his voice.

"Really. I don't mind. We'll have this cleared off in a jiffy. All we..."

Daddy didn't let him finish. Instead, he grabbed Mark by the ear and shoved him toward the newspapers. "Now, let's get this stuff out of the man's driveway so he can enjoy some peace and quiet. Now!"

Mark started grabbing as many papers as he could while the neighbor watched, an incredulous look on his face.

Once Mark had all the papers stacked on the Wilcox driveway, Daddy proceeded to, well, lose his temper. It wasn't long before Mark was sniveling and bruised.

Meanwhile, the neighbor strolled back into his house. Other people's children and other people's method of discipline really wasn't his business, after all.

Later on, after Daddy had gone to work, Mark vented his frustrations by destroying a few models, smashing a few Matchbox cars and tossing his bike into a ravine.

Danny had seen the whole thing. He watched in frustration and fear. But, there was nothing he could do. Well, except the one thing that he had recently started doing. He didn't like smashing his stuff like Mark did, although in times of hell, he had broken one or two things of his own. One time, he tossed his metal lunchbox across the street, breaking the Thermos inside. Momma didn't take too well to that. So, instead, Danny took a liking toward hitting himself in the face and pulling his own hair. He tried to hurt himself as much as he could. Fortunately, the only damage he might have suffered was mentally. But, he had to do something! He always felt terrible afterwards but it seemed to have lightened the tension in his mind.

The thing was, there was no one to talk to and there was no help on the way.

Daddy was becoming increasingly difficult to figure out. He went through the daily routines of being the type of father that he was but he just didn't seem all the way there at times. Danny suspected that Momma saw his increasing distances and silences. For the kids, it was good when he was silent because he stayed away from them, sometimes for days at a time. Yet, Momma's frustrations appeared to have been increasing little by little. He started noticing Momma change and he didn't like what was happening.

There was terror at one level with Daddy because he was a large man. With Momma, though, it was entirely different case.

The first time that he saw that something had gone terribly wrong was a clear and warm Saturday afternoon. This time, it was Louise who suffered.

The effects of the mental and physical abuse had taken its toll on her, imperceptibly, at first. This eleven year-old girl, with her learning disability, responded to the detrimental environment in the only way she knew how.

She went inside herself. She was just as afraid of her parents as the other children in the family, but the effect of that fear was more pronounced because of her disadvantaged situation. First of all, she was a girl. Boys are raised in such a manner that they are taught to roll with the punches. Girls, on the other hand, are taught to be protected. They're raised with the idea that they're fragile and recessive. Girls are taught to confide in other girls, whether it be a mother or a girlfriend or a sister. But, Louise had none of those options. While Mark and Danny were able to whisper to each other in the deep hours of the night, Louise was in her bedroom alone, with no one. To make matters worse, her learning disability constricted her even more, leaving her confused and lonely.

Her disability required love, understanding and patience to be dealt with properly. She needed those extra steps to bolster her mental stability. But, with the death of the patient who sued, Momma and Daddy had other things on their minds. And, as they deteriorated, so did Louise.

She tried as hard as she could to be what her parents wanted her to be. Day in and day out, she looked for approval in her most minor of successes. She remembered the meaning of new words. She memorized her times tables. She retained most of the capital cities of the United States.

Unfortunately, in Daddy's eyes, that wasn't enough. Her reading level was three years behind that of "normal". Daddy tried to get her to catch up by making her read in every single waking hour.

There's only so much that a child can study in one sitting. When children get tired, their attention span dwindles to the point where retention is almost non-existent. When this happened to Louise, Daddy would become infuriated. He didn't understand that he was pushing too hard. She didn't understand why he was pushing so hard. He may have been able to retain something after six hours of studying, so why couldn't she? No kid of his was going to be an idiot. He had a name to uphold and if she didn't want to learn, he'd damn well make sure that she would, after he was through with her.

Pain seemed to be the only thing that created any results. So, her learning sessions included the pulling of hair, some pinching under the arms, and the brutal slamming of her hands or her face into a book. She cried and screamed, which only caused Daddy to do it more. Why wouldn't she learn, damn it!

Whenever Louise was quizzed on her studies, she did her best to give the answers that Daddy was looking for. Rarely did the answer seem to be the right one. In that, she rarely walked away, unscathed. In the end, or the beginning of the end, her response was only natural. Rather than risking giving answers that were wrong, it was safer not to say anything. Oftentimes, because she clammed up, Daddy would send her to bed, and to her, that was better than suffering for the torture of giving the wrong answers. Sometimes it worked, sometimes it didn't...

Danny watched in terror, as her method of survival backfired. Ironically, what made it even worse, was that Daddy wasn't even there. Momma was the instigator and Danny never really recovered from the incident. It probably also marked the first time that Danny realized that they had a problem that was far too big for even *the protector* to handle. And, for years, Danny would be jarred awake from a particularly vivid nightmare that had been a recreation of that same incident. Those nightmares of his screaming voice reaching out to be heard, left on deaf ears in the frustration of watching his sister in terror, his hands tied behind his back.

It happened on a Saturday afternoon. The temperature was mild outside as a plethora of birds fed themselves on the sunflower seeds that Momma routinely made sure was filled in their respective feeders. Blue Jays, Cardinals, Redpolls, Evening Grosbeaks and Chickadees were frolicking in an abundance of food, chattering their daily conversations while an entirely different scenario was building inside the house. While other kids could be heard playing on the street, the Wilcox kids were inside, doing their respective chores. Each child was banished to a part of the house, with a dampened dust cloth in hand. Danny was told to clean the kitchen, while Mark was upstairs working on the bedrooms and Louise was elected to clean the foyer and the attached living room.

In silence, each child busily dusted and cleaned, hoping they would pass Momma's ensuing white-glove test. Danny was staring at the birds outside the bay window in the kitchen, wishing for release, while his hands mindlessly wiped, lost in a fantasy world light-years away.

"What are you doing, Louise?" he heard Momma ask her from the top of the stairs, overlooking the foyer.

"I'm cleaning," she answered defensively.

Danny looked over to the connecting foyer and saw her standing next to the black, wrought-iron railing that encircled the steps to the upper landing where Momma was. A damp rag hung limply in Louise' hand. Danny quickly made himself busy, in case Momma came downstairs to investigate prematurely.

"You were not cleaning," Momma said, sternly. "I was watching you. What were you doing?"

"Well, um..."

"I asked you a question. What were you doing?"

"I was dusting the railing."

"You're lying to me!"

"Well..." Louise stammered.

"Answer me!"

"I was...I..."

Danny knew exactly what was going on. Momma had probably caught Louise daydreaming, and Louise was afraid to admit it. So, as the pressure increased, so, too, did her inability to speak.

"You were what?" Momma pursued.

"Um..."

"I can't hear you," Momma said, threateningly. Danny could almost feel the tightness in Momma's demeanor.

"Well...I was..." Louise stumbled out again.

Danny watched Louise as she twisted the dust cloth in her hands. He wanted to rush over and tell Louise to answer before Momma got upset. He had seen enough in Momma, lately, to know that her changes were no longer just minor nuances. He wished that Louise would say anything to appease Momma. The tenseness grew by the second.

"Are you going to answer me?"

"I don't know what to say," Louise answered shrilly.

"Damn you!" Momma suddenly said, infuriated.

Danny heard her come stomping down the stairs. His hair stood up on the back of his neck while his stomach twisted in fear for his sister. He busied himself in a mock display of cleaning the rungs on the kitchen stools, while watching the scene develop out of the corner of his eye.

"I'm sorry," Louise said fearfully.

"For what? "

"I don't know," she answered.

"I'm going to ask you again. What were you doing?"

"I was...I don't know."

Momma suddenly slapped her full across the face. Danny cringed at the sound of her hand as it met his sister's flesh. "Will you stop saying, 'I don't know'! That is not an answer. Now, before I get upset, are you going to tell me what you were doing?!"

"Well, yes, I was..." Louise said, tears pouring down her face. "I don't know!"

"That's it!" Momma slapped her again, much harder this time. "What? "

"Um..."

When Louise didn't answer, Momma slapped her again, the retort echoing across the foyer. Then she grabbed Louise by the shoulders and began shaking the daylights out of her. "I can't hear you! What did you say?!"

The only answer that Louise gave was muffled in cries and screams of fright.

"I said answer me!"

Still, Louise' response was the same. She had clammed up and nothing was going to break into that shell. Momma released her shoulders and reached back and slapped her again. Louise fell to the floor, holding her stinging face.

Danny looked on, incredulous. He had never seen Momma quite like this.

Though he had grown angry and frustrated, he didn't know what anger was until he saw what happened next.

Momma grabbed Louise' head and pushed it to the floor. "Don't you fight me, you insolent little idiot!" she screamed at Louise while Louise squirmed in what little defense she had. Momma kicked her swiftly in the legs. Louise screamed even louder, not knowing what was going to happen next. She was now lying on her back, on the white tiled floor, while Momma towered over her.

"Are you going to answer me!'

Louise responded in a wail of fear.

"Fine. I'll get an answer out of you if it kills me. I won't be as patient as your father has been!" Momma took her foot and placed it squarely on Louise' chest. "One last chance!"

In bewilderment, Louise cried.

With one hand holding onto the railing, Momma placed her weight on her daughter's chest. Danny heard the air rush out of

Louise's lungs. After a moment or two, she stepped off of her. "Are you ready to answer me?!"

Louise only screamed louder. Momma promptly stood on her again, and again, and again as the repeating tirade continued.

As this was happening, Danny watched, his eyes widened in terror. He began pinching himself as hard as he could, ignorant of the blood that he was drawing from the back of his own hand. Unknown to him, at the time, Mark was simultaneously crouched in his room, hitting himself as hard as could.

While Louise continued screaming, Momma continued to repeatedly step on her.

Danny could no longer block the screams out of his head. The pain he was rendering to himself was nothing compared to the pain of what he was watching. If Danny didn't do something, he was sure that it would never end until her ribs broke. And, in the ongoing madness, he saw the telephone. It seemed to be beckoning him. He'd have to call the police. There was no other way around it. They would be able to hear what was happening, and they could stop it! He couldn't watch this happening to his sister, anymore! If only he was strong enough to fight his mother!

The telephone loomed only feet away, larger than life.

Louise continued screaming.

Danny had to do it! The phone...if only he could pick it up. It was ten feet away, at the most. But, how was he going to get past the doorway without Momma seeing him? As Louise screamed, he forced himself to stand and take the first step.

What if Momma saw him!

Thoughts rifled through his head. If Momma caught him, he would surely face a fate worse than what Louise was enduring.

Worse yet, what if Momma actually caught him on the phone? If she was angry now, imagine her mood as she caught him mid-sentence to the police! She would kill him; there was no question about that!

But, she was killing Louise right now!

Danny panicked and rushed over to the sink, discarding any thoughts of the telephone. He grabbed the dirty glasses that were lined up, ready for him to wash. With a sweep of the arm, he pushed them to the floor. They shattered everywhere, as Danny stood there in frozen concentration.

The screaming stopped.

"What the hell is going on here?" Momma questioned as she stormed into the kitchen after Danny.

"I'm sorry! I bumped the glasses. I didn't mean to do it!" Danny lied in a terrorized voice.

"You clumsy brat! Clean it up or shall I give you some of your sister's medication? "

Then, Momma was angry at Danny. Although she hit, kicked and screamed at him, he knew it was nothing compared to the fear of watching it happen to Louise.

Eventually, Danny had all the glass cleaned up. Momma banished everyone to their rooms on that sunny Saturday afternoon. She turned on the radio in the kitchen, humming to, *Sing a Song*, by The Carpenters.

It wasn't the last time that Danny was to be *the protector*. Not by a long shot.

22

SCARLET BEGONIAS

After the bullet rifled between Dan and Diana, neither one wasted any time in staying underwater as long as they could while also moving ahead. They held their breath until they thought they were about to explode. Suddenly, they risked coming up to the surface for air. Each one knew that this breath might very well be their last.

Simultaneously, they broke the surface, doing their best to keep from sputtering and coughing, making sure that their heads were above water before inhaling into their near exploding lungs.

In the darkness, Dan wiped the water from his eyes, rolling with the swells. It was difficult to see and, for a moment, he thought he had lost his bearings. In the distance, Dan saw the shadow of Captain Jones' boat, gratefully headed the opposite direction. He quickly looked for Diana. He saw her treading water between the rolls of the waves about four yards away.

"Over here!" he whispered to her.

"I see you," Diana called back. "Let's get in to shore before he sees us."

"Follow me," Dan said.

The two of them did the breaststroke the rest of the way in, leaving only their heads on the surface. A freestyle stroke would have left them as sitting ducks. Every once in awhile, Dan would look back checking on the progress of Ross. It appeared that he had lost them but was still searching, his boat going in wide circles while he scoured the water with a Maglite. For every second, they were a step closer to freedom.

Before they knew it, they could hear the waves lapping against the rocky shore. Each knew how close freedom was and it gave them the final boost of adrenaline to push ahead in the frigid waters. Dan reached the shore first, stubbing his toe on particularly large, submerged boulder. It was all he could do to keep from cussing out loud. He let the pain smart and then ebb away in his already numb body. Moments later Diana came swimming up, crawling on shore when she felt the land under her feet. Sharp rocks threatened to lacerate her feet. She pulled herself out of the water, numb to the bone.

"Jesus Christ!" Dan said, massaging his foot.

"He was shooting at us!" Diana said, still amazed at how quickly things had soured.

"Bastard," Dan said, spitting water to the ground. "Do you know that if I hadn't have heard him...?"

"Let's not talk about it," Diana said. "We need to get out of here."

"Follow me," Dan said, not needing another warning.

Both he and Diana knew that they must have looked liked patent escapees with no shoes on, haggard looks and wet clothes to boot. But, St. Ignace, being a small Northern Michigan town, rolled up it's sidewalks by midnight. In that, to their benefit, virtually no one was on the street. Only one car came down the street when they were within a block of Derry's Auto body. They dashed into the alcove of the closed Greyhound Station. The car passed, oblivious to their existence.

Not two minutes later, Dan was hurriedly tapping on Derry's door. A second later, it opened.

"Where have you guys been?" Derry asked.

Ignoring the question, Dan looked at him. "You gonna let us in or leave us out here to freeze like a couple of derelicts?"

"Yeah, come on in," he said, a confused look on his face at seeing their soggy appearance. "What happened to you guys?"

A girl appeared behind Derry. "What has happened to your manners? Can't you see they're freezing? Go get some towels. I'll put on some hot tea. The bedroom's that way, folks, if you'd like to get out of those clothes."

Dan looked at her, obviously a bit uncomfortable. "Actually, you wouldn't have separate rooms, would you?" he asked, not looking toward Diana in this unexpected uncomfortable situation.

"Oh, I'm sorry," she said. "I thought you two were, well, together."

"Well, we are, but not that way," Dan said.

The girl, dressed in shorts, Birkenstocks and a tie-dyed sweatshirt pointed them out to opposing rooms. "Excuse the mess, but you'll find towels in the bathrooms. What's ours is yours. We'll route up some clothes for you. Now, go on! We'll talk when you're dried up. Matter of fact, one of the rooms has a bath and the other a shower. Feel free," she said as she rushed off to the kitchen.

Diana looked at Dan and smiled. "Can I have the shower?"

"Sure," Dan said. "I'm still shaking, you know that?"

"No need to tell me that. But, next time that Derry gives you a referral, you better check his references."

Twenty minutes later, the four of them were in the living room. Everyone was sitting except for Dan, who was busy pacing trails on the living room floor, telling the edited story of their short-lived visit to Mackinac.

Derry took a drink of his tea and pondered the situation for the moment. "So, are you two on the run for murder?" he asked, letting the question hang in the air while, Stella Blue, played faintly in the background.

"Where'd you get that idea?" Dan asked, his guard up.

"Seems pretty obvious, man. You get a load of the newspapers, lately? This is the most talkin' that I've heard goin' on since the IGA and The First National Bank was robbed in the same day ten years ago."

"I didn't do it," Dan said steadfastly.

"But, you're suspected of it," Derry's girlfriend said.

"Ah, yeah," Dan answered. "By the way, I never got your name."

"Aw, man, I'm sorry," Derry jumped in. "This here's my girl, Althea. It was her who fixed up the interior of Blossom. Probably been on two hundred shows with me. A great road warrior and great companion!"

Althea smiled.

"And this is Diana," Dan introduced. "A good friend of mine."

"I'd say so," Derry said. "If the lady's out dodgin' bullets with you, you got a real friend."

"If I had known, Diana never would have been with me," Dan said, his eyes floating toward the floor.

"I'm an adult," Diana said. "I knew what I was getting into. Of course, I didn't quite expect this, either. I thought you said that Captain Jones was a good friend of yours," she said toward Derry.

"I never said he was a friend!" Derry defended. "You folks were lookin' for a boat and he's the only guy I could think of. I did say that he was an ornery son of a bitch. Go figure!"

Just then, they all stopped to listen to a growing sound. It built in propensity until it virtually shook the walls. Dan froze in fear but it passed overhead within a second later. It was definitely the sound of a chopper.

All of them ran to the living room window and looked out. The beacon lights could be seen disappearing over the waters of the Straits.

"Derry, I appreciate the hospitality but the longer we're here, the greater the risk that we're going to put you into danger. Do you mind if we hit the road?"

"No sweat, man. While we were waiting for you, we stocked up Blossom and threw in a full tank of gas. We kinda had a suspicion of what was going on. How are you guys set up for clothes?"

"We've got money. We'll pick some up tomorrow."

Althea got up and came back with a Marlboro Duffel bag. "We've got a bunch of stuff here that I was going to donate to

Goodwill. Well, once Derry and-I got to talking, we figured that you two might be better off with it. I've got some wonderful dresses here that might fit you a little large but I think you'll like them, Diana. Most of this, we've picked up while we were at Dead shows and at various consignments centers across the country," she said as she unzipped the bag. She started pulling out Dead shirts, flowered dresses, some well-worn jeans and a variety of aged bandanas.

"Really, thanks," Diana said. "But, those clothes aren't really my, uh, how shall I say it? They aren't my style?"

Derry laughed. "Uh, what is your style, Diana? I've got you pegged for a working class lady. Am I right?"

"Actually, I've got a Ph.D. So, I'm used to..."

"The papers say you're a psychiatrist. Correct?"

Diana blushed.

"Yeah, well, that's what we thought," Derry said. "You want to be smart about this whole thing?"

"Of course," Dan said.

Althea jumped in. "Well, then, these clothes will be perfect for you. The cops ain't going to hassle a couple of deadheads so how about dressing like one?"

"I can't wear that! I mean, I appreciate the gesture but..."

"You're gonna look kinda funny in a business suit driving a '74 VW bus. You catchin' my drift? You ain't gonna make it past the Mackinac Bridge. They got state troopers lined up there like you wouldn't believe."

"Oh yeah?" Dan asked.

"Word has it, they got cops crawlin' all over the Upper Peninsula after you two. Feds are involved 'cause they're sayin' you're armed and dangerous and you kidnapped this here doctor."

"What? " Dan and Diana said simultaneously.

"He's not kiddin'," Althea, piped in. "If you hadn't been here the other day, and Derry hadn't known you so long, well, we might not be here trying to help you. They're making this out to be a big thing. They ain't looking for deadheads, though. So what do you say?"

Reluctantly, Diana looked at Dan, then at Althea and then at the clothes. "Well, it's only temporary..."

Althea stood up, grabbed the bag and then took Diana back to the bedroom.

In the meantime, Derry looked at Dan and then reached into his wallet. "I'm not sure what kind of journey you're on, man. And I ain't sure that I want to know more than is necessary. But, me and the lady got somethin' to give you." He handed Dan two cards.

Dan looked at the two corresponding driver's licenses to his friends. "I can't take these!"

"Don't worry about it. In a week or so, we'll go re-apply at the Secretary of State's Office for new ones. It'll buy you ten days or so. We'll just say we lost 'em. You'd do the same for me. Just be damn careful. Since when does a driver's license look like the person it's supposed to, anyway?"

Dan looked at the pictures and thought they looked fairly similar with Derry and his long hair and Althea with her brown hair. "I don't know what to say..."

"Mail me the ID's when you're done. Like I said, we'll give you some time before we apply for new ones." Derry stood up and motioned Dan outside.

Derry took him through a complete inspection of Blossom. He showed him how the top went up, if they were to park in a campground. He pulled out the overhang where they could shade themselves from the rain and put it over a picnic table, if they wished. It was stocked with plenty of drinking water and water for the sink. The spare was in okay shape but it couldn't be trusted for too long. Inside, he had greased the joints for the dropdown beds and the refrigerator was in working order.

"She don't like driving in a lot of heat, though. She's got a radiator on account of her new engine, which most busses don't have. You watch the temperature and she'll do you fine."

Of course, Blossom was equipped with tape decks both in front and in back

"You remember this, Dan. As Jerry said, 'Set out runnin' but I take my time. A friend of the devil is a friend of mine'. So, here's that list of tapers.

Every one of them will help you out. Tell 'em you know me, make 'em a few tapes and they'll be all that much more grateful. Know what I'm sayin'? Jerry may be gone but the spirit's still alive."

"Like I said, I don't know what to say."

"Do what you gotta do," Derry said with a pat on the back.

The two of them walked back in the house while Derry handed Dan the keys.

Just then, Diana walked out, wearing a long brown, lightly flowered dress, beads adorning her neck. She could have been any number of twirling girls that he had seen at any given Dead show in years past. She almost looked serene in her back to the basics outfit, complete with Birkenstocks.

"You look good," Dan said.

"I can't believe I'm saying this," Diana said, looking at herself in the mirror. "I feel like a throw-back from Haight-Asbury but I'm comfortable."

"That's the point," Althea said, straightening the beads around Diana's neck.

"Too bad we ain't got a show to see," Derry said with a saddened smile.

"We've got our own show," Dan commented.

"Well, Diana, shall we? The faster we get away from here, the better. Are you ready?"

Nervously, Diana took a deep breath. "If anyone ever saw me..."

"They'd think you look beautiful," Althea finished.

The four of them shook hands and hugged. A new stretch of the journey was about to begin.

Blossom fired up on the first try, ready to traverse many unknown roads, peppy and free as a bird, surely ready to re-travel roads that the Dead had in their day.

Before they knew it, Blossom was taking them out of the driveway.

The last thing that Derry and Althea saw was the bumper sticker on the back window that read, "FUKENGRUVEN" and the license plate that read "WHRF RAT". If anyone had been watching them, they would have seen tears of remembrance in their eyes as they said good-bye to Blossom and their friends inside.

Dan and Diana were quiet as they approached The Mackinac Bridge; it's towers looming up like a guillotine. Half a mile before the bridge, they saw the state troopers' vehicles adorning either side of the roadway like a gauntlet of death.

Dan dropped the bus into second gear as he slowed the vehicle to pay the upcoming toll, his heart pounding in his chest.

The police turned to look at them as they pulled up to the bridge. Over the waters to their left, they could see a helicopter searching the frigid waters of the Straits.

Dan and Diana held their breath, afraid to break the silence.

23

JACK STRAW

The first hint that Danny had that he was supposed to be growing up was when he saw Momma loading the Cadillac when they got home from school one day. Both Mark and he looked at each other strangely as Momma loaded up bag after bag into the trunk of the car.

"What's going on?" Danny asked.

"How about helping me out?" Momma asked busily.

"With what?" Mark asked.

"Go to your room and get your toys, every last one of them. It's time that you learned how to be an adult. I expect the Lego set, Erector sets and every last toy car that you have up there. We're going to Goodwill and giving these to kids who can use them."

"But..." Danny started to say.

"But nothing! You get up to your room or are we going to have to discuss this with your father?"

There was no room for arguments when Momma put it that way. So, the two boys spent the next hour unloading the toy chest. Meanwhile,

Louise was in her room, packing her Barbie doll sets, dollhouse and various other toys. All the kids silently did as they were told. If one were to watch them carefully, they would have seen tears slipping out of their eyes.

Mark and Danny put their Hot Wheels in a bag and hid them in the back of the closet, under some shoes. They could part with anything except for their cars. There was no way that Momma was getting hold of those. At the last second, Mark decided that they should keep a couple of cars separate from the bag. Namely, the pink and blue Lincoln Mark lll's, the yellow and red Custom Corvettes, the purple and green Eldorado' and the olive green and tan Torero's were hidden under the mattress in case Momma found the stash in the closet.

Just before they left to Goodwill, Momma found the stash in the closet. It was the worst day of their lives, no question about it.

An hour later, three sullen kids were back at home feeling that their lives were over and their toys, like departed old friends, were gone forever. While Daddy was eating his dinner, the house was eerily quiet.

"What happened to your hand?" Daddy asked Momma while they were eating dinner.

Danny was tip-toeing up the stairs by the kitchen when he stopped to listen.

Mark and Louise had been banished to their rooms, a common place to be ever since Momma had lost her temper with Louise recently.

"Nothing," Momma answered.

"It's obvious that something happened, with a bandage that big," Daddy pursued.

"A couple of days ago, I was washing dishes and I cut my hand. When we were on the way to Goodwill, the wound re-opened itself. That's it," Momma lied.

"Well, you don't have to get so sharp with me," Daddy said. "I've had a rough day, too, you know."

"I know, honey. You always have rough days. Can't I have one once in awhile?"

The two of them ate in silence for about five minutes. Danny waited motionless and intently on the stairs.

"What's happening to us?" Momma asked.

"Huh?"

"I hit Louise the other day."

"What for?" Daddy asked.

"She clammed up. She wouldn't answer me when I asked her why she was rough-housing the living room. I just lost my temper..."

"Could you help it? These kids are getting more defiant every day," Daddy said. "We all lose our tempers every once in a while. My father did it all the time, but did it hurt me? Look at how I turned out. It's just discipline, that's all. One day, they'll be happy that we raised them in a strict environment. You have to remember that we're only doing the best for them."

"But, I still feel bad..." Momma said quietly.

"And didn't you feel bad when you had to smack Cookie for urinating on the floor when she was a kitten?"

"Yes, but..."

"But, nothing," Daddy said. "It's all a part of being a parent. Next time, she'll think twice about rough-housing behind your back. I think you did the right thing. We have a lot of expensive things in there that we'd be heartbroken to lose. If she wants to rough-house, she can wait until she's outside. Otherwise, we will not put up with it in my house. Next time, she'll understand that."

Momma appeared to think about it for a moment. "Thanks, I feel a little better," she said.

"So, do you want to get Danny down here to talk about what we talked about last night?"

Upon hearing his name, he quickly dashed upstairs to the safe confines of his room. What was he in trouble for now, he thought.

"Danny?" Daddy called from downstairs.

His heart leaped. "Yes?" Danny answered.

"Come down here. We'd like to talk to you."

"I'm coming," Danny called back as he ran down the stairs.

Momma and Daddy were sitting at the kitchen table, eating dinner when Danny walked in. He tried not to be jealous of the stuffed pork chops and au gratin potatoes. Pangs of hunger gnawed at his stomach, even though he had just eaten an hour before. Momma had bragged about the dinner that she had served the kids, consisting of a plate of "No Brand" macaroni and cheese. She had gotten four boxes for a dollar and learned that each box served four kids at a time. Not bad, for a quarter.

Danny still couldn't get used to the tasteless, lukewarm and unappetizing meals.

"What does trust mean to you?" Daddy asked, while stuffing a big piece of juicy pork into his mouth.

"Trust?" Danny asked, not knowing what he was referring to.

"Yes, trust, the definition of trust. Are you deaf?"

"Well, no. Trust is when you believe in someone."

"That answer will work for the time being, I suppose." Daddy looked up from his plate, pointing his fork at Danny. It was loaded with creamy potatoes. "Can we trust you?"

"Well, yes," Danny said while wringing his hands behind his back. It looked like this might pan out to be a long quiz session. God only knew where it was headed.

"Why do you say that we can trust you?"

Danny nervously pondered the question for a moment. He hated these quiz sessions. They usually never amounted to anything but trouble for him. He fumbled for the proper words. "Because I'm trying to be a good son."

"Yes, you've been trying, haven't you?" Momma piped in sarcastically. "You've run away from home, you've lied, forged and God only knows that those are only the things we've caught you doing. Are you trying to call that someone to trust?"

"Well, no."

"Do you want to be trusted?"

"Yes."

"Why?" Daddy asked.

"Um, so I won't be a bad son," Danny answered, like he thought he was supposed to.

"Oh, great. I feel safe now," Daddy said, sarcasm dripping from his voice. He looked at Momma without saying anything, as if he was having second thoughts.

Danny wrung and twisted his hands behind his back, consciously trying not to look at their dinner.

"Do you know why we took your toys away?" Momma asked.

"Because we've been bad and we can't be trusted?" Danny said as a question.

"No, Danny," Daddy said. "It's because you're now thirteen years-old and it's time that you faced responsibility. You've got no time for toys, anymore. We've decided that, as much as your mother has opposed this, we should begin to trust you. Do you think that that's a mistake?"

"No."

"I hope not because if we find out that this is a mistake, there's going to be a price to pay. Do you understand me?"

"Yes, Daddy," he answered, knowing very well what Daddy meant by saying, "a price to pay."

Momma looked at Danny. "We're going to start square dancing, again. Your father and I used to do it a long time ago, before we were burdened with having you. We think that it's time for us to start enjoying ourselves again. So, if we can trust you, we want you to babysit your brother and sister on Thursday night and every Thursday thereafter. Can you handle that?"

"Yes, Momma."

"We're going to be gone from six o'clock until eleven or twelve o'clock. There are some very strict rules to be followed and we want them followed to the letter. Do you understand?"

"Yes," Danny answered, already excited about this new prospect of freedom.

"Now, Danny," She enunciated clearly, "we've thought about this a lot and we have no choice. Our square dancing is going to be held at K.I. Sawyer Air Force Base in Gwinn. It's a long drive out there. We'd rather have sent you to Mrs. Thill's but it would make it too difficult for us. Besides, she charges a lot of money." Mrs. Thill was their babysitter when Momma and Daddy went out of town. "So, the only viable solution that we can come up with is to trust you with the welfare of your brother and sister. I'll have you know that it's against our best intentions. Is that clear?"

"Yes," Danny answered, doing his best to keep his excitement at bay.

"If you let us down, you'll be the sorriest boy on the face of this earth. We're giving you only one chance. If you ever let us down, you'll never be trusted again. But, we have to start somewhere. Can you be trusted?"

"Yes, " Danny answered again. He knew he was being trusted because of the money they would save rather than because it was an attempt at having a "normal" family.

"Good, champ," Daddy said. "We begin on a trial basis, tomorrow night."

And so, the next night, he was trusted to babysit his siblings. Momma wasn't kidding when she said that there were going to be some strict rules.

Each child was placed in a separate room in the house with Mark in his bedroom, the door shut and locked and Louise was to stay in the basement, under the same conditions. Danny was resigned to stay in the kitchen where he could monitor any attempt at misbehaving. The situation was set up so that all the kids would be as far apart as possible thus alleviating any chance for shenanigans. Momma emphasized that it was a privilege for Danny to be allowed to stay up so late, since he normally was sent to bed by eight-thirty. She also made it clear that not only was he to watch out for the welfare of his brother and sister, he was in charge of their two million dollar house.

Each rule was laid down, to be obeyed with an or else clause. Mark and Louise were to be in bed by eight o'clock, or else. They were not allowed to have any contact with each or speak with each other. Or else. They were not allowed to leave the rooms designated to them, or else.

"Is that clear?" Momma asked, after each rule was spelled out.

For the first few Thursdays, each rule was followed to a "T". None of the kids moved from their rooms and the house was just as quiet as it would have been if Momma and Daddy were there. The only thing that was noticeably different was the lack of tension when the parents were out of the house.

After a while, Danny modified the rules, somewhat. So what? He thought.

They weren't doing anything bad, they just acted like a little family. Danny would wait about an hour after Momma and Daddy left, in case they came right back after forgetting something, and, when he felt the risk was minimal for a premature return, he would let his brother and sister out of their respective rooms. At first, they were nervous as rabbits, trapped in a potential fox-hole. They'd creep out of their rooms, unsure of what to do with their newly found freedom, like a fawn wandering from the safety of a mother deer. A few Thursdays later, they found themselves getting comfortable with it, and looking forward to it. If one were to look in the windows unobserved, they would see the three kids sitting on the floor in the family room, watching re-runs of, The Three Stooges and of, The Honeymooners, laughing every time that Ralph said, "To the moon, Alice!" Or, they might be seen playing Yahtzee or Chinese Checkers. On another occasion, they might have been seen playing Frisbee or flying gliders outside.

The kids felt normal. It was great, being able to talk out loud, without disturbing their parents. If they felt like laughing with glee, no one would be any the wiser. There were no quizzes and they weren't called things like, "disobedient, lying, insolent brats."

And, a good hour before Momma and Daddy came home, Danny would make sure that each kid was returned to their respective rooms. They came to enjoy the brief, weekly respite from their parents' ruling hand. Danny always made sure to rush them off to their rooms with the admonishment that they must never tell Momma or Daddy. If they found out, it would be the end of their fun. One never knew how they would react, either.

Danny didn't want to guess at what they would do if they ever found out...

During those Thursdays, the kids became closer to each other. Thursdays gave them a break and something to look forward to. Regardless of what was happening on any given day, they always knew that they had Thursdays to look forward to.

Thursday was a day of magical escape for them and it never came soon enough and when it did, it passed too quickly.

Danny was fortunate enough to have two other escapes from the routine of their family life. The first respite was his grandmother, on his mother's side. She loved Danny although Danny wasn't sure why. She lived in Detroit, on Mulberry Drive and, every once in awhile, Momma would beg Daddy to fly the family down there. Danny was always sure to be showered with hugs, kisses and new toys. He wasn't very comfortable with the hugging and kissing but the toys made up for it. She'd take him shopping for hours at a time, a thing that Momma and Daddy didn't approve of, but there was little that they could do about it. Grandma could cook, too, making her even more endearing. On that score, Momma and Daddy would limit the kids to one serving, saying, "You don't need to be making gluttons of yourselves. That's a sin, you know. Besides, we don't want her thinking that we don't feed you, do we? Quit acting like you're starved. You know better than that!"

Of course, they weren't starving. Were they?

Danny knew that Momma and Daddy noticed how they ate their grandmother's food. How could anyone not notice how they dove into the chicken, roast beef, real mashed potatoes, homemade Lemon Meringue pie, or whatever other delights were served? Daddy was the only one who ever saw that kind of food at home. Obviously, Grandma spent more than sixty-eight cents a day on them. Danny couldn't help but notice Momma and Daddy's jealousy of her, how the kids seemed to behave perfectly without her scorning them. Fortunately, there was little that Momma and Daddy could do about it.

Grandma always wrote Danny letters, too. For some reason, although she loved all the kids, she had taken a special liking for

Danny. He could see it from the postmarks from such faraway places as Egypt, France, England, Japan and hundreds of other spots on the globe. Daddy didn't much like giving Danny his mail.

Momma contended with the letters but she withheld the money that Grandma sent saying that he didn't deserve it. Momma always said that if Grandma knew how Danny really was, she wouldn't give two cents about him. No, he never knew why she had taken such a liking to him. It didn't make sense, but it didn't stop the glow of pride on his face when he received another letter. He didn't worry about the disappearing money. It was the fact that someone loved him. Someone cared. And, he waited for the next letter...

The second thing that helped Danny escape was his old friend, Robbie Feshter. They had been inseparable best friends ever since they had moved back from Detroit. Well, Danny had known him since kindergarten, the second longest since his brother. Momma and Daddy didn't like him too much saying that he was a typical Yooper. That was because of an impression Robbie had made on Daddy, back when he was seven or eight years-old.

"Hi, I'm Robbie." He was introduced while Daddy was mowing the lawn one summer day.

"Well, hello," Daddy answered in a friendly enough tone of voice. "Aren't you the boy that I met sledding down my driveway late one night?"

Robbie blushed and extended his hand. "It's good to meet you, Mr. Wilcox."

"Dr. Wilcox," Daddy corrected. He went back to mowing the lawn, leaving Robbie standing there, his hand still extended.

Since then, Robbie was labeled a "hick" and a bad influence on Danny. Daddy figured that Robbie was just another Yooper who was ignorant of how hard Daddy worked for that town. It was just as well. Robbie didn't like Daddy much, either. He was nice enough not to let him know.

Except for Danny and Mark, Robbie and Danny were as close as two boys could get. Whenever they had the chance, they would do everything together. They looked at their first Playboy together. They were stung a hundred times each once, during an impromptu apple fight they had had in Farmer's Field. They got lost in the woods on countless numbers of adventures while they killed each other a thousand times; play fighting, in imitation of G.I. Joe. During the winter, they went sledding until their boots were packed with twenty pounds of ice.

One day, they shacked the bus, and it was the first of many secrets that they ended up sharing. It was about six-thirty in the morning when they met at the bus stop. Both of them were buried in thick parkas. Before the bus pulled up, they both hid in the bushes, undetected, waiting for its arrival. When the other kids piled on, Baldy, the bus driver, pulled the door closed. Danny and Robbie scooted to the rear bumper. As Baldy pressed the accelerator, each boy made sure that they had a firm hold as they got in a slouched over position and waited for the ride of their lives. As he drove to the next stop, the two boys could be seen laughing as they were sliding on their heels behind it. Shacking the bus was an adventure in and of itself, better than the traveling carnival that came every spring. They usually got coated with packed snow from the rear wheels but it was a thrill that only kids could understand. They went through three stops and decided to gamble on one more stretch when lightning struck.

The city had salted the roads, unbeknownst to the boys, about an hour before. Unfortunately, there was a section of the road where the salt had melted the snow, leaving a stretch of bare and wet asphalt. The boys found out quickly that bare pavement is not conducive to shacking a bus properly as they went sprawling, face first, dragging behind the bus. The next thing they knew, they were tumbling head over heels, trying to remember their prayers from catechism. The bus pulled to a screaming halt when the passengers alerted Baldy. He jumped out of the bus and came running up to them.

"Jesus, kids! You okay?" he asked worriedly.

"I think so," Robbie and Danny answered in unison.

"You scared the bejesus out of me!"

"We're sorry, Baldy," Danny said, his head down, ashamed at being caught. Suddenly, Baldy started laughing. "No harm done. I can't rightly say that I'm going to be upset 'cause it ain't the first time it's happened. I used to do the same thing. Next time, though, don't do it with me driving, eh? I'm getting too old to be picking up body parts on the street."

"You're not going to tell our parents, are you?" asked Robbie.

"Ya never know, eh?" Baldy said with a wink.

That incident marked one of their first secrets together. Much later, Danny told Robbie another secret. He told him about Momma and Daddy. Robbie listened intently, incredulous as to how parents could be like that. His parents had never even laid a finger on him. So, he suggested to Danny that he might try running away. Danny explained his failed efforts. So, Robbie mentioned that he should go to the police. Danny refuted by saying that the police would never believe him. And, every suggestion that Robbie gave, Danny shoved it under the carpet as inadequate. Danny was too disillusioned, though. At least he had someone to share his problems with.

"I've been thinking about your parents and I've got an idea," Robbie said casually one day. The two of them were fishing under the Harvey Bridge, a railroad trestle, from a stream that fed into Lake Superior. They rarely caught any fish but it was fun to hope. The animals made their noises in the woods, insects bounced off the water while an occasional train would shake their worlds, overhead.

The only time that they had ever caught a fish down there was the first time that they had been there. Somehow, Robbie managed to keep from getting hauled into the water when he snared what surely seemed as big as a shark. As it turned out, it wasn't a shark but rather a pregnant Rainbow Trout, its multi-colored scales gleaming in the sun. Robbie wanted to keep it but Danny suggested that they throw it back in the water.

"Imagine all the trout that'll be in this stream when all those eggs hatch," Danny prodded.

Robbie agreed and that had become their fishing spot from then on.

"So, what's your idea?" Danny asked while he watched his worm squirm in the abnormally frigid waters.

"About your parents," Robbie stated.

"Don't tell me. Whatever it is, it won't work."

"No, Danny, listen. I've been thinking about it and I think it could work if you did it right."

"Robbie, please?" Danny pleaded, testily. It was too nice a day to jump into a conversation about his parents.

Robbie casually cast his line a little further upstream. "Really. Don't act like you were born cross-eyed. Listen to this."

"Okay, I'll listen. But, don't expect me to follow through on it. If it's stupid, I'm going to tell you, alright? So, don't get pissed off at me."

"I won't," Robbie said. "Tape them."

"What?"

"My dad has a tape recorder. We could tape them when they're slapping you guys around."

"We?" Danny questioned. "You mean me." He watched his feet as they dangled in the water and chewed on it. "It'll never work. How am I supposed to do that? Wait for my dad to start beating the crap out of Mark and then run and grab the tape recorder and stand there while he does it?"

"Sort of."

"Forget it," Danny said dejectedly.

"Seriously, Danny. Let's just say that they start picking on Mark. You've got the tape recorder hidden in your bed or something. If Mark is getting beaten up or something, shove the tape recorder in your shirt and sneak to someplace nearby. All you have to do is hit the 'record' button."

"Oh, sure, Robbie. And what happens if I get caught?"

"No guts, no glory."

"Fine, so I tape them. What do I do with the tape?"

Robbie tugged on his line a bit. "Don't be dumb. You take the tape to the police station and make them listen to it. They'll hear it and they'll have proof that something's wrong. You'll go to court or something and then you can live with me and my parents."

When Robbie put it that way, it was too tempting for Danny to ignore. He reluctantly agreed to Robbie's plan.

Days later, Robbie took the tape recorder without telling his parents and gave it to Danny, complete with a fresh tape and new batteries. Robbie knew that his parents wouldn't even notice it gone. First, Danny hid it in the garage, behind Daddy's boat. A day or so later, he managed to sneak it upstairs to his bedroom and hid it under the rafters of his bed.

After that, it was a matter of waiting it out for the perfect scenario. Unfortunately, for the longest time, whenever Daddy would get mad with the kids, Danny was nowhere near the tape recorder. On top of that, even if it was within reach, he was too afraid to use it. So, the tape recorder remained hidden, untouched.

Then, to the disadvantage of Louise, there came an evening when Daddy began his usual fare with her while helping her with her studies. Danny had been in his room doing his studies when he became distracted by her growing screams. At the very moment that it pissed him off, he thought of the hidden recorder. For a moment, he froze. He didn't think he could do it. Then, he heard the sound of her getting smacked followed by a yelp as Daddy began pulling her hair. Something inside Danny snapped, and he reached under the bed for the tape recorder. He felt the cool plastic of the machine and carefully slipped it out. His hands were shaking as he crept over to his bedroom doorway. In the kitchen, Louise's screaming intensified.

Danny looked down the hallway, both ways. Seeing no one, he stuck the recorder out, so that it faced in the direction of the kitchen. He didn't dare creep down the stairs as it was far too risky. He pressed the 'record' button, thinking, "Scream your heart out, Louise. It'll be the last time. Scream as loudly as you can."

He heard the kitchen stool fall back against the kitchen table, as it usually did when Daddy lost his patience. Daddy hit and Louise screamed. The tape recorder was running all the while. Before the recorder stopped, Danny turned it off and hid it back under the bed.

When he went to sleep that night, he felt strong and victorious.

Although easier said than done, Danny managed to sneak the tape recorder out of the house early the next morning. Once he rounded the bend of the driveway, the recorder hidden in his shirt, he ran all the way to Robbie's house. He kept it hidden when he knocked on Robbie's door, so that his parents wouldn't see it. If they had seen it, he knew that Robbie would get into trouble and there was enough trouble going around without getting someone else involved.

"Oh, hi," Robbie said through the screen door.

"I got it!" Danny said excitedly, in a loud whisper.

"Got what?"

"I taped my dad last night!"

"No kidding?" Robbie said, disbelievingly. "Mom? I'll be right back. I'm going outside and playing with Danny for a little while."

"Don't go too far away," she hollered from somewhere in the house.

"Lunch will be ready soon. Danny? Would you like some lunch?"

"No, thank you, Mrs. Feshter," he answered. "I'm not allowed."

"Oh, Danny. You know you're always welcome here."

"I already ate," Danny lied. He didn't trust adults very much, even if it was Robbie's mom. She'd probably accidentally tell his parents and then he'd get his butt kicked for 'free-loading'.

"Have it your way," she answered with what sounded like a smile. She was like what a real mom should be.

The two kids took off into the woods behind Robbie's house.

"Well, are you going to play it or what?" Robbie asked when they found a suitable place beneath an aged Birch tree.

Danny hit the 'play' button and heard nothing.

"Did you rewind it?" Robbie asked.

"Oops," Danny said, realizing what was wrong. He rewound it. Both boys listened intently when he hit the 'play' button again. They heard the squeal of the leader and then the hiss of the tape as it began. Danny's palms were sweaty with anticipation. This would be the moment of truth. He finally had obtained proof. They sat upright and raised the volume of the player.

"Mmmmf... mmm...mf...mf...mmmf," it said, muffled.

A look of disbelief crossed Danny's face.

"I didn't hear what it said," Robbie commented.

Danny rewound it and tried it again.

"Mmmmf...Mmm...mf...mf...mmmf," the tape repeated.

Danny felt like he was going to cry in frustration, but couldn't in front of his best friend. He looked at Robbie. Robbie looked back, comprehending their failure.

"Shoot! I knew it wouldn't work," Danny said, forcefully holding back his tears. "It didn't tape good at all!"

"We'll try it again, okay?" Robbie offered supportively. "Don't worry. There'll be other times. Next time, just get closer when they do it! We'll get it right, okay? We aren't going to give up just like that!"

"Yeah, maybe next time," Danny said, dejectedly. "Maybe next time."

24

FRIEND OF THE DEVIL

Dan downshifted Blossom to blend in with the line of cars approaching the toll of the Mackinac Bridge. In the tape deck, a Des Moines, Iowa rendition of *Jack Straw* played, from June 16, 1974: *"And now the die has shaken, now the die must fall. There ain't a winner in the game, he don't go home with all..."*

Diana appeared to hug the armrest with the trembling of the vehicle. Police were lined up on either side, inspecting each vehicle casually. Her eyes made contact with an officer who passed his eyes onward to the vehicle behind them. Neither Dan nor Diana said a word as they passed through the gauntlet.

Dan reached into his wallet and pulled out the required three dollars. They crept slowly forward, nervousness being the predominant weather pattern. Finally, they reached the female toll-taker who took their money, wordlessly.

Before they knew it, Blossom was struggling back up to fourth gear as they reached the crest of the bridge. Off to their left, a helicopter searched the waters, its spotlight arching crazily in the night. For the first time in hours, they both felt the tension ebb away.

"Are you okay?" Dan asked quietly.

"I think so," Diana said. "I'm still recovering from being shot at."

"Me, too. I'm going to hate reading about this. I have a feeling that by the time the distorted story comes out, we're aren't going to look good."

"I know. My question is, is this what we have to look forward to?"

"I sure as hell hope not. But, the more miles we put between us and the Upper Peninsula, the better."

Diana looked out over the water on her side, realizing that they were probably a good five hundred feet above it. In the distance, she could see the approaching lights of Mackinac City. The monotonous hum of the grating under their wheels was slowly lulling her to sleep.

"Thanks," Dan said.

"For?"

"Back on the boat. I didn't realize what kind of hot water we were in. There's no way that I anticipated that you'd risk your life for me."

"We didn't have any other choice," Diana said. "I'm sure there's people out there who would think that I've gone stone crazy if they heard what was happening. I can hardly believe it myself. Besides, it was partly my fault for using the credit card."

"What's done is done," Dan said.

Blossom picked up speed as they went down the other side of the suspension bridge. There were no police to be seen.

"Listen," Dan said. "If you want to crawl in back and take a nap, feel free. I'm figuring that we have about an hour drive before we can find a campground that's far enough away from the heat up here. I thought about hitting Cheboygan but we'd be better off, further down the line. Does it sound okay to you?"

"It has been a long day," Diana said drowsily.

An hour later, on 1-75, they blew through Gaylord at about sixty-five miles an hour. Diana had dropped off to sleep while Dan was fighting to keep his eyes open. He opened his window to get some fresh air while fumbling with the map of northern Lower Michigan. Soon, he found what he was looking for. Ten minutes ahead, he found a state park that allowed camping, Otsego Lake State Park. If they didn't stop there, he was sure to fall asleep while driving. He didn't dare risk pulling over to sleep in a roadside rest stop for fear that the Michigan State Police would pull in.

Once they were in the park, after paying the six dollar fee with hook-ups, it took Dan about ten minutes to get them settled. Both were asleep fifteen minutes after that, lacking the energy to even wish each other a good night.

The next morning, the sun beamed through the windows while Diana was awakened to the sound of Dan brewing coffee, frying eggs and bacon and fumbling through a highway map. Dan handed her a steaming cup of coffee.

Diana sat on the edge of the bed and nursed it.

"Did you sleep well?" Dan asked.

"Like a rock. I didn't even dream anything that I can remember."

"Same here. After we eat, there's a shower just around the corner."

The two of them ate a particularly delicious breakfast ravenously. All the while, Dan spoke of the plans for the day.

"As far as I can see, our best place to start is on Mulberry Drive in Southfield, where my mother's mom lives. I haven't seen her in years but she should surely know something about Dad and Louise. We only have ten days to two weeks so don't mind me if I'm focused on making tracks."

At eight-thirty, they were back on the road, facing a new day. They were looking at a three hour drive down 1-75 before they were to hit Southfield, on the outskirts of Detroit. For a long time, neither one said much as the Grateful Dead played out of the stereo.

"I don't know if I've ever asked you this," Diana said as they cut through Flint.

"What's that?"

"Do you believe in God?"

"I'm not a theologian, if that's what you're asking."

"I didn't expect you to be. Are you still Catholic?"

"I was labeled a Catholic, yes," Dan said, skirting the issue.

"Well?"

Dan chewed on it as he deftly passed a Hyundai loaded with goggle-eyed kids. "For a long time, I didn't. I'm sure you can understand why. Then, I went on the road. The writing played a huge part and so, too, did the Grateful Dead. I think that people have drifted away from structured religion because it wasn't giving us the answers that we wanted it to. I mean, we were taught that God was to be feared and we were constantly warned about the terrors of hell. Well, there's hell on earth that can be worse than any hell that I can imagine. In that, it puts a hole in the story. How can God allow Charles Manson? What of Oklahoma City? And, well, what of our parents? Is that what religion is all about?"

"You tell me."

"If I were to haphazard a guess, I'd say that my religion is a cross between, *Celestine Prophecy*, *Embraced By The Light*, and *Soul Mates*. God exists but he's not going to tell us how to live our lives. We have to learn to take control of our lives by understanding ourselves through our mistakes. Further, you can't stop believing, no matter what. So, in an unconventional way, I have my own religion. We talk but I don't need a church with steeples to do it. I take care of my fellow man like I would take care of myself. That's the essence of the Ten Commandments. Maybe it's sacrilegious, I don't know. But, who makes the rules?"

"Who?"

"We do, as individuals. If you don't have a code of ethics inside, then you have a problem."

"Hmmm. Don't you think there's more to it than that?"

"Probably," Dan said, smiling ruefully. "But, for now, until I learn more, it's keeping my life together."

"How does the Grateful Dead fit into this?"

"You'll see," Dan said. "You'll see."

Just before noon, they stopped into a Bob Evan's to have breakfast. Diana couldn't help but notice the strange looks that people gave her and Dan with his tie-dye and her Birkenstocks.

She couldn't eat quickly enough to get out of there. Dan appeared to be perfectly comfortable with his outfit. The only time that he was shaken was when he saw two troopers stop in for breakfast, sitting only three tables away.

An hour later, it was obvious that they were headed into Detroit with the increased amount of traffic and their corresponding high speeds. Even though the speed was supposed to be fifty-five, Blossom hung in with the flow of traffic at seventy-five miles an hour. Every once in awhile, a car with a younger generation would fly by with a honk of a horn, their car adorned with Grateful Dead memorabilia.

Dan always beeped back.

They drove into the sprawling estates that adorned the street of Mulberry drive. One house after another followed with perfectly manicured lawns adorned by homes that made Dan's parent's home look middle class. It seemed that every home had a flowing fountain in front with a beautiful river in the back. They were definitely in the country club realm of wealth, with two golf courses in the neighborhood.

Dan looked at the address and found his grandmother's home without a problem. They pulled into the semi-circular driveway and turned the engine off. A wealth of birds chirped in the trees while the sound of lawn mowers could be heard buzzing in the distance.

Diana followed Dan to the door. He had been quiet for the previous fifteen minutes and Diana knew it best not to say anything. She could only imagine what was going through his head. It was one thing to have lived the childhood that he had, while it must have been an entirely different thing to be abandoned by your family for fifteen or twenty years.

He took a deep breath and rang the doorbell. He waited a couple of minutes and wiped his hands on his pants and rang it again. After a third time, he dared to peek in the windows.

"Shit," he said quietly.

"What is it?"

"It appears to be a dead end. The house is empty."

"Meaning what?"

"I would say that either she's moved away or she's passed away. Neither scenario would surprise me."

Suddenly, an older lady from next door came stomping across the lawn.

"What are you doing?" she screeched. "You get off this property. Do you hear me? We don't want your kind around. Go on. Scat!"

Diana could hardly believe that she was speaking to them. "You don't understand, ma'am. All we're trying to do is..."

"I'm calling the police! There will be no hoodlums around here! We have a neighborhood watch program and we don't look kindly on your sort of people. Get out of here or you're going to have a whole lot of trouble on your hands! You have one minute!" she screamed at them. She turned around and started storming away.

Dan looked at Diana, confused. Then, he looked at the attire they were wearing and understood. It's exactly what a black man would have felt in that very same neighborhood. He motioned for Diana to wait there and ran off after the lady.

In spite of Dan's wishes, she ran after Dan, anyway. She was not going to be treated like that. She was just as involved as Dan was.

"Ma'am, please? Just one minute of your time!" he called out after her. "The lady that lived there, she was my grandmother! Please!"

The lady stopped in her tracks and turned around. "Do you have some sort of identification?"

"In the car, I do. Although, I'm not sure what good that'll do as I haven't seen her in over twenty years. Besides, she was from my mother's side," Dan said quickly.

A frown crossed the lady's face. "What's your name?"

"Dan. Dan Wilcox. I was her oldest grandson."

"Do you have any brothers or sisters?" she asked, suspicion still in her eyes.

Dan told her about Mark and Louise.

"Is that Louise?"

Dan turned around, surprised to see Diana there. "Well, no," Dan said cautiously. "She's a friend of mine."

The lady crossed her arms over her chest and studied the two. "Well, if you're here to collect some sort of inheritance, I'd say you're about a year too late."

"She's passed away?"

"I went to the funeral myself. What took you so long to get in touch with her?"

"It's a long story," Dan said softly. "We weren't a close family." He didn't want to go into details with a stranger.

"Well, my name's Mrs. Lee. I'm sorry to give you that news. I was her best friend in her final years. I've heard your name mentioned. I can't say as I agree with how you folks handled everything. She died a lonely lady."

Diana introduced herself. "Do you know where the rest of the family might be?"

"She's got a son in Florida, as far as I know. He's the one taking care of the estate. Like I said, she died a lonely lady, especially considering who her husband had been. I still can't see why you couldn't get in touch with her before this. Maybe you've learned a lesson. You've only got one family."

"I understand, Mrs. Lee," Dan said. "Is there any way that you can give me his phone number and address?"

"I'll give you his address but I don't have a phone number. Besides, I wouldn't waste my time trying to get hold of him. He's pretty angry at the family. You should understand why. If you weren't out doing whatever drugs you kids do nowadays, maybe I wouldn't have had to give you that kind of news," Mrs. Lee said scornfully.

"Now, listen, Mrs. Lee. I resent the implication. I'm a psychiatrist, a doctor. This isn't how it looks," Diana said, not hiding the vehemence in her voice.

"Sure, lady. And I'm a Senator, too. Now how about you get off of this property, now that your business is done!"

"Can we have the address and you'll never hear from us again?" Dan asked, as politely as he could, his teeth gritted.

"Humph!" she said. "Stay where you are. I don't want anyone seeing the likes of you on my porch!" She stormed off and returned a couple of minutes later with a name and address written on a scratch piece of paper.

"Thank you," Dan said. "You sure you don't know of any other family?"

"Like I said, she died a very lonely lady. Now that your business is done...?"

They didn't need to be asked again. Moments later, they fired up Blossom and found their way out of Southfield.

Dan was silent and Diana followed suit. He fingered the piece of paper that listed the Florida address.

"It seems that death don't have no mercy," Dan said quietly as they entered 1-75.

Diana had no idea what he meant except that it sure didn't feel like they were getting anywhere.

Slowly, but surely, Dan began talking, launching into one of the most terrifying stories of his life...

25

BUILT TO LAST

For months, Danny and Robbie tried to conceive ways of how they could finally nail Momma and Daddy. One time, because Danny said that his father was in a bad mood, Robbie stood under one of the eaves of the house in the backyard, tape recorder in hand. It was Robbie's idea to hide out back there. He figured that he could be a witness in court, in the event that something happened. Well, Robbie's hiding turned out to be to no avail. Since it had been drizzling all day long, the only thing that Robbie got out of it was a whopper of a cold. It was just Danny's luck. Just when he wanted something to happen, nothing did. His parents were too damned unpredictable.

Although Danny told Robbie a hundred times how much he appreciated his trying to help, Danny knew that Robbie would eventually begin to doubt his word. Before something really bad happened, Danny felt that he had to prove his case to someone. To Danny's discouragement, something always got in the way. Either Danny was not close enough to the incident when it happened, whereby the taping of it proved useless, or the incident was too minor for the taping of it to be worthwhile.

It frustrated Danny to no end. His father's reputation was no help, either. Who would believe that a doctor, one who provided such a service to the town, was also the same man who beat his children? Was there child abuse occurring on "Doctor's Row" in Shiras Hills, the affluent neighborhood of the city? Who would take a child's word over an adult's? Nobody.

Unless …. Danny could prove it.

Danny also worried over the increase of the incidences. It seemed like it was happening all of the time, never when he could prove it, and each incident was getting a little more ferocious than the incident prior. He worried so much that he couldn't sleep with the intrusion of terribly vivid nightmares. Something inside was telling him that something really bad was about to happen. It was inevitable. All it would take is one time where just a fraction of strength was just a little too much, like the straw that broke the camel's back. If that happened, Danny thought, he would surely never be able to live with himself. He'd feel responsible because he was sure that there was a way he could stop it, but how? If he worked just a little harder, the inevitable might be averted. Danny thought that somebody could die, somebody who was frail and defenseless, like Louise. He wished, a thousand times, that he could walk in to the police station and get it over with. But, if the police didn't believe him, he would surely be sent back home to face a father who would most certainly take it out on his hide. If he thought that missing school for a couple of weeks was bad, imagine what would happen when he came back from trying to turn his father in to the police.

Everything was going to hell in a bucket and he was powerless to stop it.

Summer merged into fall and fall blew into winter, always returning much faster than anyone wanted. The thing about winter in the Upper Peninsula was that it was about seven months too long with temperatures that would freeze an ear in a minute and bring pain to your fingers. It kept people in the house, for months at a time, waiting anxiously for the first spring thaw, which was always too far away. When Stephen King published, The Shining, people in Northern Michigan understood cabin fever. And cabin fever, in a house like that of the Wilcox's, could be life-threatening, no question about it.

So, it was in the middle of one of the coldest February's on record, with temperatures plummeting to well below zero, that Daddy got a call from Marquette General Hospital for an emergency. They needed him right away, as a man had just attempted to drink a bottle of Drano, in a failed suicide attempt. As Daddy had said, the liquid never made it down the man's throat. The acid reduced the man's tongue and jaw to nothing more than dangling flesh. Daddy had to go to the hospital to attempt some sort of reconstruction, something he didn't relish at the time. It was too damn cold out to go anywhere. Besides, Daddy knew that it would be a time-consuming effort, probably taking him the better part of the night. Momma had hoped for a quiet evening with him and, again, she would be deprived.

Danny did make a mental note never to attempt suicide via the Drano method. It sounded gruesome and, most importantly, it didn't work.

As soon as Daddy left, the tension in the house dissipated. It was always worse when both parents were home. When only one parent was home, it seemed that the chances of getting smacked were greatly reduced. The only other time that the children did not feel the overbearing nervousness and tension, was when Daddy was sick in bed with the flu, a common occurrence during those frigid winters. Of course, the kids were quiet while he was in bed recovering, but that meant that Momma also had to be quiet. She wouldn't dare hit the kids while Daddy was sleeping for fear that they'd wake him up. Daddy wasn't in a good mood if he was awakened prematurely, as everyone was well aware.

It was strange, the way Momma was changing. One could never predict her moods. One day she would be great, the next, she would be down and the kids would suffer for it. On that particularly frigid Friday night, an icy wind blew, driving temperatures well below thirty degrees below zero, which magnified an already touchy situation.

Cabin fever had drawn itself to a fever pitch.

Danny was in the study downstairs, looking through Daddy's books for a book to read. He had finished his nightly chores while Mark and Louise were still working on theirs. Louise was supposed to be cleaning the bathroom, adjacent to the study, while Mark was supposed to be cleaning the laundry room, next to the bathroom. Instead, Danny could hear Mark and Louise playing "tag" in hushed tones in the laundry room. Danny listened with amusement while they played, thinking that it sounded like fun, but not daring to get involved. Like his brother and sister, he had let his guard down for a moment.

"You're it!" he heard Mark whisper excitedly.

"No, I'm not! You didn't touch me!"

"I did, too!"

"No, you didn't!" Louise corrected, playfully. "It's still your turn to get me!"

The sound of pattering feet followed, as they chased each other around the laundry room. Danny could hear that each one was running out of breath. Every once in a while, he heard an occasional giggle.

"I gotcha!" Mark said, the sound of victory in his voice.

Then, the sound of a crash followed, as one of them fell into the laundry room closet doors. The sound seemed to reverberate down the hallway. Obviously, someone had been attempting to avoid a tag and had miscalculated their step. Danny froze, as did the occupants of the laundry room. They all waited in silent panic for Momma to come rushing downstairs, demanding to know what the noise had been.

Silence permeated the air for one infinitesimal minute.

"We better stop," Danny heard Mark whisper to Louise. "Let's get back to doing our duties before we get into trouble."

"Okay," Louise said. "But you're still it!"

"Am not!"

"Are so! "

"Am not!" Mark whispered back.

Danny was just pulling a book off of a shelf, when he saw Momma's shadow go fleeting by in the direction of the laundry room. His stomach lurched.

"What the hell is going on here?" Momma asked, breaking the silence.

"Nothing!" Mark answered defensively. Danny knew that he must have just about dumped in his drawers with Momma's unexpected appearance. He could hear it in his voice.

"Then what was that big crash that I just heard?!"

"I don't know!" Louise answered in a guilt-ridden voice.

"That's alright, Momma," Mark defended. "I don't know what you heard, either!"

Danny crept over to one side of the den where he could observe the developing situation, undetected, by looking into the hallway mirror which gave him clear sight to the laundry room. It was at a moment like that that he wished that he had the tape recorder within easy access. But, it was all the way upstairs and he didn't think that Momma knew that he was in the den. He hoped that it wouldn't be one of those times.

"And what are you two doing in here together, when I specifically separated you by putting you in the bathroom and you in the laundry room?" Momma demanded to know.

Mark tried to exit the situation by saying, "I'm sorry, we'll finish right now!"

"Oh, no you won't. Not until I have an answer out of you! What happened here?"

"I don't know," Louise repeated, her voice level rising to a light screech.

Danny watched Momma walk over to Louise and grab her under the arm.

He was very aware of the pain that Louise was feeling as Momma dug her fingernails into the tender flesh under her arms. Louise winced in pain, squirming to get away.

"You nincompoop! I want an answer out of you and don't you dare say, 'I don't know'."

"Oww...it hurts...please, Momma, don't!"

"You disobedient little retard!" Momma shouted at her, shaking the daylights out of her. With her other hand, she started slapping Louise in the face. "Fine! Don't answer! I'll keep doing this until you do!"

"Cut it out, Momma!" Mark suddenly yelled.

Momma let Louise go and looked at Mark, her face turning red. "Well, I'll be," she said. "Have we got a tough boy here?"

"No," Mark answered, his courage greatly diminished. He had a look on his face that said he had just realized what a grave mistake he had made.

Momma placed her hands on her hips and looked at him, as if she was trying to determine what form of punishment best suited his crime.

Danny watched the rest happen, as if it was in slow motion. Disbelief painted his trembling features, like a slowly advancing shadow. He shouldn't have been shocked at the sight; it was practically status quo, except for Thursday nights. It was to be expected, ignored and forgotten.

Momma's hands suddenly reached out, one grabbing Louise's head and the other, grabbing Mark's. She brought both heads together, which created a resounding crack. They both answered in simultaneous cries of pain.

Danny, the onlooker, was biting his lip in a fit of anger and frustration, not even aware of the blood dripping down his chin. Bitter tears flooded his eyes. And he watched, while his brother and sister stood there in a sobbing daze, when she lost her mind like he had never quite seen before. Her feet started kicking them repeatedly while her clenched fists flailed over their heads.

An overpowering sense of anger blossomed in Danny with every second increasing its intensity. His role as the protector resurfaced: he had to stop it! The first thought was that he could run in there and overpower her. He quickly dismissed that in watching how angry she was, though. She was too angry and she would surely kill him. What she was doing to Mark presently, because of his attempt to stop it, was convincing enough. He thought of the tape recorder, but that was upstairs. There was no way that he could get out of the study without her seeing him. Once again, he felt like his hands were tied behind his back.

The wind howled outside, causing the windows to rattle.

As he watched in eye-widening horror, Momma grabbed the mop that Mark had been using to clean the floor. She raised it above her head and cracked the handle down on the helpless children. Danny wanted to scream but fear constricted his throat. He grabbed the hair at his temples and began pulling as hard as he could. His eyes were squeezed shut, oblivious of his own pain, as he tried to block out the sounds of their echoing screams. As the screams increased in intensity, Momma seemed to increase the frequency of blows with the mop handle.

Suddenly, Danny turned around toward the desk. The telephone sat there, its black surface reflecting the glow of the incandescent lights. He had to do it now! Danny found the drive to dash over to the desk, making sure that his movement wasn't seen. He picked up the receiver and dialed the number to the police department as fast as he could. It took him three times to dial the number because of his trembling fingers. His tears also made it hard for him to read the sticker on the base of the telephone, which had a listing of all the emergency numbers. That sticker had been placed on all of the telephones in the house when Danny had started babysitting. Danny never realized what he would really use that number for.

"Hello?" he said in hushed whisper, his hand cupped over the mouthpiece.

"Yes, this is the Marquette County Police Department," a lady's flat and disinterested voice repeated.

"I have to report something right away," Danny said quickly. His brother and sister were still screaming in the background, telling him that he was safe from Momma's attention for the moment. As long as she was hitting, he still had time. He kept glancing toward the mirror in the hallway but the angle prevented him from seeing what was happening in the laundry room. He didn't have much time. If Momma heard him...

"How can we help you?"

"My mother is beating my brother and sister to death!" Danny said urgently. "You have to help us!"

"If this is some kind of joke," she said, irritated.

"It's not! Listen!" Danny said. He held the phone in the direction of the echoing screams for about thirty seconds, time enough for the person on the other end of the line to understand what was happening. "Did you hear that?" he asked.

"I couldn't hear anything," she answered, obviously unshaken.

"What do you mean you couldn't hear anything?" Danny asked in exasperation. "Please! I'm serious! She's going to kill one of them any second now!" Danny begged.

"Let me speak to one of your parents, son," she demanded.

"You don't understand..." Danny said, stopping. He hung up the phone, knowing that there was no point in continuing the phone call. Damn, he thought, why won't anyone believe me? Then, he heard the sound of a crash as somebody fell into one of the closet doors. He crept over to where he could see what was happening in the mirror.

Momma was repeatedly slamming Mark's head into the closet door.

It was then that Danny saw a sight that he would never see again. Louise reached out to Momma's back. Although she did it very hesitantly, she did it.

Danny knew exactly what Louise was doing in that simple gesture. She was reaching out to plead with Momma to stop it. Danny could read it on her red and tear-stained face. At that moment, Louise looked incredibly small in size compared to her mother but her courage made up for it. She paused a moment then, slowly, reached over and tugged on the back of Momma's blouse.

And, Momma turned around. It was if she knew the exact intentions that Louise had at that moment, as if Momma couldn't believe that Louise could be stupid enough to show such belligerence and gall. She went to slap Louise, but Louise quickly raised her arm up to defend herself, as if she knew Momma would react in exactly that way. Momma's hand collided with her arm.

"You little creep! You hurt me!" Momma screamed at her. Momma turned around to grab anything she could. Danny saw that the mop was a discarded weapon, lying on the floor, the handle broken in half. On the washing machine, Momma's hand found an aerosol can of Spray 'N Wash. Using the can like a club, she brought it down upon Louise's head. A popping sound followed...

Blood suddenly showered the flowered, wall-papered walls. It squirted straight up from Louise's head, bringing the room to silence as droplets hit the door and sprayed Momma in their ferocity. And Danny was watching it all, frozen in shock.

Louise's knees collapsed, bringing her to the floor. The spray can dropped out of Momma's hand, as she stood there, watching the blood spray, maybe wondering if she had just killed her daughter. Maybe realizing that, this time, she had gone too far.

"Danny!" Momma screeched. "Get down here!"

"Yes, Momma," Danny answered after a few moments. He quickly wiped the drying blood off of his own chin and ran into the laundry room.

"Start cleaning up this blood!" she ordered him. "We have to get Louise to the hospital." She grabbed a towel and wrapped it around Louise's head. Louise's face was becoming pale and lucid, with a lack of any emotion except what appeared to be shock. "See! This is what you two get for not doing what you're told to do! If you hadn't have been rough-housing, this would never have happened. You remember whose fault this is!" she reminded them. "Mark! Take a good look at what you've done to your sister. I hope you're happy!" she screamed.

"Yes, Momma," Mark answered with a confused look.

"Damn it!" Momma said to no one in particular. "When we get to the hospital, after Danny finishes cleaning up this mess, I had better hear all of you telling the doctor that this happened while you were playing. Do you understand me?!"

"Yes, Momma," Danny and Mark answered simultaneously.

Danny cleaned up as fast as he could, all the while, scared for the life of his sister. What if she died while he was still cleaning? He was angry at the police, too. If they had listened instead of jerking him around, this never would have happened, he thought frantically. Danny stood up when he finished wiping the blood up, dropping the rags in the laundry room sink.

"Don't forget to wipe it off the door!" Momma ordered him. "I don't want your father knowing about this!"

Danny did as he was told. Once Momma passed inspection, she and the children got into the car and drove silently to the hospital. Momma made sure that they didn't go to Marquette General Hospital, where Daddy was working, but rather to Holy Cross Hospital, an extra fifteen minutes away. On the way over, the only sounds that could be heard were the weeping and groaning noises made by Louise, as she held the towel to her head. Danny watched her white blouse darken with the growing stain of blood. Danny and Mark looked at each other, communicating their sentiments without opening their mouths. The same question was conveyed in each other's eyes: Was Louise going to die?

When they got to the emergency room, Momma walked Louise in while Danny and Mark followed silently. When they finally talked to a doctor, after Momma explained who her husband was, Danny listened to the lies that poured out of Momma's mouth.

"Oh, you know kids," she said nervously. "They're always getting into some sort of mischief. Look what happened. Her brother, evidently, took a thong and smacked Louise with it. I can't tell you how many times that I've told them to stop hitting each other but they just won't listen," she explained quickly. "It's not bad, is it? I love her so much! She'll be okay, won't she?"

Momma talked like a completely different person, especially compared to the one she had been an hour prior. She assumed a persona likened to that of their babysitter, Mrs. Thill, only the kids knew better. Although it made Danny and Mark angry, their primary concern was over whether Louise was going to live or die. It was not the time to deal with the truth. At least that's how Danny rationalized it. He didn't have the guts to tell the doctor the real truth. Sadly enough, he saw that the doctor appeared to have believed his mother's lies. Momma even went so far as to look like she was going to cry over Louise's fate.

The doctor went off with Louise, sending the rest of the family to the waiting room. Momma spoke only once, looking at Mark with a vengeance in her eyes, "I hope you're happy with what you did to your sister. Doesn't disobedience pay?!"

Mark's eyes dropped to his lap, feeling responsible for everything that had happened.

Danny clenched his fists silently in hate and anger, while his tongue played with the delicate area inside his lip. It was from that point on, after reliving the memory of what he had seen in laundry room, that he decided that he hated his mother. Everything that had been taught to him of God and religion was all garbage. How could God allow something like that to happen to his sister? How could God make the police ignore him? If there really was a God, Danny though angrily, he would kill Momma for what she had done!

As it turned out, an hour and a half later, Louise received twenty-two stitches in her head. The doctor had said that it had been one of those freak things, her head getting cut where it had. The contact point had been directly over a blood vessel, which explained the profuse amount of blood. Again, it crossed Danny's mind to blurt the truth out to the doctor, but he kept his mouth shut knowing that it would have been an exercise in futility. If he was ever going to say anything, it had to be said when he knew that he wasn't going to be sent back to his parents. Little did he know that an opportunity to do that was closer than he could have thought. For the moment, he had chickened out again, and that made him feel like a spineless piece of trash.

The returning drive home was completed in silence as Sammy Davis, Jr., sang *The Candy Man* on the radio. Louise had a gauze bandage wrapped around her head and face, making her look like a mummy in a scary Saturday night movie. The doctor had told Momma to keep her head bandaged for the better part of a week, not wanting to risk the re-opening of the wound.

As soon as they got home, Momma sent Danny and Mark to bed. Just before sending Louise to bed, she looked at her.

"That looks ridiculous," she said in reference to the bandages. "We are not having the town asking questions about this. It looks like I beat you up all of the time. Well, you'll be fine. There's no need to keep these bandages on."

She removed the white bandages. "You had better not say a word about this to anyone, including your father," she warned.

"I won't, Momma," Louise answered obediently.

While Danny and Mark were in bed, silence settling over the house, they waited a long while before whispering. The bare branches of a tree scraped against the window in the winter wind.

"Danny?"

"Yeah?"

"It's gotta stop."

"I know."

Neither one of them had anything left to say that night. Each had cried silently, remembering the confused and dazed look that had been on Louise's face when they had been driving back in the car. The only thing that could have been seen on her face, through the bandages, were her eyes, distant and sad, which seemed to ask, "What happened? I didn't mean to do anything wrong. I'm sorry."

Yes, Danny thought, it's gotta stop. But how?

26

HELL IN A BUCKET

For the next hour, Dan was quiet as they passed through the busy freeways of Detroit. To Diana, it seemed that he was hell-bent for leather in getting out of Michigan, maneuvering Blossom as if he had been driving her for years. His face was tense but his hands moved her gears gracefully. For a short while, she thought that he was going to crack but, being occupied with the road, she saw the tension ease.

He looked at his watch as they crossed the border into Toledo, Ohio. Dan pulled out his map and saw that he had no map of the new state they were entering. He looked at his watch, again.

"We don't have much time," he said. "It's four o'clock and I've got to get Blossom in somewhere."

"Is something wrong?" Diana asked, not noticing any changes in engine pitch.

"Thankfully, not yet. But, no one's looked over this vehicle and I don't want to get stuck in the middle of nowhere. Besides, we need to find a couple of newspapers and find out how far word has spread about us. The further we get away from

Michigan, the less chance we have of finding out how far Robinson has taken this murder."

The first thing that Dan did was to find a busy truck stop. He parked Blossom and busily wrote out a list of items that they would need. He explained that the less stops that they had to make for supplies, the better that they would be. There was no need to risk unnecessary contact with people if they didn't have to. While he was taking inventory of everything on board, Diana wrote notes in a notebook, intending to keep a record of the things that Dan had told her.

Dan checked the money in his wallet and ran into the store that was adjacent to the station. There, he picked up a set of jumper cables, plenty of bottled water, a container of anti-freeze, some spare belts, bug spray, three cans of Fix-A-Flat and plenty of extra food. After that, they found their way to a Valvoline Station where he had the oil changed, the tires checked, fluids filled and had the transmission checked. Once they pulled out of there, Dan walked around the vehicle, inspecting under the engine and underneath her.

At a certain point, Diana began to get irritated. "What are you doing?"

"I'm making sure that we can make it to Florida. There's no need in taking unnecessary risks," he said firmly. "If there's one thing that my father taught me, in spite of what a creep he was, preparation is the key to everything. You have to know your adversary. In his case, it was the weather and his airplane. In our case, it's Blossom and the police. If we run pell-mell south, sure as shit, we'll get caught with our pants down. All we have is two weeks with Derry and Althea's ID's, so let's make the best of the time by finding the problems before they happen."

"Do you mind if I make a suggestion?" she asked carefully.

"Sure," he said, busily charting out a map.

"Don't you think we might be better off to hit the airport here in Toledo. We could be in Florida by late this evening. When we're done with business, we'll just fly back up here."

Dan stopped writing for a moment. He casually got out of the VW Bus and went around to the other side, opening the sliding door in back. He dug through their freshly bought groceries until he found the bag that he was looking for. He pulled out a couple of local newspapers, along with a USA Today.

"Get a load of this," he said, handing her the stack.

Diana looked at him questioningly as he walked around to the driver's side and hopped in. He returned to his work on his Rand McNally Deluxe Motor Carrier's Road Atlas with a grease pencil working dutifully over the laminated pages. Next to him, he was also working on a gas mileage chart. It looked as if he was setting up pre-flight plans for an airplane ride.

She started looking through the papers one by one. It didn't take her long to realize that they were bigger news than she had anticipated. One headline read, Fugitive Murderer Kidnaps Psychiatrist, while another headline glared, Psychiatrist and Author On The Run. On yet another paper, Murderer and Psychiatrist Hijack Boat Captain while the cover of USA Today claimed, Accused Murderer and Psychiatrist: Innocent or Armed and Dangerous?

"You have got to be kidding me," she said.

"No shit, huh?" Dan said, looking up for a moment. "There's no turning back now. I would have told you earlier but we had to get Blossom taken care of. I got the general idea of the articles and, basically, they've got you lumped in with me because of the boating incident with Captain Jones. He slams us pretty good, blowing the whole thing out of proportion by saying that we had automatic weapons, we hit him and a whole bunch of other nonsense. The fortunate thing is that we've had no contact with anyone since, except for the neighbor of my deceased grandmother."

"I'm sure she'll go to the press," Diana said, not bothering to hide her frustration.

"Actually, I don't think so," Dan said, curiously optimistic. "Take a look at the pictures of us."

Diana put aside all parts of the papers except for their front sections. Each paper displayed pictures of them, separately. Her picture was from an antiquated picture from her yearbook of her Northwestern days, a good ten years younger, dressed in formal attire. Dan's pictures, on the other hand, were publicity photos from the jackets of Rusty Wallace novels, which the papers referred to obliquely as dime store novels. The pictures barely resembled them in either age or the style of clothes they were wearing.

Then, it settled on Diana when she thought of the granola girl outfit that she was wearing. Further, Dan's long hair was hidden in his publicity shots.

"So, they're not looking for a couple of Deadheads..."

"Exactly," Dan said, a grin on his face. "Thing is, if we were to hop on a commercial plane, there's manifests and things like that. I also have a feeling that any airport is going to be a hotspot for cops. That's the first thing that anyone with money would do. We can't even risk it. Besides, Blossom's in excellent condition, much to our advantage."

One by one, Diana started reading the articles. Each one had the general idea but had a variety of different sources listed. Every once in awhile, when she particularly flared, she'd read a line to Dan. "Here's a comment from my wonderful husband," she said, infuriated. "I had noticed my wife becoming increasingly distant in the past few months. She had spoken of this character Dan Wilcox and I had a feeling that they were having an affair. Shortly before we separated, I saw that alcohol was interfering with our marriage and I had to let her go on her spiral downward."

"Are you kidding?" Dan said. "An affair?"

"That isn't how this happened at all and he knows it. By defaming my character, he thinks he won't have to pay out in the divorce. Not that I want his money but..."

"You still love him," Dan completed for her.

"Not at all," Diana said. "He was having an affair. It's the principle of it.

Where does he get off? "

"Sorry," Dan said.

Diana continued reading. "Here's a juicy quote from Robinson. 'We must consider both parties armed and dangerous. We have reason to believe that the psychiatrist's moral character is questionable. We also have reason to believe that she may have been in cahoots with the accused in the murder of his mother, a completely innocent woman'," Diana read, becoming more incensed by the moment. "Do people actually believe this?"

"That's the law for you."

As she continued, she found a quote from Dan's brother. She read it aloud, "Mark Wilcox, the brother of the accused, residing in Southern California, has alerted police to the possibility that he may have fled the country. Police have a twenty-four hour watch at all airports handling foreign flights."

Dan smiled. "Go Mark! He knows what's going on. See, there's even more reason not to take a plane!"

"This is absolutely incredible," Diana said. "They've got the story contorted in such a way that there's no way that a jury will look at us unbiased!"

"They aren't looking for a murderer anymore because of the clothes that Robinson got out of my house," Dan said. "Now do you understand why I'm taking all these precautions?"

"I wouldn't have believed it unless I saw it myself."

"Exactly."

He spent another forty-five minutes planning their route while Diana finished reading the papers. After awhile, she tossed them in the back of Blossom with disgust.

Dan looked up from his work. "Do me a favor," he said.

"What?"

"We have to be extremely careful. As a Deadhead, we're a target to be pulled over. Even though we have these I.D.'s on us, I don't think we should keep the newspapers in the vehicle. There's no need for a cop to make the connection by seeing those in the back."

"What? We're a target in these costumes?"

"A different sort of target. Hopefully, we won't experience it. How do you think I got busted for having a joint? It sure wasn't because I was wearing a business suit," Dan said, referring to the Chicago show years earlier.

"That's right," Diana said. "I read about it in the paper where they said you had prior drug busts. I didn't want to ask because I didn't want to know. Is that the only time?"

"Yep!"

"So, you're not a dealer?"

"Nope! Never was, never will be. Matter of fact, I haven't smoked pot in a few years. Remember? I used to have a career as a mystery writer. The two don't go hand in hand. Well, unless, it's a social thing..."

"What's supposed to mean?"

"I'm kidding, okay?" Dan said. "Let's take it easy on each other. The better we get along, the faster that we're going to find our murderer and get off of this hell-ride, alright?"

Diana hopped in back, grabbed all the newspapers and walked them over to a dumpster, glancing at them one more time, one by one. It was hard to believe that a week ago she had been married to a cardiologist, living in upper middle-class affluence.

Shortly thereafter, Dan was driving Blossom up to an ATM machine. He pulled out his card and slid it into the machine. Moments later, a slip came back. Dan crumpled it up, obviously upset.

"We've gotta go, now!" he said.

"What's wrong?"

"First of all, in no time at all, the police will know that we've been here. Second of all, it appears that the state has a lock on my accounts."

"What are you saying?" she asked as Dan hightailed Blossom out of the driveway, heading in the direction of 1-75 south.

"Well," Dan began slowly, "it appears that we have only about three hundred dollars left to work with."

"Are you trying to say that we're almost broke?"

"It appears that way," Dan said.

"How are we going to make it?"

"I don't know," Dan said. "I really don't know."

While Blossom entered the interstate, a golden sun was setting on Diana's side of her, a Grateful Dead tune twinkled out of the stereo, *Built To Last: "Don't waste your breath to save your face when you have done your best. And even more is asked of you, fate will decide the rest."*

27

LOSER

It was inevitable that somebody would throw a rock at the glass house that the Wilcox family lived in and it was only right that Danny be the one to shatter it.

After the incident with Louise and her going to the hospital, Danny felt like they were a walking high wire act. A thin line of reality was keeping him in his maligned home.

Of course, he hoped that his parents would learn from their mistakes, but they didn't. As the mistakes were made, Danny, Mark and Louise could feel their time running out, with Thursdays as their only respite from hell.

Louise showed the worst signs of wear by withdrawing into a shell that no one could seem to penetrate, including her siblings. She hid in the dark territory of her mind, scared to move without having some sort of repercussions from Momma and Daddy. Her grades in school slipped with silence as her only armor of protection. If she did talk, it was only prompted by the continual ritual of quiz sessions from Momma and Daddy, ending in the same results. If she gave them an answer, it was always the wrong answer and she paid for it. It was not uncommon to see Momma operating on her bruises with a dab of make-up for school, the admonition clear: "If you say a word about this to anyone..."

Well, Louise didn't say a word about anything to anyone. She was becoming a recluse who believed she was retarded, making her an easy target for childhood schoolmates. She wasn't loved by Momma, who said she wanted to give up on her while Daddy had become sour and bitter, believing that he was undeserving of such a defective daughter. They didn't have to tell Louise that. She felt it every time that she was banished to her room.

Mark wasn't spared from the tiring effects of their environment, either. At times, an air of defiance showed, as if he was prompting Momma and Daddy to continue their charade. There was many a time that he, too, could be seen whipping his lunchbox, in frustration, across the street, only to have to face Momma and explain why his Thermos was broken, again.

Spring was melting into summer, the period that none of the kids relished for they didn't have the salvation of being at school five days a week.

Summer was a tirade of dealing with Momma and Daddy on a twenty-four hour basis, seven days a week. The pressure would build until one of them, in a cesspool of hate and fear, would snap. Mark finally ran away after Momma tirelessly whipped him with an evergreen branch. He couldn't take it. He just ran with only the clothes on his back. What surprised Danny was that Momma didn't even act phased by it.

She called Danny downstairs. "Do you see what you've done?" she asked calmly.

"No, Momma," Danny responded.

"You're the one who made Mark run away. I would suggest that you get him back here as soon as possible or you'll have to deal with your father when he gets home. You wouldn't want that would you?"

"Mark ran away?"

"Yes, Mark ran away. He thinks he can do that because of the example that you've set in this household."

"I didn't make him run away," Danny answered, keeping his defiance at bay. His dark side was threatening to surge.

"Don't you talk back to me, young man," Momma warned. "You're going to have something to run away for if you don't get him back here, pronto! Are you going to go get him, or are we going to wait until your father gets home and see what he thinks? "

Danny left, obediently, his head hung in shame.

He pretty much knew where Mark was and why he had bolted but he didn't relish the thought of bringing his brother back. Heck, he wasn't too pleased himself about living at home. For the moment, though, he knew that he was stuck with this shitty duty. For him to be blamed for it, made it all that much more worse. So, on the way, he stopped at a local convenience store, King's Korner, and shoplifted a couple of Swingin' Wing Hot Wheels, a sort of barter gift. After that, he made his way to the infamous St. Peter's Cathedral.

As he walked up the steps leading to the huge oak doors, he couldn't help remembering the distasteful experience he had had there, on a rainy night a long time ago. Sure enough, he saw Mark's shadow in one of the pews.

"Hi, Mark. What's going on?" he asked as he slid into the pew next to him. He didn't bother to genuflect, after all, it was only a building, and its meaning lost a long time ago.

"How did you find me?" asked Mark, none too pleased at seeing his brother so quickly.

"You told me that this is where you'd go if you ever ran away."

"Me and my big mouth," Mark said sullenly.

"Hey, I got you something," said Danny. He pulled out one of the Spectraflame Hot Wheels. "Here."

Mark's eyes lit up for a second. He ripped open the package, rolling the car on his hands. "Cool."

Danny followed suit with the other car. "I got one for me, too. Compliments of King's Korner."

They sat in silence for a moment.

"Go away, Danny."

"I can't, Mark. I'm your brother."

"Not anymore," Mark said. "I'm not going back." His voice sounded ghostly as it echoed off the walls of the ancient Cathedral.

"You gotta come home," said Danny, something he didn't want to say.

"I'm not going home. Ever!"

"Mark, please listen to me."

"I can't take it anymore, Danny. They're too mean to us. I'm scared all of the time. You're not supposed to be scared of your parents. You're not supposed to beg for food from other kids. It isn't right! They hit, scream and yell so much, it's like everything's out of control and they can't see it. It wasn't always like this," Mark said. He thought about it for a moment. "And how do you explain what happened to Louise?"

Danny couldn't say anything because he knew that his brother was right. He was torn by what he was supposed to do and what he wanted to do. Heck, he wanted to run away himself but it wasn't the right time. On the other side of the coin, there stood images of what his father would do if he didn't return Mark to where he belonged.

"It was an accident," Danny said as convincingly as he could.

"Yeah, right," Mark returned scornfully. "And what about next time? Will it be an accident if they kill one of us? I just wanna be normal, like other kids. This isn't fair and you know it!"

"I know it isn't fair, but we have to stick it out."

"I don't wanna stick it out," Mark said. He proceeded to start bawling, oblivious of the echo chamber that they were in.

Danny put his arm around his little brother's shoulder, allowing him to let out some of the pain and frustration. He looked at the immense crucifix hanging over the altar, the blood dripping from the various wounds, and wondered if Christ's pain was anything like theirs.

He looked at his watch, figuring that they had an hour before Daddy got home. They didn't have much time. "We have to go back," Danny said quietly.

"Please don't take me back," Mark begged. "If you were any kind of big brother, you wouldn't do that."

He felt like he had been stabbed by his brother's stinging words, but he pushed. "Mark, listen to me. I have to take you back. I promise that I'll get you guys out of there, I just can't do it right now."

"You promise?"

"I promise but we have to tough it out just a little while longer."

Mark appeared to ponder the pros and cons of the situation. "Am I going to get the belt for this?"

"No, Mark. I promise that you won't get the belt."

"Well, okay," Mark said with a hint of relief. "You're a great brother, probably the best that one could have."

"Thanks, Mark."

"And thanks for the Swingin' Wing. I don't know what we'd do if it weren't for you and me and our Hot Wheels. I just wish we had our other collection back, the ones that Momma gave away."

So, Mark and Danny took their time walking home, trying not to think about the parents that they didn't like, anymore.

Danny tried not thinking about the promises that he had made to his brother, promises that he wasn't sure he could follow through on. He was feeling like he had tricked his brother into coming home.

Well, when Mark got the belt that night, Danny felt each blow ten times over. For every crack that Mark received, Danny was upstairs, hitting himself as hard as he could.

Push came to shove, not too long afterwards. The bits and pieces that Danny wasn't around for, he pieced together from

Mark many months later. Danny's wish was going to come through, much sooner than he expected. He would be handed a silver platter with the opportunity to get the kids out of there. It all began with a conversation that Momma had with Louise.

It was a hot mid-August day, the type of day where the heat caused tempers to flare at the littlest of things. Momma was testy, in part because Daddy had been working a lot, leaving her with the responsibility of watching the kids, a chore that she was tiring of. Danny had been in the garage, going through his meager collection of glider parts in the toy box, hidden away so that Momma couldn't find it and dispose of it. Mark was upstairs in the bedroom, grounded for shoplifting King Don's at King's Korner, piecing together a puzzle that he couldn't have cared less about. Louise, meanwhile, was delegated to cleaning the kitchen.

Momma watched her for a long time before speaking. When she did speak, it was in a mock-friendly manner, her voice dripping with a sweetness that was buried in bitterness and trickery. "You know what, Louise?"

"What?" Louise responded, much like a normal child.

"I remember when I was a little girl like you, my parents used to take a lot of vacations, like we do on Thursday nights. They used to leave us at home with a babysitter. Boy, we used to have all sorts of fun."

"Yeah?"

"Oh yes. I remember my big brother," of which Momma never had one. That was how Mark knew that trouble was brewing. "He used to take care of us. Boy, oh boy, did we have a good time. We used to get wild and crazy, and my parents never knew about it. You know what? When my parents did find out, they weren't even mad. I bet you kids have fun when we're away square dancing, don't you?"

"Well..." Louise responded, hesitantly.

"Oh, don't worry, Louise. If you kids do have fun, it's okay," Momma said very sweetly. Mark knew that Momma was warming Louise up. Whenever someone was nice to her, she came out of her shell. Momma tugged on another string. "Here. Do you want one of Daddy's donuts?" she offered.

"Oh, yes," Louise said, taking the bait.

"Here you go," as Momma watched her eat it. "I bet that after we leave the house, Danny lets all of you out, doesn't he?"

"Well, yes," she answered.

Right about then, Mark was upstairs, feeling like he was ready to take a dump in his shorts.

"Well, that's okay. You kids should be allowed out. I bet you have a lot of fun, don't you? I mean, you probably watch television and go outside and play, huh?"

"Yes, Momma, we do," Louise answered. "But we're careful."

"Uh huh. I bet you have food out of the cabinets, too."

"Oh, no. We never do that," Louise defended. "We play and things. Sometimes, we just talk. Other times, we even play hide and seek except that Mark and Danny never let me win," she said, opening up. It was obvious that she enjoyed this rare, personal talk with Momma.

"Does Danny tell you that he's disobeying us?"

"No."

"What does he tell you?" Momma asked. Was her voice sounding somewhat strained?

"He tells us that we should never tell you what we do when you're gone."

"I'm sure he does. Now, why don't you go to your room and play?"

"But I'm not finished with my chores in here."

"Yes, Louise, you are finished," Momma said, an edge in her voice.

"Don't worry, Danny will take care of it."

As Louise went upstairs, Mark felt a panic well up inside the deepest reaches of his gut. He never had a chance to warn Danny. As he told Danny many months later, he had no idea that Momma would react quite the way she did. If he had, he would have jumped out the window to warn Danny of his impending doom.

"Danny, can I talk to you?" Momma asked Danny from the doorway to the garage. He was still digging through his box of toys when Momma appeared, causing him to jump involuntarily. At first, he thought that Momma had busted him with his hidden toys.

"Yes, Momma," Danny answered obediently. He walked over to where she was standing. Judging from the look on her face, he had a feeling that he was in trouble for something. He knew that he had to watch his guard and he knew that something was wrong. The butterflies danced in his stomach while he tried to maintain a mask of composure. It was as if she could look right through into your soul sometimes and this was one of those times. He could feel it and it was immediately apparent that it wasn't about his toy box.

"I was just curious. How is the babysitting going for you?"

"What do you mean, Momma?"

"Does everything go alright? You don't have any problems keeping your brother and sister in line?"

"No. They're good," Danny said. He wasn't sure at that point where she was heading, but he wasn't pleased with where she was steering. He did his best to keep his eyes focused on her eyes. She could tell you were lying the moment that you looked down.

"So, Louise stays in the basement and Mark stays in his room, right?"

The way that she had asked the question made Danny even more suspicious. The thing was, he didn't think that there was any way that his brother or sister would divulge their Thursday night secret. The only people who knew what was really happening were within their triangle. Even so, he had this strange feeling that he was walking into a trap, but what else could he say? "Yes, they stay in their rooms like they're supposed to."

"So, you have no problems and you conduct yourselves in the manner that you were told to?"

"Yes, Momma."

"And you think that you're doing a good job, obeying us?"

"Yes, Momma. We're all good when you're gone."

Suddenly, the smile fell away from Momma's face and Danny knew that he was in for it. He had walked into many a trap and he knew, instantaneously, that he was deep into it. So, when she raised her arm to belt him, it was as if he knew it was coming. He did only as was natural, raising his arm in defense, and Momma's forearm crashed into his.

If anything was a precursor to trouble, bad trouble, it was when a blow was shielded off. At that moment, Danny knew that things were going to get out of hand. It was the look of surprise in Momma's face and then the look of her own pain in realizing where the blow connected.

Mark and Danny had spent many a late night conversation talking about the beast or the rage. One could never guess when it would come out. But, they remembered times like the laundry room when it had flooded and Daddy's beast had come out. It was the difference between pain and sheer, irreversible terror. Daddy, when he was under an extreme amount of outside pressure, was the first to let this uncontrollable rage out. Momma's beast had only shown as far back as when they were sued and Daddy had become distant. It was as if violence was the only way that she could keep the fragments of their family together. But, if a blow was shielded off, it was elevated to something higher, unsurpassed in intensity. And Danny saw it coming in the redness of her face and the smallness of her eyes. It was the same look that Louise must have seen when Momma lost her mind on her in the foyer. The only thing he felt was fear, clean and crisp in clarity. The type of fear where the bowels would let go without your even realizing what was happening. The worst part of it was that once the beast was released, there was nothing that anyone could do to stop it. It fought against all reason and rationality and the best that one could hope for, was to live through it.

To a child, under those reigning blows, death was a nearby and close companion.

And, as Momma backhanded him across the face, her diamond ring sliced through his cheek as if he was a tender piece of veal. She lunged at him and threw him to the ground.

"You damned liar!" she screamed. She grabbed him by the hair and dragged him over to the cement threshold between the garage and the laundry room. He tried to stand, but he couldn't quite catch a grip. He could feel the edge of the threshold digging into the back of his head. The next thing that he knew, Momma was standing over him, her hands in a death lock on his ears and in his hair. She lifted his head up and slammed it into the threshold. Again and again, she did it while Danny flailed uselessly. White sparks flared behind his eyes every time his head slammed into the cement. He fought the urge to throw up as the pain echoed in his mind. He started screaming as loud as he could, his head threatening to explode. Spittle sprayed on his face in her anger.

The beast was loose and God was nowhere in sight.

Then, she yanked the dazed and bleeding boy to his feet and pulled him into the laundry room, slamming the door. His screaming would surely have gotten the neighbors' attention. But, with the door shut, his cries fell on deaf walls. Danny wet his pants, something he hadn't done in a long time. When Momma saw that, it was as if her rage was turned up one more notch. And, he had never been that scared in his life. Momma began smacking and hitting him until he was cornered by the walls.

"So, you like babysitting, huh? " she said, cuffing him on the side of the head.

"Please...!" he tried to scream. His voice sounded muffled while his ears rang.

"You like disobeying?" she yelled, her foot slamming into his shin.

"Owww!!"

"You like to lie? " she asked him at the top of her voice. Then, blow after blow rained down on him, until he fell to the floor. "You piece of shit for a son! We trusted you and this is what we get?" she screamed at the cowering figure in the corner. Momma began kicking him like a useless piece of meat, with no area protected, as hard as she could, in the shins, the ribs and even his face wasn't spared.

"Stand up!" she ordered him, grabbing him by the hair at the top of the head and yanking him to his feet. She clenched her fist, while yanking on his scalp, and rammed it into his face. In a reflex, his arm came up and hit her in the chest. Blood poured from his nose and splashed on the yellow-tiled floor.

His head was reeling yet she wouldn't stop. He screamed as loud as he could, praying that someone would intervene, praying that it would stop.

He felt himself slam into the wall. He dimly saw Momma's face pressed close to his own, sweat smearing her make-up, distorting her features. He could smell her breath and hear the rasping of air as it ran in and out of her lungs.

"We warned you, didn't we? You lying sack of shit! You have destroyed this family! You pathetic excuse for a human being! We warned you, didn't we? " she screamed.

"Yes!" Danny wailed.

For the moment, Danny lost track of time. The ringing grew to a continuous muffle while she slammed him into the wall repeatedly. He felt the blackening rushes threaten to overtake him. He would pass out at any second.

He wasn't sure when, but it stopped. All he felt was her yanking him out of the laundry room by the ear and upstairs to the main foyer. He could feel the wetness of the blood on his face.

"Get undressed!" she ordered him.

"Wh...w...what?" he asked, his breath coming out in short wheezes.

"You heard me, you despicable piece of shit! Get undressed!"

Danny stood there in disbelief. He thought that he was really going to get it now.

"I...I...I..."

"Don't you pull a Louise on me! You're dripping blood all over the floor!" she screamed. Then, she grabbed his shirt and literally tore it off. She began to roughly wipe his face, smearing his features. "I am not going to have you run away again! Let's see how far you get when you're in the nude. Now, are you getting undressed or am I going to have to do it for you? "

"No, I'll do it!" Danny screamed back, wanting to die rather than go through any more torture. He took all of his clothes off, hurriedly, and stood cowering in front of her.

Momma grabbed him by the ear and yanked him into the kitchen. She got a mop bucket out of the pantry and put it into the sink, turning the water on full blast until billows of steam rose from it. She threw a sponge in and set it on the floor.

"When your father gets home," she said, with a bloody fierceness in her eyes, "he's going to kill you! You think you got it from me? Huh? Well, it was nothing in comparison to what he's going to do you! While you're waiting for him, you can scrub every inch of this floor on your hands and knees. Do you understand me?"

"Yes!"

"Listen, you naked ninny! While you're busy cleaning, you had better be saying some prayers because you haven't seen anything, yet!" Momma grabbed him from under the arms, digging her fingernails into his flesh. He screamed in agony as shockwaves of pain ran from his biceps to the tips of his fingers. "Now, get on your knees and clean!"

She threw him to the floor. Then, she grabbed him by the head and dragged him to the steaming bucket of water, yanking his arm and diving it in. Danny cried as the white-hot heat stung and then numbed his hand. "I said, clean the floor! Now!"

Danny's numbed hand found the sponge, pulled it out. He started scrubbing as fast as he could. Momma kicked him the ribs one last time and stormed out of the kitchen, making her way upstairs.

"And don't you dare think about running away, you little creep," she screamed down from the balcony at the top of the stairs. "Remember, I have all your clothes and the only way that you'll do it is naked. If I catch you even thinking about it, I'll kill you before your father has a chance to lay a finger on you! Is that clear?"

"It is!" Danny yelled up to her.

Danny fumbled with the sponge, his breath still surging in and out of his lungs, heaving. As he cleaned, he saw that he was wasting his time. For every wipe he made, blood dripped, making fresh marks on the floor. His nose ran and his body ached.

There was only one thing on Danny's mind as he mindlessly wiped. He had to do it! He was more than thinking about running away, he knew that he had no other option! If what Momma had done to him was any indication of what was to come, he was not going to be around when his father came home.

Every limit had been crossed in human decency and there was no way that he could live through it again. He had to get out of that house quickly, naked or not!

He scrubbed and mumbled uncontrollably to himself. "Oh God, please help me! Please don't let it happen anymore. Please! Please...!"

After gaining some control, he crept to his feet and looked around the corner, up the stairs. He listened, fighting to keep his teeth from chattering. He couldn't see her but knew that she must of have been in the master bedroom. He could see the doorway to his room but it was shut. There was no way for him to get in there without Momma seeing him or hearing him. Clothes! Where was he going to get some?

He heard the sound of the toilet flushing from Momma and Daddy's room.

It was then or never. The reverberating sound of the toilet would mask the sound of his naked feet running across the tiled floor of the foyer. He bolted, not worrying about his nakedness. He ran through the foyer and down the stairs toward the family room and, in no time flat, he was headed toward the laundry room, pausing at the adjacent bathroom. He dashed in and grabbed a towel, hurriedly wrapping it around his waist. He listened for the sound of his mother.   He heard nothing, thankfully. Then, he saw his blood-smeared face in the mirror. Quickly, he used the towel to wipe his face and then wrapped it around himself again. Knowing that there was no time to waste, he ran into the laundry room, pausing to open the door to the garage very slowly so as not to attract the attention of Momma. He pulled the door closed behind him and made his way to his bicycle. He grabbed it by the handlebars and ran it out of the garage. He clumsily hopped on and started pedaling.

Unfortunately, the damn thing was in tenth gear and it was a struggle to get it moving. He yanked the shift levers down, panicking when his saw the chain threatening to slip off of the gears. Suddenly, they caught themselves as he gained speed heading down the driveway. As the bike picked up speed, he almost spilled himself on the street by taking the turn at the bottom of the driveway a little too fast. The bike skidded crazily. He regained control, trying to think of where he was headed.

The only thing that was on his mind was getting out of under that roof as fast as he could. Then, the towel almost blew off. He grabbed it in time as he tried to maneuver the bike, picking up speed with every passing second, his mind, a jumbled panic of thoughts.

Robbie! The thought of his best friend flashed through his mind in an instant. He was there through the failed tape recordings and he would be there for this, Danny thought. He pushed his legs as hard as he could as he blew through "Doctor's Row" and down toward Brule road, where Robbie lived. He kept looking behind him, expecting to see Momma chasing him in the car. Danny bucked the wind and pushed himself even harder until his legs began feeling like lead.

Before he knew it, he was at the bottom of Brule road, with Robbie's house in sight. He hit Robbie's driveway a little too fast, skidding wildly and then losing control. The bike crashed into the bordering bushes while Danny flew over the handlebars. He didn't even feel anything. As soon as he hit the ground, he was jumping up just as quickly as the accident happened, the pain being nothing in comparison to what he had been through. Quickly, he wiped his face and then ran up to the front door, pulling the towel tightly around his waist. He pounded on the door, a little too emphatically.

"Yes?" Robbie's mother hollered from somewhere in the house. Danny looked toward the cement steps, attempting to regain some semblance of control. He wasn't running away, he...he had been swimming. That's it!

"It's Danny. Is Robbie around?" he asked, trying to keep his rushed breath at bay. It was difficult, especially knowing that Momma might be coming around the corner at any second.

"Sure, Danny," she answered cheerfully, upon opening the door. He saw a funny look cross her face. He looked toward the ground, shielding his face.

"Oh, I've been swimming and I wanted to tell Robbie about it."

"That's nice," she said, sounding as if she bought the story. "Do you want to come in?"

"No, thank you," Danny said, fighting the urge to check for Momma behind him.

"Suit yourself. Let me get him for you."

Danny stood there, for what felt like an eternity. Every sound made him think that it was the roar of Momma's car. Where the hell was Robbie?

"Hi, Danny," Robbie said, startling him with his appearance.

"It happened," Danny said in a panic, through the screen door.

"What did?"

"I've gotta hide, Robbie!" He reached in and pulled Robbie outside as fast as he could. He just about yanked Robbie off of his feet as he pulled him around to the side of the garage, out of the sight of the street and any neighbors who might have been watching.

Robbie's face had a hundred questions written all over it. "What happened to you?"

"My parents! My mom! She lost it. Then, she said that my father's going to kill me!" he said quickly. It was as if he couldn't get the words out fast enough. "I ran away! You've got to help me! I don't have any clothes!" To prove it, Danny pulled the towel away and quickly put it back around him.

A look of disbelief was on Robbie's face. "Did you tape it?"

"How was I supposed to tape it? It happened so quickly that I didn't even have a chance to think about it!"

"Jesus, Danny!"

"You've gotta help me, Robbie!"

"I don't know what to do!"

"Just hide me! Please!"

"Okay! Okay!" Robbie answered.

And so, the adventure began.

28

FOOLISH HEART

Beads of sweat dripped slowly off of Dan's face as he maneuvered Blossom through Cincinnati. Periodically, he picked up the large map book as they arched their way through one construction zone after another.

"Are you okay?" Diana asked after a long string of silence.

"I suppose," Dan said ruefully.

Diana didn't believe him. She could see it in his eyes and in his movements. He appeared nervous and fitful, as if their ride had made him curiously claustrophobic. On top of that, he wasn't as graceful with the bus as she had gotten used to, with his pounding on the accelerator and jamming on the gears. "Do you want to talk about it?"

"That leaves only me to blame cause Momma tried," Dan quoted.

"What?"

"The Grateful Dead tune playing right now? It's called, *Mama Tried*. Want me to turn it up?"

Diana felt his edginess. "Look, Dan, I'm just trying to help. If you want to speak in cryptics, go ahead. I'll shut up."

"Sorry," Dan said. "I'm getting frustrated. Do you think that these are stories that I want to talk about? I've spent fifteen years running from them and I don't want to go back, you know? Besides that, do you think I'm pleased in running from the law? Well, I'm not. I've gone through enough shit without this to top it off."

"What bothered you so much about the story you just told me?"

Dan turned down the Fillmore, April 27, 1971 show, so he could think a moment. "I would guess that it was the intensity of it. Not only do I question how a human being could do that to another human being, I'm still wondering why. Part of me says that we were despicable children, that we deserved it in some fashion or another. Then again, we were just children. Our parents were our point of reference. If they did that to us then what's there to prevent us from doing it to our children?"

"Acceptance," Diana said.

"Acceptance? Meaning what? That we accept what they did as wrong and go on with our lives? I accept the fact that we got the shit kicked out of us and that leaves me absolutely nowhere."

"Well, listen a moment. For you to accept this in a healthy manner, you have to have understanding. The first thing that you need to understand is why your parents were the way they were. I think that you've accepted your father and his faults but I don't feel that you've accepted your mother in the same fashion. Am I reading that correctly?"

"I'm still pissed," he said softly.

"Good. That's a start. Now, you need to understand her intentions."

"We're not getting anywhere. I don't want to understand her intentions. I want to find out who killed her so that I can get on with what's left of my life. I want to let all of this go."

"But," Diana said fervently, "You can't let it go. You must drop the guilt that you're feeling inside. It's still there. I can see it as clearly as I can the car in front of us. It's not healthy. You'll never have a family until you..."

Dan slammed Blossom down one gear when the car in front of him abruptly slowed. "Dammit! Who's talking about my having a family? I'll have a family when I want one. I'm not ready for that stage. Don't you think that I don't know that? Big deal. So I don't understand why she was the way she was. Maybe it's because she loved my father so much that we, as kids, got in the way of that..."

"But weren't you a product of their love?" Diana questioned.

"Product, property, whatever. Why don't we say that she was just nuts and that's that?"

"Because that's not healthy."

He eased Blossom back into fourth and turned up Loser. "You've got all the answers, don't you? Well, try this on for size. I haven't thought of that story in, probably, twenty years. As a matter of fact, I could easily say that I've forgotten it. It's been blocked out. So, for you to tell me what I think of my mother is not healthy, imagine remembering the kind of shit I'm remembering. Like I've said, it's not a nice place to go, okay? "

"Have you ever heard of battered child syndrome?" Diana asked.

Dan started shaking his head, a sarcastic chuckle coming out of his mouth. "Oh good, another label. And what psychiatry book did you get that out of? Does everything have to have a nonsensical name? This is reality, Diana, and it isn't a pretty picture and it isn't a name from a book. Did you ever consider that people just happen? They don't have to follow some rule out of a schoolbook. You wouldn't understand unless you've been there. You've got your pretty little house and your pretty little office and a lot of opinions that haven't amounted to a hill of beans. Have you noticed that?"

Diana looked out the side window, an array of cones making a continuous orange flash alongside the bus. Ahead, the skies were darkening, threatening rain. When she began talking, it was slow and with a self-assurance just shy of speaking with clenched teeth. "Well, Dan, I don't have that pretty little house, anymore. Nor, might I remind you, do I have a pretty little office. Has it crossed your mind that I've risked everything for you?"

Dan looked at her but didn't say a word.

"Have you given a moment's thought as to why I've risked everything?"

"Look," Dan said, "if you'd like me to let you off right now..."

"That's not what this is about, dammit! The answer is not in running and it's not in our separating ways. It's about that thing called battered child syndrome, a catch-all phrase for a lot of things that we don't understand, yet. The thing is, we can't have understanding until we look at each individual's response to abuse. Abuse comes in many horrid colors, shapes and forms. People react differently, depending upon if they are male or female, depending upon the intensity and frequency and, finally, upon how strong we are inside. That strength comes from a logical realization as to what kind of abuse occurred and how we're going to learn from it."

"Very good, Diana. And what chapter of what book did that come from?"

"It didn't come from a book," she answered, her eyes reddening.

"Then, what professor taught you that?"

Diana fought with the growing image, *a warm and calloused hand moved up her leg, ever so slowly.*

"Well?" Dan prodded. "You're telling me doctrine after doctrine about abuse but I don't think you really understand it. I think you came along because you want to understand it. The fact remains; you'll never understand it unless you've been through it! If I may give you my learned opinion, that is."

For a moment, Diana was as angry as she had ever been. She couldn't look at him. She couldn't. He didn't understand and it wasn't his business to understand. She thought of Clinton's warning of counter-transference, a term she had studied and had carefully avoided. Yet, it was happening and she knew it. This exchange between two people was requiring her involvement. It was pulling her in as surely as a magnet would attract a nail. She fought it as hard as she could, trying to focus on something else. But, that image was pulling her in.

You can sit on my lap. It's okay. I like it when you sit with me. Come here, Precious. It's okay. Remember, don't tell anyone, though.

"Diana?" Dan asked, pulling her from a long time ago.

"I'm fine," she said sternly.

Ahead of them, a storm line approached, causing Dan to turn the headlights on. Then, the rains came, splattering the bus with golf-ball sized rain drops, slowly at first, until the rain became a pounding rhythm, drowning out the music, the sound of the engine and their conversation. Dan slowed the bus dramatically because of the reflecting brake lights ahead of him. They pounded through growing pools of water, threatening to stop the bus in their depth. Dan worked Blossom carefully. In exasperation, he gave up when he saw an exit for a rest area.

Meanwhile, Diana was fighting images that she thought that she had forgotten years ago.

You're very special to me. Precious. Don't you know that? We have something special between us, don't we? Answer me! Don't we?

Yes, Uncle Bill.

Good, Precious. We have something so special that it's a secret, isn't it? A secret that's just between us, don't forget that. We can't have this secret if you tell anyone. Do you understand me? You like me, don't you?

Please, Uncle Bill. I don't want to be in the barn, anymore. Can't we go in? Please?

Sure, we can go in. But not until you do what Uncle Bill likes so much. Come here, Precious. Touch me. Then, you can go in.

I don't want to do that...I don't want to do that...Please, let me go! You're hurting me! Stop it...Stop it!!!

"Diana, are you okay?"

Diana looked up at Dan, momentarily disoriented. Suddenly, she grabbed the handle to the door and ran out into the pounding, warm rain. Blindly, she ran toward the restrooms. She slammed into the door and pushed it open: unsure of whether it was the tears or the rain blinding her eyesight. She ran into a stall, lifted the toilet seat and threw up. Her stomach heaved until nothing was left and, yet, her insides continued convulsing wildly. She flushed the toilet continuously until she gained comfort in the coolness of the porcelain.

Fifteen minutes later, she heard a light tapping at the bathroom door. She stood up on weakened legs and made her way to the mirror. Her eyes were sunken and her hair was askew, still wet from the downpour. Diana hardly recognized the figure that looked back at her.

"Diana," Dan said, cracking the door open only enough for his voice to echo inside. "Are you okay?"

"Yes, Dan. I think so. Give me a minute to get my composure."

"Sure," Dan said. "I'll be out in the bus."

"Thanks," Diana said. "Uh, would you mind grabbing my bag out of there? I got a bit wet."

"You got it," Dan said. Moments later, he set it inside the door.

Diana spent a few minutes cleaning up, brushing her teeth and drying her hair under the electric hand dryer. Focusing on her facial needs, took her mind off the re-surfaced image.

When she got back in the bus, Dan looked at her. "I'm sorry," he said.

"Just don't ever tell me that I don't know my business. I know very well what abuse is. It may not be the same type as yours but it's still abuse," she said firmly, the tone of a psychiatrist clear.

"I didn't know," Dan said.

"Well, now you do. There are very precise reasons why I chose psychiatry as a profession. One of those reasons has to do with understanding why it happened to me. Further, I knew that there was no way to stop it. So, I help victims. I help them because I know how deep that pain can go. I understand the varied reasons for drug abuse, alcohol abuse and suicide. Maybe, that's why I think that I can help you. Unfortunately, like you, when it comes back, it can be catastrophic. It doesn't mean that I'm a weak person and neither are you. But, the first thing that you have to understand is that it will always be there. Always."

"Sorry," Dan said. "I mean it. We've spent so much time going back where I haven't wanted to go that it, well, it just never occurred to me."

"It's alright, Dan. We live, we learn and we take it all one day at a time."

"How did you cope with it?"

"I did what everyone else does. I pretended that it never happened. Then, one day, I told my mother."

"What happened? I mean I don't want to get too personal. If you don't want to talk about it..."

"I went through sexual abuse from an uncle for about two years from the time when I was ten years-old. I remember telling my mother about my uncle and me and seeing the look on her face. At first, I thought it was anger at my uncle. It wasn't. In fact, she was angry with me. It's the only time in my life that I remember getting hit by my parents. I swear that I can still feel that slap across my face. It was pushed under the carpet and my uncle moved away not long after that. No, it was a taboo subject. I don't blame them, anymore. I did for a long time, though. Then, I pushed it out of my mind."

Dan had started preparing some franks and beans on the stove. "But you didn't forget."

"No, and it came back at times when I least expected. At the time, I was an undergraduate. I went to a psychiatrist because of the fears I was having. I believe those fears were most dramatically pronounced when I began dating. Well, this psychiatrist, Dr. Clinton, pulled me out of it. It took a few years and, eventually, I switched my goal to becoming a psychiatrist, all due to that great man."

"If you don't mind my saying, I think you've worked things out pretty well."

Diana smiled. "Thank you. It all comes from facing what you fear the most."

"I know," Dan said. "I came to that realization when I first saw you. How long did it take me to finally visit my parents after seeing you? Six months?"

"That's about right."

"Hmm. Look the way things turned out. The only thing that bothers me is that if I had waited just one month less, she might not be dead right now," Dan said.

"You don't know that."

"You're right. I don't know that but I do know that it'll always be food for thought. Speaking of..." Dan said as he plated their quick meal.

They ate in silence as Dan pondered over the map. Outside, a rainbow crossed the horizon behind the storm front. Sunlight danced off the beads of water in the grass and in the trees, greatly uplifting their spirits.

Half an hour later, they were back on the road again. But, Dan wasn't too much in the mood for driving and neither was Diana, so they agreed to cut across the 14 to Interstate 27. Dan smiled when they exited at Kincaid State Park, surrounding an oddly shaped lake. Dan opened the doors and pulled out the shade over a picnic table.

The day melted into night, as a campfire crackled and snapped. *Me and Bobby McGee* played softly in the background while Dan stared intently into the fire. A look of confusion crossed his face. He raised his finger and then stood up. He was sure that what he was picturing wasn't from a dream. It gnawed at the back of his head like a woodpecker poking at unseen parasites in a tree.

Go back to where you belong, you loony bird! Go! I thought that I had gotten rid of you. Get out of my sight before I call the police! You damn loony bird!

"What is it?" Diana asked.

"The night of the murder!"

"Yes?"

"She called me a loony bird!"

"Who did?"

"My mother. She told me that I was a loony bird. I know it!"

"Why?"

"That's just it. I don't know. Why would she call me that?"

The campfire chewed on the wood as Dan tried to reconcile with his latest memory, confused as he ever was.

You're a damned loony bird! That's all you are! Stay away from me! Just stay away from me and go back where you belong!

29

ESTIMATED PROPHET

"The first thing that we gotta do is get some clothes for you. Hold on a second, I'll be right back," Robbie said.

"What about your Mom?"

"What about her?"

"Don't let her catch you," Danny warned.

"Aw, Danny, don't worry about it. I've got normal parents, remember?" Robbie said. "But, just in case, I'll be careful, anyway." He gave Danny a quick supportive smile and went back into the house.

Danny sat down by the wall on the side of the garage, his towel still wrapped around him. He felt oddly vulnerable and his hands were still trembling uncontrollably. There was only one thing that he was still sure of at the moment: he was glad that he had run away and he was resolved in the decision that he was never going back. At that point, he wouldn't have cared if someone had told him that he was going to be living in a dumpster for the rest of his life. The only thing that nagged at him was that he didn't exactly feel free. He felt like a dog that was on the loose who knew that his captors would be back to get him. As he looked into the shadows of the trees, he couldn't shake the image of his mother screaming, "When your father gets home, he's going to kill you!"

It seemed like forever and a day before Robbie returned. Danny had been daydreaming of various scenarios of his imminent capture when he suddenly appeared, startling the hell out of him. He jumped.

"God, you scared me? And what took you so long?" Danny asked.

"Sorry about that," Robbie answered affably. "Here, put these on. I snuck them out of the house without my mom seeing me."

Robbie handed Danny a faded pair of jeans, an orange t-shirt (which didn't amuse Danny with its billboard effect), some old white socks and a pair of dilapidated tennis shoes. Danny wouldn't win any fashion contests but the clothes sure felt great after he had put them on. It took the feeling of vulnerability away.

"You look kind of funny," Robbie said.

"I do? Why?"

"Those clothes are way too big for you, for one thing. What's funny is that I haven't worn them for years because they're way too small for me."

"Hey, I'll invite you over for dinner at my house for a few weeks and I bet you'll fit in them in no time," Danny said sarcastically.

"The food that your parents serve is that good? No thanks," Robbie said.

"You're missing something, though."

"What?" Danny asked. "I know what it is. I need those shoes like John Travolta wears in Saturday Night Fever.

Robbie took his Detroit Tiger's baseball cap and dropped it on Danny's head. "There, perfect."

"I can't take this," Danny said. "It's your favorite hat!"

"Not anymore. It's your favorite hat, now."

"Look, Robbie," Danny said, a serious tone to his voice, "thanks for the clothes and stuff."

"Aw, no sweat. You may not be able to wear them to your senior prom, but they'll work. That's what friends are for, you know? Besides, my mom will throw a fit if she sees you running around naked. I get into enough trouble as it is," Robbie said with a smack on Danny's back. "Hey, let's go out back in the woods so we can talk. I don't want your parents seeing you here. Now that would be trouble!"

The two boys trekked to the woods behind the house, to the fort that Robbie and Danny had built years earlier. It was made from excess lumber from a new house that had been built. It didn't look new anymore, though, with its rain streaked walls and warped curves. Danny and Robbie couldn't have counted the number of secrets that they had shared there over years past.

The thing was, those secrets were pretty minor compared to the secrets that they were sharing now.

Once inside, they settled on the dirt floor. To anyone else, the fort might have looked ratty and run down but to Danny, it was a great haven from the terrors of the outside world. Robbie pulled out a couple of pieces of Watermelon Jolly Rancher candies that had gone soft and gooey from being in his pocket all day.

"Here," he offered Danny.

"No thanks," Danny said out of habit.

"Would you just take it?" Robbie pressed him. Remember? You're not with your parents anymore."

"Sorry," Danny said. He proceeded to delicately work the cellophane off and then popped it in his mouth. Robbie followed suit.

"So, tell me what happened?"

Danny began the story with how the day had begun without any sign of danger. Then, he proceeded to tell Robbie about the babysitting questions and then, finally, about Momma's explosion of anger and how it was nothing in comparison to what his father was going to do. He left out the parts where he had cried; giving Robbie the impression that he had done his best to take it like a man but it had gone too far. The rest was history. That's how he found himself at his best friend's house.

"Geez, Danny, that really sucks," Robbie said, snapping a twig in half.

"Robbie, I don't know what to do. The worst part about this whole thing is that I feel like a coward for running away."

"Why should you feel like a coward? You didn't have a choice. You were scared."

"Yeah, but my brother and sister are still there and I hate to think about what's going to happen to them. My mom wasn't kidding when she said that my dad was going to kill me. He's going to kill them instead! I know it!" Danny said vehemently. Then, he embarrassed himself in front of Robbie by breaking out in tears. It felt like he was always crying. For once, he wanted to take things like a man and quit acting like a baby.

Robbie sat there, without interfering. He munched on his Jolly Rancher thoughtfully. "They're bastards, man."

"Yeah," Danny agreed.

"We shouldn't have bothered taping them. We should have just killed them, like setting the house on fire when you guys were supposed to be at school," Robbie said with a manly determination. "Man, can you imagine what would have happened if they had ever caught you or me taping them? We would have been dead meat for sure!"

"I told you that it was risky, didn't I? You didn't believe me. You kept telling me to get closer and closer and now you know why I was scared," Danny said.

"Okay! Okay! I screwed up, all right? I didn't know that they were quite that bad. Give me a break! Most parents..."

Danny cut him off. "Yeah, well my parents aren't most parents. The question is, what am I gonna do now?"

"I'm not sure," Robbie said flatly.

The two boys sat in silence with Danny picking at his shoelaces and Robbie tracing trails in the dirt with his finger.

More than anything, Danny wanted to disappear, pretending that all of this was someone else's dream. He felt tired and worn out with nowhere left to turn and no one left to help him. Part of him was tempted to lie down and go to sleep so that he could pretend that his life wasn't happening. But, he knew that he had to be an adult about the situation, especially considering that he didn't have a choice. He was in a state of flux in trying to think of what to do but nothing came to mind, deepening his resentment for what his parents had started.

"The worst part of it is," Danny said, "that I don't even have any proof that anything happened."

"Yeah, you do," Robbie retorted quickly.

"What kind of proof? I never had a chance to tape it."

"Your face!"

"Huh?"

"Danny, do you know what your face looks like?" Robbie asked.

Then, Danny had a brief image of all the blood. There was the cut on his cheek from Momma's diamond ring. Then, the bloodied nose, not to mention all the spots on his body where he had been kicked and bruised. "Yeah! That's it!" Danny said ecstatic at the thought. "Come outside where it's light and take a look at me!"

The two of them crawled out of the fort and found an area where the sun went through the trees, unobstructed. Danny took off his newly acquired shirt, while Robbie proceeded to look at his back, much like a fellow baboon might preen another.

"Jesus, Danny!"

"What is it?"

"You've got red marks all over your back! You got the shit kicked out of you!" Robbie said, not hiding his surprise.

"Is it that bad?"

"Big time! Those marks may be red right now, but I can tell you from experience that they're going to turn into some mean looking bruises. I bet they get all purple and blue and they'll look even worse than they do now! Let's look at the rest of you."

Danny stood there as Robbie slowly walked around him, quietly inventorying the damage. He looked under Danny's arms and found the bloodied cuts where Momma's fingernails had gouged him. He looked at Danny's legs and saw where he had been kicked repeatedly, swelled in spots and the skin torn and bloodied in others. Then, with Danny's permission, he felt around the crown of his friend's skull.

"Owww!" Danny protested vehemently.

"What'd I do?"

"Be careful! My head hurts!"

"Hold still," Robbie ordered him. His hand gently moved along Danny's head.   "Yeah, you got a really good beating this time. Wow! If my mom ever did this to me..."

Every once in a while, Danny would jump involuntarily as Robbie's hand went over a particularly tender spot.

"Your head is full of bumps. It's got little red dots all over it, too. Is that from where she pulled your hair?"

"I guess so," Danny said. "Owww! That hurts!" Danny repeated again.

"Sorry."

"Just be careful!"

"Man, Danny. We gotta do something about this. I hate to say it, but it's gotta be soon."

"Why's that?" Danny asked.

"Because this is the evidence that we've been looking for. If we're gonna do something, we can't wait until it heals up. Somebody has to see this!"

Robbie said. "Let's go back to the fort and figure something out."

The two made their way back and crawled in. They sat in silence, contemplating their plight. They both knew that they had an opportunity to do something and they had to do it right and they had to do it quickly. They knew that in a matter of days, the evidence would quickly disappear in the healing process.

One by one, Robbie placed ideas on the table and, just as quickly, Danny would shoot them down. First, Robbie said that he could show his own parents. Surely, they'd understand. Danny argued that it was too risky. How could they be sure that Robbie's parents wouldn't just call Danny's parents?

That would put them right back at square one. Robbie then suggested that they go to the police. Danny reminded Robbie of the phone call to the police, the night that Louise went to the hospital. The police wouldn't listen while it was happening, so why would they listen after it happened?

"Maybe I should just leave to another town," Danny said, the futility of his situation settling in.

"No, you can't do that. What about Mark and Louise?"

"I know, but I can't think of anything else to do."

"We have to think of somebody who'll listen," Robbie pursued, not ready to give up the fight that easily.

"I don't know of anyone."

"Danny, there's got to be someone we can tell. Don't you have any adult friends who'll listen?"

"No."

"What about one of our teachers?" Robbie asked.

Firmly, Danny said, "I don't trust teachers."

"Okay. How about a grandmother or grandfather?"

"I have a grandma, but I doubt that she'd believe me. Besides, she lives too far away, in Detroit."

"Hmmm," Robbie said, contemplating.

"See what I mean?"

"How about babysitters?" Robbie offered. "Don't you guys stay with one when your parents go on vacation?"

"They barely ever go on vacation."

"Oh. Well, how about..?"

Danny interrupted, "Wait a second!"

"What?"

"A babysitter! There is one that my parents always choose. Two years ago, when my parents went to Europe, we stayed with this really nice lady named Mrs. Thill. I don't know if she would work or not, but I just got to thinking that she likes us. She might listen, I'll bet on it!"

The boys discussed the pros and cons of telling her. Danny had known her before the problems had gotten as severe as they did. What he did remember, clearly, was that she had liked the kids. He remembered wishing that he had parents who were like Mr. and Mrs. Thill instead of who he had gotten stuck with. Danny was starting to think that she might be his best shot at resolving his predicament.

"No guts, no glory," Robbie stated.

"I've heard that before."

It was resolved. They were both going to make the trip across town to Mrs. Thill's house. Robbie left Danny in the fort while he ran home to ask permission from his mom if he could go out and play for a while. A short time later, he returned, knowing that his mother wouldn't go out looking for him. They both left, on foot, to Mrs. Thill's.

It took the better part of the afternoon to get within a few blocks of where she lived, since they had to minimize their risk by using all side streets to get there. Suddenly, Danny suffered a case of cold feet.

"I can't do it," he said firmly.

"You have to, Danny."

"I don't have to do anything," Danny said adamantly.

"Fine, Danny," Robbie said, not hiding his irritation. "Why don't you go back home so that your parents can continue beating the shit out of you over and over again, until you're dead? If you don't want to grow up and be a man about it, then there's nothing else that I can do," Robbie said, heatedly.

"I'm scared, that's all."

"I'm as scared as you are. I don't even know why you're still alive. If I were in your shoes, I don't know what I would have done. All I know is that I'm lucky to have gotten the parents that I did," Robbie said. He took Danny by the shoulders. "The only way that we're going to have a chance for you to live with me is for us to do something about it. We've got to take the first step and we have to be strong about it. You've gotta stand up for your rights!"

"I know, Robbie. But, it's easier said than done."

"Listen to me," Robbie continued. "What has happened to you is wrong. I'm sure it is. A family isn't supposed to be like your family. All kids screw up once in a while. That's the point of being a kid. But, you're not supposed to end up in the hospital for it. The right people have to know about this! You're in control and you're strong. You're stuck with the job of helping your brother and sister, too. If you don't do something, what's going to happen to them? You told me that yourself! You need to find the right people through Mrs. Thill."

"I'll never find the right people," Danny said pessimistically.

"Maybe not, Danny. But we have to try."

"I know."

Robbie reached into his pocket and dug for his house key. He pulled it out and took it off the ring, handing Danny a white rabbit's foot.

"Here," he said. "This always brought me good luck. I think that you need it more than I do."

Danny took it and rubbed the soft fur beneath his fingers. "Thanks,

Robbie. First the hat and now this?"

"You've been the best friend that a kid could ask for, you know? You'll always have me as a friend," he said, looking toward the ground. Danny thought that he looked like he was going to cry.

"You'll always have me as a friend, too," Danny said.

The two boys gave each other a hug, something that Danny had rarely done with anyone. Robbie shook his friend's hand and wished him the best of luck. He turned around and began his walk home.

Danny watched his figure grow smaller and smaller in the distance, all the while, rubbing the rabbit's foot between his fingers. When Robbie was out of sight, Danny felt a loneliness that seemed to rip into the deepest part of his heart. He had no choices left. He had to see Mrs. Thill, alone.

Butterflies churned in his stomach as he walked the final block to her house. His palms were sweating as he made his way up her cement steps. He rang the doorbell, pausing momentarily, making sure that he knew what he was doing. His head and his back ached and throbbed. He could either be walking into a new life of freedom or he could be headed straight back to the unwelcome arms of his parents. If the latter were the case, those arms would kill him next time.

As he waited for someone to answer the door, he rubbed the rabbit's foot furiously.

He was scared. It was now or never.

30

EYES OF THE WORLD

The next two days were spent in the tediousness and monotony of driving. Although Blossom was doing her best to keep up with the time schedule, her age and wear was beginning to show. The first thing that Dan noticed, as they were leaving Kincaid Lake, is that she was having problems going into first gear. Considering their money situation, this wasn't good news. To Dan's best calculations, they would have a little less than one hundred dollars in their pockets after reaching Sarasota, Florida. So, if this was a major transmission problem, they were in trouble, as if they weren't in trouble already. The best that Dan could hope for was to ride it out and hope for the best, keeping their stops as minimal as possible.

Then, the lighter went out. Normally, this wouldn't be a big deal except that Dan smoked a good pack a day in normal life but, while driving, this increased to an easy two packs a day. This inconvenience left him searching for his lighter at the worst of moments. He learned quickly that it didn't pay to be looking for a lighter while a big rig was blowing by them or while going through construction zones. If he was particularly annoyed with trying to find a lighter, he'd call Blossom a lighter-eater and somehow, the lighter would show up.

They took I-23 down to where it hooked up with 1-68 and got on Paris Pike just outside of Lexington. The two of them saw loads of Highway Patrol cars and, fortunately, nobody gave them a second look. Once they got back on I-75, Dan figured it would be smooth sailing from there. It was for a couple of hours. Then, the flatlands turned into slow rolling hills that eventually increased their grade upwards. They were headed through the Daniel Boone National Forest. As the elevation increased, so, too, did the vast array of colors. The higher points on the mountains showed that fall was around the comer. It concerned Dan because that meant that snow would be on the way soon, something he didn't want to struggle through with Blossom's first gear acting up the way it was.

"Don't you play anything else besides "The Grateful Dead?" asked Diana after a particularly long stretch of silence. After their recent experiences with the resurging of the past, neither one had much to say, lost in their own worlds.

"You don't like them?" Dan asked in return.

"Well, it's all I've heard for the last three days. Where did you get all these tapes?"

"Trading, mostly. I've traded with people that I've met at Dead shows, or met in head shops and, friends within that circle. To be honest, five hundred tapes is nothing in the scheme of it all. By my best estimate, there are probably five to six thousand tapes out there that I don't have."

"You've got to be kidding me. What's the fascination with it?"

"It feeds my compulsive personality," Dan said with a smile. "The band performed over three hundred and fifty songs on a regular basis. You never knew what they were going to play, how they were going to play it and when the next time was going to be. I mean, think about it. They never repeated the same show twice, nor did they do the same song in the same way twice. Compound that with thirty years of bootlegs, I've got a very entertaining hobby. I know it sounds crazy but...they were crazy times. Besides, no other band ever reached the levels they did as far as durability and uniqueness. And, well, it takes me away and makes me smile."

"I still think it's nuts," Diana said, shaking her head.

"Do you want to channel surf on the radio?"

"What? You're actually going to let me play with the radio. The next thing you know, you might even consider letting me drive!"

"You're upset, aren't you?"

"I'm not upset, I'm just getting tired of sitting here. You're getting tired, too and I can see it. How about letting us switch off once in awhile?"

"No problem," Dan said. "Right after we get out of the mountains."

"Fine, when we get to the easy stuff, right?" Diana said, not hiding her dissatisfaction.

"Okay. Okay. At the next rest stop, you take the wheel. You're right and I could use the rest. Do you want to alternate in six hour shifts?"

"How about five hour shifts?" Diana asked.

"Well, the reason that I said six hour shifts is because it equals both sides of four ninety minute tapes. It'll prevent me from clock watching. You can play the radio all you want when you're driving," Dan offered.

"Oh, gee, thanks," Diana said.

When it was her turn to drive, though, she rode the radio waves to Marty Robbins' *El Paso*, Bob Dylan's *It Takes a Lot to Laugh, A Train to Cry*, Bonnie Dobson's *Morning Dew*, Chuck Berry's *Johnny B. Goode*, Buddy Holly's *Not Fade Away*, Muddy Waters' *Smokestack Lightning*, and Joan Baez singing a live version of *Fennario*. At one point in time, she couldn't help laughing when she ran into David Gans doing his weekly radio show, on none other than, The Grateful Dead Hour. She appeased Dan's wishes by leaving it on, featuring a January 22, 1968 show in Seattle, Washington.

So, for the next two days, they power drove in six-hour shifts. They crossed through the rest of Kentucky, through Tennessee and through the interminably long stretch of Georgia. On September 18, they finally crossed the border into Florida, facing another four hours before they reached Sarasota. The air was hot and sticky and Blossom's temperature gauge was beginning to show the same thing. Dan wasn't happy with having something else to worry about. For a time, he was wondering if they were ever going to make it there.

As soon as they reached Gainesville, they pulled off in Paynes Prairie State Preserve and shut Blossom down for the night. That's when her sliding door latch decided it didn't want to work well, anymore. So, the only way that one could close the door was to warm up and give it a mighty push so that it would catch. Sometimes it would, other times, the door would bounce back, the latch unyielding. In essence, it, too, had become a pain in the ass.

The next morning, they didn't leave the park until almost 11:00 in the morning. They were too exhausted to leave any earlier. Besides, their brief visit with a bird-ravaged park was a nice respite from being on the run.

"How long before we get to Sarasota, do you think?" Diana asked while they were packing up.

"Three hours, give or take," Dan said as he was doing a walk around the bus. It was a ritual. Religiously, every time they prepared to go anywhere,

Dan would take a cursory inspection of the exterior of Blossom, checking things like the tires, underneath for leaks and so on. Yes, it was just like doing a pre-flight inspection of an airplane. To Dan, it relieved impending stress.

"Well, I'm thinking that this uncle of yours might be a little more responsive if we dress appropriately."

"Meaning?"

"Well, the obvious," Diana said. "Is he going to talk to a couple of deadheads in tie-dyes or will he talk to a couple of normally dressed people?"

"I'm not wearing a suit coat," Dan answered back. "It's too damn hot."

"I didn't say you had to wear a suit coat. But, you've got to shed the Jerry shirts for the time being."

So, they agreed. Once they got into the outskirts of Sarasota, they would change clothes and look respectable.

"And I'm not cutting my hair," Dan said.

For the next three hours, neither one had a lot to say. Dan thought about this uncle that he was about to meet. Not that there was a lot to think about. As far as he could recall, he believed that he had only met the man once, about twenty years prior. It was on a trip to Detroit not too long after Dan's family had moved back to Marquette. The purpose of the trip was a funeral for his grandfather, on his mother's side. Dan never liked to think about that trip. It was the only funeral that he had ever been to.

He remembered the wake on the night before. His grandfather had been dressed in a conservative pin striped suit with his glasses perched upon his nose. He remembered wondering why anyone would want to wear their glasses in their casket. He was kneeling in front of the casket. He looked around him to see if anyone was looking and, seeing that he was safe, reached over and touched the waxed and hardened skin. He remembered jumping at the feel of him, as if he had just been bitten. It was about then that the surprise and fearfulness of death had hit him, causing him to break out in tears. He wished and prayed that God would bring this man out of his sleep, but nothing happened. And then, he felt a firm hand over his shoulders.

"Are you all right, son?"

Danny looked up at the man. He had soft blond hair and a smooth face accented by dark, brown bushy eyebrows. "I think so."

"He'll be okay. He's with God now. As a matter of fact, I bet he's looking down at us right now."

"How do you know that he went to heaven?" Danny asked.

"Because I know. He was a good man. All good men go to heaven."

"Why is he wearing his glasses?"

"Because nobody would recognize him without his glasses. Did you ever see him without his glasses?"

"Sure," Danny said. "Mostly in the morning. Or, before we went to bed."

"Well, most people didn't see him that way. He was a very public man. I bet you never saw him without his glasses on when he left his home, did you?"

"Well, no," Danny said.

The two of them stayed kneeling in front of the casket for another five minutes. Every once in awhile, Danny would look over at the man next to him, wondering who he was.

"Name's Uncle Harold," he said, as if reading Danny's mind.

"Mine's Danny."

"Pleased to meet you, son."

The funeral was the next day at St. Mary's Holy Cross. Danny only got a glimpse of him once, just outside the cathedral. He was busy organizing the occupants of one limousine after another for the upcoming three-mile procession through Detroit to the cemetery. Danny had never seen so many limousines in his life. There must have been thirty or forty black Cadillacs lined up as far he could see. Momma got to ride in a limousine, but Danny and Daddy had to follow in their own Cadillac. Daddy wasn't part of the immediate family.

And that was all that Dan could remember of his Uncle Harold.

Meanwhile, Diana stared out the window, lost in thought. She thought about her husband for awhile. She wondered what had made him have an affair in the first place. Part of her knew that it was the ennui of marriage that can sometimes settle in. On the other hand, she found herself blaming her career. If she had paid him a little more attention, maybe he wouldn't have gone off with some floozy. If she weren't so headstrong about everything she did, including her psychiatry, maybe the marriage would have worked. Somewhere deep inside, she hurt. It was only natural and she knew that. But, the pain didn't want to go away.

She looked over at Dan who was intent in his driving. She admired him in a lot of ways. The thing that she found the most comforting was the fact that he didn't seem to stress over what surely would have stressed anyone else. The coolness with which he had handled Blossom; the way he had spoken with Derry only an hour after being shot at. Then, there were both of their childhoods, surprisingly parallel in the depth of their injuries. As a matter of fact, she was starting to see him as one of the sanest people that she had ever met, but a murderer? Her doubts grew with each passing moment.

To be honest, though, she really wasn't into this Grateful Dead thing. Then, she smiled upon hearing some words in, *Crazy Fingers: 'Gone are the days that we stopped to decide, where we should go, we just ride. Gone are the broken eyes we saw through in dreams, gone both dream and lie.'* She couldn't help thinking that the tune was right on the money.

Before they knew it, they were exiting 1-75 into Sarasota. Dan pulled Blossom into a Circle K and filled her up. While he was fueling, Diana used the opportunity to change back into her old clothes, something she had looked forward to for a long time. She was surprised that once she was dressed, she was not as comfortable as she thought she would be. The most noticeable difference was in her feet. Whereas the Birkenstocks, with their sandal design, allowed air and freedom, her pumps felt tight, constricting and awkward. The same thing applied to her clothes. The loose fitting dresses were comfortable to walk around in while even the buttons on her blouse seemed to fit too tightly. One thing for sure, she wouldn't say a word about that to Dan.

"Well," Dan said, after they were back on the road, "we have ninety dollars left. I don't think that that's going to get us very far."

"I don't know if I like the sound of this," Diana said. "What are we going to do?"

"Wing it," he said casually. "First things first, though. We'll deal with that issue after we deal with this uncle. Don't sweat it. We'll make it. I promise."

Diana tried to take faith in his words.

The address that they were looking for was in Gulf Pine Circle, a wealthy retirement community and country club, located on the Gulf of Mexico, just north of Siesta Key. On one side, sprawling homes bordered the white sand beach while, in the center; homes bordered an 18-hole golf course. Upon entering the gated, security complex, Dan was glad that they had changed clothes. The guard gave Blossom a couple of funny looks before he hesitantly let them in. Dan was sure that the man had second thoughts when he saw Blossom jump into second gear and speed off.

Dan parked Blossom about two addresses down from where they were headed. She looked strange in a neighborhood that was occupied by Cadillacs and Lincolns, with an occasional Mercedes to break the mode. If there was a neighborhood watch program in the area, he was sure that the phones would be buzzing over the VW bus.

"So, how do I explain you?" Dan asked. They were walking toward his relative's house, marked by two black porcelain sentinels standing out front, lamps in hand, guards of the southern rich of the past.

"I could say that I'm your sister," Diana offered. "Or, if you're uncomfortable with it, I could wait in the car."

"No, I don't think that either is a good idea," Dan said. "First of all, they might know who Louise is, which is our purpose in this and, second of all, I'd rather have you with me. But, not as my psychiatrist." He looked at her left hand. A rather large diamond adorned her finger. "How would you feel about being my wife?"

"Nice proposal," Diana said, a small grin on her face.

"Just for the moment," Dan said, surprisingly quickly.

"Well, I think that I could go along with it. No funny stuff, though."

It was nice for both of them to allow a little light-heartedness enter their conversation.

They walked up the semi-circular driveway in silence. Dan looked at the sprawling estate with awe. It would have been his father's dream to retire in such a community. But, life deals its cards and those were dreams that were lost in a grave a long time ago. The hum of air conditioners could be heard like the consistent sounds of Floridian birds in the hot and grueling rays of the sun. The home looked surprisingly cool with its soft white and gray tones accented by a freshly cut lawn.

For some reason, Dan's hands started shaking, just as he knocked on the door of an uncle that he hadn't seen in twenty years. A warm sweat broke out on his forehead.

"Yes?" a Mexican lady asked, cracking open the door only enough to see outside.

"We're here to see a gentleman by the name of Harold," Dan said. "Uh, we're relatives."

"One moment, Senor," she answered, pushing the door closed.

A minute later, a short, blue-haired lady opened the door again. Wariness and suspicion were prevalent in her voice. "May I ask who's calling?"

"My name's Dan Wilcox and this is my, uh, wife," Dan said, trying to keep his nervousness at bay. "I'm a nephew. I was wondering if we might spend a few moments with my uncle. It won't take long at all."

The lady appeared to scrutinize Dan and Diana before opening the door wider. She raised her finger, as if she was grasping a long lost memory.

"Are you the son of Mary Wilcox?"

"Well, yes," Dan said.

"Wait a minute. Didn't you become a journalist or something like that?"

"I'm a mystery writer," Dan said, a little surprised that she knew of him at all.

"Well, I'll be!" she said with a smile. "Come on in out of the heat, please!" She hurriedly pushed the door closed behind him. "Harold! Harold! We have a surprise!" She quickly lead them to the living room, adorned with a cool, plush beige carpet and matching white, nouveau furniture, stylish about ten or fifteen years prior.

Amidst their surprise at being welcomed warmly, they heard a resonant hum as it came around the comer. There was Uncle Harold, looking completely different than the way Dan had remembered him from so many years before. Not only was he in a modern, motorized wheelchair, his blond hair had virtually disappeared leaving only the bushy eyebrows as a reminder of who he once was. He maneuvered his scooter up to where Dan was and extended a warm handshake.

"My God," he said slowly. "Danny?"

"Well, I prefer Dan, actually. It's good to meet you again, Uncle Harold," Dan said, the words sounding strange coming out of his mouth.

"Maggie," he said to his wife. "Get these folks some refreshments, will you? They look tired from the heat."

Maggie looked at both of them, surprise still glued to her face. "If you only knew," she said. Suddenly, she hurried off in the direction of the kitchen.

Dan watched her disappear, thinking about her comment. "If we only knew what?"

"Well, son. I don't know how to put this but..."

"What?" Diana asked, curiosity getting the best of her.

"Well, we thought that you had died years ago. My sister said that..." his voice faltering. "Well, she said that you had passed away in a car accident."

Dan took the words like a stab. It seemed that every time that he turned around, he was learning about a mother who was attacking him, even from her grave. Dan was at a loss for what to say.

"Look, I'm sorry," said Harold. "You have to understand that we didn't know any better. I hope there's no offense taken."

"No, actually," Dan said slowly.

Moments later, the maid hurried in with ice teas for all of them, silver spoons adorning the glasses. Maggie followed behind her and walked up to Dan.

"Did you tell them, Harold?" she asked, never taking her eyes off of Dan.

"Yes, dear."

"I thought that I was looking at a ghost for a moment. I mean, we didn't have any reason to believe otherwise," she said, a nervous flair at the edge of her voice. "After all these years? It's Harold's sister. We've spent many an evening talking about her. And we didn't believe her, if you want to know the truth. But, I'll tell you this. When we weren't asked to go to the funeral, I told Harold that there was something fishy going on. We knew it, didn't we Harold?"

"Well, let's say that we just suspected something. Really, if you think about it, how could you say something like that about someone? I have half a mind to call her right now," Harold said angrily.

Dan looked at Diana and then put his head down. "I've got some equally bad news for you, too."

"What is it?" Harold asked, concerned.

"Your sister passed away a number of weeks ago. She was buried in Marquette."

Maggie hurried over to Harold and put her hand on his shoulder. "How did it happen?" she asked.

"She was murdered," Dan said quietly.

"My God," Harold said. The two of them sat quietly for a moment, taking in the news.

"Are you okay, Harold?" his wife asked.

Harold lightly stepped on the accelerator of his wheelchair and buzzed across the carpet toward the living room window. Maggie and the others watched silently as all the sound appeared to have been sucked from the room.

Diana looked at Dan, as if to obtain permission to step in. Dan nodded his head. She walked over to Harold. "We need your help. Anything that you can tell us about her would help greatly."

"You know," Harold began slowly, his voice softened, "we were close at one time, before she got married to that doctor. But, that was thirty some odd years ago. A lot of time has drifted away since. Year after year blended into decades. She was unreachable. I don't know if it was her husband or the anger within herself."

"Why do you suspect her husband?" Diana asked.

"I'm not sure that suspected is quite the right word," he said. "You see, we all looked at him as a sort of black sheep in the family. He was always bucking the system. There's nothing wrong with being a doctor, mind you, but we had created a position for him. Our family knew his family. He came from a family where his father had been a foreman on the assembly line for General Motors. When he and Mary began courting seriously, we thought it only proper to offer him a position with the company. Instead of being grateful for the offer, he adamantly refused."

"What kind of position," Dan asked, his curiosity aroused.

Harold turned around in his chair. "Do you know who your grandfather was?"

"As far as I knew, he worked in the auto industry also."

"Oh, he worked there, all right. Let me show you something," said Harold. He buzzed off to another room and returned with a fairly large photograph album. He opened it and showed it to Dan.

Dan looked at the pictures, one by one, of a man who was much younger, a man that he didn't remember at all. The pictures were obviously from a time when Dan wasn't even born yet. The bulk of them were black and white from the late forties or early fifties. Some were grainy and some were clear. They all showed virtually the same idea, that this man was well respected in his field being the recipient of one award after another. In each, he smiled modestly, while holding a plaque for design, or mechanics and even sales, in later years. The company was Cadillac Corporation.

"Do you get the idea?" Harold asked after a time.

"He was obviously well respected."

"The man retired as Vice-President of Cadillac. Now, mind you, this was an accomplishment from the son of immigrant parents from Germany years before. He had achieved the proverbial American dream. He went from starving to being one of the most influential men in an industry that was growing by leaps and bounds. So, when he made it his business to bring your father into the industry, and your father turned it down, well, let's just say that we thought your father was the black sheep in the family."

"But he became a doctor," Dan said in defense. "Didn't he do what my grandfather did? He reached the American dream in his own way."

"Some would argue that," Harold said. "I believe that I remember a time when he went running from Detroit with his tail between his legs, virtually broke. Am I right?" Harold asked pointedly.

"Well, there were hard times," Dan said quietly.

"But, you see, he could have had a piece of the business. It did well for all of us. And, I believe he turned it down because of basic pride. Do you really believe that anyone wants to be a dentist?"

"An oral surgeon," Dan corrected.

"What difference does it make? The fact remains; he became a dentist in an attempt to show us up. Well, Grandfather had a daughter that he wanted taken care of. That was the reason the offer was made to begin with. Instead of going with the family's business, he decided to break from the family and no one ever forgot it," Harold said with a firm finality.

"Where does your sister fit into this?"

"Inside, I think she was, well," Harold said, struggling for the right word, "resentful. She could have had a life of luxury unsurpassed by few. Instead, she married him and was forced to struggle with his decision. So, over the years, it was as if she was embarrassed to speak with us. She knew what she could have had. But, we're devout Catholics and once you marry, it's for life. She had to live with that."

In those few thoughts, Dan thought he was beginning to understand something that he had been quite unaware of until that moment. He understood the long line of Cadillac limousines at his grandfather's funeral. He also understood his father's drive and obsession to prove, not only to himself, but also to his wife and her family, that he could reach what was called the American dream. But, in that obsession, he had gotten lost. Dan knew that his father knew what he had to live up to and it was virtually insurmountable. His mother, on the other hand, was forced to live within the confines of a lifestyle that wasn't easy to obtain and was difficult to maintain. During all that time, they had to ignore the thought that it could have been easy, very easy.

"How did it make you feel?" Diana asked of Harold.

"Sad, I think. We knew what was going on. I mean that you couldn't hide the struggle on your faces, when you were kids. You didn't look happy and content. There was stress in that family, to be sure. But, what could we do in the face of your father's determination?"

"Do you know what was going on with the kids?"

"Mary kept her private life to herself," Harold said as he took a drink from his iced tea. He set it down on a crystal coaster on the coffee table while the maid came around and refilled everyone's drink. "It was as if she wouldn't let us in, any of us. I'm not sure what happened to all of you but, again, I suspect it wasn't good."

"It wasn't," Dan interjected.

"Well, if it's any consolation, we're sorry. But our hands were tied. Consider your father and his stubbornness, what could we do? The best we could was to keep our noses out of where it didn't belong. Grandfather told us that years ago and that's how he got to where he was. Keep your nose to the grindstone and worry about your own life and your own family. Anything else would have been a waste of energy," Harold said, steadfast in his opinions.

"Didn't you wonder what happened to us?" Dan asked earnestly.

Maggie stepped in. "Of course we wondered. But, as Harold said, it wasn't our business. Your father and mother made their own decisions and their own failures. She didn't want our help when it was offered. Besides..." she said, her voice trailing.

"Besides what?"

"There was something that happened in your household that, well, they were embarrassed about. We had the feeling that you were in jail. Whether it was from truancy or what, they would never speak about it. I asked her after your father's funeral and she stood her ground, refusing to talk about it. We got the feeling that you kids were troublemakers. Am I right?"

Dan faltered. "There was trouble..." He struggled to grasp something that bordered the edge of his memory, but it was elusive in surfacing.

"Are you okay?" Maggie asked.

"Yes, I am. Just thinking. Let me ask you, how was my father when he died?"

"You weren't at his funeral, were you?"

"No," Dan said, his voice greatly subdued. "I didn't know about it."

"I'm sorry," Harold said.

"The best that I can say," Maggie said, "is that he died a very bitter man."

Diana walked up and put her hand on Dan's shoulder, a gesture of comfort and support.

"I have one more question," Dan said.

"Sure," Harold answered.

"I have a sister that I've lost contact with and I wonder if you could help us out."

"You're referring to Louise?" Maggie asked.

"Yes."

"Of what I remember, she was the most troubled of you children. Unfortunately, we don't know what's become of her. That's not to say that we didn't wonder. We wondered about all of you over the years. We truly did," said Maggie, earnest in her words. "But, so many years have gone past. And, the way that your parents kept to themselves, we had to put our faith in God that you were all right. She was introverted and shy, the last time we saw her. That would have been in the late 70's or early 80's. After that, we lost track."

Dan wasn't pleased. It was appearing that they had hit another dead end as to finding her whereabouts.

"Harold, wait a moment. Let's call Stacey," Maggie interjected. Stacey was their daughter, a cousin that Dan vaguely remembered as his first love, when he was about eight years old, until he found out that one can't marry your first cousin. "She seems to know a little more about where some of the family has gone. She's loves gossiping," she said toward Dan.

Maggie disappeared to find the phone. Dan casually looked at the coffee table and noticed a hardbound edition book lying there, it's gold embossed lettering standing out remarkably loud, *Profiles In Courage*. It had been years since he had seen that book, a stern reminder of his father, a man lost in his pursuit of courage.

Moments later, Maggie walked in, speaking on the cordless. Her movements and tone of voice were erratic and excited with a tinge of nervousness. "You're not serious, are you? Well, no, we haven't heard from a detective, yet."

Harold looked up from his scooter, question marks in his eyes.

"You think that your phones are tapped? Stacey, calm down. I'm sure that there's a reasonable explanation for this. Have you called your phone company? Maybe there's some sort of malfunction in your phone lines," Maggie said, obviously trying to calm a distraught woman on the other end.

Dan looked at Diana, slightly pale.

"So, you're saying that this detective, Robinson did you say, is looking for Dan Wilcox?"

Harold looked at Dan, wondering what was up, suspicion crossing his face. Dan looked toward the ground, unable to keep eye contact.

"Well, no, we haven't seen him, yet," Maggie said, staring at Dan and Diana. "Armed and dangerous? Are you sure that that's what he said?"

It was obvious that the answer was in the affirmative.

"Of course I'll call you if I hear anything. Please, don't worry, Stacey. I'm sure that there's a logical explanation for this. Look, the reason we called is, we happened to be wondering if you knew where his sister is. Her name's Louise..."

Harold didn't look pleased at all.

"So, she is alive and the detective knows where she is?"

Dan looked up. Maybe, just maybe...

"Oh, but she's not a suspect, anymore? Well, where is she? Are you sure that you don't know? Of course, we'll call you if we hear anything about Dan...No, no, we won't let him in. We'll call the police the moment that we see him...Yes, we'll be careful. Look, Stacey, may I call you later? Harold is calling me..."

The moment that Maggie hung up the phone, the tone in the room had completely changed from white to black. All Dan could say was, "I'm sorry. It's not how it looks."

Harold moved his scooter toward the door and opened it. "I don't think that you should be here any longer than you have to."

"We're sorry, too," Maggie said.

"I don't know what you have going on, son, but be grateful that we're not calling the police," Harold said, steadfastly holding the door. "This is all we have left in the world and we can't risk becoming a party to whatever you have up your sleeve. If you want to know the truth, I don't believe that you're capable of murder. On the other hand, you deceived us. You knew that you were a suspect all along, didn't you?"

"Yes," Dan said, "but I had nothing to do with it."

"She was my sister," Harold said. "If I find out any different, I will have you put away. You know that I don't have any other choice. Until then, do what you have to do and thank the Lord that we're giving you this chance."

Dan and Diana needed no more coercing. They walked out.

"We're sorry," Maggie said again, pressing the door closed.

The two of them walked back toward Blossom, shaking their heads. "I can't believe that that just happened," Diana said.

"No shit," Dan said. "But, we did learn a few things. My question is, why isn't Louise a suspect?"

"Well, she's alive," said Diana. "That's a start. Do you think we should call the detective?"

"No, we can't risk his tracing our call. But, there's no question about it. We have to find Louise. One way or another, she fits into this story. I can feel it," Dan said with determination.

"I feel the same thing," Diana said.

The two of them hopped into Blossom, wounded by a simple twist of fate. The tinge of nervousness was back, unrelenting in its silence. They both felt that they were being watched from unseen corners of the world and they didn't like it. The worst part was they knew that they were victims of something greater than themselves. But, it was beginning to feel like they had nowhere to run.

Dan mentioned that they should change before they hit the road again.

Diana agreed, seeing the importance of their outfits, a blanket of safety in another identity. But, she knew without saying anything out loud, that they were into something far deeper than she imagined. This Robinson fellow, a pillar of the law, had become the unseen enemy in a matter of minutes and she didn't like the feeling of claustrophobia that seemed to encompass them.

They hit the road out of Gulf Pines Circle, with a strengthening *Estimated Prophet* playing out of the tape deck, *"My time comin' any day, don't worry about me, no. It's gonna be just like they say, them voices tell me so. Seems so long I felt this way, and time's sure passing slow..."*

Dan pulled out of the wealthy suburb, Blossom's first gear screaming agonizingly. He thought about the measly ninety dollars in his pocket, at a complete loss as to where they were going. The fear was back and they were running out of time and contacts and he knew it.

And then, the worst thing that they could have wished, happened. It was in a stunning and slow motion like clarity. Although he had seen and felt fear before, it still scared the living shit out of him. He saw that same fear in the face of Diana as they pulled Blossom over to the side of the road. He didn't have a choice and he knew it. Blossom just didn't have the engine power to run. Facts were facts.

He and Diana thought about that and a host of other things as they watched the blue and red lights twinkle in their rear-view mirror. The officers stepped out of the police car; stern looks upon their faces, as they began their walk up to the two fugitives from the law...

31

FEEL LIKE A STRANGER

"Danny?"

"Hi, Mrs. Thill."

"What in the world are you doing here?"

"I just thought that I'd come by and say, 'Hi'."

"Well, come on in."

Mrs. Thill was just as Danny had remembered her. She was a large woman with light brown hair, which she usually left curled in a bun over her head. Whoever said that fat people were jolly, was right in Danny's eyes. Mrs. Thill was the epitome of that and more, being a loving and tender person. It was exactly why Danny had chosen her as his last resort. During the times that the kids had stayed there, Mrs. Thill was never seen without a smile on her face, being the exact opposite of who Momma was. She also served the best food that Danny had ever tasted, next to Grandma's, of course. No wonder that Danny wished that she had been his real mother "Would you care for something to eat?" Mrs. Thill asked, the first thing that she always asked the kids when they were there for a stay, as if food was as standard as saying, hello.

"Sure," Danny said, happy with the stall for time. As much as he wanted to be comfortable with her, he found it difficult to quell the butterflies in his stomach. There was so much he had to say, but he didn't know how or when to start.

Moments later, Danny had a plate of homemade chocolate chip cookies in front of him, complemented with an ice cold pitcher of lemonade.

"I thought that this might do the trick," Mrs. Thill said with a smile. "It's so damn hot out there that the heat is enough to drive a crazy man crazier."

"Thank you, Mrs. Thill," Danny said as he hungrily bit into a cookie. It felt like he hadn't eaten in years. The last thing that he had had was a bowl of puffed wheat for breakfast, which was akin to eating air, and his stomach seemed to remember that.

After Danny had voraciously munched down about eight cookies, Mrs.

Thill, watching him with praise, asked what brought him to her house.

"Ah, nothing. I just wanted to visit."

"Danny. I know children, and they don't walk all the way across town just to visit. Or, did you take the bus?"

"I walked," Danny said.

"So, what's wrong?" Mrs. Thill asked perceptively.

"Nothing. Really," Danny answered. He had lost his nerve in telling her and he didn't know why. What did he have to be afraid of? His mind answered back just as quickly as the question had arisen. Remember Father Regan? She would love his mother's house and birds, just like he had.

"Is something wrong at home?"

"Well, um, not really."

"Danny? Tell me."

"I don't know what to tell you."

"I can see that there's something on your mind. Don't be afraid.

"I am afraid," Danny admitted.

"Why don't you start wherever you want and I'll listen. Now, what is it?"

"I ran away."

"Oh, no," Mrs. Thill said, leaning forward. A look of concern and worry settled on her face. "Why?"

"Well..."

And then he talked. He spit everything out, beginning with the belt and proceeding through his previous adventures with running away and why he had run away. He told, with increasing intensity, of how everything had escalated into something that he couldn't hope to control, anymore. He told of Mark's running away, and of Louise's visit to the hospital. He even told her of his empty promise to Mark and how he didn't think that he could have kept such a promise.

Mrs. Thill was obviously shaken at his tale. "And what made you run away today?"

"Because my mother lost her temper with me, the worst that I've ever seen.

Well, next to what happened to my sister. Then," said Danny, trying to catch up with his breath, "after she was done with me, she said that Daddy was going to kill me when he got home! I'm scared because I know that she was serious. So, I had to run away," Danny said emphatically. "Mrs. Thill? We have to do something!"

"It's okay, Danny," she said. "Sometimes parents will get a little upset with their children. When we warn you to be afraid of your father coming home, it's only a figure of speech. It doesn't mean that it's really going to happen. Raising kids is a lot more difficult than it looks. You have to be more understanding," Mrs. Thill said, much to Danny's consternation and frustration. Evidently, she saw it on his face. "Look, Danny, I can talk to them and we can work all of this out. I've met your parents and I'm sure that they don't mean to hurt you. Lord knows, I've dealt with enough children to understand that much. Why don't we..."

Danny tried to interrupt her. "But, Mrs. Thill..."

"But, nothing, Danny. Look, I think that the best thing that we can do for you is to call your parents. You can talk to them over the telephone."

"Wait, Mrs. Thill..."

"Danny, this is for your own good. Don't worry," she said. "I know what I'm doing. They're probably worried sick over you right at this moment. What's your telephone number?"

"No, Mrs. Thill," Danny defiantly said. "I won't give it to you."

"Danny, please don't make this any more difficult than it already is," Mrs. Thill countered. It became obvious to her that Danny wasn't willing to cooperate with her. She picked up the Marquette telephone book and rifled quickly to the "W's".

Danny watched her, growing angrier by the second. He couldn't believe that she was doing the same thing to him as the others had done. Had he miscalculated? Was she like all the rest of them?

Feeling cornered and frightened, the first thing that was on his mind was that he needed to escape. It was time for him to leave.

Mrs. Thill picked up the rotary telephone and started dialing.

Suddenly, Danny jumped up in protest. He couldn't watch it happen. "No, Mrs. Thill!" he yelled. Without his realizing it, he jumped up and yanked the phone out of her hands. "You haven't listened to a word that I've said. Louise just went to the hospital! My parents are mad and there's something wrong with them. Nobody else's parents are like mine! Now, you want to send me back to them? No way, Mrs. Thill. I thought that you cared about me. I thought that you cared about kids!"

"I do, Danny."

"No, you don't! You're like everyone else!" Danny yelled with intensity that he didn't know he had inside of him. Then, in a role reversal, he mimicked what he had seen his father do to him so many times, "Oh, Danny reads too many books. Oh, Danny has such a wild imagination! Well, tell me, Mrs. Thill, did I get these from books? " Danny screamed.

Much to the shock and surprise of Mrs. Thill, Danny suddenly began tearing his clothing off, article by article, until he was standing in front of her in his underwear. Then, he turned around so that she could see his back. "Did I get this from a creative imagination?!"

He was trembling from head to foot in anger and determination. He knew that he had been taught to treat adults with respect. He had never so much as even raised his voice to an adult, at least not the way he had to a stunned Mrs. Thill. He felt slightly remorseful for yelling at her, a lady whom he truly cared about, but his anger had overtaken all of his senses. The adrenaline rushed through his body, marking a trail of frustration. He stood there and tried to calm down but his legs were shaking so badly that he could do nothing but remain silent.

Evidently, it worked because Mrs. Thill was walking around him, her hand cupped over her mouth. "Oh, my," he heard her say, faintly, as if her breath was gone.

As she looked him over, gingerly touching the fresh wounds, she asked him to explain the origin of each, as best as he could.

Carefully, Danny reiterated everything that had happened on that nightmarish morning.

"I'm so sorry for not listening to you," she said tenderly.

"I'm scared of them, Mrs. Thill. Nobody has ever believed me. The best that anyone can do is to keep sending me back. I'd rather kill myself than go back to them!" he said vehemently. "It's usually okay for a while and then everything starts all over again. You've got to help me! I don't know what to do, anymore!"

Mrs. Thill embraced him into her full chest as he let his tears flow. She held him tightly as he fell apart, although he was partly grateful that it appeared that he had an impact on her.

After he had calmed down significantly, her hands running through his hair, she told him to put his clothes back on. "I've got to make a phone call to work."

"Why?" he asked suspiciously, wondering if he was about to be tricked.

"I have to call my boss at work. Do you know what the Department of Social Services is?"

"No," Danny said, thinking that it sounded like a fancy name for the police department.

"We handle special cases like you. You aren't the only child to have suffered the things that you have," she explained carefully. "What has happened to you is very serious. You've convinced me that we have to do something. We want to help children like you."

"Are you going to send me back to my parents?"

"I don't think so, Danny. If we can prove that your parents have, in fact, abused you, which appears to be the case, then there's a good chance that we can get you into a foster home. Is that what you want?"

"Anything, Mrs. Thill," Danny said gratefully, relief in his voice. "Remember that my brother and sister are going through it, too. If I go anywhere, they have to go with me. If they stay there, they'll get killed by them! None of us should have to go back there. Ever!"

"Leave it up to me, Danny," Mrs. Thill said. "Let's see what we can do." She picked up the phone and called her work from memory.

"Hi, Charles," she said when she got the proper person on the line. "I've got a problem here. I've got a young man here by the name of Danny Wilcox, whom I've babysat for in the past. Ah, he's in a bit of trouble."

Danny looked on, praying that he was doing the right thing.

"No, no. He hasn't done anything wrong. He's run away from home and I believe that he's had reason to."

She squeezed Danny's shoulder in support.

"Yes, Charles, I'm serious. He's got marks all over him, the type that couldn't have been self-inflicted. I think that you had better take a serious look at him."

Danny wiped his hands on his pants.

"Yes, Charles. I'm quite aware of who he is. I also know that it's not going to be easy to file a six-fourteen against Dr. Wilcox but it has to be done and there's no other alternative. When you see him..."

Mrs. Thill stood up, as if she was emphasizing her point. "Charles, listen to me! I don't care if he's the son of the President of the United States! What has happened to this boy is wrong. This kid has been brutally beaten," she said emphatically in defense of Danny. She was pacing with the phone coil dangling behind her, an exasperated look on her face.

"No, Charles. We would not be liable. No one can sue an agency of the government so your fears are unfounded! You must give me the benefit of the doubt and see him. Rest assured, that once you do, you'll understand."

Mrs. Thill listened for a moment and appeared to calm down as a deal was struck.

"Thank you, Charles. And Danny thanks you ahead of time. We'll be down tomorrow afternoon."

She hung up the phone and looked at Danny, her hands on her hips.

"What's wrong?" Danny asked.

"Nothing, Danny. It just took a lot more work than I thought it would to convince him to, at least, take a look at you. It seems that your father extracted his wisdom teeth a number of years back. Can you beat that?"

"Everybody knows my father, Mrs. Thill. That's half my problem. Everyone thinks he's perfect."

"I gathered that," Mrs. Thill said supportively. "Anyway, here's what's going to happen. Tomorrow, you're coming down to my office. There are some people there who are going to look you over. As far as tonight is concerned, Charles is going to contact your parents and let them know that you're okay."

"Oh, no!" Danny said, a frightened look on his face.

"Whoa! Don't worry. He's not going to tell them where you are, if that's what you're worried about. I convinced him that you'd be in danger if you were returned home. At least I was able to get through to him that far. Legally, we have to tell them that much. We'll worry about the next step tomorrow, okay champ?"

"Please don't call me champ," Danny said. "My dad calls me that when he's upset at me."

"I'm sorry, Danny. Do you trust me, yet?"

"I think so, Mrs. Thill."

The rest of the night went without incident. Mrs. Thill made a feast for kings by cooking up a load of spaghetti covered with as much Italian sausage as he could eat. He watched The Three Stooges on television afterwards, curiously wondering why he was amused at their beat-em-up antics when he didn't find it anywhere near amusing at home. When he crawled into bed, he felt as if he had a new lease on life but wondered when it would end.

His dreams were filled with his parents. What if they caught him? What were they thinking now that he had gone so far?

There was many a time that he found himself tossing and turning, vivid dreams capturing his imagination with colors of hitting, smacking and hair pulling, a fate that his brother and sister were forced to reckon with. When he woke in the morning, he felt more exhausted than anything, especially with the anticipation of what he was going to face that day.

It was Danny's turn to speak now.

The day broke as overcast and dreary with a threat of rain as Danny and Mrs. Thill made their way to the Department of Social Services. It turned out a more harrowing day than Danny could have imagined with one counselor after another interrogating him relentlessly. Pictures were taken of each and every bruise. As they pursued their investigation, a tape player recorded Danny's explanations. He wondered, for a time, if they weren't trying to catch him in a lie. But, Danny's stories remained consistent, although he had repeated the stories so many times that he felt like he couldn't even think anymore.

"So, why are you doing this?" a nameless counselor asked, his jowls bouncing with the question.

"Because I don't ever want to go home again," Danny answered firmly.

"Well, don't you think that you and your parents could work things out?"

"No, we tried that," Danny answered. "The only thing that ever came out of this was more beatings. I was the one who had to see the counselor, not them. Now, ever since my sister went to the hospital, I'm afraid that things are going to get worse."

"What hospital did she have to go to?" the counselor asked, his pen dutifully transcribing every word into a notebook.

"Ah, the hospital on Spruce Street, near the high school."

"And what night was that?"

"About six weeks ago, on a Friday night, I think..."

And so, the interrogation and barrage of questions continued throughout the day, for three days in a row. Danny tirelessly answered each question, fulfilling his ultimate role as the protector, all in the hope that he would never have to live at home again.

After the third day of questioning, Mrs. Thill squeezed his shoulder supportively. "Well, Danny, it seems that the department believes you."

"Really?"

"Yes, really. Our counselors have been working overtime on this. They've talked to Father Regan, they talked to the doctor that worked on Louise and they've talked to your neighbors. We finally got some corroboration to your story."

"What's that mean?"

"It means that other people have stepped forward to back up your statements."

"You mean that I have proof?"

"It looks like it, Danny. People were pretty shocked with your allegations. Everyone seems to know your father and it was pretty hard for them to believe that you weren't lying. See, people expect child abuse to happen only in high-risk families, where alcohol and drugs are abused, and in families that are broken and poor. What you've shown is that it can happen anywhere, regardless of social stature. You should be proud of yourself."

"Yeah?" Danny said, greatly encouraged.

"It took a lot of courage to stand up for your brother and sister. It takes an adult to do that."

"So, what happens now?" Danny asked.

"Somehow, we have to get through to Louise and Mark. It appears that they won't talk to us."

"I don't understand why not," Danny said. He figured that they would gladly step forward, if Momma and Daddy weren't sitting there.

"Well, the problem is that your father has gotten himself a lawyer. He's claiming that you made all of this up. We're trying to work around the law but it's turning out to be pretty difficult to speak to them."

"You'll be able to do something about that, won't you?" Danny asked, feeling insecure about the situation.

"I think so, Danny. You have a lot of people on your side."

"So, are we coming back here for more questions tomorrow?"

"No, we aren't," Mrs. Thill answered.

"Then, what are we going to do?"

"We're going to court. You're going to be able to tell a judge and a jury exactly what you've told us. Do you think you can do that?"

"Yes," Danny answered, determination in his voice. "I know I can."

It was the moment of truth, finally.

32

DESOLATION ROW

Dan gripped the steering wheel, his palms sticky with sweat. "Shit. Shit, Shit!" he muttered as he watched the two police officers approach.

Diana was frozen with fright. "Stay calm, Dan. Stay calm; let's not over react.

"I don't even know why we were pulled over," he said with clenched teeth. "Remember who you are. And you're not a psychiatrist for the moment. Do you know what I mean, Althea?"

Diana was glad that he reminded her, although it served to only increase the tension that she felt. What if they were caught?

One officer approached Dan's side of the bus while the other warily approached the other side where Diana was. Each had one hand resting on their holsters, serving to frighten Dan and Diana even more.

Dan turned the stereo down to a low muffle.

"License and registration, please," the fair-haired officer said to Dan, two paces from his door.

"Sure, officer," Dan said as calmly as he could. "What'd we do wrong?" he asked as he carefully popped the glove compartment door open for his registration.

"We received a call about a suspicious vehicle in Gulf Pines Circle. You mind explaining what you were doing in there?"

"Sure," Dan said. "We were passing through and I've got an uncle who lives there." He immediately regretted divulging that information. What if the officer checked his sources? His license wouldn't correspond to who Uncle Harold thought he was. He handed the officer the required information, fighting the trembling in his fingers.

"You seem a little nervous," the officer said, never taking his eyes away from Dan's.

"Well, you know how it is, officer. We don't often get pulled over."

"Hmm. Would you mind stepping out of the vehicle? Slowly," the officer commanded, his hand still resting on his holster.

Dan looked nervously at Diana as he felt his bowels drop. He slowly opened the door and stepped out. "What's going on? We haven't done anything."

"Put your hands up and spread 'em," the officer said forcefully. He kicked Dan's ankles apart as he searched him.

"Officer," Dan said as politely as he could. "I'm not sure what this is about but..."

"Ron," the officer said to his partner. "Get her out, too. Search her."

"Gladly," his partner said.

Diana needed no prodding. For a moment, she wanted to voice her protest and then thought better of it. She got out and turned around, in exact replication of Dan. The officer briskly searched her.

"She's clean," he said.

"Before we look in your vehicle," the fair-haired officer said to Dan, "is there any stuff we should know about in there?"

"Stuff?" Dan asked. "Are you referring to drugs?"

"Oh? Are you telling me that you've got drugs in there?"

"No, officer. I'm just asking why you want to search the vehicle. You haven't even given us a good reason for pulling us over."

The officer looked at Derry's driver's license. He leaned forward toward Dan's ear. "Look, pal. You think we were born yesterday? I see the stickers on your car and I can see the clothes you're wearing. We don't like your sort around here. As a matter of fact, this community doesn't like hippies too much. So, you got a problem with that, you can explain it to a judge. Comprende!"

Dan knew that if he argued with the officer anymore, the officer would do anything to get them in jail. What kind of defense would he have if the officer said they were trying to resist arrest? Besides, he wondered about the risk of sitting in jail with an alias to his name.

"There's no problem here, officer. Feel free. But, there's nothing in there. We don't do drugs. We're clean. I swear it."

"Yeah? Well, we'll just see about that. Ron, watch'em both, I'm going to take a little look see."

Dan and Diana watched as this twenty-five year old representative of the law began scouring the interior of Blossom. He began by picking through the ashtray, then moved to the glove compartment and finally he stepped into the vehicle and began pulling up seat cushions and rifling through their luggage. He was none too polite about putting anything back, leaving everything disheveled and torn apart. He backed himself out of the bus, sweat on his forehead.

"What's up?" the other officer asked.

"Looks clean," he said. "Wait here, I'm going to run their licenses," he said, stalking away, obviously pissed that he hadn't found anything.

Dan did his best to keep his legs from shaking. A plethora of thoughts ran through his head. What if Derry did have a violation on his record, like a warrant for missing some minor court date? Even worse, what if Robinson, somehow, had figured out about the switch in I.D.'s? Or, what if Derry and Althea had turned their licenses in for new ones, leaving Dan and Diana with the appearance of using false ID's? To make matters humiliating, he watched one passing car after another gawk at their vehicle and the two deadhead detainee's standing outside. He knew what they were thinking, that they didn't belong in a rich affluent area.

Moments later, the officer walked back up. "You staying or going now that your business is done?" he asked, his intentions clear in his eyes.

"We were just leaving, officer. Like I said, we were only passing through."

"That's good to hear. Need I remind you, if we see you around here again, we don't need a lot of reason to pull you in for something. Have we made ourselves clear?"

"No problem," Dan said.

The officers handed back their ID's and watched them carefully as they got back into Blossom. Dan turned the key in the ignition and was grateful that she started right up. It appeared that Blossom didn't want to be there any longer, either. They sped off a second later, aiming for 1-75. It remained unsaid that they weren't pleased with their welcoming committee.

"What was that all about?" Diana asked.

"It's part of being a deadhead and having long hair," Dan said truthfully. "Thank God for Derry. I think that somebody upstairs is watching out for us. Now, my question is, what next?"

As they hopped on 1-75, Dan proceeded with the business of talking over their options. With everything that they had learned over the last few hours, there were a few things that presented them with problems. The first and foremost problem was their lack of funds. Blossom's tank was nearing a little less then half. With her next fill-up, this would leave about seventy dollars in their pockets which would barely get them out of Florida. So, money was priority number one.

Secondly, for the moment, they literally had no direction to go. This problem was compounded by the fact that they knew Robinson was searching for them, obviously playing some heavy tactics if he was attempting to tap the phones. Dan figured that going across state lines, that the phones weren't tapped but rather the calls were being traced. If that was the case, he could probably risk calling Mark. The way he would do that is through a ten minute phone card from a Circle K or 7-11. He would have to keep the call under a minute, if not thirty seconds. He was sure that Mark would sport him a few bucks.

Next, there was the problem with the location of his sister. Diana brought up the fact that with her being a doctor, she could probably slip into a hospital and get permission to sit down at a computer for a couple of hours. If Robinson was able to find Louise, then there was a chance that she could find her. She couldn't see that he was going to be all that bright, given some of his apparent strong-arm and desperate tactics. Dan liked the idea. Although it wasn't much to go on, there was a chance that it would work. The question was, where to start.

As they were flying up 1-75, making tracks from Sarasota as fast as they could, Dan looked at the map. They were tired and exhausted from the past five days and they needed some rest. They were getting slightly irritable with each other at the littlest of things and that wasn't good for keeping a clear head to face what they needed to do. Dan decided that they were headed toward Hillsborough State Park. It was just outside of Tampa and would only require another hour's drive to get there.

In an effort to kill time, Dan decided that what they needed was a good case of brainstorming. So, he went back as far as he could to the scene of the murder and tried to piece together what he already knew. What they knew, so far, was that his memory was inhibited by two factors. The first, and most likely irrecoverable, was that he was suffering from amnesia, from the moment that he was hit. The question remained, who hit him? Dan's memory of a woman at the scene led to the possibility that it was either her, the mystery woman, who hit him or his mother. But, because of the memory limitation, that didn't bar out the fact that someone else could have been there, also. But, trying as hard as he could, he couldn't remember anyone else at the site.

The other factor that played a role, that Diana emphasized as very possibly recoverable, was his case of Post Traumatic Stress Disorder, which was allowing small tidbits to come back; for instance his being called a looney-bird. It still remained as elusive a clue as before but Dan had a feeling that it was extremely important.

"The trick with the disorder," Diana said, "is not to push it. It must come back naturally. I'd like to hypnotize you but..."

"I know," Dan said, "I don't know what I saw. But, if worst comes to worst..."

"No, I still won't do it," Diana said. "It's too dangerous."

"All righty, then, tell me what you know about memory. How does it work? What enhances its ability to work? And, what's going to work for me?"

"The first thing that you should know is that memory is not an exact science by any means. We're dealing with theory here. In the center of your brain, is an area called the hippocampus. It's a seahorse shaped section. This is the area where new information is processed and then dispersed throughout the brain. It's thought that nouns and verbs are stored in separate parts of the brain just like plants and animals might be stored in another part of the brain. These connections, upon recall, are made through neurons," she said, feeling like she was rehearsing studies learned in school many years before. She continued steadfastly. "Now, once a connection between certain neurons are made over and over again, those memory surges become stronger. It's thought that a person who is well educated has stronger connections, thus better memory recall, because those neuron connections are constantly challenged. Hence, a more educated person loses their memory later in life than someone who's less educated. Now, we're speaking in the purest sense of memory. This bars such things as Alzheimer's disease and, what you've got, PTSD. Obviously, we haven't discovered exactly what causes some people to be inflicted with either."

"Now, why do you say that my memory is recoverable?" Dan asked as he flew by a station wagon loaded with a bunch of kids. One particularly daring kid flipped them the finger, unbeknownst to his parents.

"Well, past history. I'm not saying that all people who suffer from PTSD get their memory back but many do, sometimes partially and sometimes completely. It depends upon how strong they are mentally and it depends upon the severity of the incident that they've blocked. I hold to the theory that psychotherapy will unlock it because you are changing the routes between neurons by testing various sources of what you remember. Somewhere in there, you literally stumble upon the lost memory because the hippocampus has inadvertently placed it somewhere else inside your head."

"Keep going," Dan said. He was intrigued by the thought that the murder was truly back there somewhere.

"Well, there are five types of memory. You have your semantic memory, which is confined to the general meaning of basic words like "wedding" or "college." This memory is constantly filled until death and tends to be the words that you'll never forget. You've also got your remote memory, the type of memory that wins Trivial Pursuit games. It's unknown why some people retain nonsensical details better than others. Again, education is probably the biggest factor. But, this memory, you lose first," Diana said.

While Diana was talking, the first thing she noticed was that she felt like her skills were being honed again. She also realized that she did, in fact, enjoy her profession immensely. That immediately led her to feel that she might not have a career when they got out of this mess.

Dan's eyes remained glued to the road, pensive yet curiously recharged. They were going to get through this if it was the last thing he did, which, hopefully, wasn't too close to the truth.

"Another area of memory is called your working memory. Do you remember the last time that you shifted Blossom into third gear?"

"Of course," Dan said, "just after I shifted into second and before I shifted into fourth."

"And where were we?"

"Good point," he said.

"Exactly. This area of memory has to do with the day to day workings of functioning but is not important enough for the brain to store. It all depends upon an auto-pilot maneuver, so to speak. Your mind somehow deems what is important to save and what isn't. You aren't likely to remember a license plate number of a car in front of you even though you may have read it, unless there is something distinctive about it. Then, there's your implicit memory, which has to deal with never forgetting how to drive a car or ride a bike."

"But, where do I fall?"

"Let me finish," Diana said. "The fifth area of memory is called your episodic memory, which is the one that I'm most concerned with in your case. In a way, it's a cross-section between your working memory and the events that happen in your life. Can you make a fusion between both and, if you do, it's likely to be recoverable. For instance, you remember how to drive a car but you can't remember where you put your car keys. The loss of this memory can be attributed to age, a traumatic experience like you went through, or even just basic distractions. Too many charges are going through millions of neurons at the same time and you have a short circuit, so to speak."

"So, I've had a short circuit. How can I get it back?"

"My best suggestion would be relaxation and discussion. Again, it can't be forced."

"A lot of good that does me," Dan said. "We're running into the law, we have the law chasing us and you're telling me that relaxation is my best medicine? Beautiful," he said sarcastically. "As if I'll be able to relax. Damn it all to hell!"

"See?" Diana pointed out. "You can't get frustrated. Let it come naturally."

"Thank you, Doctor Powers," Dan said, dutifully well-spoken.

When they hit Tampa, Dan exited at a truck stop and fueled Blossom, cringing upon the realization that they had a measly sixty-eight dollars left. He found a payphone off to the side after purchasing a phone card. It was time to call Mark to see if he could get some money wired to him. He dialed the number, praying that he would be home.

"You have reached the residence of Mark and Connie. The thought for the day is that Jack Straw will be meeting you at the time that the mystery train lands here in the Promised Land in four days time. I'm sure that we'll be happy to hear your message. Beep!"

Dan looked at the receiver, completely confused. He placed the phone back down. Now what was that all about, he thought? He dialed the number again and got the same recording. Again, he hung up the phone.

He walked back to Blossom, scratching his head. First of all, if his brother ever left a message on the machine, it was short and sweet, usually something like, "You have reached the number you called, please leave a message." As a pilot, he liked things right to the point in everything he did. He also didn't like phone calls from sales people. But, thought for the day? Now, Dan was more likely to leave a thought for the day, being a writer. Puzzled, he wrote down the message.

"What do you make of it?" Diana asked after Dan showed her the mysterious message.

"That's just it. I don't know. It doesn't make any sense..."

"A coincidence?" Diana offered: "Maybe you're reading into something that really isn't there."

"That's a possibility," Dan said, although his tone of voice suggested otherwise. "But, it still doesn't change the fact that we're almost broke. There's gotta be a way that we can get a hand on some cash. There has to be!"

At that moment, Diana was frustrated, too. If her parents were still alive, she was sure that they would have helped. Unfortunately, what remained of her small family was scattered throughout the country, and she'd had little contact with them over the years. She also couldn't very well call up her in-laws and ask them for money, knowing that her husband had probably destroyed her name with his lies. She decided to mention Clinton, her friend who was handling her affairs.

"I don't think that we want to risk it," Dan said. "Although, if we're desperate, we can try him. But, Robinson must have gotten to him by now. He has to know that by cutting off our funds at the source, that..." his voice trailed off as his eyes brightened.

"What is it?"

"The source. Jesus! Why didn't I think of that before?"

"Dan, you're speaking in riddles again."

"You know?" Dan said as he hurriedly began looking through his bags. "Sometimes the most obvious of things can elude you without your realizing that you have an answer, clear as day, right in front of you." Suddenly, he came out of the back of Blossom, a phone number in hand. "I'm a writer, remember? Which means, I have royalties coming. It's never a lot, mind you, but I could usually count on a couple of thousand dollars every month or so. I'll be right back." Just as soon as he said that, he was headed back toward the pay phone, leaving Diana standing there, in a quagmire of confusion.

Dan's agent was a small, squirrelly guy out of New York. He had never met the man, but knew him through his signing of contracts in the mail, first through representation and then through his four consecutive Rusty Wallace book sales. If he had been a Stephen King, a Tom Clancy or a John Grisham, it would have been another story. But, Dan hadn't hit the big-time and neither saw it necessary to meet. His books sold, and that was enough to get him off the ground and keep him going. He had a feeling that he probably wouldn't like the guy much anyway, there was something annoying about his personality, like how he was always asking when his next book was coming. It wasn't Dan's favorite question to answer.

He picked up the phone and called Meredith, Lazarus and Nevin Inc., his agency, which sounded more like a law firm than a literary agency. Unfortunately, his agent, Sam Crown, wasn't one of the names listed on the letterhead. He had been delegated to handling the books "of lesser revenue but good potential." After going through two secretaries, using the name, Rusty Wallace," Dan heard Sam hop on the line.

"Where the hell have you been, old boy?" Sam asked excitedly. "Murder seems to have put you on the map, did you know that?"

Dan didn't appreciate the light-heartedness but held his tongue. Politely, he said, "I didn't murder anyone, Sam."

"Well, no matter, Dan. But, I'll tell you this. Murder sells books and you'll be delighted to know that you're in demand! My God, I can't believe you called me. This is great, Dan! Where are you calling from?"

"Out of town," Dan said elusively. "Listen, I was wondering if..."

"Is it true, Dan? You've kidnapped your psychiatrist?! Do you know how good that this looks in print? Get a load of this, every one of your books has gone into a new printing! The whole country is interested in you! *Hard Copy* and *Current Affair* want exclusives with you. What do you think? "

"You know me, I like to keep a low profile. I told you that a long time ago," Dan said.

"Low profile? Well, Dan Wilcox, your cover's blown. Come on, old boy, run with it! You get this opportunity once in a lifetime! I'll meet you anywhere!"

"Sam! Listen to me! Just for one moment, will you?" he asked irritably.

Sam quieted down. "Anything, Dan. Anything you want. I'm here for you."

"Good. I need some money. Have I got any royalty checks there?"

"Well, give me a second and I'll look up your account on the computer," Sam said.

Dan could hear him banging away quickly on a keyboard, an occasional "bleep" breaking the silence. He crossed his fingers in anticipation. Please let it be good news, he thought.

"Oh, Dan, it says here that we mailed out your check for over five thousand dollars just over a week ago."

"Damn it!" he muttered, upset that it was probably in his mailbox at home, in Marquette. "When's the next one coming out?"

"Well, after the new printings, you can look at another check in about a month. Can you hold out that long?" Sam asked, a tinge to his voice.

"No," Dan said dejectedly.

"Good, then it's a deal. Hard Copy will give you twenty-five thousand up front to do an exclusive. Your problems are solved. When do you want to meet?"

Dan didn't like his agent's aggression at all, which surprised him. Why hadn't his agent been like this two years ago? If he had, maybe he never would have visited his mother in the first place, being too busy with fame and all that comes with it. "Sam, I appreciate it. Really, I do. The fact is that I can't do any interviews. Well, not at this moment. But," he said carefully, baiting a hook, "I might consider it shortly down the road if you can sport me a little advance? Is that a deal?"

"Ah, gee, old boy. In the old days, I might have thought of it, but we're a corporation now. You have to explain every dime that comes in and every dime that goes out. You know how it is. I've got people that I have to answer to."

Dan banged his fist against the wall. "Look, Sam, how about a personal loan? You can take it out of my royalties. How does that sound?" he asked, trying not to give the appearance of begging.

"I wish I could. The wife's just had a hysterectomy and I've got two daughters in college. These are expenses that..."

"Yeah, Sam, I know," Dan said, against the wall.

"Like I said, Dan, think about it. *Hard Copy* is the way to go. Now, tell me where you are and I'll..."

"Yeah, yeah," Dan said. "Look, I'll call you when I can. I've gotta go."

He hung up the phone in exasperation. His agent could have gotten him money if he wanted to, he knew it. On the other hand, he knew that everyone reaped the rewards; the more desperate that he was. He had this feeling that Sam thought he would call back begging for the interview anytime now. Well, twenty-five thousand was tempting but not tempting enough for him to risk the rest of his life in prison. For the moment, he would have to find another alternative.

He walked back to Blossom; his head hung low, his spirits temporarily shot. He told Diana of his exchange and then got in and started her up. He fought the urge to break something.

"We will get by," he said, in line with the song, *Touch of Grey*.

They took the 301 to Hillsborough State Park in silence. Dan fumbled with the piece of paper denoting his brother's message, reading it and re-reading it until he had virtually memorized it accidentally.

Jack Straw will be meeting you at the time that the mystery train lands here in the Promised Land in four days time.

What in the hell kind of message was that? Further, with sixty-eight dollars in his pocket and Blossom playing little engine games, their time was quickly running out.

Then, Dan thought bemusedly, Diana tells him that relaxation would unleash his memory. Now, how the hell was he supposed to relax? This didn't look like any vacation to him!

It looked more like a nightmare that you couldn't wake up from...

33

DARK STAR

"Are you sure that you want to do this?" Mrs. Thill asked, as they were preparing to leave for the courthouse.

"Yes, I'm sure."

"You're being quite a man about everything."

"Thanks, Mrs. Thill," Danny said. "It doesn't mean that I'm not scared, though."

"Remember, there's nothing for you to be afraid of. We're all here to protect you. Do you remember what to do?"

"Sort of."

"Let me tell you again," she said, placing a steaming plate of scrambled eggs and grits in front of him, heavy on the melted butter over the grits. "Now, eat this. You'll need the energy for today."

Danny dove in hungrily, smiling at the thought that nobody had to force Mrs. Thill's food down his throat. It was too good and probably explained why she was so ample in weight.

Mrs. Thill continued, pecking at her own plate, distracted by what they were going to face that day, "We're going to court to bring charges up against your parents. Those charges are going to state that you have been subjected to abusive behavior and that, in essence, the goal is to have you and your brother and your sister removed from that household. Do you understand that much?"

"Yes, Mrs. Thill. We've been through this a hundred times."

"If we have to, Danny, we'll do it a hundred more times. This is very important. Now," Mrs. Thill continued, determined that Danny was going to do everything right, "I'm sure that they're going to put you up on the witness stand. There'll be a lawyer on your side and there'll be a lawyer on your parent's side. Each, in turn, will be asking you questions. Answer them as honestly as you can, and be as accurate as you can on any details."

Danny looked at her and smiled nervously. "Boy, do I have details."

"Don't be afraid to tell every one of those details. This time, there isn't going to be a jury there. We have to prove that these charges have merit. So, your attention should be focused on the judge. If he believes you, then formal charges will be brought against your parents."

Danny finished a long drink of apple juice. He wiped his lips, saying, "I've got it so far."

"It's not going to be easy. You'll get a lot of pressure from the lawyers, both yours' and your parents'. I'm warning you ahead of time, your parents' lawyer is going to try as hard as he can to prove that you're lying."

"I'm not lying," Danny said defensively.

"I know that, and you know that. Your job is to make sure that the judge knows that. Don't be afraid if a lawyer tries to intimidate you, he's just doing his job. Most importantly, don't be afraid of your parents. They can't touch you in a courtroom. So, when you tell your story, stick to your guns. The moment that you think that you're starting to feel insecure, just look over at me," Mrs. Thill enunciated. "I'll be right there, giving you support. Just be strong."

"Believe it or not, Mrs. Thill, I will."

"Somehow, I know you will, too," she said, smiling with admiration.

"I have a question, though."

"What's that?"

"Will my parents try and come after me?"

"The only way that they can do that is through their lawyer. Don't think about it," she said. Mrs. Thill paused to straighten the buttons on her red dress. She had worn red so that, no matter where she was sitting in the courtroom, Danny would be able to pick her out easily. She took a deep breath and held Danny by the shoulders. "Let me be very honest about something, so that you're not surprised in the courtroom. Your parents are claiming that they have never harmed you at all, even on the day that you ran away to me. They said that you only got slapped on the back once, because..."

"That's a lie!" Danny said, infuriated.

"See? You mustn't do that in court," she pointed out. "Now let me finish. They said that you accidentally got a slap on the back because you hit your sister."

"Where do they think that I got all the bruises from?"

"They're claiming that you must have done it to yourself," Mrs. Thill explained.

Danny looked down, his appetite shot.

"Danny, you and I know that that would have been impossible to do. We also know that you're telling the truth. As long as you tell the truth, nothing will go wrong. Remember, we have pictures of what they've done to you. We have tapes of your testimony, although their lawyers are arguing that they can't be submitted. We also have the hospital reports from Louise. Don't worry about a thing! There's so much evidence against them that there's no feasible way that they can lie their way out of it!"

"I'm worried," Danny said. "Things have never worked out the way that I've wanted them to."

"Well, this time, they will work out. Be strong on the witness stand and stick to the truth."

"I will."

"Are we ready to go to court?"

"Yes, we're ready."

Mrs. Thill straightened Danny's tie, a conservative striped tie complementing a navy blue suit that she had purchased for him at J.C. Penney's. Shortly thereafter, they were in her car, headed toward the courthouse. Danny kept to himself for virtually the whole trip, still feeling exhausted yet apprehensive at what he was about to face. His world had been filled with imagining every possible scenario as far as what was going to happen. He figured that it was best if he didn't look at his parents. If he did, he knew he'd break down and they would surely come after him. He'd resort to suicide before he ever went back to them.

One slap? He thought. That pissed him off. How could they say that? All of his life, he'd been taught to obey the Ten Commandments. Now, maybe he wasn't the best at following the Ten Commandments, but what about them? They didn't obey the Ten Commandments so well. On the other hand, there was no commandment that said "Thou Shalt Not Hit Your Kids" even though there was a commandment that said "Honor Thy Mother and Thy Father". But what else was he supposed to do? Maybe God would understand and be on Danny's side for a change.

The courthouse was located a block from St. Peter's Cathedral, a lot smaller in comparison to the church. Its red brick facade loomed ahead, its walls about to hear the tale of Danny's harrowing experiences. For a moment, while Mrs. Thill parked the car, Danny thought that the building, with its dusty red stone exterior, looked almost ancient and forbidding to him. Mrs. Thill must have sensed his apprehension because she stopped to give him a firm hug before they walked up the steps to his fate.

As they walked through the brass embossed glass doors, Danny felt miniscule and unimportant. All around him, people hustled around in preparation for the day's proceedings. Then, he saw a sign directing them toward a room straight ahead, its sign glaring in black and white: The State of Michigan v. Wilcox. Danny's stomach rumbled with a zillion butterflies. He dropped his eyes to the orange marble floor as they walked in, not wanting to make eye contact with his parents.

With a squeeze of his shoulder, Mrs. Thill whispered to him, "Remember to be strong, Danny. There's nothing to be afraid of."

"I will," he whispered back.

Out of the corner of his eye, he accidentally saw the rest of his family. Then, he couldn't take his eyes away from them, wondering what his brother and sister must have been thinking. They were standing quietly in a group on the other side of the courtroom, their faces showing no sign of emotion. Louise and Mark were dressed appropriately, in new clothes, as if they were going to attend midnight mass on Christmas. Daddy stood behind them, dressed in a dark brown suit while Momma stood by his side, wearing a black skirt with a light blue blouse.

Daddy's eyes made contact with Danny's. His jaw, ever so imperceptibly, jutted forward, not enough so anyone else would know, but enough to let Danny know, he wasn't pleased. Those eyes said if I ever get my hands on you...

Danny squeezed Mrs. Thill's hand. She returned her support.

Daddy and Momma then said something to the man who was standing next to them, in the blue pin-striped suit. Danny surmised that man to be the lawyer that Mrs. Thill had spoken of. The man nodded his head toward Daddy, as if extending his permission for something. To Danny's discomfort, Momma and Daddy strolled over to where he and Mrs. Thill were standing. He felt like he was going to wet his pants as a ripple of fear ran through him.

"Thank you, Mrs. Thill, for watching our son," Daddy said, sarcasm ringing in his voice. "We really should have guessed that it was you behind these antics. How is he doing?"

"Fine," Mrs. Thill answered, her voice as cold as a stiff winter chill.

"Have you fallen for Danny's wild imagination, too?" Momma asked. "Or, should I say his lies?"

Daddy appeared to have nudged Momma into silence with a whisk of his hand.

"Maybe you know, that's for the courts to decide," Mrs. Thill answered.

"Hmmm, we'll see," Daddy said.

For a moment, silence hung in the air until Daddy focused his attention on Danny. "How are you, son?" Daddy asked.

In the lousy fourteen years that Danny had lived at home, his father had never referred to him as "son".

"Fine," Danny answered, trying to be strong yet, at the same time, afraid for his life.

"Why are you doing this?"

"I have to," Danny responded firmly, his eyes averting Daddy's.

"Danny, Danny, Danny," his father said, shaking his head. "We're your parents and we love you. There's no reason for you to continue this charade, now is there? It's all over now. We want you to come home and we can straighten this out."

Obstinately, Danny answered, "There's nothing to straighten out."

"Look, if we've done something to hurt your feelings, we're sorry," Daddy said, extending his hand. "Let's call it quits, champ. Are we still friends?"

Danny looked at his father's hand and looked toward the ground.

"I'm offering my hand," his father said firmly.

Danny continued to ignore him, the tension growing with each passing second, not daring to give him the satisfaction.

Momma broke the silence, watching Mrs. Thill. "Poor Danny. He has a lot of problems, Mrs. Thill. It's sad to see that you were taken in by his stories, too. We're really very nice people once you get to know us. You should know better than anyone, that kids tend to exaggerate even the most simplest of things. We haven't done anything that any normal parent wouldn't do. Why don't we just brush this under the carpet and we can all resume being friends, huh?"

Danny felt Mrs. Thill's hand tighten on his shoulder. She was as mad as he was.

"As I've already said, Mrs. Wilcox, that's for the courts to decide."

"If that's how you want to play," Daddy commented tightly, "then so be it. Oh, and Danny?" he added, "we'll talk to you later!"

Danny responded by blocking his father's voice out. His parents turned on their heel without another word and returned to the company of Mark, Louise and the man in the blue pin-striped suit. He looked at his brother and sister and, for the look that he got in return; he may as well have never been a part of the family.

"Are you okay?" Mrs. Thill asked.

"I'm more scared than before," Danny said softly. He couldn't get a grasp of what was going on. People seemed to be milling about, with no particular reason. He fought the urge to run off to the bathroom.

Then, a man in a tan uniform walked up. He had a badge on his shirt and a very intimidating gun in his holster, giving him the appearance of being a policeman. "Are you a Danny Wilcox?" he asked, a formal tone to his voice and demeanor.

"That's me," Danny answered, apprehensively looking at Mrs. Thill.

"The judge would like to see you in his chambers. Come along with me," he said.

Danny didn't remove his eyes from Mrs. Thill, as if to ask what was happening now.

"I'm the guardian of the boy," Mrs. Thill said, intending to accompany him.

"I'm sorry, ma'am. The judge would like to see the boy alone. He'll be out in a short time," the bailiff said. "Come along with me, son," he said toward Danny.

"It's okay, Danny. I'm sure that everything will be all right. I'm right here, if you need me. Now, do as the man tells you," Mrs. Thill said with a squeeze of his hand.

Even though Mrs. Thill had said those words of encouragement, he didn't like what was going on. He felt like a lamb must feel like when he's headed toward the slaughterhouse. Her smile was weak and her eyes were as uncomprehending as Danny's.

Nervously, Danny followed the man through the double doors at the front of the courtroom, not daring to look toward his parents who were off toward the right. They entered a small, windowless room where the walls were lined with more books than Danny had ever seen, except for the Peter White Public Library. A man, dressed in black robes, was sitting studiously behind a large and ornate walnut desk, the cushion of a mahogany leather chair rising up behind him.

The first thing that Danny noticed about the judge was that he was surprisingly young given that he thought that all judges were old and gray-haired, if they had any hair at all, that is. This man was as young as Father Regan.

"Have a seat," the judge said, motioning him toward a chair seated in front of his desk. "Do you know why you're here?" he asked, with a shuffle and a stacking of his paperwork.

"Um, to go to court," Danny answered in a tiny voice, noting the judge's nameplate as reading, The Honorable Judge P. Ferguson.

"Why?"

"Well, I'm not sure," Danny said nervously. "I guess it's because I don't want to live with my parents, anymore."

The judge leaned forward on his desk. "And why don't you want to live with them?"

Danny knew that this was an important answer for him. He used his words carefully and deliberately. "Because I'm scared of them. They're always hitting us and I'm afraid that it's only going to get worse."

The judge took a deep breath and pondered Danny's response. He removed his glasses and started cleaning them with the cloth of his robes. He then held them up to the light, checking their cleanliness. Satisfied, he put them back on and leaned forward on his elbows. "Do you realize what the implications are in regards to what you're saying?"

"Yes," Danny answered.

"Danny, let me explain something to you. These charges that you claim to have happened, well, they could get your parents into a lot of trouble. Your father has an impeccable reputation in this town. He's a very well respected man. Are you aware of that?"

"I know that," Danny answered, not particularly liking the direction where their conversation seemed to be headed.

"I'm not sure that you do, in fact, understand, son."

Danny sat there, picking at the cloth of his armrest. He was doing his best to remain firm and strong, the way that Mrs. Thill had trained him. *As long as he told the truth...*

The judge restacked some papers and sighed deeply. "Do you know what perjury is?" he asked, a careful tone to his voice.

"No, sir."

"Well, when you walk into a courtroom, you're required to take an oath. You agree to telling the whole truth and nothing but the truth in front of the court and in front of God. Perjury is when you lie."

"I understand," Danny said, feeling as if he may as well have been standing on the moon.

"Do you know that I can put a person in jail for committing perjury?"

"Yes, sir."

"You don't want to go to jail, do you?"

"I don't understand, sir. Why would I go to jail?"

The judge adjusted his glasses on the bridge of his nose. He took a deep breath and let it out slowly, never removing his eyes from Danny's eyes. "For perjury."

To Danny, it felt as if a gavel had just made its impact upon his head.

"Now, son," the judge said slowly, "if I were to allow you to walk into my courtroom to continue saying the things that you have been saying, you would be committing perjury. I can't allow that to happen."

"You mean...are you saying that I'm lying?"

"The real question, it seems to me, is, why are you lying?"

"I'm not lying!" Danny said adamantly.

"Danny, I'm giving you a chance to come clean. As a representative of the law, I can't watch you destroy your father. You're a young man with your whole life in front of you and I'd hate to see anything get in the way of that. But, if you continue with this kind of talk, I'll be forced to do what the law mandates me to do. So, how about telling the truth?"

As the judge waited, Danny sat there, shock and disbelief across his face. This isn't how Mrs. Thill told him it would happen! He was supposed to be on a witness stand and the judge was supposed to hear his story. He was supposed to hear what happened, how it happened and why it happened.

Danny exploded, knowing that it was his last chance to do anything. "Judge Ferguson, you've gotta listen to me! I'm not lying! I never did lie! Everything that I told Social Services was the truth. I swear it was!"

"This hurts me, too," the judge said. He directed his attention toward the man who was standing behind Danny. "Bailiff?"

The officer stepped forward and motioned for Danny to stand up. Danny turned around as his hands were put behind his back. He could hear the sound of metal and chain clinking as he felt the cold steel of a pair of handcuffs, tightening around his wrists. He was stunned.

"Son, this is a serious matter here," Judge Ferguson said sternly. "You've left me no other choice but to sentence you to six months at St. Mary's Juvenile Delinquency home in Houghton. Your actions, of late, are not befitting to your living with your parents. This is for your own good. After some time there, I hope that you'll understand the ramifications of your actions. Unfortunately, I think that this is best for all parties concerned."

"But...?" Danny tried to say.

"Bailiff, you had better take him," Judge Ferguson said, closing the matter once and for all.

The man pulled Danny out of the judge's chambers. All the while, a million thoughts ran through Danny's head. The first was disbelief while the second was the fast realization that he had just been railroaded. Sadly, Danny never found out exactly what happened on that fateful day. It could have been that his father had thrown some money around. Or, it could have had to do with the man in the blue pin-striped suit, more than likely a lawyer, who pulled a nice tricky maneuver. Or, it could have been that Danny's story was so incredible, against a man of such a worthy reputation, that nobody would believe it. The fact was: Danny felt like he had been made a mockery of, and he was back to square one, meant to suffer the consequences.

As soon as the bailiff got Danny back into the courtroom, Danny surprised the officer by breaking free of his grasp.

"I never lied!" he screamed as he ran pell-mell across the courtroom. The officer unsuccessfully tried to grab him.

Everything in the courtroom dropped to a hushed silence as everyone's eyes turned toward this fourteen year-old boy who looked as if he was losing his mind.

"Come on!" he yelled to no one in particular. "Somebody has to believe me! Please!"

Suddenly, he was in front of his parents, still handcuffed. "How could you do this to me? "

Momma looked down, as if embarrassed by the sight. She shook her head and managed an uncomfortable smile as if to say, where did this deranged boy come from?

"Mark!" Danny said to his brother. "Tell them that I was telling the truth!"

Mark's eyes looked at Momma and Daddy and dropped to the floor.

"Louise! Tell them about the hospital! Tell them about the foyer! You could have died!" Danny screamed.

Although her eyes were red, flooded with tears, she, too, looked away.

Suddenly, the officer grabbed Danny. Danny was no match for him, subdued into a horrifying silence.

"I'm sorry about that, Dr. Wilcox," the bailiff said, pulling Danny away.

"Heaven help the fool," Daddy responded, shaking his head sadly, "Tsk Tsk Tsk."

The bailiff walked the boy down the main aisle of the courtroom, a hundred eyes watching but no one saying a word. A movement toward the doors, revealed Mrs. Thill, fighting her way down the aisle.

"Danny! Danny! What happened? "

"Ma'am, please step back. We're taking the boy into custody," the officer commanded.

"Mrs. Thill!" Danny interjected to the protest of the bailiff, "They don't believe me! You told me that they'd believe me! They're taking me to jail!"

"What? You can't do that!" she said loudly. She reached forward, to pull Danny toward her.

"Ma'am! Step back!" the officer commanded. "We'll have you arrested for obstruction of justice!" he said, yanking Danny away. He called toward the front of the courtroom. "I need another bailiff over here, now!"

Another officer ran to his assistance, pushing Danny ahead of them.

The next thing that Danny knew, he was being escorted out of the courtroom doors, his energy sapped and drained. The last thing that he heard as he left with the law were the shrill screams of Mrs. Thill.

"Danny! Danny!"

At the bottom of the courthouse steps, a police car waited, an officer standing behind the opened rear door. One of the bailiffs grabbed the top of Danny's head so that it wouldn't hit the roof of the car, and pushed him inside. The door slammed shut as the waiting officer ran around the front of the car and hopped in, slamming the car into drive.

Danny looked out the back window only to see Mrs. Thill running down the steps, her red dress blowing in the wind. It would be the last time that he'd ever see her.

The rest of the afternoon was spent in driving to the juvenile delinquency home in Houghton, about two and a half hours from Marquette. They drove up U.S. 41 into the deep reaches of the forest covered Keweenaw Peninsula, with both the officer and Dan enjoying a stony silence.

Dan didn't think much of cops, anymore.

He stared out the window as his wrists ached uncomfortably. And, he was as angry as he'd ever been. What went wrong? How could they not go to court, with all the pictures of his bruises? What happened to the hospital records? Did he have to die to save his brother and sister? And, while he was in jail, what was to become of Mark and Louise?

The car slowed when they reached County Road 33. In the distance, Dan could see a whitened steeple framed against a cloudless sky, above a gray weatherworn church, the only structure that could be seen for miles, excepting the towers of the bridge that connected Houghton to Hancock. The police car slowed and turned into the gravel driveway. The officer stepped out and opened the door, removing Dan's cuffs immediately.

"Well, you're home, Dan," the officer commented.

A fairly young, bearded priest casually walked to the car where they were standing. "Hello," he said affably. "You must be the visitor that I'm expecting. What's your name?"

"Dan Wilcox," he answered sullenly.

"Well, the pleasure's all mine. Why don't you come in and meet the rest of the boys? We're excited to have you as a part of the family. My name's Father Healy," he said, extending his hand.

Dan shook it weakly, not pleased about being the middle of nowhere with a bunch of strangers; and jail, to top it off, although it didn't look much like one.

"The boys are in the living room. I want you to introduce yourself, okay?" the priest said.

"Sure," Dan responded coldly.

The officer waved and backed out of the driveway while Danny and the priest walked up the steps toward the rectory. He was led into the living room where he saw ten or fifteen boys waiting anxiously, some sitting on ragged furniture while others were parked on the floor. They all looked older to Dan, being sixteen or seventeen years-old...and they looked tough and street-worn. Father Healy led Dan to the front of the room, under the close scrutiny of their watchful eyes.

"Now, tell your new roommates who you are," he instructed firmly.

"I'm Dan Wilcox."

"And tell them why you've been sentenced here. Don't worry, it's a ritual. Every one of your roommates has had to do the same thing upon their arrival."

Dan could feel their eyes watching him but he couldn't return their stare. He was ashamed and embarrassed. "I don't know," he finally mumbled.

"Dan!" Father Healy commanded sternly. "Tell us why you are here!"

Dan bit his lower lip, determined not to start crying. He had no other alternative, again. These people didn't know him from Adam and they didn't care. It was a new world now with a new set of rules. The cards were dealt the way they were and he had no choice but to play them out, one by one.

He cleared his throat, holding his head as high as he could muster. "I'm here because I lied about my parents. I told everyone that they beat me and it was a lie. I committed perjury," he said. "It's nobody's fault but mine."

"Good, Dan," the priest said. "It's a start."

"May I go to my room?" Dan asked, his eyes dropping to the floor.

"Yes, you may. I'm sure that it's been a long day for you, hasn't it? It's down the hallway and it's the second door on the left."

"Thank you," Dan mumbled. He thought about saying, "You win again," but kept his mouth shut.

He stepped out of the living room and walked down the hallway, fighting the tears the whole way. The walls were colorless and grimy, flecks of paint peeling and worn. The bed was un-sheeted and stained.

He sat on the bed and then lay back as the filtered sun warmed his face. He turned on his side and stared at the wall, silent and determined.

He wasn't going to cry.

In the background, in a distant room, he could hear a tape playing, tinny and live, *"I have never been so lonesome and a long way from home. Somebody help me...somebody help me..."*

His tears made the mattress wet.

34

NOT FADE AWAY

Dan prodded the campfire with a stick sending a shower of orange sparks cascading upwards while Diana chewed on the remnants of his story. She wasn't sure, but it looked like his eyes were glistening.

"It made you angry, didn't it?" she asked.

"Of course," he answered.

Then, she drew the sword. "Were you angry enough to kill her?"

Dan dropped the stick in the fire and watched the flames lick it and then consume it. "I might have considered killing the judge or my father but my mother? No, I didn't have a motive for it. You see, she couldn't help who she had become. Then, consider that this happened twenty years ago. I never would have begun seeing you to begin with if I had harbored that kind of resentment. It doesn't make sense. There's an important factor that we're missing, something that we haven't considered."

"Is it possible that you stumbled upon the murderer, that it was just coincidence that you happened to be there?"

"One of the things that I've learned in life is that there are no coincidences," Dan said, his eyes reflecting the flames. "In one odd way or another, everything happens for a reason. I believe that I was meant to be there and I was meant to go to jail. Not because I was a bad person but because I was meant to learn something from it. You want to hear something really strange?"

"What?"

"That song that was playing in the background was a Jerry Garcia Band song. It was the summer that I learned that there were other things out there besides my parents. I learned about taping and I learned about making friends through taping. Twenty years later, it's still the biggest influence in my life and there's a reason for that. No, there are no coincidences," he repeated thoughtfully. "Can we move on to another subject?"

"Sure," Diana said.

"Excuse my frustration at this situation but we're looking at a pretty severe problem," he said. He pulled out his wallet and counted their funds. "Well, with fifty-six dollars left, we're in a bind."

"Do you know anyone in Tampa?"

Dan thought about it for a moment and then his eyes suddenly lit up. "You know, I just might at that!" He jumped up and ran into the back of Blossom, digging furiously through his Marlboro luggage. Moments later, he hopped out with the list of names that Derry had given him back in St. Ignace, Michigan.

"What's that?" Diana asked.

"Well, I have five hundred tapes on board," Dan explained. "This here is a list of tapers. The universal connection between all of us on the road was the tapes. It doesn't matter if you've ever met them before. Once you start trading, you're friends for life! If I sold them..." Dan said. He looked at his watch. It was only 9:30. He pulled out his phone card and ran to the park's washrooms, where he found a pay phone.

Dan had about twenty people on the list from Florida alone; six were in the Tampa-Clearwater area. He hit pay dirt after he called the third name on the list, a guy by the name of Eric. Once he got him on the line, he explained their financial predicament, leaving out the part about the police chasing them.

"I'd be willing to sell them for two or two-fifty a tape," Dan said, trying to keep the desperation out of his voice. "Essentially, we're stranded here. I've never sold a tape before. All you'd be paying for is the cost of the tape."

"Aw, man, that sounds like a deal. I can't afford any five hundred tapes. I'd be interested in twenty dollars worth, though. You want to meet at the show tomorrow?" Eric asked.

"What show?"

"Isn't that what you're in Florida for? There's a huge Jerry Tribute at Tampa Stadium tomorrow. Why don't you meet me there?"

"Tampa Stadium? I can't afford tickets to the show," Dan said. But, the temptation was too great. "Who's playing?" he asked.

Eric didn't hide his excitement. "The rest of the band's going to be there. Also, Hornsby's playing, the Allman Brothers, Carlos Santana, David Crosby and a whole shitload of others. If you want, I'll trade you a couple of tickets for, say, thirty tapes. See, then afterwards, we're all headed to a place called Maggie's Farm. I don't think they're allowing vendors at the show but I bet you can sell tapes at there."

"Really?" Dan said to his newly found friend. He liked the idea. It would get them out of their primary problem for the moment, finances. Once again, Derry had helped them.

Dan agreed to meeting Eric in the parking lot after giving a brief description of Blossom. He told Eric about his license plate, WHRF RAT and promised that they'd look for each other at about 1:00 in the afternoon.

Dan felt like he was rejuvenated. The next thing he did was to call his brother, again, praying that he would answer the phone.

Jack Straw will be meeting you at the time that the mystery train lands here in the promised land, where the hound broke down, in four days time, the message said, slightly edited from before. His brother had changed the message which meant that he had been home! Also, Dan noticed a pinging sound emitting from the receiver. He wasn't sure what a trace was going to sound like but he had a feeling that that's what he was hearing.

Was the message meant for him?

He hung up the phone and ran back to Blossom and began diving through his tapes. One after another, he dropped them in the deck, searching for certain songs.

"What's going on?" Diana asked finally.

"I'm beginning to think that we might be out of hot water," Dan said. He told her of the concert the next day and of the possibility of getting cash back in their pocket. "But, take a look at this message," he said.

"I don't get it."

"There are three songs in this message," Dan explained excitedly. "If the phones are being traced, I don't think Mark is going to want to risk contact with us. But, he's making a point here. Listen to this," Dan said. He began reading the lyrics to certain Dead songs, *Jack Straw*, *Promised Land* and *Mystery Train*.

"It doesn't make sense," Diana said, still entirely confused.

"Oh, yes it does. My brother and I have been trading tapes for years. He's also a pilot, as you know. Why does he say that the "mystery train lands here"? A train doesn't land. So, I'm thinking about an airport, right off the bat. He wants to meet us at an airport in four days time. Now, I've got to ask where the airport is and where we are to meet him."

"What's he mean when he says, 'the hound breaks down'?"

Dan flew through one tape after another until he found a *Promised Land* on a Passaic, New Jersey Show from April 1,1980. He rewound it and played it four times, scribbling the lyrics down to the fast driving song. "Here it is," he said, thrilled. He read the lines that carried the significance to the message. *"Had motor trouble, turned into a struggle, half way across Alabama. The hound broke down, left us all stranded in downtown Birmingham!"*

"Okay," Diana said. "So, we meet him in Birmingham."

"That's correct," Dan said. "I've got to think that our time schedule begins from the moment that I leave him a message."

"What are we supposed to do, going wandering all over the city until he finds us?"

"No," Dan said. "We're meeting him at the airport. The next question is, at what time are we meeting him? Well, our answer is in the song, *Mystery Train!* So, Dan searched down every Jerry Garcia Band tape that he could find until he found the song from a live performance at Chico State on March 17, 1982.

Diana watched his apparent madness with interest as he played the song, his pen scribbling furiously.

He rewound the song for her. "Listen!"

A segment of the lyrics played back: "*Well, I went to the station, to meet my baby at the gate. Asked the station master, 'is your train runnin' late?' She said she'd be waiting on the 4:44...*"

"Hah! What do you think of that?!" Dan asked.

"So, we're meeting your brother in four days at 4:44 in the Birmingham airport? I would assume that the airport's going to be a good size, wouldn't you?"

"I'm sure that it's a good size," Dan said. "Listen to this, though..."

He dropped in a Boston Gardens' show from December 2, 1971. The tune played, an excited audience in the background, "*Jack Straw from Wichita cut his buddy down....One man gone and another to go, my old buddy you're moving much too slow.*"

"I don't get it," Diana said.

"Well, I know this sounds like I'm reaching but it's telling me that Mark's hooked into something or he wouldn't have implied that we're moving much too slow. Remember how Mark and I used to have dreams of flying together?"

"Yes," Diana said, trying to follow.

"Well, we dreamed of doing that in a Beechcraft. Wichita is where the headquarters to Beechcraft is. In other words, if I'm reading this right, we're meeting in the private sector of the Birmingham airport and we're looking for a Beechcraft at 4:44! That's gotta be it! I'll be right back!"

"Where are you going?"

"Back to the phone. We have four days to get to Birmingham. If I can sell the tapes tomorrow, then we're scot-free. Let me let Mark know that I've gotten his message!"

Dan took off, wound up like rubber band on a Sleek Streek glider. He could barely dial the phone fast enough. Then, the message repeated itself: *Jack Straw will be meeting you at the time that the mystery train lands here in the promised land, where the hound broke down, in four days time...*

When the machine beeped, Dan returned his message, cryptic and mysterious, knowing that his brother would figure it out. He pulled a quote from *Desolation Row*: "*Yes, I received your letter yesterday. Don't send me no more letters, no, not unless you mail them from Desolation Row.*" As soon as he finished it, he hung up the phone.

Maybe they would be all right, after all.

The next day was one of the strangest days that Diana had ever spent with anyone. It began with their meeting Eric in the crowded parking lot of Tampa Stadium. Everywhere around her, people were dressed just like them, a culture and a society blown back from somewhere in the '60's. Blossom fit right in with hundreds of VW busses in every imaginable condition and color parked everywhere. There were RV's and beater cars. There were yuppies and long haired people, all of them equal. Instead of it being a tribute to death, it looked more like a tribute to life, everyone wearing smiles and anticipating a concert that "generations would remember."

Eric, looking like a beach bum from California, his matted blond hair lying askew on his head and an attitude to match, handed them two tickets in trade for thirty tapes of his choice.

"Just listen around, man. You'll hear where Maggie's Farm is. Just get down and have a good time."

Dan exchanged addresses with him. "Well, I'll send you some blanks, if you don't mind. If we didn't need the money so bad..."

"I'll take care of you, man. We've all been there. Glad to help you, dude!" he said with a smile, disappearing into the crowd.

Their two links were poverty and the tapes, a bond that united most of the people there.

The police were surrounding the stadium in full force but Dan and Diana didn't have to worry about a thing. They were too busy trying to monitor twenty-thousand Deadheads gone rampant in laughter and anticipation. Dan overheard one of the cops talking to another cop, "What the hell is going on in this city? And, where did all these damned busses come from?"

People bumped and pushed each other as they made their way to the gates, but nowhere was there a fight or a harsh word said. It was as if the air was filled with an electrical charge, all united by their homage to this man by the name of Jerry Garcia.

If Jerry was in heaven looking down, he would have been pleased as a festival of his musical counterparts from years past, one after another, appeared on stage on that great Saturday afternoon.

Ken Kesey opened the show with an exhilarating poetic tribute. Then, came the Allman Brothers doing a sweet rendition of *St. Stephen* followed by Bruce Hornsby settling into a tearful but joyous *Sugar Magnolias*. After that, came one guest artist after another performing with what was left of the band. People sang and danced with the guests, the band and themselves until it became a blur of images and smiles. In one moment, there was Bob Dylan with Clarence Clemens yanking out some phenomenal saxophone solos in *Knockin' On Heaven's Door*. In another, David Crosby was singing *Eyes of The World* with Suzanne Vega. And, the list went on to dizzying heights with Boz Skaggs, Pete Townsend, John Fogerty, Neil Young, The Neville Brothers, David Grisman and The New Riders of the Purple Sage jamming the day away.

It was a tireless afternoon of jazz, blues, rock, folk and psychedelia. The tapers sat in their section, mesmerized, monitoring and taping each minute of the show, knowing that it would live on to infinity, with their fourteen and sixteen-foot microphones attached to expensive DAT recorders.

In another section, yellow balloons with the Alcoholic's Anonymous triangle floated above the fans, marking the attendance of the "Wharf Rats," those who took their twelve-step meetings on the road. Signs waved frantically with such slogans as, "One Show At A Time", "Another Dopeless Hope Fiend", and, "Let Go...Let Jerry, You Know Our Love Will Not Fade Away!"

For the whole of the afternoon, they were lost in a world that might never be the same again. Most importantly, they smiled. A man next to them leaned over, a computer analyst in his real life saying, "I'm jonesin' for a *Dark Star*, bad!"

Dark Star was played, everyone united in guitar riffs that never seemed to end.

The closing of the show was marked with a tearful *So Many Roads*, flowing into *Tomorrow Is Forever* and ending with the classic, *Broke-down Palace*. Thousands of people held hands, united by an unbroken chain, Dan and Diana included.

When the show was over, it took Dan no time at all to find out where Maggie's Farm was. He asked six different people and five people gave the same response. It was about twenty miles north of them in a remote area just west of Lutz. It was said that ten thousand people were going to show up.

Blossom made it there without a problem acting right at home when she pulled in the fifty acre piece of property. Dan knew exactly what he was looking for in order to sell his tapes. They had to head toward an area that would be called *Shakedown Street*, typically where vendors of all sorts would set up shop for selling and trading, an impromptu business area. Blankets were laid out in front of VW busses lined with every imaginable item such as "kind" imports, jewelry, bongs, incense, tie-dyes, hand-made Guatemalan sweaters, lyric books and, of course, tapes.

Aromas of food and smoke filled the air. The smoke was from campfires, kind bud and incense of all sorts. Cabbage and onions sizzled in woks mixing with the smells of plump burritos, ganja brownies, grilled cheese and garlic bread. Down the dirt road, about four city blocks long, a man was selling oatmeal-chocolate chip-raisin-banana cookies while across from him someone was selling a virtual plethora of homemade ice cream in flavors like Amaretto Getaway, Beat It On Down The Lime, In The Mint Chip Hour, Touch of Grape and Wharf Raspberry, not to mention the ever popular Cherry Garcia.

Smiles were exchanged and stories of first shows were traded, each a unique experience in itself. And Dan ran into a hundred friends that he had met on the road while following the Dead and writing his books. There was Eric and Mila, of which he traded a couple tapes for tie-dyes. Over by the lake, he ran into Brad, Mike and Don, whom he hadn't seen in years. They bought fifteen tapes from him at two dollars a shot. At another point, Mike and Laura showed up, offering to trade tapes for some killer mushrooms, which Dan turned down but gave them a couple tapes anyway, for old times sake.

Everyone had music playing, the unifying tunes being bootlegs of the Dead from over thirty years of time. Some were scratchy and hissy, signifying a bad audience tape, while others were clear and crisp, heavy on the bass, indicative of soundboards traded country-wide.

At one point in the evening, Diana decided that she wanted to take a walk. Dan was busy selling his tapes, lost in conversation with Kelly and Jerry, a couple which heralded themselves from Michigan. She walked down *Shakedown Street*, in utter amazement at this counter-culture. It represented everything that she didn't expect to see. For one thing, she noticed that alcohol was virtually non-existent except for a vendor or so who was selling chilled "kind" imports, enough to break the dryness of a parched throat. Cars drove by at a slow pace, careful not to hit any of the pedestrians while the pedestrians were just as careful to allow the cars to pass. She saw people smiling and laughing and telling stories. Campfires burned while people, strangers, told stories, eager to share their own. In other spots, she saw drum circles, with six or eight people sitting around a fire constructing resonant rhythms that seemed to orchestrate a heartbeat of what the evening was. Yes, she smelled the scent of marijuana and watched curiously, other folks running around with full multi-colored balloons. At one point, she found herself standing alone, lost in a gypsy world of sellers and spirits wandering in their world, happy and content.

"Hard to believe, isn't it?" a lady asked, sitting comfortably behind a card table loaded with an array of beaded jewelry.

"I've never seen anything like it," Diana said. "So many people..."

"Oh, yes, dear. And there's many, many more. I got started in this circle in 1970. How long have you been into the scene?" she asked, lighting an incense cone.

"Actually, this would have been my first show," she said.

"Really? Well, it looks like it might be your last. Things are never going to be the same after this. After Jerry..."

"That's what I don't understand. What's the fascination? I mean, the man was only a musician, wasn't he?"

"If you want to look at it that way, you're right. He was only a musician. But, he was also an ideology."

"Or a cult," Diana added.

The lady started laughing. "A cult? No, my dear, you are far from the truth. These people, this feeling in the air is far more than that. If you want to know the truth, I believe that we'd all live in a better world if more people believed in this. You will find environmentalists and you'll find the studious. All around you are people who care about life, life as it was meant to be. Nowhere on this earth will you find a more trusting and caring group of people. My name's Brenda," she said, offering a hand.

"Diana," she said returning the handshake. "Where are you from?"

"Here, there and everywhere that goodness prevails," she said with a wink.

"Actually, I'm from Bricktown, New Jersey. Haven't been home in five years. I hate the city. Give me an open road and new experiences and, well, I guess it explains why I'm here. Pleased to meet you, Diana."

"Likewise," Diana said, watching as two guys walked up and purchased a couple of necklaces. Friends were made and gone just as fast as they arrived.

Brenda reached into one of her bags under the table and pulled out a tie-dye, handing it to Diana. "I want you to have this," she said warmly.

"On, no. I can't take this."

"Take it after you read it. Maybe it'll make some sense to you."

The shirt was a multi-colored die in yellow, orange and red colors. On the back, it was a twenty-fifth anniversary shirt while on the front, there showed a calendar written in the cycles of the year: fall, winter, spring and summer. Below it, there was the definition of the Grateful Dead.

Diana read it aloud to Brenda. "The Grateful Dead: The motif of a cycle of folk tales which begin with the hero's coming upon a group of people ill- treating or refusing to bury the corpse of a man who had died without paying his debts. He gives his last penny, either to pay the man's debts or to give him a decent burial. Within a few hours he meets a travelling companion who aids him in some impossible task, gets him a fortune, and saves his life. The story ends with the companion's disclosing himself as the man whose corpse the other had befriended."

"Do unto others..." Brenda said with a smile. "And that, my dear, is what it's all about."

"If more people believed that, then..."

"Exactly, my dear. It was wonderful meeting you."

Diana walked away, her shirt in hand, still amazed.

Somewhere toward the end of evening, while Dan was stoking the fire, she found the energy to smile. She wondered how many more people were out there like these. Dan told her that she'd never know. But, if you ever see someone in a tie-dye, you know what it means. All of them were bonded by something much greater, much more universal. They had money in their pocket and full stomachs. To top it off, there was an unexplainable peace in their souls.

But most of all, for the first time in over a week, Dan and Diana were relaxed.

Dan counted the money in his pocket. He had just over five hundred dollars and twenty tapes left. Next to him, he had a list of the many people that he had sold his tapes to, a phone number and address next to each, so that he could contact them down the road to get copies of his tapes back. He folded up shop and put his things back in Blossom.

"You want to go for a walk?" he asked.

"If I have the energy to," she said.

The two of them walked through the rest of *Shakedown Street* and found themselves walking a dirt road into a field surrounding a pond. A full moon was shining, sparkling off the early morning dew on the grass. A white mist rose over the pond, a ghostly image of a wonderful day and era drawing to a close. Dan led the way down the slight embankment toward the water. He turned around just in time to catch Diana as she stumbled over a small rock.

In the moment that he caught her, she knew that she should have stepped away. But, in those brief minutes, she was no longer a psychiatrist nor was she on the run with a suspected murderer. She was a woman like any other woman at Maggie's Farm, free of everything except for the time and place that they found themselves at.

An easy wind coursed through the air as time came to a halt. She looked up at Dan who held her firmly. A surge of electricity ran through her as her eyes connected with Dan.

They drew closer, their lips only a hair's breath away from each other. Her rational side was telling her that they shouldn't be doing this but another part of her wanted and needed the closeness, the tenderness. Their lips touched, soft and warm, as a tingling ran up her spine.

Very slowly, Diana brought her hands up to the firmness of Dan's face. Carefully, she pulled back. "Dan, stop," she said softly, her breath light.

"What is it?" he asked, running his hand through her auburn hair, tinged by the whiteness of the moon.

She could feel the beating of her heart and the warmth of his skin. "I don't know how this happened but...we can't."

Dan carefully stepped back, looking over the soft fog of the pond. "I'm sorry. I don't know what came over me. It was my fault."

She reached out and touched his arm. "If things were different..." she said, leaving the words in the air.

"You're a special lady, Diana Powers," Dan said. "I promise you, if we ever get out of this..."

She took his hand and held it.

Dan returned the squeeze. Suddenly, he squeezed it tighter and then let go, wiping his forehead.

"What is it?" she asked.

As clear as day, he could see her face. The sun was ebbing through the kitchen window, sparkling orange rays off the chrome of the sink. He was lunging toward her. She had a knife in her hand, the serrated edges reflecting the soft light.

The knife came forward, threatening to kill her. He could hardly believe that it was happening. His arm caught her arm with a brutal force. The knife came down, sticking and then tearing into his shirt.

He stumbled backwards, backwards even further, threatening to lose his balance.

She came at him again, her teeth showing, an angry grimace on her face. He tried to scream but, like a nightmare, nothing came out. Behind him, he heard the shrill wail of his mother, screaming at him.

"You looney-bird! What have you done, you Goddamned looney-bird...!

Dan stumbled backwards on the grass. His head threatened blackness as his nightmare faded. His forehead broke out in a sweat while his legs became weak. In a faraway distance, as if down the long expanse of a tunnel, he could hear Diana calling him but the words were stuck in his throat.

Diana reached over and grabbed him, settling him into the grass. "Are you okay? What happened?"

All Dan could say was, "I could see her face!"

"Whose face?"

Dan reached for the memory again. It was startlingly familiar- thin, pale, drawn and, yet, older. He was almost sure that it looked like what he imagined his sister to look like. "Louise's," he said, breathlessly.

"Are you sure?"

"Yes, I think I am," he said.

"Dan, listen to me," Diana pressed. "Are you sure that she called you a looney-bird and not her? Or, was it the other way around?"

Dan thought about the voice that was behind him when she had lunged. Diana might have been right. How did he know who his mother was referring to? "Maybe," he said softly.

Diana sat down next to him and held him close. "We have somewhere that we have to stop tomorrow," she said.

When they returned to Blossom, a hint of twilight was cresting the horizon. Both of them retired, choosing to leave words unsaid.

Two hours later, Dan and Diana were awakened by an irritating tapping on the door, growing steadily more intense.

Dan opened the door to see his old friend, Kevin, standing there, one of the myriad of people that he talked with the night before. He had a worried look in his eyes. As with most fellow Deadheads, Dan didn't know Kevin's last name. The first time that he had met him was about ten years prior, at an Oakland show. Periodically, Dan had run into him over the years in many different parts of the country.

"What's up?" Dan asked.

"You might have some trouble headed your way, dude," he said. "There's a word being passed that they're looking for a green VW Bus with the plates, "WHRF RAT". I remember seeing yours, so I had to come tell you. There's, like, four cops about five aisles up, headed in this direction."

Dan must have turned a few shades of white.

"Don't worry, man. We'll stall for you but you better pack your shit and hit the road. Hey, uh, if you don't mind my asking, you aren't the two that have been in the news, lately, are ya?"

"I'd rather not say, Kevin. You know how it is," Dan said.

"You got it, man. As far as anyone here is concerned, we never saw ya. Now pack up and git. Nothin' personal, mind you but we gotta take care of each other. I don't think that people's gonna much like cops hanging around, know what I mean?"

"Diana? " Dan called, waking her up. "We've gotta go." He turned back toward Kevin. "Well, guess we gotta BIODTL, know what I mean?" he said, in reference to the song, *Beat It On Down The Line*.

"See ya at the next show, if there is one. Like I said, we'll distract them as long as we can. Peace man," he said, throwing them a sign and splitting as fast as he had appeared.

Dan didn't take long to batten down the hatches. Blossom started in a heartbeat and headed away from the direction that the police were coming. How the hell did they find out about them? He asked himself.

They pulled out of Maggie's Farm at about eight o'clock, the sun just over the horizon, illuminating what would promise to be a beautiful day. On the deck, *Fire On The Mountain* played, from

October 14, 1994 at Madison Square Gardens: *"Drowned in your laughter and dead to the core. There's a dragon with matches, that's loose on the town. Take a whole pail of water, just to cool him down. Fire, fire on the mountain..."*

At least they had money in their pocket, a tank full of gas and some memories of a disappearing eon. But, how long would it be before the dragon caught up with them?

The worst part was, as Dan accelerated Blossom out of The Farm, he couldn't shake the image of what he thought looked surprisingly like his sister. He could vividly picture her jet black hair, stringy and long and he could even see the detail of her face, crow's feet at the comer of her eyes.

The worst part of the image was her eyes, cold, black and heartless in their intensity.

The knife glistened in the afternoon sun as Dan stumbled backwards, fear consumed his entire being.

She lunged...

35

SAINT STEPHEN

"Dan?"

"Yes, Dad?"

"Didn't we ask you to do something today?"

"Um...I don't remember."

"Why don't you try and think about it?"

"Ah...I'm not sure what you're talking about."

"You don't know what I'm talking about," Dad said sarcastically. "Didn't we ask you to clean up the garage?"

Dan suddenly remembered upon his prodding. "Oh yes, I'm sorry."

"Oh good," Daddy said. "The idiot has a memory. Why didn't you clean up the garage like you were asked to?"

"I'm sorry, Dad. I didn't mean to forget."

"But you don't forget to eat our food or sleep in our beds, do you? Just what the hell do you think it is around here? A damned country club?" his father asked angrily, while they were in the kitchen.

"Well, no."

"Then why wasn't the garage cleaned? Didn't we ask you nicely enough?"

"I'll clean it up right now," Danny offered quickly.

"No, you won't clean it up right now! You'll tell me why the garage wasn't cleaned!"

"I forgot."

"You forgot?" Dad mimicked with a raised eyebrow. "No, I think that you purposely disobeyed us!"

"I didn't mean to," Dan answered in high-pitched voice.

Things hadn't changed much, Dan realized, as he watched the typical performance play itself out. His father's jaw jutted forward and his fists clenched at his sides. He raised an arm, as if he was about to backhand Dan across the face. Dan, in defense, backed up against the wall and cringed, waiting for the blow to connect.

When Dad was only inches from his face, he suddenly backed up. "Oops! Oops!" his father suddenly said, his hands upraised as if to show their cleanliness. "I'm sorry! I'm sorry! I didn't hit you, did I?"

Dan stuttered, a confused look on his face. "Well..."

"No, I didn't! I didn't lay a finger on you, did I?" his father said, taking another step backwards. The sarcasm was thick in his voice, humiliating Dan with his words. "Please, son! I'm begging you! Don't report me! I didn't do anything! Please don't tell the authorities that I did something! I didn't do anything, did I?!"

"No," Dan answered, meekly.

"Oh, good," his father said, pretending he was relieved. Then, he got on his knees in front of his son, clasping his hands together as if he was in prayer. "I'm sorry, Dan. Don't report me, please!"

For the next three years, Dan was reminded in that way of his reporting his parents to Social Services. Every time, his father made a point of humiliating him and degrading him as much as possible, in retaliation for what Dan had done. His father had found a way of getting to him that was almost more painful than actually getting hit. His father made it look like Dan was the informant and he was at the complete mercy of his son, which made Dan feel worse every time he was taunted with it. Dan almost wished for the old days when his father would lose it on him. The way it had become, Dan felt like trash and it made life virtually unbearable.

But, his father wasn't hitting them anymore, or was he?

When Dan was released from the juvenile delinquency home, back to the custody of his parents, things had been like walking on eggshells. At first, his father wouldn't talk to him at all, keeping his resentment to himself. Then, his father slowly allowed his anger to show, in little ways. There was a look in his eyes and it said that he was furious. Dan hid and cowered at the sight of his parents, feeling as if it was a time bomb that was ready to blow at any second.

The irony was that Dan's summer in Houghton had turned out to be the best summer that he had ever lived, contrary to what he had thought it would be like. Father Healy became a friend and a father to Dan, promoting activities with the other boys in the home. Dan learned how to ride a motorcycle, a Kawasaki 125 dirt bike, his first ride ending in a resounding crash into a garage wall. He learned how to play pool, darts and how to interact with others, honesty always being the rule of thumb. He went on camping trips with boys who, in their earlier lives, had been harbingers of trouble by committing B and E's, and being a general nuisance to society. Much to the chagrin of his parents, these "thugs," as Daddy referred to them, became his friends, regardless of their pasts.

To Dan, that summer was the precursor to what life would be once he was out of the shadow of his parents' control. He would be free to live without the fear of being hit or humiliated. He counted the days until he would be eighteen and on his own. Then, he could be normal, like he was for that incredibly short summer.

And, in the early hours of the morning, Mark would beg him for another Father Healy story, a story of what it was like on the outside, where kids could be kids, no fear attached. Dan told those stories over and over again, reliving each detail for the ears of Mark, providing a brief and short respite from their intimidating lives.

Sadly enough, Dan's return home began a nightmare with different colors. His parents never hit him again, although there were many times they came close to blowing up. But, the suffering was delivered in a different way, by being constantly reminded of his words to Mrs. Thill. His lies, Daddy said, had caused irreparable damage to his father's reputation and Dan would never be forgiven for that. He was a sick excuse for a son and God bless the day that he graduated from high school, for his parent's responsibility for him would be through.

Don't worry, Dan thought many a time over, he looked forward to that day of graduation, too, free from ever talking to his parents again.

Dan couldn't count how many times his parents would scream at him, "I wish that you'd never been born!"

For the next three years, Dan suffered the verbal punches, his strength growing day by day. But, that wasn't to say that those punches wouldn't hurt more than the actual act of getting hit. They eroded his self-confidence just as rust would surely tear apart a chrome bumper left in the rain, slowly but surely marring what was once shiny and bright. His parents were smart in not laying another hand on him because they knew that he could do nothing in a court of law. Who would believe that it had actually become worse?

Who would believe that talking could hurt more than a fist?

He hurt so much that when his parents called him scum or told him that they wished that he'd never been born, Dan would go to his room and start pulling his own hair or hitting himself, much like the old days. He regretted the day that he ever went to court. He regretted being alive. So, in the only way he knew how, he punished himself.

It was about two years after the court incident that Dan learned something that made him just as angry as when he left for court. One afternoon, he came home from Rob's house. Somehow, to the chagrin of his parents, he had managed to maintain the friendship with Rob, with Rob still serving as a buffer between Dan and his parents. Dan walked into the garage and was just about to go into the house, when Louise came out of the laundry room.

"Oh, hi," she said, surprised at seeing him. She ducked her head away from him.

"Hi, Louise," Dan said, instantly suspicious that something was dreadfully out of line. "What's wrong?"

"Nothing," she answered a little too quickly.

"Louise, tell me. What's wrong?"

"Dan, nothing's wrong. Leave me alone."

He reached over and lifted her chin toward him. "Let me see your face." Her hair was tussled and her face was reddened in spots. He couldn't believe it, knowing what the tell-tale marks were from. "Louise, please tell me what happened!"

"Nothing happened," Louise answered, tight-lipped.

As firmly but as caringly as he could, Dan pursued the issue. "Tell me who did this to you?" he said, knowing the answer.

"I said that nothing happened, Dan. Can't you just leave it alone? What if something happened? Would it make any difference? Are you going to go to the police and tell them?" she asked, a piercing glare in her eyes. "And, tell me, where are you going to be when we get punished for what you've done? Can't you see? There's nothing that you can do for us anymore!"

"But I can help!"

"Dan, the best way for you to help is to not tell anyone about this. You don't know what it was like the summer that you were in jail. Those were the worst times that we ever had. Mark and I suffered for what they wanted to do to you. Please," she implored, "you can't do anything anymore."

"I'm sorry," Dan said.

"I am, too," she responded, breaking out in tears and storming away.

The next morning, after he had whispered another Father Healy story to Mark, long before their parents were up, Dan asked Mark about it.

"I don't want to talk about it," he said firmly.

"Please, Mark. I know what's been going on. Louise told me yesterday. All I'm asking is for you to tell me, is it true?"

Mark swung his legs off of the side of the bed. "Follow me downstairs," he whispered softly. It was about 6:30 in the morning, a safe time zone before their parents were out of bed.

They quietly creeped downstairs to the lower bathroom, Mark's index finger over his lips, signifying a warning of silence. He opened the vanity drawer and dug around in back. He pulled out a clump and handed it to Dan.

"What's this?" Dan asked.

"Every time that I get my hair pulled, I save the leftovers, the stuff that comes out of the comb," Mark whispered to him.

Dan was virtually repulsed by this thickened ball of hair that his brother had painstakingly saved over the past two years, a wad of compacted violence, still alive behind Dan's back.

As Dan held the ball of hair, he felt worse for the mileage with proof that it was still happening. What ever happened to the belief that, someday, everything's going to be different? It wasn't different at all. It was a deadly cycle that had been kept at bay enough so that Dan wasn't aware. Why Dan had believed that he could change things, he would never know. With the ball of hair in his hand, he understood the resentments of Mark and Louise. Dan felt worse in knowing that his parents would never hit him again, but what about what his brother and sister must have felt?

Finally, graduation from high school was around the corner for Dan, with his father's admonishment, "Don't forget, the day after you graduate, our responsibilities are over. I hope you know that you're to be packed and gone! Is that clear?!"

It was crystal clear and Dan couldn't wait for the day to come.

Dan graduated from high school with honors, his parents' presence, nonexistent. They felt that he went to a Yooper school anyway, so his grades were nothing to be proud of. Dan went to college, scraping up every penny to pay for it himself, his parents making it clear that "he was on his own".

Fine, Dan thought, he would show them what he was worth. So, for the next four years, he obtained almost perfection in his G.P.A. He joined the swim team, debate team and forensic team, all in an effort for them to notice. He even got into the most prestigious fraternity on campus.

The anticipated day of graduation came four years later, with him dropping an invitation in the mail for his parents. They would see him in his robes and braids and they would finally be proud of him. Hopefully, they would forgive him for what he had done in court. Well, he never got the satisfaction because he found himself standing alone. No one showed up and no one called. The odd thing was, he took it in stride. He wasn't hurt because they couldn't hurt him anymore than they already had. It was clear that he had to move on with life. Moments before the ceremony, he disrobed and went back to his apartment and ordered a pizza. The next day, his bags were packed and he was in his car, headed to California, where he could start a life of his own, his parents deceased in his mind.

In the meantime, Mark had graduated from high school. He skipped college and, behind his father's back, he joined the Air Force. The next thing he knew, he was stationed at Edwards Air Force Base in California. It allowed the brothers to remain close, the rest of their family forgotten like a fading bad dream.

Mark pursued his dreams of being a pilot with a voracity that matched Dan's in college. Mark was going to show his Dad what he was made of. One day, he would brag, he would drive up Dad's driveway in a spanking new, red Porsche. He would get out of the car proudly and walk up and ring the doorbell, waiting for Dad to answer. When he answered, he'd say, "See, I made it. You never thought that I would, did you?"

Dan knew that all those thoughts were wishful ones. Their father would never be proud and Dan should have known it from the day before he had graduated from high school, when his father had pulled him aside,

"I hope you know, you'll never be what I am today. Never! Enjoy your last night in this house because, after this, you're on your own. We've done our job."

Well, Dan's resolve was to be more than what his father was. It took him a few years to realize, though, that it would have been fruitless to go back to his father and shove it down his throat. Dad would have found some way to reduce his accomplishments to meaningless feats and that's exactly what Mark would have faced. Dan never had the guts to tell Mark, though. He just told Mark, "Yeah, it'll be great to see Dad's face when he looks at that Porsche."

Five years later, *the beast* emerged, when they least expected it. Dan had finally found a niche in his writing, completing his first Rusty Wallace book, *Confessions of a Dead Man.* It received moderately good reviews, getting him a second advance that kept him alive for six months. Dan's resolve to be something in life was no longer focused on proving something to his father but rather in proving something to himself. Seeing that book in print put Dan at the top of the world. Nothing would ever change the fact that he had finally accomplished the first step.

Then, the telephone rang. It was Mark's girlfriend of two years, Michelle.

"Well, I'll be," Dan said to her cheerfully. "What a surprise to hear from you. What's going on?" he asked.

Her voice cracked. "I think you had better get over here."

"I can get up there this weekend," he said in reference to the two hour drive to Palmdale, "but right now is a bad time. I have to get..."

She interrupted him. "Dan, you had better get over here right now! I mean it!"

Dan knew that something was up by her ghastly tone. "I'll be there this evening," he said.

It took Dan record time to make it up there. What should have taken two hours to make it, took him about an hour and fifteen minutes. He pulled up to their modest home and ran up the front steps to the door, knowing that something was terribly wrong. Michelle opened the door, revealing a bruised and reddened face. Dan looked at her, not hiding his surprise.

"He's in the living room," she said, turning her face downward.

Dan reached out to her. "Are you alright?"

"Don't worry about me," she said. "It's him who needs your help. Please, you need to talk to him. I can't reach him, anymore." She walked away, leaving Dan standing there to deal with the situation.

Dan walked toward the living room, noticing that their normally well kept house was in disarray. He was almost afraid to say anything to his brother, who was sitting in an easy chair, channel surfing on the television. Next to him, a half empty bottle of Early Times sat, as if it were a guarding soldier.

"Hi, Mark. How are you doing?" Dan asked tenderly.

"Hey, bro, what's shaking?"

"Not much," Dan answered. The two of them sat quietly. Mark looked drunk. Dan could see Michelle lurking in the hallway. The silence became overwhelming, almost deafening.

"What happened to Michelle?" Dan asked.

"I fucked up, bad," answered Mark, a slur to his words. "You wanna drink?"

Chuck Woolery babbled about some nonsensical date on the television, while Dan stared at a picture of an F-16 that was hanging on the wall.

"You want to tell me about it?" Dan asked.

"There's nothing to say," Mark responded. He took a drink straight out of the bottle. "How rude of me. Can I pour you one?"

"No, thanks," Dan said. He thought about it and then stepped into the subject, as carefully as he could. "Did you do that to Michelle?"

"Yeah, I did. I don't fucking know why."

"Tell me about it," Dan prodded again.

Mark stood up on shaky legs. He walked over to the television and shut Chuck Woolery off. "I don't know what to say, Dan." He stumbled as he made his way back to the couch. He picked up the bottle and raised it to his lips. "Fuck!" he spat.

"Come on, Mark. Tell me what's going on."

"Everything's falling apart. You know? I love her. She's been everything to me and I'm throwing it away. I can't stop it. It doesn't go away."

"What doesn't go away?"

"My fucking temper. You don't know what it's like. It takes over, like there's something else inside of you. There's a point where you get mad and there's a point where it gets...crazy. Like, you start hitting and then you hit harder and harder and you can see nothing but fury. It's a beast that lives there, inside of me. I feel...despicable," Mark said, a blackness surrounding him.

"How did it start?"

"I don't know, I really don't. Two months ago, I was happy. Then, I got this idea in my head that Michelle and I should get married. We've been dating for two years and we love each other, you know? I mean, that's what you're supposed to do, isn't it? Get married?"

"Yeah," Dan said hesitantly. He lit a Camel and watched the rings curl off the end.

"I was riding the crest of a wave. I was happy. Then, what did I do? I called Mom and Dad." Neither one of the boys had dealt with their parents in the previous four years, eliciting Dan's interest. "Mom answers the phone...I'm excited as you can get. I tell her the good news, and at first, she doesn't react. I'm thinking that she's surprised and happy to hear from me, ya know?"

"What'd she say?"

"She says that I can do anything that I want. She says that I excluded them from our lives, so she's excluding us from theirs. I apologized. I was really sorry about everything that happened. She says that my apologies are no good. She says that I'm a miscreant son, that you were a bad example and that Louise is just plain crazy. She didn't deserve to have children like us, ya know?"

"Then, what happened?"

"I lost it," Mark answered stoically, facing the facts. "I was fucking pissed. I told her that she and Dad could go to hell and I slammed the phone down, never wanting to speak to them again."

"I see that Mom and Dad haven't changed."

"No, they haven't. But I have. It's like I'm becoming just like them. I don't want to be like them! But, there's this temper, deep inside, that I...I can't control it." Mark took another drink from the bottle, wiping his lips with the back of his hand. "I can't understand what's happening. Now, I get ticked off at the littlest of shit. If the bathroom's dirty, I get annoyed. If she uses the wrong tone of voice with me, I bark back. If Michelle says or does something that doesn't suit me, I feel my fists clench. I wanna beat the shit out of her."

"Did you do that to her?" Dan asked, taking a deep drag off of his cigarette.

"Yes," Mark answered. "I did and I feel terrible about it. I'm not like that, am I? I'm not like Mom and Dad. Please don't tell me that!"

"I think that if we're not careful, we could end up that way," Dan remarked as honestly as he could.

"Take a look in the kitchen," Mark said, lazily pointing Dan in the right direction.

Dan got up and walked toward the kitchen. The sight took him a moment to comprehend. On a cutting board were a loaf of bread, a package of lunchmeat and a bottle of mustard, which were all stacked on top of one another, a butcher knife pierced through them. Below them, on the floor, were blood drippings mixed with mustard. Dan walked back to the living room.

"You like that?" Mark asked. "Don't worry. I cut my hand, not her."

"What the hell?"

"I lost it, ya know? What the fuck is my problem? She comes in looking for some lunchmeat, this afternoon. I told her that I ate it. She gets all pissed off because she had to make another trip to the store. It's my house! I can eat what I want. It's such a dumb thing but it got me so infuriated that I couldn't even see straight. Then, she tells me that I'm crazy! I don't know what happened after that except that this girl, the love of my life, is standing there bruised and crying. What's happening to me?" Mark asked, his eyes brimming with tears. He picked up the bottle and took a long swig, as if to drown everything away. "You got a cigarette?"

Dan shook one out of the pack and gave it to him.

Mark lit it, coughing on the first hit. "So what do I do? The same thing that we hated from Dad, am I nuts? Do I actually belong on this earth?"

"Don't talk like that," Dan said, becoming more concerned than he already was. "I think that you need help."

"I don't need help."

"Mark, that's the only way that you can control it. You've got to stop it before it starts."

"Are you saying that I'm crazy?"

"No, Mark, you know I'm not saying that. I'm not saying anything except that, if you love Michelle, and if you hope to do anything with her, you need to speak with someone. There's nothing to be ashamed of. We all need to speak with someone at one time or another."

"Damn you, Dan!" Mark said, jumping up from the couch. "You're always the one with the answers, aren't you! Well, I'm not crazy!" He grabbed his bottle and ran out the door, jumping into his Iroc Z, parked outside.

"Mark! Wait!" Dan hollered after him. He was drunk and upset, the two worst combinations for driving.

The key turned in the ignition followed by a black belch of smoke behind his Camaro. "Fuck you! I'm not crazy!"

Before Dan had a chance to reach the car, Mark slammed the shift into reverse, laying rubber in the driveway. He peeled down the street, shifting gears until he was out of sight.

Michelle was standing behind Dan. "You didn't do too well, did you?"

"Dammit!" Dan said.

"He's been that way. I can't seem to get through to him."

"Neither can I," Dan said with remorse in his voice. He turned around and looked at Michelle's puffed and tear-stained face. For a moment, she resembled his sister, Louise, whom he hadn't seen since he had last seen his parents. Dan put his arms around her. "I love him, you know."

"I love him, too."

"It might take some convincing but he's got to see someone about it. Why didn't you tell me that this was going on?"

"I thought that it would go away," Michelle answered, holding herself under control.

"Well, it hasn't. I thought that it would go away with our parents, too. It doesn't disappear."

That night, Dan stayed at Michelle's, waiting for Mark to come home. She retired to the bedroom, while Dan fell asleep on the couch. At two-fifteen in the morning, the telephone rang. Dan picked it up sleepily.

"Hello?"

"This is Officer MacDonald, California Highway Patrol. Is Michelle Sheldon in?"

"How can I help you?" Dan asked. "She's asleep."

"This is very important," the officer said. "It's regarding Mark Wilcox..."

Suddenly, Dan was awake, fearing the worst. "I'm his brother, Dan."

"I'm sorry to tell you this, Dan. There's been an accident."

Dan felt the world sway beneath his feet. "What? Is he okay?"

"I'm afraid not. Judging from the scene, he was drunk; his car was found wrapped around a tree. There was a fire, evidently from the impact. He was thrown about fifty feet from the vehicle. He's in a coma at Palmdale General Hospital..."

Dan dropped the phone and staggered backwards. He fell onto the couch, in a daze. Mark may have been drunk, but he knew what he was doing, Dan could feel it as he remembered those last words of his brother as he peeled out of the driveway. That car had not accidentally careened into a tree. Mark had done it on purpose, just as blindly as he had beaten Michelle. *He had been trying to kill that beast inside.* He did it because he couldn't control that monster, a monster inherited from his father, a monster that they had both faced many times before. It was the very same monster hat Dan and Mark had whispered about in the early hours of the morning and in the deep hours of the night.

Even though the two of them had escaped from their parents, the wounds ran deep and wide.

The worst part was, the beast would always be there...

36

ALTHEA

Dan decided that their best bet was to stay off the well-travelled roadway of 1-75, taking the 19 up the gulf coast of Florida. Both of them could feel the exhaustion from the day before and the lack of sleep that they had had that morning. The thing that was on Dan's mind was in how the police figured out to look for their bus. His uncle couldn't have given away the connection, they had parked a ways from the house and they weren't in their Deadhead clothing. Not being able to contain his perturbation any longer, he pulled into a station in Spring Hill.

He called Derry in St. Ignace.

"Derry's Auto Body," Derry answered. "How can I help you?"

"Hey, Derry. It's Dan. How are you doing?"

"Jesus, Dan. How are you doing? I know a lot of people who want to talk to you, man. You're famous up here!"

"I've gotten the idea," Dan said. "Listen, uh..."

"Dude, I'm really sorry! We had a little glitch in our trade. Did you realize that we forgot to trade license plates?! I got pulled over yesterday and the fucking cavalry showed up to have me arrested! Then, I had your license on me, which I could hardly show these guys! Shit man, if I had known, I don't think I ever would have gotten involved in this," he said, slightly out of breath.

"I'm really sorry, Derry. So, what happened?"

"I told them that I bought this car from you. They didn't believe me. Then, last night, while I'm sitting in the slammer, I meet this asshole named Robinson. If anyone wants to say that the police don't use strong arm tactics, anymore, I'm going to tell them to kiss my ass..."

"Derry, please get to the point. What happened?"

"Let's put it this way. Your cover's blown. I didn't have a choice, man! I told this Robinson asshole that I had met you on the road and you offered a sweet deal for Blossom. I figured it best to pretend that I didn't know you except as a passing acquaintance, you know? So, he knows Blossom's plates but he doesn't know about the driver's license. In other words, you've got a marked vehicle. He's after your ass something fierce."

"Shit," Dan commented, chewing on a fingernail.

"By the way, how's Blossom doing?"

"Touch and go," Dan said. "But, she's still running."

"Good to hear from you, Dan. But, I've got a word of advice. Don't come around here, like The Dead say in the song, *Bertha*. Cops are on my ass like stink on fucking shit, man. You doing alright, by the way?"

"I'm hanging, Derry. We went to a Jerry Tribute last night and the police marked us this morning. I guess I know why, now."

"You in Florida? I heard one of the cops say that Blossom was pulled over down there, through the license plates."

"Let's just say that the less you know, the better off you are. Derry," Dan said, "I didn't want you to get caught in the middle of this, you know? I'll mail your ID 's as soon as I can."

"No sweat, man. You take care and watch your ass!"

"You, too, Derry."

"Peace, pot and microdot. See ya," Derry said, hanging up the phone.

As soon as Dan got back to Blossom, he told Diana what had happened.

"So, our time's up, isn't it?"

"Not until we get caught," Dan said. "You've got to make a deal with me. If I should get caught, you're to say that you're a hitch-hiker. I picked you up and you didn't know who I was. There's no point in both of us going to jail. Is that a deal?"

"I can't do that..."

"Dammit, Diana. This is why I didn't want you to go along to begin with. I have enough troubles without being responsible for you, too. Please, go with me on this one. You'll use Althea's ID, if need be. Please!"

Hesitantly, Diana agreed, feeling the noose tighten around their necks.

That afternoon, they made tracks, going through one small northern Florida city after another. Yankeetown, Gulf Hammock, Shamrock, Tennille and Athena flew by, ignored and unseen in their desperate run. Blossom's temperature was rising and that only served to increase the pressure they were going through just a little more. The good thing was, they didn't see one cop along the way.

At one point, Diana asked Dan to recount everything he remembered about the murder, all the way down to the last detail. Of course, Dan spoke of the possibility that the face he had seen was his sister, a little older and a little grayer. He remembered the glint of the knife and his losing his balance when the knife cut through his shirt. He filled in the part where he had gotten hit, his memory washed afterwards.

"And you woke up in your house?"

"That's right," Dan said, wiping the humid sweat from his brow.

"Hmm. And when did you realize that something was wrong?" she asked, taking notes.

"Well," Dan said, thinking back to that Thursday afternoon. "I remember that my contacts were in and that I could barely open my eyes. I stumbled to the bathroom, being blind and I remember tripping over my shoes. When I got to the bathroom, it was all that I could do to get my contacts out. They hurt something fierce. Then, once they were out..."

"Your shoes?" Diana asked.

"Yeah. They were next to my bed. Which, now that I think about it, was kind of odd. I have a habit of taking my shoes off when we go into the house. I mean, well, when we were kids, we were raised that way. So..."

"So," Diana said slowly, "how did your shoes get there?"

"I don't know. I don't even know how I got there."

"That's what I'm saying," Diana said. "Listen, you know that you were knocked out from the welt on your head, right? Well, is it possible that the person who knocked you out is the same person who got you back to your house?"

"Why would anyone do that?" Dan asked.

"Exactly," Diana said. "In that one little detail, I think that we can comfortably assume that it's someone who knew you. It seems to me that if it was a genuine murderer who attacked your mother, they would leave you at the scene of the crime, drawing the attention toward you and away from them. In your case, however, this person went through a lot of trouble to get you out of there. All they had to do was to look through your wallet to get your address. You stumbled in on something where you didn't belong. Further, didn't the detective say that there was no sign of a robbery yet it was made to look like a robbery?"

"Yeah, he did," Dan agreed.

"This was set up. But, the key is that if you didn't know the killer, the killer knew you. I think the killer was trying to protect you. It couldn't have been easy getting you back to your house. If anything, they would have left you there. Wait a minute!" Diana said, flipping through her notes.

As they headed toward Perry, the landscape looked like the Everglades, swamps galore, a peeping alligator sneaking through the canals that ran along side the road. Blossom bounced, sounding rough at times. Dan tried to ignore it.

"Let's get back to this looney-bird thing. It's been bothering both you and me because it never made sense from the beginning. You remember being called a looney-bird and we decided that your mother could have called the other person in the room a looney-bird, right?"

"Like I said, it's possible."

"Uh huh. And, didn't you say that when your brother called home, your mother referred to your sister as crazy?"

Dan thought for a moment. "Yeah, I said that, didn't I?"

"You sure did!" Diana said excitedly. "Well, in the beginning of all of this, that detective couldn't find your sister by normal techniques. There were no marriage records, no criminal records and no driver's license records, right?"

"Well, I'm not sure of the exact details but..."

"But!" Diana marked pointedly, "in a normal investigation, the usual records didn't seem to exist. Think about this theory. Is it possible that she was put into a sanitarium? Didn't your uncle make a reference to her being withdrawn and unsociable, as if he couldn't figure out what was going on with her?"

"Yeah?" Dan said, shifting Blossom down to third to avoid some roadkill.

"Anything regarding mental health is kept extremely confidential. Her name wouldn't show up on a roster unless you specifically were looking in that direction. We have never looked specifically at a mental health institution. She's not in jail or Robinson would have found her immediately!"

"But, she's not crazy!"

"Who says she is! If she was committed before she was to the age of eighteen, in a private institution, she might very well still be there!"

Dan didn't like the thought or the direction that Diana was headed. But, he couldn't turn down the logic of it. "Maybe..."

"Maybe?" Diana questioned sarcastically. "It makes perfect sense!"

"Yeah, but it's a moot point. How can we find her now?"

Diana crawled into the back of the bus and began rifling through her clothes. They were a bit wrinkled but they would have to do. "What's the next big city that we're headed to?" she asked.

Dan didn't have to look at the map. "Tallahassee," he said.

"Great, can we stop at a major hospital? I can walk in as if I'm a visiting psychiatrist. All I need to do is get near a computer and we're home free. Do you want to try it?"

"Okay, I'll bite," Dan said quietly. "If she is in a sanitarium, I'm going to be pissed."

"Yeah, but at least we'll know."

"Wait a minute," Dan said. "If she's in a sanitarium, then how the hell can she be the killer? That's about the best alibi that one can get, isn't it? It'd be like being accused of a crime when you're in prison!"

Diana hadn't thought of that. On the other hand, the curiosity was insurmountable. They had to, at least, look into the matter.

An hour later, they drove into Tallahassee and proceeded to get lost right off the bat. Then, Blossom blew a front tire, sending them into a crazy figure eight off the exit ramp.

Dan surmised the damage. Her tire was shredded, her treads exposed like the innards of a robot. "Dammit!" he said furiously. He walked around to the front of the bus and removed the "Steal Your Face" cover, relieved that the spare was in decent shape, although far from new. He scurried around in the front compartment for the jack set-up.

Meanwhile, Diana was looking down the road, seeing signs for a Florida State University. She looked at her wrinkled outfit in back and weighed the issue as to whether she should change. "I have an idea," she said.

"Yeah?"

"They've got a library at the university which means that they'll have a computer. While you're doing that, how about I save some time and take a walk over. Meet me in the parking lot of the library."

"You sure?" Dan asked, wiping his hands on his pants. She wouldn't have been much help, anyway.

"It'll save time," she said.

"Go ahead," Dan said. "I'll be fine. I'll grab some gas, too."

An hour later, Dan was baking in the sun in the parking lot of the library. He didn't want to risk going in.

He was just beginning to doze when Diana hopped in. She handed him a computer print-out.

"Bingo," she said.

There was Louise's name, clear as day, at an address in Houghton, Michigan: Shady Hills Mental Health Hospital.

Dan was pleased to find his sister's whereabouts but he wasn't very pleased at the results. "This leads us back to square one," he said.

"How so?"

"Well, here's her alibi. If she's in a hospital that's over one hundred miles from where my mother was killed, then who did it? Who was the woman that I remember? Further," Dan pointed out, "who went through the trouble of bringing me back to my place?"

"I don't know," Diana said.

Dan fingered the edge of the printout. The only thing that they had to look forward to was meeting Mark in two days time. Hopefully, he knew something.

"Is it possible that I imagined this lady attacking me with a knife? Is it possible that I did it myself, my memory maladjusted by the effects of this Post Traumatic Stress Disorder?"

Diana didn't want to answer his question. It was quite possible and was something that wasn't unheard of. People, in their effort to block the terribly traumatic, experienced such traits. The mind could do anything that it wanted to, if it had reason to believe that the being couldn't face the inevitable truths.

"Diana?" Dan asked. "Is it possible?"

Quietly, avoiding his eyes, Diana answered. "Yes, it's possible."

Dan thought of his brother and *the beast*. Who was to say that *the beast* wasn't inside his soul? What if, in all their running, that it was he whom he had been running from?

Dan knew who the beast was from his mother, father and his brother. Had the beast found him on that fateful afternoon?

He had to face the facts. Maybe...

37

THE WHEEL

After Tallahassee, Dan and Diana decided to take 1-90 headed west, which was less travelled than I-10. Although it was significantly slower than taking the main highway, it was best for getting as little attention as possible. They passed through the northern Florida town of Chattahoochee and then crossed the Apalachicola River before Dan became concerned with Blossom's temperature. The needle had only risen to half way but it was enough to prompt Dan to pull off to the side of the road to check the engine over.

He hopped out and opened the compartment to the back of her. That was when he noticed the oil leak coming out of one of the valve lifters. Slowly, it dripped to the ground as the engine crackled in the heat. He wiped the excess oil from the engine and walked to the front of her.

"Is everything alright?" Diana asked.

"I guess so," Dan answered hesitantly. "I'm not a professional in regards to engines but I've found an oil leak. Let's have something to eat and let her cool off a bit."

If it wasn't in the middle of the afternoon, he would have packed the trip up for the night. Unfortunately, the heat in the late September day was enough to deter that thought. It was better to be driving, with the wind whipping in through the windows than to sit there and roast. They munched on some beef jerky and drank warm Cokes to pass the time while Blossom's over-worked engine cooled itself to silence.

Before they got back on the road, Dan looked underneath Blossom one more time. Three innocuous drops of oil spread on the pavement underneath her, doing little to relieve Dan's concern.

He looked up toward the sky, saying a silent prayer. "Please, all we have to do is to make it to Birmingham. That's all I'm asking." He slapped Blossom on the side and hopped in.

As he drove, he kept the radio low in order to hear any nuances in the engine that might give an indication for any problems. He didn't know why, but he was nervous about her. He knew that for the last week, they had run her hard, much harder than dashing off to Dead shows across the country. Doing shows, allowed the vehicle plenty of time for rest. Running from the law, on the other side of the coin, pushed the vehicle to limits of unknown stress. One had to consider, in spite of Derry's work on her, that she was over twenty years old and one ever knew what could happen. The thing that elicited the most fear was that they were in the middle of nowhere and if something went wrong, well, he didn't want to think about it. So, he drove her and hoped for the best.

Forty miles later, in virtual silence, they came upon the hole-in-the-wall town of Cottondale. For a moment, Dan thought about banging a right on I-231 which would have taken them north, across the Alabama border to Dothan and then straight up to

Montgomery. Unfortunately, it looked like it would be a little too well travelled for their needs. He didn't want to draw attention toward them if he didn't have to. So, they continued west on 1-90 with the intent of taking the less travelled 1-331 north, which would have taken them directly into Montgomery without going through any major cities.

Just past De Funiak Springs, they came upon the fork in the road for 1-331. Dan hung a right, lurching Blossom out of first gear. An hour and a half later, they saw a sign stating that they had reached the highest point in Florida, a whopping 345 feet above sea level. It was literally the size of a hill that wouldn't even have been a bump if they were in San Francisco. Ten miles after they went through Florala, just past the Alabama border, they ran into a lengthy construction zone.

Blossom bounced along, avoiding one pothole after another. It kept Dan and Diana's attention as they weaved through a web of orange cones while also watching for craters. Sweat beaded on their eyebrows. No matter what, they were going to make it to their destination. Off to the left, Dan watched as a band of severe weather headed their way. The sun was eventually blocked out with a wall of black darkening the highway.

"Think I should pull over?" Dan asked, the first words to come out of his mouth since being in Alabama.

"I don't like how it looks," Diana said.

Dan looked at the temperature needle, which was still holding at the halfway mark. He also considered the fact that they were in this seemingly endless construction zone. In his mind, he flipped a coin. Do they try and outrun it or do they pull over and wait it out? Dan decided on the former. A good amount of luck had run their way in avoiding any major road problems, so he stepped up her speed to seventy miles an hour.

The darkening clouds closed in on their left. Dan's best guess was that it was still ten miles away and all they had to do was get another ten miles north and he could be past the threat, where he could lower her back down to more engine-acceptable speeds. He was just looking back toward the road when he saw they were headed directly toward a crater-sized pothole. He tried to jam her toward the left but it was too late.

Blossom's tender, right-front tire connected the foot deep hole squarely, bouncing the occupant's heads off the ceiling, with their stuff bouncing everywhere in back. For a moment, he lost control of the steering wheel, scaring the shit out of him. Diana slammed against the passenger door. Crazily, Dan got ahold of the wheel as they heard fragments of the asphalt from the pothole break apart underneath Blossom. Then, just as quickly as the accident almost happened, they were back in control. Their speed had dropped to about fifty miles an hour.

Dan's breathing had just returned to normal, when he glanced at Blossom's gauges. It appeared that they had escaped blowing a flat, the steering wheel solid in his hands. But, the damage had been done.

The temperature gauge, which had been hovering at the halfway mark, was now grilled to the maximum. She felt alright but there was something wrong and Dan knew that they had to pull over and check it out. Diana looked behind them, seeing billows of white steam trailing behind them. Dan saw it at the same time.

"Shit," he muttered furiously. The storm threatened to their left, ebbing closer with each passing second. Dan didn't like the feeling deep in his gut. They were in the middle of nowhere facing mechanical troubles and a weather front that could hold tornados and high winds, was leaving them in inclement danger.

He pulled his foot off the accelerator, letting her coast to the shoulder. As soon as Blossom was stopped, he hopped out to check the rear engine compartment.

The moment that he got in back of her, he knew that their problems were bigger than what he had anticipated. She was hissing wildly, steam spurting from under the engine. Dan prayed that it was just a hose or a clamp.

"Stand back," he told Diana, who was by his side.

Dan carefully unlatched the engine compartment and opened it.

The temperature of the engine was probably running close to three hundred degrees. Further, when they had hit the pothole, a chunk of asphalt had run under her tires and had popped up and punctured the radiator. Compound that with the heat of the anti-freeze in her, the sudden entrance of oxygen from the door being opened and the flammable alcohol on the overly hot engine, the result was disastrous.

Dan heard the air connect and saw, in one infinitesimal second, the resounding explosion as he was thrown back, landing on the pavement. Fire exploded out of her rear end. It took Dan a moment to realize what was happening and another moment to realize that they had nothing to put the fire out. He scurried to his feet and started grabbing handfuls of sun-baked gravel and began tossing as much as he could on the engine.

Heat pulsated out of her, the gravel having no effect in putting the fire out. Black smoke began billowing out of Blossom as the various hoses began melting. Before they could do anything more, the fire on the engine was burning out of control. The heat grew and the rear tires, one by one, exploded and then settled her rear end to the ground. Flames licked at the stickers on the back of her; the FUCKENGRUVEN sticker was the first to turn black and melt away.

"Come on!" Dan yelled at Diana. "Let's get our shit out of there, now!"

They ran pell-mell toward the side door. Of course, it decided that it didn't want to disengage. Dan opened the front door, a belch of heat pouring out of her. He had enough time to grab whatever was in front, tossing it out past the shoulder of the road. He got ahold of his knapsack, a case of bootlegs, Diana's purse and his wallet, which was under his front seat. Suddenly, black smoke ate him up inside as the cushions caught on fire, made before a time when fire-retardant materials were required. He stumbled backwards, choking, as Diana caught him and dragged him away from the inferno that was engulfing her.

The storm approached but the ensuing rains were too late to save Blossom as she died in flames and smoke. They watched their bus, which had become a part of them, become eaten alive. The windows grew black and then, a crack, flames shot out with the new influx of oxygen. Then, the front tires caught on fire, heated up, exploded and settled her carcass completely on the ground. The ensuing death was short-lived as her shell was pattered with the driving rain, the flames strangely and stubbornly staying alive.

Lightning cracked and thunder rolled across the sky while the skies unleashed the pounding rain. Dan and Diana stood there with nowhere to go and nothing to do but get wetter and fight the brief wind bursts without any protection whatsoever. Their belongings and memories were gone; and they are left in the middle of some God-forsaken territory of Southern Alabama.

Eventually, the storm subsided, leaving a rainbow on the western horizon. Neither one saw the beauty of it.

All they saw was the blackened shell of Blossom, melted and stinking of burned rubber. They had a day and a half to get to Birmingham, which, an hour before, should have been an easy task. An hour later, though, it may as well have been Alaska for all that it mattered.

Diana watched as Dan lost his mind.

He walked up to her remnants and looked inside, wiping his rain-soaked hair from his face. He looked in and saw that there was nothing left except what looked like irreparably lost, burned toast.

If Diana was back in her old, normal life, she might have labeled Dan as suffering from Dementia Praecox, a complete loss of identity in his own mind. His eyes were glossed over and his hands shook. There was a combination of rage and frustration that she had never seen in him before. This normally stable man, who looked at life as if it was a challenge, was suddenly in the face of complete and irreversible defeat.

Dan gave the shell of Blossom a swift kick in the side before he stormed down the road. He looked toward the skies and began screaming. "Is this some kind of joke? Is it? Because I'm telling you, I've had it! This isn't funny, anymore. Have I been so bad that I deserve this? Come on!" he yelled as loud as he could.

Diana had to look upstairs, too. Dan had a point. Two weeks ago, she had a normal life. She had a husband, a practice and a home. She even had a car. But, to be stranded in southern Alabama somewhere, with no one to turn to and nowhere to go, she had to wonder. Then, for a moment, she had the urge to laugh as she watched Dan. In its own bizarre way, the situation was almost humorous.

In the back of her mind, she pushed away the thought of the kiss at Maggie's Farm. On one hand, harmless...

"Haven't we been through enough? Haven't we?" Dan yelled toward the skies, with only snakes and lizards hearing his voice. "What do you want me to do? What have I been doing wrong? Am I not nice enough? Will you please give us a fucking break! Dammit!" he yelled as he threw his backpack as far as it would go, reminiscent of when he and his brother had the same tantrums when they were young. "Fine, you wanna fuck with us! Go ahead! See if I care, you mean old son of a bitch! Go ahead, throw us some other fucking problem and see how we deal with it! You just see! Because you know what? You can't knock us down! You can't! No matter what, we're making it to Birmingham and let's see you just try and do something about it! Just try it!"

Dan sat down on the side of the road, glaring off into the flatlands.

Diana waited a moment and then walked up to him. She sat down next to him without saying a word. She knew it was best to let the anger ebb away with time. There was no use in sparking things up again.

Dan's breath rushed in and out in short staccato bursts. Slowly, it returned to normal as he picked at the gravel at his feet. "You know what's really odd?" he asked, not looking at her.

"What?"

"We went through all that work to get some money in our pocket and it's doing us absolutely no good whatsoever. Go figure, huh? Not one car has passed us, we're in the middle of nowhere and this money may as well be firewood. Think there's something to be said about the pursuit of money? That, in the end, it really is meaningless?"

"Could be," Diana commented.

"Fuck!" he said. "Sorry, excuse my language but I'm a little pissed off right now."

"It's understandable."

"Listen to you. Don't you ever get upset? Don't you ever get pissed? Don't you ever want to scream?"

"Of course, Dan. But, rage makes you blind. You have to see past it. You have to see where it comes from and then move beyond it. That's what I do. I know what anger is and I know what rage is. Lord knows, when I told you about my uncle, I lived with that for years," Diana said thoughtfully. "You're a strong man, Dan. You truly are. Live off of that strength. Don't give up! Aren't you the one who's shown me that?"

"Yeah, but this is utterly ridiculous."

"So, what are you going to do?" Diana asked. Without waiting for an answer, she continued talking. "What you're going to do is walk over, pick up your backpack and we're going to walk in the direction that we were headed in the first place. Look what we've done so far. We've avoided the law and we've kept ourselves alive. Isn't that what the Grateful Dead has taught you, that in the face of adversity, you keep a smile on?"

Dan looked up at her. "Are you saying that you like the Grateful Dead?" a small smile tickling the edge of his lips.

"No, I never said that!" Diana said, teasing him. "But I do like the spirit. Let's pick up our stuff and get to walking. Something will happen, you'll see. This isn't the end of the world. Look at it this way; we could have been seriously hurt. We really could have. The fact remains, we have to be grateful for what we do have and, we have our health. Please, Dan, don't give up on me now. We've made it this far."

Dan chewed on it. He took a deep breath and pulled himself up on his feet and walked into the brush where his backpack was. He walked back where Diana was standing and proceeded to dig into his bag for a pen and some paper. Finding both, he made a sign and pinned it on the back of his pack and slung it over his shoulders. Meanwhile, Diana picked up her meager belongings.

"Hey lady," Dan said toward Diana, "you headed toward Birmingham?"

"Matter of fact, I am," Diana answered with a smile.

"Wait a minute," Dan said. He ran back to Blossom's rear end. He pulled out a Swiss Army Knife and detached the blackened rear license plate and jogged back up to Diana. "No need in taking any risks. Let's go," he said.

For the next two hours, they walked the dusty highway north. Not one car passed in either direction and both tried not to think about where they would sleep that night. The thought of being "Gator Bait" was not a thought to relish.

For a while, Dan sang the words to *Friend of the Devil,* an effort to pass the time and to avoid thinking about their predicament, *"Got two reasons why I cry away each lonely night. The first one's named Ann Marie and she's my heart's delight. The second one is prison, babe, the sheriffs on my trail, and if he catches up with me, I'll spend my life in jail."*

Awhile later, five miles under their feet, Dan started talking. Maybe it was because of the stress that they had just gone through and maybe it was because his mind was entirely focused on where their journey had begun. But, something inside his brain had found what it had been looking for all along. Neurons sparked and the memory of walking up the steps of his parents' house came back in a wave, surprising both of them. Slowly but surely, Dan let the memory out, unafraid and firm in his belief. He talked to the cadence of his or her feet, staring at the ground all the while, as if he was talking to no one other than himself.

On his back, his sign flapped in the wind, its message clear: "I NEED A MIRACLE: BIRMINGHAM, ALABAMA.

Dan waited for the brass embossed black door to open. He rang the doorbell again, fighting the urge to run back to his car and get the hell out of town. What was he afraid of? He was too old for them to hit him, anymore. So, why was his heart racing and his stomach lurching? Why did he feel guilty? They were the ones who had kicked him out of the house? They were the ones who had forced him to go to court. He didn't have a choice at that time. He had been just a kid for chrissakes! What did he have...

The door opened, revealing his mother standing there, a look of confusion yet recognition on her face. She didn't look as fragile as she had when she was taking the trash out the night before. She looked almost intimidating, eliciting that same age-old fear in Dan's heart. Yes, he felt like a little kid, again: afraid and small with nowhere to turn.

"Can I help you?" she asked.

Evidently, she didn't recognize him, after all. "Hi, I know it's been awhile. I'm Dan, your son," he said. His voice sounded foreign to him, as if it was coming from someone else. It was hard to believe how much work had gone into the saying of those words; the trip to Marquette, the psychiatrist and the many nights that he had stood at the bottom of the driveway. Once he had said it, it was funny how easy it had come out.

His mother stared at him, as if he had said those words in another language that she wasn't familiar with. "You've got to be kidding me," she finally said, disgust in her voice.

"I know that it's been a long time," Dan said. "We've all made some mistakes and I'm here to admit to mine. Can we talk for a moment?" he asked her carefully.

"This has got to be some kind of joke. I thought that we made it clear where we stood. You are no longer welcome in my house. Need I remind you of the destruction that you caused in this family?"

"But, I was young. I didn't know any better," Dan said, wondering why he always felt it imperative that he apologize.

His mother held the door, making it clear that he wasn't coming in. "I have nothing further to say to you. You will please leave my property or I will be forced to call the police," she said, beginning to push the door closed.

"Wait!" Dan said, sticking his foot part way in, preventing the door from closing. "Can I, at least, talk to my father? Is he home?"

"Is he home? How dare you ask a question like that?"

Momentarily confused, Dan asked her what she was talking about.

"Your father's been dead for four years? It's a little late for a reunion, isn't

it?"

Dan stood there, not knowing what to do. He had never imagined that his father would have passed away. In all the *scenarios that he created in anticipation of that day, it was the one thing that hadn't even occurred to him. "Dead? You couldn't even tell your son that he had passed away?"*

"Don't you come into my house and tell me what I should have or should not have done. You destroyed that man! Destroyed him! You didn't sit with him for three years while cancer ate him alive! You were nowhere to be found!" she retorted.

"But I sent you a copy of every one of my books! If you look in the front covers, you will see my address and phone number! You could have contacted me!"

"You call that trash literature? Your father wouldn't allow them under our roof. As far as he and I were concerned, you were dead and dead is what you shall remain! Now, get out!" she screamed at him, slamming the door closed.

Dan fell back, disoriented and confused. The worst of his nightmares was true. Inside, he was angry but the hurt ran deeper into his soul. Desolate and shaken, he began walking the steps to his car, tears flooding his eyes. Why was he so upset? He had lost nothing more than what he had to begin with. He should have felt relief in knowing that he had tried.

Then, he heard the sound of a crash and a piercing scream. He stopped dead in his tracks, chilled to the bone. It was his mother's voice but it sounded strange. Or, maybe his mind was playing tricks on him. Then, he heard another crash and he knew that something was wrong. He turned and ran back up the steps, listening with his ear pressed to the black door.

He could distinctly hear two voices, both female although he couldn't understand what was being said. His palms broke out in a sweat. Should he open the door? Should he ring the doorbell? Was her life in danger? That scream echoed shrilly in his head.

Dan pushed the door open after hearing another crash, despite his mother's admonishment.

The noise was coming from the kitchen.

"You looney-bird! What are you doing?! Get out! Get out of here!" his mother screamed.

Blindly, Dan ran into the kitchen. A dark haired lady was grabbing a knife from the cutting board by the sink, flailing wildly. Without thinking, Dan tried to jump her. She turned in half-surprise as she raised her arm, knocking Dan off of his feet by hitting him squarely in the chin. He scrambled to his feet as he saw the glint of the knife coming toward him. They connected arms as the knife sliced through his shirt causing him to jump back, looking to see if she had cut him. Then, he realized that her face was familiar. It was the stringy black hair, and the thin frame. He could see the crow's feet at the corners of her eyes and the depth of her anger.

She swung back and connected him squarely in the forehead with the butt of her arm.

Dan saw a flash of white and felt the strength disappear in his legs. His last thought, before he hit the ground was that she looked surprisingly like his sister...

Dan stopped walking, looking straight ahead. "The next thing that I can remember is that I woke in bed and it was four days later. But, I remember that face. I really think that it was my sister. I know that time changes things, and it was fifteen years later..."

"But, you're sure it was your sister?"

"I won't know until I see her again. But, if I did, I would recognize the face. I'm sure of it! The whole thing happened too damn fast. One minute, my mother's telling me that my father's dead and that I'm no longer welcome in the house and in the next moment, I'm trying to save her life. And, you're right, it wasn't me that she was calling a looney-bird! It was Louise, it had to have been. This makes sense," Dan said, fitting the pieces together. "Or, at least I think it does. Who else would bring me back to my place? But, murder? What the hell drove her to murder?"

"Well," Diana said, "you have had a colorful past, haven't you? I can see a lot of resentment and anger would be created in Louise." Adding, "If she was placed in a sanitarium against her will..."

"Then, she had a motive," Dan said, finishing her train of thought. "Which leaves me in another interesting predicament..."

"Which is?"

"How am I supposed to tell the police that it was my sister, huh? How can I live with that?"

"You're jumping to a conclusion," Diana said. "Listen to me. You don't know that it was her, do you? Are you absolutely sure? No, you're not. It's possible that it wasn't. So, what I suggest is that once we're on our way, we decide when we see her. In the meantime, let's not waste a lot of energy getting worked up over it. Chances are, with her being in sanitarium, it couldn't have been your sister."

"I hope you're right," Dan said. "I'll tell you this, if it came right down to it, I couldn't turn her in. It'd be the same if it had happened to be Mark who had been holding the knife. This might sound cruel but the lady was not a good lady. I don't want to say that she deserved to die but I can't help wondering. It gives me chills. What next?"

"I don't know," Diana said, as she watched a lonely roadrunner scurry into the brush.

"I don't either but please don't let it be her who killed. I don't know what I'd do..." Dan said, his voice trailing off.

The two of them walked the next three miles in silence. Each was getting hungry and they couldn't avoid the fact that they were getting thirsty. On top of that, once Dan scared a nest of Black Racer snakes, they were realizing the dangers of wildlife once darkness settled on the highway. Then, they heard the unmistakable sound of a truck coming up behind them.

Dan yanked the sign off of his backpack and walked backwards, holding the sign up for the trucker to see. At first, they thought the semi was going to blow by them, going at a speed far in excess of the speed limit. Suddenly, they heard the sound of brakes and the rumble of the diesel exhaust as it slowed down to a stop, an eighth of a mile ahead of them. Although Dan and Diana were tired, they found the energy to sprint up to the cab.

"What the hell you folks doin' way out here?" asked the driver, who resembled Kris Kristofferson.

"We broke down a way's back," Dan said. "You headed toward Birmingham?"

"Actually, Montgomery," the driver said. "I can get you as far as that. Take it or leave it."

And they got their miracle, sort of...

38

RUN FOR THE ROSES

At 3:30 in the afternoon, Dan and Diana were sitting on a bench in the private aircraft segment of the Birmingham Municipal Airport. Both looked weary and exhausted from their excursion on the road, finding little to talk about. A white and orange striped, twin engine Seneca II taxied past them, preparing to head out to the main runway.

They should have been well relaxed after spending the night in a Ramada Inn in Montgomery. They had managed to get an early Greyhound out of Montgomery to Birmingham and then a taxi from the station to the airport. Considering how the rest of their trip had gone, the last segment had been the easiest part. Both of them were happy to be back in new civilian clothes that they had picked up in a mall on the way there. Once Blossom was gone, there was no longer a point in hiding out under the ruse of being Deadheads.

Dan watched the skies with anticipation, praying that his brother would be piloting one of the planes coming in. For a time, he doubted the phone message that had brought them to this spot. Could he have misread it? Could he have jumped to the island of conclusions? Was it possible that in their anticipation, they were supposed to be in a completely different city? Dan could only rely on his intuition regarding his brother's mysterious message. He couldn't count how many times that he and his brother used coded messages as kids to warn each other of impending doom. He only hoped that he was on the mark this time.

Plane after plane made their approach on that afternoon. Dan named them off just like his brother used to do when they were standing at the end of the runway in Marquette, when they were watching their father practice touch and go's. There were just as many twin engine planes coming out of the sky as there were single engines. They watched Piper Cubs, Malibu's and Cherokees make their approach while a loud and raucous Cessna Skymaster took off behind a Shrike Turbo Commander. A Beechcraft Baron made a particularly rough landing behind a sleek Piper Navaho. In the distance, a Cessna Skyhawk II was in a holding pattern while a twin engine Westwind accelerated down the runway. For every plane that Dan remembered Mark naming, he was just as discouraged to find that Mark was not in the pilot's seat.

At 4:40, Dan looked at his watch with anticipation. Come on, he prodded with gritted teeth. Let this plane be the one. In the distance, he saw a dark blue Beechcraft King Air arch its way toward the landing strip. It drew his attention just as fast as the Beechcraft Baron had. The propellers increased in pitch as its nose approached the land. A resounding "cheep" was heard as the wheels touched the concrete of the runway.

Dan stood up as the plane approached the tarmac where they were sitting. He couldn't quite see in the window where the pilot was. All he could tell was that it appeared to have a single occupant in front, piquing his attention a little more. He crossed his fingers as the plane turned around and stopped, the propellers shutting down.

Two minutes later, a rear door opened with steps extending to the ground. Dan's heart leaped when he saw the face of his brother.

Neither one wasted any time when they saw each other, running up with a solid embrace.

"It's damn good to see you," Dan said with a tired smile.

"You, too," Mark responded warmly. "Well, I guess you figured out the message.

"It took me about four times to figure it out, you know that?"

"I had a feeling when I heard the hang-ups. That's why I added the part where 'the hound broke down'," Mark explained. "Well, it's good to see you. I guess we're calling this *Desolation Row?*"

"Yeah, and we're pretty close to that as we speak. By the way, this is Diana," Dan said, introducing her.

The two of them shook hands. "Ah, the infamous psychiatrist. I hope you took care of my brother."

"Well, I think we took care of each other," Diana said with a smile. "I've heard a lot about you. It's good to finally meet you."

"Likewise," Mark said. "Listen, I know where Louise is."

"We do, too. Diana figured it out," Dan said. "She's in a sanitarium in Houghton."

"I know. I was notified by a lawyer as to her whereabouts. By the way, we're not in the will but Louise is. Evidently, Mom willed everything to her and her care. I guess she had a heart, after all," Mark said ruefully. "But, more on that later. Listen, are you ready to get out of here?"

"You're damn straight," Dan said. "Do you want to grab something to eat first?"

"I'd like to but we don't have time. There's a weather front moving in from Canada. We're headed to Houghton and I'd like to beat it. If you don't mind, I've got to cancel this flight plan and set up a new one. I was thinking that I wouldn't go see her unless you were there. If you weren't here, I was about to turn around and head back toward California," Mark said while a fuel truck pulled up behind them and began filling up the plane.

"Nice wheels," Dan commented.

"Thanks. I borrowed her from a colleague. Isn't she a dream? She flies at a sustained 490 knots and, boy, is she smooth. Why don't you get your stuff loaded in the back and I'll be right back," Mark said.

Dan didn't bother to tell him that they had nothing of significance to load except what was on their backs.

Ten minutes later, Dan was following Mark around while he did his preflight procedures. "I've got some interesting news for you," Dan said.

Mark was moving the ailerons, checking their mobility. "Oh, yeah?"

"Try this on for size. I think that it's possible that she was the one who murdered Mom." Dan then told his brother about the flashback and the familiar face compounded by his remembering the term, 'looney-bird'.

"Well, then," Mark said with a sigh, "Robinson's in for a surprise. He's dead and determined to believe that it was you. He got ahold of our cousin in California, Stacey, and strong-armed her pretty good about your whereabouts. Further, although I can't prove it, I think he's been tracing our phone calls. From what I've gathered, one can tap a phone from in the house while a trace is done through the outside line. That's why I left the cryptic message. He's also made it clear that he has your clothes from the night of the murder. Of course, the Michigan State lab was able to prove that the blood on those clothes are from both you and Mom, which doesn't look good for you," Mark explained as he checked underneath the plane for any residual oil leaks.

"Which goes to show that I'm in a hell of a lot of trouble."

"Oh, I wouldn't doubt that at all," Mark commented. "But, there's one thing that I don't understand. If she's been in this sanitarium for the last ten years, how could she have left to commit a murder? Isn't that a pretty tight alibi?"

"I'm not sure," Dan said. "I guess that's what we have to find out. But, I can tell you this, I know that I didn't kill her."

Mark was looking at the T-tail, checking for any marks that might indicate damage. "I believe you, Dan. For the last two weeks, I've tried to imagine what I would have done if I were in your shoes. I should have been on the road with you."

"No, don't worry about it," Dan said. "There wasn't much you could do, for one thing and, on top of that, it wasn't very much fun. Well, except for the Jerry Tribute in Tampa."

"Speaking of that, "Mark said, pausing on his pre-flight, "did you know that you were spotted by a news helicopter doing a story that wasn't related to the murder? From what the ensuing news reports said, Robinson saw the clipping and now they're looking for you all over Florida. What were you doing down there?"

Dan quickly told him about Harold and Maggie, completing the story with who their grandfather was.

"Which explains why Mom wasn't too happy with the life she had chosen with us and why Dad was driven so hard," Mark added.

"Exactly. But, that still leaves Louise hanging in the balance and me under the shadow of a murder."

"So, let's fly up and see Louise and we'll go from there. I've hired a lawyer, also. He doesn't know about this trip but I promised that if we hooked up, I'd get you in under his protection. He's a good man and he knows his shit. I just wish that there was more that I could have done."

"Your being here is good enough for us," Dan said.

Twenty minutes later, after Mark had filed the new flight plan, the three of them were in the King Air with Mark and Dan in front and Diana, resting comfortably, in back.

Before starting up the left propeller, Mark followed proper procedures by yelling, in a loud and boisterous voice, "Clear!" outside his window. Dan watched the rest with growing interest as Mark pushed the throttle forward. A whine slowly increased as the first propeller started to turn. Once it was going at the proper RPM's, he repeated the same process with the other propeller.

He switched the frequency on his Collins radio and called the Air Terminal Information Service for the latest updates on weather. He wrote down the corresponding information on the small clipboard attached to his right leg.

"Ground Control," Mark said formally after another radio channel switch, "This is King Air November eight-seven-three-six Yankee, permission to taxi to runway."

"Three-six Yankee," the tower answered, "Taxi to Charlie niner and turn left."

Mark released the brake and pressed the throttle forward slowly as they moved off the tarmac to the taxi area parallel to the runway. Once they were on the run-up area, third in line, Mark fired up each of the engines to their near maximum RPM's. He got another update on weather. Satisfied, he called Air Traffic Control.

"This is King Air November eight-seven-three-six Yankee, ready for takeoff."

"Three-six Yankee, you are cleared for take-off."

Mark looked over at Dan and smiled. "Kind of reminds you of when we were kids, doesn't it?"

"Sure beats a Sleek Streek," Dan commented. He couldn't believe that a mere ten years prior, Mark had been in a coma, fighting for his life. The recovery had been arduous and slow but once Mark had gotten his will to live back, he had attacked his career with perseverance unmatched by few. He had gone from the lowest point in his life to fulfilling a childhood dream, that of owning the skies. Dan could see it in his pride as he attacked every detail with relish.

Mark took a deep breath and released the brake, pressing the throttle forward, the engines increasing in a solid purr as they pulled forward. The King Air smoothly took the length of the runway and lifted into the air, headed for the deep, blue skies.

Once they had maintained an altitude of sixteen thousand feet, Mark set the plane on auto-pilot, comfortably set for the next three hours. He poured two cups of coffee, seeing that Diana had fallen sound asleep.

The rest of the flight was spent in catching up on everything that happened in the past three weeks.

"Tell me," Mark said softly, "do you like her?" he asked at one point.

Dan looked at him, surprised. "I do. But, with the way everything is, there's not much that I can do," he said, an element of worry in his eyes.

Mark thought about it for a moment. "Don't worry. I'll do whatever it takes to get us out of this mess. We've been through worse, you know."

Dan tried to take solace in his words, remembering their being kids. He looked back at his road companion, thoughts of the kiss at the pond resurfacing. He vowed that if he ever got his life back, he would, at the very least, ask her out. If of course, she agreed to it.

For the first time in weeks, Dan felt safe and relaxed in the solitude of the airplane, content that someone else was behind the driver's seat, so to speak. He looked down over the sun washed plains, farmland charted out like the squares of a checkerboard. Occasionally, the passing shadow of a cloud moved its way across the land. The hum of the propellers pulled Dan in with their hum, lulling him to sleep. His dreams were fitful and jerky, a constant reminder of the shadow that was following them.

Hours must have passed by the time that Dan awoke, momentarily confused by his surroundings. He looked over at Mark who was busy making calculations on his kneepad. The sounds of the propellers increased and decreased as they maneuvered around mountains of threatening clouds, crystalline white on top while dark and foreboding on the bottom. Every once in awhile, he could see lightning as it sparked its way toward some unknown location on the ground.

"How was the nap?" Mark asked as he banked the plane between a sharply defined thunderhead.

"Good, I think," Dan said.

"Well, I hope you enjoyed it because I doubt you're going to get much sleep for the rest of the flight," Mark said, adjusting his Collins radio to the proper frequency.

Without being asked, Dan connected his seat belt, suspecting what was going to happen next. He turned around and shook Diana by the shoulder, jarring her awake. Her eyes read disorientation, also.

"You better fasten your seat belt," he said. "I believe that we've got some turbulence coming up."

"Sure," she said, grogginess in her voice.

"How far away are we?" Dan asked his brother.

"We should be going into final approach in about fifteen minutes," Mark answered. "Dammit, I was hoping that we'd miss this front line," he added.

As if on cue, they hit a pocket of air, dropping the plane a good five hundred feet, as if they were on a freefall roller coaster, slamming the plane into a jolting bounce. Dan gripped the handle as tightly as he could, hating the feeling and wondering when the next bump would rock their senses.

"Houghton tower," Mark said into the small microphone around his chin, "this is King Air eight-seven-three-six Yankee, inbound for land."

"Roger, three-six Yankee. Descend to 2500 feet for downwind leg," a deep and resonant voice responded.

Mark adjusted various controls on the panel as they descended into the clouds below, maneuvering his ailerons. The sun disappeared above them as they sank into the billowing white clouds, occasionally bumping their way along. Thin streams of water ran alongside the windows as the clouds grew thicker. Beads of sweat worked along Mark's forehead.

"Three-six Yankee, this is Houghton tower," the voice said formally, "Turn left on final, cleared to land on runway one-three. Wind at two-niner-zero, five knots, gusting to twenty knots Northeast. Temperature fifty-four degrees, dew point at fifty-one, cleared to land."

"Roger, Houghton Tower," Mark answered as he banked the plane to the left. He looked over at Dan. "Welcome back to the warm and balmy temperatures of the Upper Peninsula."

Suddenly, they broke the ceiling of thirty-five hundred feet, descending to another thousand feet below the clouds. Lightning lit up the land below them, a sea of dark green trees, interspersed with a dotting of lakes and ponds. The engines whined as they hit another pocket of turbulence. In the distance, Dan could see the twinkling of lights, marking the towns of Houghton and Hancock. Just off the nose, a string of white beacon lights directed them to where they would be landing.

Mark compensated, occasionally, with the cross winds, aiming the King Air where she was supposed to go. The ground edged closer and closer, revealing details of small farmhouses and the movement of traffic two- thousand feet below.

The familiar voice of Houghton Control broke the silence in the plane. "Three-six Yankee, we need you to make a go-around. Ascend to twenty-five hundred feet and maintain pattern until further notice."

"Dammit," Mark muttered. "Roger, three-six Yankee."

"What's wrong?" Dan asked.

"Hell if I know," Mark said as he pulled on the yoke. "I'll tell you this, the last thing that I want to do in this kind of weather is to make laps of the airport. Either there's an obstacle on the runway or we have opposing traffic."

Mark got the plane back up to the required altitude, obviously displeased about the circumstance. He looked at the fuel gauge and was just as upset. "I can't afford a holding pattern of more than five or six laps. This damn weather has eaten us alive."

Above them, the ceiling was dark and blackened as they arched a turn, as if the tip of the wing could touch the ceiling at any second. White light splashed over the airport as a crooked shot of twisted lightning sparked across the sky.

Mark looked down outside his side window as they were turning. "Son of a bitch," he muttered quietly.

"What is it?" Dan asked.

"You are not going to believe this," he said.

"What?"

"What's going on?" Diana asked from the back, obviously aware that something was up.

"Take a look down, out my side of the plane," Mark pointed. "We've got company."

Dan and Diana looked where Mark was pointing. What they saw made their stomachs lurch with a burst of acid and adrenaline.

It took Dan a minute to let the words slowly come out of his mouth. After all the work that they had done, he could hardly believe their luck. It was not a coincidence and Dan knew it. There was no other way that their situation could be explained. It was blatantly clear why the tower had told them to circle the airport.

Below them, a stream of traffic was pouring into the airport. The problem was that on each of these vehicles, blue and red lights twinkled as if to mock their very existence.

"Dammit!" Mark said, furiously. "I can lose my license for this!"

Dan knew, in that second, that harboring a fugitive was probably a felony and a federal offense. He didn't need Mark to explain any strict Federal Aviation rules. They were on the run from the law and Mark had gotten caught in the middle.

"What if we abort this airport and go to another," Dan offered, lacking any other option.

"First of all," Mark said, "we don't have the fuel for it and, second of all, no matter what airport we pick, I'd be violating a flight plan and you can be sure that they'll be waiting for us there."

"Maybe it's a coincidence," Diana said from the back. "Maybe there's some sort of emergency and we're jumping to conclusions. How could Robinson find us up here?"

Mark looked back toward Diana and then looked at Dan, as if he was scolding them silently for getting him into their mess. He banked the plane to the left as rain drilled the windshield.

"She's right," Dan said. "How could he know that we were arriving here?"

"If the bastard's got my phone traced, there's no doubt in my mind that he had someone watching me, waiting for me to move."

"I don't see what you're talking about," Dan said. "Wouldn't we know if a plane was following us?"

"There's no need for a plane to follow us," Mark said. "All he has to do is get ahold of my flight plan."

The reality of the situation hit Dan. Robinson had a good three hours to maneuver his forces since they had left Alabama. So, while they were flying, Robinson was setting the trap all the while.

They had just broken into their second go-around when the radio barked at them, "Three-six Yankee, you are cleared to land on runway one-three. Wind at two-niner-one, seven knots, gusting to twenty-two. Temperature at five- three degrees with dew point at five-zero. Cleared to land."

Dan looked at Mark as he gripped the handle next to him. Five minutes before, they would have been happy to land the plane. But, since seeing the trap that was lying in wait for them, they were facing an entirely different and unappetizing situation.

Mark set his flaps and proceeded to work on bringing the plane down to one thousand feet above the airport, silent in his anger.

Dan stared at the blue and red lights, knowing his end would be in that barrage of vehicles.

To say that he was frightened couldn't nearly touch on the rim of his emotions...

39

WOMAN IN WHITE

"Three-six Yankee, you are cleared for one more go-around and then cleared to land on runway one-three."

"Roger, Houghton tower," Mark said, maneuvering the controls. "We've bought ourselves about four minutes," he said to Dan. "What do you want to do?"

Dan looked at their impending doom of blinking lights on the ground; sure that Robinson was part of the party. "I can't believe that we've come this far only for it to end here. Shit!"

"I'm going to lose my license for this," Mark reminded him.

"I know, Mark," Dan said testily. "Give me a moment to think."

The plane bounced to a particularly strong gust of wind as if it wasn't pleased at the situation, either.

Diana piped in from the back, leaning up between the two brothers. "There's a door back here. Do you think we might be able to escape that way?"

"With what? A parachute?" Dan remarked.

"No," Mark said. "She's got an idea. If I can let you out at the end of the runway without stopping, you could escape. All you have to do is to unlock the door and I'll hit the safety release lever from up here. We do it just as I pivot the plane at the end of the runway. The two of you will hop out and then I can reclose the door without anyone being the wiser. When I pull up to the tarmac, the police will find nothing but me in the plane. Hence, my license is safe. The way I look at it, you don't have any other choice."

"Where the hell are we going to go?" Dan asked.

Mark pointed downward toward the end of the runway, just below them. "Look, it's dark over there except for the blue runway lights. Keep yourself low and go over the fence that surrounds the perimeter. As a matter of fact, if you look over there, where the main street is, we can meet at that Holiday Inn," he said, pointing to a location that appeared to be about a mile away, down a golden lit main road.

"Do you think that it'll work?" Diana asked.

Mark looked back at her. "Like I said, we don't have another choice. I'm sure they have a lounge there. I'll pick up a rental car, set us up with a room and, if it's safe, I'll be in to pick you up."

"What if you get arrested?" Dan asked.

"What's he going to arrest me for?" Mark pointed out. "If you two are out of the plane, he's got nothing on me. Just keep yourselves out of sight until I arrive. Dan, get yourself in back and make sure you take everything that belongs to you. I'm about to bring her in."

Dan wasted no time in getting toward the back, grabbing what meager things they had.

"Just in case," Mark said, "strap yourselves in. The moment that I'm almost at the end of the runway, be ready to haul ass."

"Mark, thanks," Dan said. "Good luck to you."

"You need it more than I do," Mark commented.

The King-Air banked its way in for final approach, the stripes of the runway becoming clearer with each passing second. Here and there, the plane bounced agonizingly with the opposing cross winds.

Dan looked at Diana and crossed his fingers. She looked back at him with a small smile of support. "This is unbelievable," she said quietly.

"You're telling me," Dan returned nervously.

Moments later, the large plane touched the runway, raised itself and then settled back down as they met the ground at ninety knots.

"Get ready!" Mark called back. "The moment that I hit the end of this stretch, just after I turn, you better be out of the plane. Remember; keep yourselves low and out of sight. You'll have about ten seconds to work with."

While they were racing down the runway, Dan undid his belt, grabbed his knapsack and unlocked the rear door. Diana waited behind him as their speed slowed. The moment that Mark hit the end of the runway, he hit the safety release, allowing the door to come open as he turned the plane around.

"Go!" he commanded.

Dan needed no further prodding as he grabbed Diana's hand and hurriedly led her down the steps. They had no sooner touched the wet asphalt than the door closed behind them. The wind of the props threatened to blow them right off their feet.

In a crouch, they ran toward the grass as the plane moved away. A hundred yards in front of them, they could see the fence that Mark had spoken of. They sprinted, fighting their way through the rain. Once they got there, Dan tossed Diana's purse and his backpack over to the other side. Their fingers grabbed at the wire mesh as they somehow pulled themselves over, dropping on the wet grass.

Dan looked back where Mark was headed, half expecting the police cars to come screaming after them. It appeared that they weren't moving as Mark's plane pulled closer to the mess of trouble.

Moments later, they reached the main road, soaked and dripping to the bone, but relieved that no one appeared to be in pursuit. Dan thought about sticking his thumb out for a ride from a passing motorist but decided that they shouldn't push their luck. In the distance, he could see the familiar lights of the Holiday Inn that they had seen from the air. As if to push them along faster, a car blew by, showering them in a spray of water.

"Asshole!" Dan yelled after him.

Diana plodded her way in front of him, pushing away the thoughts of their absolutely absurd situation. If she could have told Clinton what they were going through, she doubted that he would have believed a word of it.

Lightning, and a resounding smack of thunder ripped across the sky just as they reached the alcove of the hotel. Both of them stopped, shaking from not only the cold but from their near brush with the unwanted lawmen.

"We're soaked," Dan said. "There's no way that we can sit in the lounge like this. Let's find the pool area and hope that they have showers. At least we can dry up a bit."

"I could really do for a hot bath," Diana commented. "Do you know that?"

"I couldn't agree more," Dan said. "Hopefully, you'll get your wish soon."

Dan lead the way through the lobby, watching for signs directing them toward the pool while avoiding the curious eyes that observed the two dampened visitors. Dan kept his head high as if they were making their way to their rooms.

Just as Dan suspected, the pool area was located in the center of the hotel, surrounded by three stories of hotel rooms. Children gave them nary a look as they played in the water. Fortunately, the shower rooms were adjacent to the pool. Both of them bolted into their corresponding areas, relieved to be out of the public's eye. With the help of hotel towels and a hot-air hand dryer, they did their best to look like two human beings again. It wasn't much but it was enough to break the shivering coldness that encompassed them.

Twenty minutes later, they were sitting in the Ship's Lantern Lounge, steaming Keoke coffees in front of them. They found themselves a darkened corner where they could watch anyone enter the sparsely filled lounge while a guy named Chuck, his eyes closed, strummed away on stage, playing a rendition of Curly Putnam's *Green, Green Grass of Home.*

"Which reminds me," Diana said, "Do you remember when we were trying to get off Mackinac Island and we were looking for that creep, Captain Jones?"

"Of course," Dan answered. "What about it?"

"Well, I thought you had stopped drinking," she said cautiously.

Dan looked at his coffee and then looked across the table at her. "You have one hell of a memory."

"It's part of my job. So, tell me what the truth is."

Dan ran his hands through his hair and took a deep breath, looking her straight in the eye. "Can you imagine if my father drank?"

"He didn't, did he?"

"Thankfully, no. If he had, none of us would have lived. So, when you told me to lay off, I did. I know the terror that one human being can inflict upon another and he was sober. I have enough of a problem trying to quit smoking without getting involved with an alcohol problem. I've been all around this world and I've seen what it can do. It would be too easy to slip onto another path to hell," Dan said. "For the life I've had, caution is the operative word."

Diana looked across the lounge, understanding his words. She thought of the two times that she had been hit in her life. The first was when she had told her mother about Uncle Bill and his atrocities. The second had been with her first husband, Tony. Alcohol was the sole reason for the undermining of her marriage, culminating when he had belted her, one too many Rusty Nails in his system. After that, the damage was irreparable

"There are only three things that I trust in life," Dan continued. "Myself and my brother. Who needs alcohol to screw that up?"

"What's the third thing?" Diana asked.

"Well, you."

Diana smiled weakly and looked down at her coffee, holding the warmth of it. She pushed away the thought of an innocent kiss at *Maggie's Farm.*

Dan looked at his watch, a shadow crossing his face. "I hope to God that Mark's alright. It's been over an hour."

Diana held her thoughts at bay as she watched Chuck on stage, lost in his world of music as he glided into Dylan's *Positively 4th Street.*

"You know, I'm nervous about seeing Louise," Dan said. "Half of me won't even know what to say to her."

"I've given that some thought on the plane," Diana said. "Are you sure that it's a good idea for you to see her?"

"What are you getting at?"

"Consider this, for a moment. Let's go on the assumption that she was the one that you remember. Do you think that she's going to admit it if she was the killer? And, would she admit it to you? She has no commitment to you if you haven't seen her since she's been there," Diana pointed out. "Ten years is a long time."

"And?"

"Well, if I were the one to see her, especially as a psychiatrist, I would have a greater chance of getting the truth out of her. I was thinking about learned traits earlier. All of you, as children, learned to lie for self- preservation. If she went from the home environment directly to this hospital, who's to say that she won't lie for fear of punishment? As far as all indications lead, I think that we can safely assume that she'll lie to save herself, if she was the murderer."

Dan took a sip of his coffee and pondered it for a moment. "You might be on to something."

"I could be wrong, I suppose," Diana said, "especially if it was your brother who did it."

"What? That's ludicrous!" Dan said vehemently.

"Is it? He had a motive just as strong as Louise did. Look how you were raised."

"No, I don't buy it. Look at Mark now. Besides, he has an alibi if you want to get down to the obvious. On top of that, I'm positive what I remember."

"It was a point that I had to bring up," Diana said.

"I appreciate the thought but it wouldn't fit. He wouldn't have flown us up here. He would have run just as fast as I have. I think that we should stick to our original plan of action, excepting the fact that I'm the one to see Louise. You may be right. If you can somehow get into Louise's head, releasing that fear of punishment, maybe we can get the truth out of her. Do you have any idea how you could do it?"

"Not yet," Diana said. "Let me sleep on it and I'll see what I can come up with."

"Is your name Jack?" a man in a front desk uniform asked Dan out of the blue.

Dan looked up and was about to respond in the negative when he thought of something. "Uh, Jack Straw," Dan answered carefully.

"I've got a message for you," the man said, handing Dan an envelope.

"Thank you," Dan said, reaching into his pocket for a couple of dollars for a tip.

"It's already been taken care of. I appreciate the thought, though," he said, walking away.

"It's gotta be from Mark," Dan said as he tore open the envelope. Inside, the message read, *Room 353 - be discreet and make sure you're not followed, Mark.*

"What is it?" Diana asked.

"Let's go and watch your back," Dan said. "He's here."

With their drinks unfinished, they left a couple of dollars on the table and went upstairs, making sure that no one was behind them.

After checking the peephole, Mark opened the door almost immediately. "It's good to see you guys. I was too afraid to risk us meeting together in the lounge."

"So, what happened?" Dan asked hurriedly.

"The son of a bitch had a warrant to search the airplane. You should have seen his face when he didn't find anything."

"Oh yeah?" Dan said, smiling at their little victory.

"Don't get too comfortable, Dan. He's out there and I know he suspects your being in the area. Carefully, take a look out the window," Mark said over by the hotel drapes, pulling it open a crack. "The rental car is that blue Cutlass over by that far streetlamp. Now, look about two aisles back and what do you see?"

Dan looked to where Mark was directing and saw a man sitting in a red station wagon, a map light on. "Who's that?"

"It's the goon that followed me here. It's not Robinson, though."

"Shit," Dan said. "So, you're saying that we're trapped here."

"Correction, brother. I'm trapped here. Remember, he only suspects that you're around. I left him with the impression that I didn't know what he was after. As long as my rental doesn't move, you're fine. You're set up with a room down the hall. In the morning, I'm going to take a taxi and get another rental. That'll be your car to get up to see Louise. It's the best that I could come up with on this short of a notice."

"I appreciate it, Mark."

"None necessary," Mark said. "But, we need to get to the bottom of this quickly. Robinson's pissed and the longer that we drag this out, the bigger the risk I have in getting caught. The FAA doesn't like the word felony too much and I don't want to lose everything that I've worked so hard for."

Dan told Mark about their successful escape and of Diana's idea to see Louise instead of Dan.

"I think she's right," Mark said. "If I had killed Mom, and I had been stuck in a sanitarium for ten years, you're damn right, I'd lie my ass off to get out of there. We can't know what she's like, anymore. She could be a vegetable or she could be fucked up and angry. I don't think she'd look too kindly on us for not visiting her, either. Do you want to go alone?" Mark asked Diana.

"I think that it would be best," Diana answered. "If she was..."

"No," Dan interrupted, "this is my problem. If we need to get out of there quickly, you'd be better off with me behind the wheel. Diana doesn't go alone. You stay at the hotel, Mark. Your ass has already been on the line."

The matter was settled. All of them were tired and decided to retire to the comforts of their rooms. Room service was ordered and Diana got her bath. In that brief respite, they had enough time to clear their heads for the next day, although sleep was evasive at the thought of the goon outside watching Mark's car.

The next morning broke without a cloud in the sky, looking warm and inviting. Unfortunately, the scene was deceiving because once Mark got outside, it was barely fifty degrees. An hour later, he returned with the keys to a black Mercury Marquis.

"The idiot is still out there, so watch your step," Mark warned as he handed the keys to Dan.

Diana was on the telephone, a formal tone in her a voice, inflections that Dan hadn't heard since he had been in sessions with her back in Marquette, eons ago. "Is this Margaret Fishman, the hospital administrator?" she asked, putting her finger to her mouth, quieting Dan and Mark's conversation.

"Good. I'm calling from the Michigan State Board of Mental Health Services. It seems that Louise Wilcox's case has come up for review since the demise of her legal guardian. I've been sent from Lansing to meet with her at ten-thirty. I just wanted to confirm our appointment before I drove over."

Dan and Mark looked at each other, pleased at her tactic.

"What do you mean that she doesn't have an appointment scheduled? This was booked over three weeks ago!" Diana said, as if upset at somebody's mistake.

"Doctor, I've been on a flight since the early hours of the morning and I'm not about to head back to Lansing because of some clerical error. How would you suggest that we work this out?" she asked firmly.

Dan sat on the edge of the bed, watching her carefully.

"So, ten-thirty would be fine, then?"

Mark breathed a sigh of relief.

"Yes, it's greatly appreciated, Doctor. If I may, though, is there an office I could use? In my rush off this morning, it seems that I left my file of standard examinations on my kitchen table. If I could get access to some of those tools..."

Diana wiped her forehead, hoping her plan was going to work.

"Your office? Why thank you, Doctor. I'll see you shortly. Your assistance in this matter will be noted in our files. Thank you," she said, hanging up the phone. "We're in," she said to Dan and Mark.

"Good job," Dan said, looking at his watch. It was a little after nine o'clock.

"Now, if we're going to pull this off right, I need clothes and I need a briefcase. I can hardly go in looking like this," she said.

Dan smiled. "Ah, you need to disguise yourself as a psychiatrist."

"Something like that," Diana said. "I told her my name was Doctor A, for Althea, Reed. It has a nice ring to it. I was thinking that my name might be a little too well known."

"I think you're right," Dan said. "Well, we better get going. We don't have much time."

Mark reached over and squeezed Diana's hand. "Good luck to you."

"Thank you," Diana said. "I believe that we might, finally, have luck on our side."

Under a low profile, Dan and Diana got out of the hotel and into the Marquis. An hour later, a cool gray business suit on and an imitation leather briefcase in hand, they pulled up to the front of Shady Hills Mental Health Hospital, an imposing gray building that looked very much like a large retirement home. Dan parked on the street.

"Do I need to say good luck, also?"

Diana looked at Dan and, for a moment, thought she saw the eyes of the boy who had been yanked from court years earlier. "Hopefully," she said, "we can repair the damage of a judge who should have been shot for what he did to all of you."

"Hopefully," Dan answered.

Diana walked through the lot, looking around. If she were to guess, she would expect the facility to house about five hundred people in various arrays of mental disrepair. Delivery vehicles were just making their drop-offs of linen and food. A shift change was in order with both male and female nurses entering and leaving the hospital. Diana kept her head high, pretending that the last three weeks of her life didn't exist. Momentarily, it felt strange as she re-assumed her role as a psychiatrist. She longed for the run to be over as soon as possible.

Diana pushed through the glass doors of the modem facility. A guard directed her toward the administrative offices, up the stairs and the first door to the right. A receptionist, a pretty redhead with a talent for keeping perfectly manicured nails, picked up the phone, calling Dr. Fishman.

Moments later, a sharply dressed lady walked up to Diana, extending her hand. The doctor appeared to have been in her late forties and still held the looks of what was once an obviously striking lady, formal in approach but soft in her eyes.

"Dr. Reed?"

Diana took her hand. "You must be Doctor Margaret Fishman."

"Yes, I am," she said warmly. "Listen, I apologize for the mix-up this morning. I'm still trying to get to the bottom of it. This is a fairly substantially sized hospital, so I hope you understand..."

"No harm has been done," Diana said.

"I've pulled Louise's file. Unfortunately, she's in the middle of a therapy session. She'll be out in about fifteen or twenty minutes. If you don't mind, follow me to my office and you can get a handle on her file. I'll also show you where we keep some of the standard tests. If you don't mind my asking, have you got an idea of how long you'll be with her?"

"It usually depends upon the patient, but I can get by with about two hours. It's sometimes more and sometimes less," Diana said.

"I may put the two of you in a board room, then. I'd hate to be running in and out. Follow me, Doctor."

Doctor Fishman's office was small and unassuming with an array of degrees lining the wall behind her desk, similar to the way that Diana's office was set up, without the skeleton in the comer.

The doctor left the office as fast as she had appeared. Diana sat down behind her desk, diving into her file immediately. If she were there under a different premise, she might have looked through the vast array of tests that Louise had taken over the years. It wasn't her concern at the moment; it would have taken too long to decipher her varying degrees of improvements and setbacks.

Her most important concern was not establishing motive; she knew that a motive was obvious. What she needed was opportunity. Was Louise ever allowed out of the hospital? Her experiences with sanitariums, especially with those patients who were long-term, were that they were either within the realm of hopelessness or their improvement allowed them to be trusted in small increments of freedom. Those pieces of freedom could have been in group outings to begin with and eventually progressed to singular outings. Some patients were eventually allowed to acquire jobs, part time at first, and eventually moved to full time jobs, groomed like a fawn getting used to its new and underdeveloped legs.

As far as Diana could see, in the first five years, there was little to no improvement in Louise's condition. Also, it didn't appear that she was allowed out of the hospital except in groups. It wasn't until the past two years that Louise had scheduled days to go to town, whether it is Houghton or Hancock. In some cases, she found records of a trip to get a haircut. At other times, there were trips to town to go shopping for clothes. In another instance, she was allowed to see a dentist or even an eye doctor. All of these things could have been done at the hospital but the value was not in the service but rather for the independence and knowledge gained in doing these things for herself; an integral part of therapy and eventual release.

In the past year, though, a pattern had developed. She went to town every Friday for almost seven months. Recently, her day off had been changed to Mondays. Diana wished that Dan were there because she couldn't remember the date of the murder and, more importantly, she couldn't remember the day. Thus far, though, the news was more than intriguing. The opportunity to murder was there. It seemed that her alibi wasn't as tight as one might suppose, adding support to Dan's theory.

She was just about to look into the battery of test results when there was a knock at the door. Diana closed the file and excitedly walked over to the door, looking forward to meeting Louise.

She pulled the door open and took a few steps back, her stomach jolting in shock and surprise.

"We meet again, Dr. Powers," the man said.

Behind him, Doctor Margaret Fishman stood there, mirroring Diana's surprise.

"The lady was kind enough to contact me in the event that there were any visitors for Louise Wilcox. I must say, Doctor Powers, you've had a lot of people fooled."

Diana took another step back, trapped and at a loss for words.

Robinson stepped into the room, assertive in his walk, dangling a pair of handcuffs. "Will you please turn around, Doctor? You are under arrest for harboring a fugitive, assault and battery, impersonating an officer of the state and a host of other things that we will be talking about."

Diana turned around, silently.

Robinson deftly took her wrists in his hands and snapped the cold and hardened steel of the cuffs around her, tightly. "You have the right to remain silent..."

Without looking at him, and hardly hearing his words, she knew that he was smiling.

40

MISTER CHARLIE

The door slammed shut as Diana walked away, toward the sanitarium. Dan took a cursory look around, just in case the cops were somewhere in hiding. All that drew his attention, though, was the bustle of activity going in and out of the hospital. All he prayed was that Diana could get to Louise so that they could end this nightmarish ride. Of course, that was assuming that they were headed in the right direction in their train of thought.

Dan rolled the window up in the Marquis. It didn't help that he was sitting in the shade, where it was a good fifteen degrees cooler. If they were lucky, it might hit the upper sixties that day, a big change since their little Alabama getaway. He turned on the radio and channel surfed for a while. Same shit, different day, all the songs played reminding him of a different time in his life. Then, there were the numerous morning shows on the radio going blah-blah- blah.

He reached into the back seat and pulled out his Marlboro backpack, digging inside, rifling around for a tape. It was hard to believe that he went from five hundred tapes to a mere thirty in a matter of days. Well, at least he had the addresses of those whom he had sold them to, allowing him to recoup his losses down the road, given that he ever got out of this shit. He found the cover to a Shoreline Amphitheatre tape, from August 16, 1991, discouraging him a little more. The damn tape, with the sweet *Scarlet-Victim-Fire,* had been in Blossom's deck when she met her unfortunate demise.

Okay, so he had twenty-nine tapes left.

Dan took a quick look around and, seeing nothing of threatening interest, found set two of a Princeton University show from April 17, 1971 and slid it into the deck. He supposed that if none of this worked out in his favor, he knew what his last wish might be before he was made to sit in the lap of Old Sparky, as King might have put it. He could see himself requesting that his last meal be served with the Grateful Dead in the background, breakfast served at dawn. Wouldn't that get some stares from the prison staff, he thought bemusedly.

As the tape played, his thoughts drifted toward Diana. It was hard to believe how much things had changed in the last forty-eight hours. The one thing that he couldn't seem to erase from his mind was the moment that he had kissed Diana. Of all the unexpected things to happen, it surely topped the list. There are no coincidences, he thought. Maybe, just maybe, it was supposed to happen just as it had. Was it a *Celestine Prophecy* type of thing? He didn't know. But that image, of the moonlight cascading off her brown eyes, the softness of her hair and the warmth of the kiss had left him wondering. He knew that she was avoiding the subject and rightly so. But, had she felt the electricity in the same way he had? It frustrated him that he was the main suspect of a murder that he didn't commit. On the other hand, if they hadn't gone on the run together...

Twenty-five minutes had passed as The Dead went from *Sing Me Back Home* into *Goin' Down The Road Feeling Bad* into what he thought was going to be *Not Fade Away*. He was just beginning to hear strains of *Turn On Your Lovelight* when he looked toward the hospital doors. At first, he didn't notice anything out of the ordinary. But, sometimes, even the smallest of details can be the most important. What was it about the dark green sedan, parked in front of the entrance? He wasn't sure if he remembered seeing it parked there fifteen or twenty minutes ago. The hairs rose on the back of his neck, which was never a harbinger of good times to come.

He had a quick flash of his ex-girlfriend, Rita, the cop. Now, why the hell was he thinking about her now? He couldn't remember the last time that he had thought about her and he didn't want to start thinking about her now. Except, there was something she had said about cop cars years ago, something that had stayed in a back corner of his mind, collecting dust. She used to say that you can spot a cop car by its wheels. For some unknown reason, no cop cars have white walls.

He looked at the car in the front of the hospital and it sure as shit didn't have white walls. He sat up in his seat, looking behind him quickly, as if he thought someone was going to jump up in the back seat. He looked back toward the sedan and noticed the small antenna on the trunk, lacking the characteristic curl of being from a cellular. He looked back toward the wheels and saw that it had caps on it instead of rims, making the black walls stick out even more.

Suddenly, he didn't care to hear music, anymore. It seemed distracting and clearly out of context. He let the tape play but turned it down to indiscernible levels, as if every sound was suddenly important and not to be missed. He looked up and down the street but everything appeared normal.

Dan turned the key in the engine, allowing it settle into a soft idle. It was that damn car in front of the hospital, gleaming in the morning sunlight. It really could have been nothing or, at least, that's what he sincerely hoped.

But, when he saw the first of a string of police cars streaming down the street toward him into the parking lot of the hospital, he knew that his world had taken an abrupt change for the worst.

He was frozen in his seat, unable to move. If he pulled out now, they would surely notice him. Further, it was Diana's ass on the line in there. He could hardly leave her. What if the cars were there for some completely unrelated incident? It was a hospital, wasn't it? He didn't have to think about the fact that it was a sanitarium to boot. Anything could happen, he thought. He couldn't let an over-active imagination get the best of him at this stage of the game.

Just in case, Dan backed the Marquis up about two feet, as close as he could get to the car behind him. If he had to bolt, two feet could make all of the difference in the world. He returned the car to neutral, praying that his instincts were off the mark.

There are certain feelings that a person never forgets. At that moment, a host of memories came back, reminding him of a time when he would be having late night conversations with Mark in the dark, and the light would snap on, his father standing in the doorway. Or, when he had been digging through his toy box in the garage and his mother stepped out, unleashing a wrath of hell. Of course, he couldn't forget the hot flash that had enveloped him when that damn sponge had flooded the laundry room, leaving him out of school for a couple of weeks. It wasn't the ensuing event that was the most terrifying, it was the moment that you looked through the doorway and knew what was on the other side, like it or not. It was the waiting for the first blow to connect, the others being diminished in strength by their volume and lack of surprise. But, the waiting for the first blow was always the worst.

All of those images flashed through his mind when he saw Robinson leading Diana out of the hospital. The other feeling that encompassed him was that terrible void of helplessness, like when he had to lead Mark back home from when he had run away, only to see him get *the belt,* anyway.

It had been a long time since Dan had been frozen in fear. He didn't relish its return. To make matters even worse, he knew that it was his fault.

Then, Dan thought of Mark waiting innocently at the hotel, unaware of the events that were in full bloom. There was a goon outside, waiting for the opportunity to haul Mark in for questioning. If Robinson hadn't called him by now, he would call him as soon as Diana was settled in the back seat.

Dan wiped his hands on his pants and slipped the car into drive. If he had ever been asked, he would have said that there weren't enough words in the world to describe how he felt in leaving Diana to the wolves. But, what the hell was he going to do? Walk up to Robinson and say, "Hey, sorry, detective, it's my fault." It may have been his fault but they still didn't have a resolution to where they were three weeks ago.

If anything, he had to get the word to Mark. He had to warn him to get out of there. If Mark lost his license, Dan would never have been able to forgive himself.

The last thing that Dan saw as he pulled away, was the rear door being opened to the green sedan and Diana's head being protected, as she leaned down to get into the back of the car, a perimeter of police around her, their guns horizontal and steady on their target.

It was everything that Dan could do to keep from flooring the Marquis the hell out of sight.

As soon as he hit the main road, he pulled into the first Holiday Station that he saw, aiming a bee-line toward a payphone. He felt as if every eye was upon him as he fumbled with his change to drop into the phone. Finally, he got the front desk and then he was patched through to Mark's room.

"Hello," Mark said, calm as day.

"It's Dan, Mark. Get out of there right now!"

"What's going on?" Mark asked, irritatingly sedate.

"It's Diana. The police have her. Look out the window," Dan said to him quickly. "Is the goon still out there?"

"The last time I looked, about ten minutes ago, he was," Mark said. "Hold on, let me go check."

The phone thumped down on a dresser, leaving Dan standing there in suspense.

It felt like a year later, before Mark got back on the line again. "Aw, shit, I don't need this, Dan. He's not there."

"I'll bet that he's on the way up. Grab your shit and go!"

"Where am I supposed to go, Dan? I've got a million dollar airplane at the airport that I'm responsible for. If..."

"Mark!" Dan barked at him. "Please get out of there! We'll talk about it. If they catch you there, you'll never see that plane again. Uh, let me think," Dan said quickly. "Meet me at the Houghton-Hancock Bridge. Take a taxi, whatever! I've got the other car. Now, go!" Dan said, slamming the phone down.

Slowly, he looked around him, half expecting a crowd of people to have seen his display. Fortunately, no one appeared to have seen a thing. He wiped the sweat from his brow as he made his way to the car. The moment he got in, he lit a Camel Light hurriedly, with trembling fingers. He started the car and pulled out to the main road, headed south, toward the Houghton- Hancock Bridge, the dividing line between the northern Upper Peninsula and the *really* northern part of the U.P.

He had been waiting there a good half an hour before he saw an Arrow Taxi-Cab drop his brother off, a bewildered look on his face.

Dan wasted no time in picking him up. "Hop in," he said as the passenger's door flew open.

Mark tossed his flight case into the back seat and jumped in.

"I was getting worried," Dan said.

"Do you know that I missed the idiot by about twenty seconds? You weren't kidding when you said that he was on the way up!"

Dan pulled onto U.S. 41 and turned south, toward the small town of Chassell.

"Where are we headed?" Mark asked.

"I need to think," Dan answered.

"That still doesn't tell me where we're headed. Don't you have a plan or something?"

"A plan? No, Mark, I don't have a plan," Dan said, trying to keep his frustration at bay. "All I know is that we need to get as much distance between Robinson as we possibly can."

"It doesn't sound like much of a plan to me," Mark said.

"I'm aware of that."

"Well, you can't keep running forever, Dan."

Dan looked at his brother and then back at the asphalt of the road in front of him.

He knew that Mark was right.

41

THEY LOVE EACH OTHER

Diana risked looking across the street, where the Marquis had been parked. She was relieved to see the tail lights of the car as it slowly pulled away, inching its way down the street, in the opposite direction.

"Do I have to have these cuffs on?" Diana asked Robinson. "You've got me. I'm not going anywhere."

Robinson turned around. "Regulations, Doctor. Sorry."

"Where are we going?"

"To jail. You're my prisoner, remember? That's where prisoners go," he said, stern in his response.

Diana sat back, slightly twisted, to keep from sitting on her bound wrists. She hated the smell of his Old Spice cologne.

Robinson picked up the two-way radio receiver. "Car twenty-five, Forty- four here. What's your twenty?"

"Twenty-five to forty-four. I'm at the Holiday Inn. Subject hasn't moved. Over?"

Robinson looked back at Diana, who was purposely ignoring him, her face glued to the passenger's window. He smiled and squeezed the receiver. "Forty-four here, bring him in for questioning. Over?"

"That's a Roger, forty-four. I'll let you know when the bird is in the cage. Twenty-five out."

"Ten-four," Robinson said, placing the receiver back on the hook. He followed between a line of police vehicles, and pulled out of the hospital parking lot. He reached into his glove compartment and pulled out a bottle of Excedrin and shook three pills into his hand and snapped the lid back on, returning the bottle to its home. He cupped the pills to his mouth and began chewing them thoughtfully. In a matter of minutes, they were crossing the Houghton-Hancock Bridge.

Diana looked out over the river, wishing she could jump in, ending the whole charade.

They headed south on U.S. 41, through the small town of Chassell, in the direction of a slightly larger city, Baraga.

"So, what makes a high-falutin psychiatrist go on the run with a killer?" Robinson asked as they were making their way alongside the Keweenaw Bay, its dark blue waters reflecting the glow of the late morning sun.

"You wouldn't understand," she said quietly.

"Oh, you shouldn't underestimate me," Robinson commented. "Really, I'm curious."

"He's innocent, if you care to know the truth."

"He's got you fooled, doesn't he?"

Diana was still upset at being a mere one hundred feet or so from Louise, before she was so rudely interrupted. She had no urge to share anything with this detective. "You think you're smart, don't you?"

Robinson looked back at her and was just about to answer when his two- way squelched to life. "Forty-four to twenty-five. Come in?"

"Twenty-five, go ahead," Robinson said.

"The bird has flown, over?"

Robinson muttered what sounded like, "fuck" under his breath. He sighed, thought about it, and then squeezed the microphone. "Forty-four, I hope I didn't hear what I thought I heard, over?"

"That's a Roger. Subject has flown the coup."

"Forty-four? Hold your position until I advise. I'm ten-eight to Marquette County. Keep your eyes open, would you? I'll be out of range in ten, so landline in two-hours. Immediate contact requested on sight of principal suspect. Is that clear?"

"Ten-four," the voice on the other end said. There was a slight delay before the man could be heard saying, almost inaudibly, "Sorry, detective."

Robinson settled into the art of driving, casually looking around, lost in thought. Every once in awhile, he would look in the rear-view mirror at Diana. Finally, he broke the silence. "So, where is he?"

"I'm sure that he's long gone by now," Diana said, her irritation clear.

"Now, why do you want to make things difficult for yourself? Don't you know that cooperation goes a long way in front of a district attorney?"

"I'll take my chances," Diana returned.

"So, let's get back to earlier. We've got a two-hour drive in front of us. Tell me why you think he's innocent. I'm listening, really."

"I don't trust you," Diana said.

"You don't trust me? I've done nothing more than is required for me to do within the confines of the law. What have I done to lose this trust?"

Diana pondered the moment and came up with the first thing that she thought of, a story told to her by Dan, ages back. "Well, for one thing, what was the point of sending Dan to see his father's grave as if he had still been alive?" She struggled for the words. "Isn't that...unprofessional?"

"I forgot all about that," Robinson said, surprise in his voice. "Maybe it was, how did you put it, unprofessional. But, see, I didn't believe him from the start. Maybe I wanted to see how he would react."

"Detective, how would anybody react when you pull a stunt like that? It was completely unnecessary!"

"You may be right," the detective said, slowing down to avoid a road-slain deer, its carcass half on the road and half on the shoulder. "I'm sorry, if that's any consolation. Now, let's get back to why the psychiatrist thinks that her patient was innocent."

Diana took a deep breath as she watched the tinges of fall colors touch the edges of the trees that were racing alongside. "Did anyone consider the sister, the girl in the sanitarium?"

"Of course," Robinson answered. "Do you think we fell off a turnip-truck?

Have you met her?"

"No. I would have except that someone didn't let me finish what I was doing," Diana said smugly.

"Hmm. And I'm supposed to allow you to go gallivanting across the country, making the department look like a bunch of incompetent idiots? I apologize for interrupting your busy schedule."

"See? There you go. Why do you have to be sarcastic and presumptuous?

If you don't want to hear what I have to say..."

"No, Doctor, go ahead. I'm curious."

"Well, consider the fact that the girl had an eight hour leave once a week for more than a year. Doesn't that prove that she had the opportunity?" Diana asked pointedly.

"There's a little more that goes into a murder than opportunity, Doctor. I had the opportunity to do it, also. But, I'm not the suspect because I don't have the motive. Further, I'm not in a sanitarium. You should know that you have to have the mental capacity to do it. I believe, if I'm not mistaken, that the girl has an I.Q. that barely borders three digits. I don't buy it, Doctor. Not by a long shot," Robinson said firmly.

"So, you've talked to her?"

Robinson slowed the car back down to the proper speed when they went through the sleepy town of L'Anse. He looked at her in the rear-view mirror, inspecting her. Once they were clear of the town, he resumed his speed to just above the limit.

"Yes, Doctor, I've talked to her. She can barely make it through breakfast, much less execute a murder as gruesome as that one was."

"He remembers her face," Diana said. "It couldn't have been anyone else."

"You really believe what you're saying, don't you? He remembers her face? Are you trying to tell me that you believe him?" Robinson asked, pulling out a Camel Filter.

"I do believe him."

Robinson sparked a flame and cracked his window open. "Hope you don't mind," he said. "I know that it's a nasty habit." Suddenly he started laughing. "Just like the tabloids have said, you've slept with him, haven't you?"

"Tabloids?"

"Oh, you folks are the biggest thing that's happened out here since the discovery of copper! You haven't been keeping up with the news? This is as good as O.J. on his suicide run. Be honest with me, you've slept with him, haven't you?"

"No!" Diana said vehemently, disgusted that he made everything seem cheap and sleazy.

"Okay, I'll bite. You didn't sleep with him yet you believe every word he says. Do you know anything about him?"

"Yes, I know a lot about him. Enough where I know that he didn't do it."

"Let me tell you what I know about the man and let's see which story that the jury is going to believe. Are you game?"

"I don't want to hear it," Diana said adamantly.

"Well, maybe it's time you did hear it, Doctor. And maybe you can get yourself out of this without too much residual damage. As far as I can see, if any of these charges stick, you'll be lucky to get a job as palm reader in a swap meet. I think it's time that you hear what you're up against," Robinson said, then added, "Doctor."

Just after Alberta, they changed direction from south to west, staying on U.S. 41.

"Can you loosen these cuffs, please?" Diana asked.

Robinson looked back at her, and then pulled the car over to the side of the road. He reached over the seat, undid her seatbelt, and dropped the key in the cuffs. "These go back on just before we get to the jail. It'll look better for the press," he said.

"Thank you," Diana said.

Robinson dropped the car back in drive and pulled his speed back up before he started talking. "All of this is State's evidence. I didn't create it and I didn't make it up. First of all, the man was a juvenile delinquent. Are you aware that he was in jail for perjury a number of years back?"

"Perjury? You don't know what happened," Diana defended. "He was cornered by a rotten judge. He had a case! There were pictures. If you'd listen to me, you could find out what really happened. It was in 1976 or 1977..."

"Uh, huh," Robinson said, interrupting her. "That was twenty years ago. Let's look at the pattern here. He was not only in jail; he was a runaway, a problem child. The whole city knows it. Secondly," Robinson pointed out with an upraised finger, "he was also a drug user. I have him on record in Chicago for possession of marijuana. Shall we explain that? No, I'm sure that was some sort of trumped up charge, wasn't it? So, let's talk about the murder, okay?"

Diana sat there in silence, knowing that it wasn't looking good.

"The brutal murder of his mother, whom he hated. I don't need to look around much for a motive. Ask anybody in the city of Marquette! Now, let's talk about his nonexistent alibi. He was at home reading or some such bullshit. His sister's alibi is air-tight in comparison. He just happened to have moved within miles of his mother only months before," he said with a residual bite of sarcasm. "Coincidence? Well, Doctor, I've got the very clothes he was wearing with both his blood and his mother's blood all over them."

Diana jumped in, "Which you took out of his home without a warrant."

"Wrong, Doctor. I had a warrant which will stand up in a court of law. I'm afraid that if we were to balance the information that you've given me and the information that I've obtained, well, it's obvious who our man is," he said. "Besides, he ran."

"Meaning what?" Diana asked.

"O.J. Simpson ran, didn't he?"

The car settled into silence as they motored through Negaunee and then Ishpeming, headed for the straight-away into Marquette. Robinson lit a few cigarettes while Diana sat in back and stewed. She couldn't help having a few doubts about her belief in Dan's innocence. After all, she hadn't quite talked to Louise. Maybe, in his desperate run for freedom, he had been grasping at straws. But her instincts told her that her doubts were unfounded.

"So, what's going to happen to him?" she asked.

"He'll be tried in front of a jury of his peers. I think you know the rest," Robinson implied stoically.

"What's going to happen to me?" she asked, halfway knowing the truth.

"Well, Doctor, it depends upon how you want to play the game. If you would like to tell me where I can find him, I'll request leniency in the charges that are being brought up against you. Sound fair?"

"I don't know where he is," she said.

Robinson smiled knowingly. "Well, once we get you to jail, he'll know where you are. You see, the press is on this like smell on shit and they'll give us some free advertising. You know why that's good for us?"

"No."

"You're bait, that's why. If you two did sleep together, he'll be coming this way, back to his home town. He won't be able to do anything for you but, if he's got a heart at all, he'll be here and we'll be waiting. On the other hand, if he doesn't come running for you, you'll know what a slimy piece of human trash he is, and we're guaranteed your cooperation when there is a trial. I think you'll change your tune when you find out that you're about to lose that medical degree. You like how we think? Murder is big news around here, considering how rare it happens. And," he said with a delicious smile in his voice, "I always get what I'm after."

As promised, Robinson pulled over just before they got to Marquette, replacing the steel of the handcuffs around her wrists. Diana didn't even give him the benefit of a grimace.

When they pulled up to the police station, it looked as if a circus was being set up. Every media source in the state was waiting for them, like horseflies buzzing around steaming manure on a humid summer day. Whether it be television stations, radio stations or the local paper, The Mining Journal, representatives were eagerly awaiting their arrival. To make matters worse, reporters from the Detroit Free Press and The Chicago Tribune were waiting with pens in hand, as cameras aimed at them, hoping to get the perfect shot at this breaking story.

The car pulled up and stopped as a crowd of reporters gathered around them. In the distance, Diana could see a row of white vans, satellite antenna's probing high in the air, as reporters from both, A Current Affair and Hard Copy, competed aggressively for her attention. She had had no idea how big that they had gotten. Robinson shielded her through the throng of reporters and down the steps where she was to be incarcerated.

It took a little over two hours for her to be processed. She relinquished all her personal items, including her shoelaces. Nobody wanted her committing suicide. Her fingers were smeared with black fingerprint ink. She was searched and handcuffs were placed back on her wrists. In the end, the iron bars of her cell enclosed her.

Robinson stopped down and visited her an hour after that. "How are the accommodations, Doctor? Do you have everything you need?"

Diana returned him a cold stare.

"Well, I guess you have everything you'll need for the weekend. Your arraignment's not until Tuesday, being that

Monday's a legal holiday. I hope you enjoy yourself," he said, leaning against the bars.

"This solves nothing, Detective," Diana responded, tight lipped. "Go back and look at the court records. You'll see what happened. That's where all of this began. If you were a decent detective, you'd listen to me..."

"Are you sure that you don't know where he is?" Robinson prodded.

"I already told you that I don't," Diana said, gritting her teeth.

"Well, have it your way," he said. He jangled his keys lightly and started walking away, whistling some unknown tune, the echo fading in the distance.

Diana sat on the thin padding of her bed and put her head into her hands. They had run out of time and they had run out of luck...

<u>42</u>

GDTRFB
(Going Down The Road Feeling Bad)

"Are you hungry?" Mark asked Dan, just outside of Three Lakes, on the border of Lake Michigamme.

"Not really," Dan answered.

"Well, if you don't mind my saying it, I am. Do you mind if we pull over in the next town?"

"No sweat."

Up until then, the ride had been filled with silent tension. Not only did they have to keep their eyes open for anything that looked like a police car, they felt like they were wandering aimlessly.

Dan felt as if the world was riding against him, a repeat of his life at home. The worst part was that Diana had been taken down with him. It tore him apart that she was in jail. Diana had put herself on the line for Dan and it was Dan who should have been in jail. He knew that she had chosen her own risk when she decided to go along with him but that didn't erase the guilt Dan felt.

The other worry was that he now had his brother, who had risked everything for him in danger. If Mark went to jail, Dan wasn't sure he could deal with it. Well, deep inside, he knew that he would, without question, turn himself in. That time was drawing nigh.

Dan wasn't hungry because his stomach was churning with anticipation and fear.

They pulled over at an IGA in Three Lakes. Dan waited in the car while Mark ran in. He slid himself down in the seat, keeping himself out of sight of any peering pedestrians that might pass.

Mark came out ten minutes later, a satchel of supplies in his arms. He hopped in the car and opened up the bag. Inside, he had two packs of Camel Light 100's for Dan, mandatory items for being on the road again. He pulled out two chilled Cokes and a couple of deli-made subs wrapped in cellophane, complemented with packages of mustard and mayonnaise. Two bags of Big Grab Doritos finished the quick lunch off. Mark hungrily tore into his food.

"Eat, Dan. If you don't eat, you can't think," he said. "Right now, we need to think."

"Thanks," Dan said quietly. He unwrapped his food and started eating, forcing each bite of the tasteless food down his throat.

"I was standing in line and I happened to look at the magazine racks, you know the ones that are by the aisles," Mark remarked.

"Yeah?"

"Well, get a load of this," Mark said, handing him a pile of newspapers and weekly magazines.

Dan set his food down after a quick swallow of Coke. He began leafing through the papers, picking up the gist of the stories. They all rang the same bells.

The article on the front page of The Mining Journal read, "Killer and Psychiatrist Continue to Elude Police". In the left comer of The Milwaukee Journal-Sentinel, "Manhunt Nationwide for Northern Michigan Murderer" glared obtrusively. The Detroit Free Press was no less kind with their local interest headline, reading, "Suspected Murderer Spotted in Florida". Even the miniscule Munising News splashed their lead story as, "Marquette Residents Held Hostage By Fear".

Dan's appetite was quelled further by the rising juices in his stomach. A quick scan of the articles had him convicted. There was even talk of reinstating the death penalty in Michigan for crimes of a heinous nature, like Dan's. He looked over at Mark, fear in his eyes.

"You okay?" Mark asked.

"Holy shit, I'm dead."

"Yeah, that's what I thought when I got a look at them. If you don't mind, I think I'm going to call that attorney that I got for you," Mark said, wrapping the remnants of his food.

"Do you think he'll be able to help?"

"He said that he would. I don't think that we have any choice but to give him a call now."

Dan set the papers down and looked out the window. "And we have no way of getting to Louise, do we?"

"I think that you're going to have to give it up. Face it, if she's been in a sanitarium, you have to admit..."

"I know," Dan said, dejectedly.

Without saying another word, Mark got out of the car to call the lawyer.

Dan sat there silently, realizing that Mark had no other choice. He also knew that with his brother's airplane at the airport, Dan couldn't string him along any further. It was time to throw in the towel. Maybe it wouldn't be so bad, he thought. If the lawyer was decent, he could figure things out. The situation had gone far beyond Dan's reach.

He looked at his watch and was quickly reminded of the moment that he had first picked it up on that terrible Thursday afternoon. It had become a moot point, though, after the detective had recovered the torn and bloodied clothes. Dan cursed himself for being such an idiot for keeping the clothes in the first place. If only he had thrown them away. If they hadn't been recovered, would he have been in this situation right now?

He picked up The Mining Journal, attempting to steer his mind away from the thought. A cool breeze stirred the air, although Dan didn't notice. He casually glanced through the paper. He wasn't really reading; he was more focused on keeping his hands busy. He was tired of thinking about the murder and he was tired of the guilt sitting inside of him. Worse, yet, the thought of Diana being imprisoned bothered him the most.

She had been his only hope and, now, she was as gone as a deer in the face of an eighteen-wheeler's speeding headlights.

He was glancing over the local insert of the paper when he ran across a lengthy article about a man who had committed his sixth "B & E", convicted by a Superior Court judge. Not only had the man received a sentence for that offense, the judge compounded the sentence by nailing him as a habitual offender, adding another ten years onto the felon's term. The judge was being praised for his crackdown on crime. The paper said that after the completion of his fifth term, he was expected to run for political office, possibly as a representative for Northern Michigan. Finally, drawing much political capital was the fact that he was a supporter for the Upper Peninsula becoming its own state, the state of Superior.

Dan looked up, seeing Mark making his way back to the car, discouragement on his face. Dan knew, without asking, that he wasn't carrying good news with him.

Mark opened the door and hopped in, looking stern.

"Don't tell me," Dan said.

"He's on vacation because of Labor Day. His associate says that you should turn yourself in right away and they'll be in contact after the holiday. What kind of shit is that?!"

"I think he's right," Dan said.

"What?"

"I've done enough damage for one month," Dan said resolutely. "First, I put Diana's ass on the line and look what's happened. Second, there's you." Mark sighed deeply. "You want to know something?"

"Hmm?"

"If we lived in a perfect world, I suppose it's feasible that an innocent man would have nothing to worry about. I've heard it but I've never believed it. Do you remember the court shit from years ago?"

"You don't have to remind me," Dan said. "Shit happens."

"It may happen but it doesn't make it right. I remember standing there with Dad, after watching you get steamrolled, like Jeff Gordon on a racetrack, and I never trusted the system again. It's about politics and money but I don't think it has anything to do with what it was intended for," he said, his lower lip strained and whitened.

"I know," Dan said flatly. "Look, maybe we should get out of here. I really think that it's best for everyone that I bail out of this. Things will work out in the end, really."

"Fine," Mark said. "Let's go."

"We need to face the music, Mark. I can't stand the thought of Diana sitting in jail because of me."

Without saying another word, Dan pulled the car out of the parking lot and headed back out on U.S. 41, toward Marquette.

They were driving through the quiet town of Champion when Mark looked over to his brother. "I really care about you, Dan."

Dan looked over at his brother, then back on the road. "I care about you, too. I'm sorry about all the shit that I've gotten us into."

Mark picked up the stack of papers, flipping through the headlines. "If somebody told me that, a month ago, I'd be running from the law, I would have laughed in their face."

"You're telling me."

For the next ten minutes, Dan looked at the forests that lined the two-lane highway, the birches tinged with yellow and hints of red on the maples. If he were in another world, it might have been nice to pull over at any of the roadside stops, and enjoy the serenity that made the Upper Peninsula, a vast haven of nature, seemingly untouched by human hands.

Mark looked up, puzzled from what he was reading.

"What is it?" Dan asked.

"Did you read this article about this judge and a guy who went to prison for a bunch of burglaries?"

"Yeah? Something about the kid getting a bunch of extra time on his sentence?"

Mark was thinking; his brow furrowed in concentration.

"Well?" Dan prodded.

"Do you want to stop by the house?"

"In Marquette?"

"Yeah."

"For?"

"Well, do you remember the name of the judge that put you in jail when you were a kid?" Mark asked.

"That was a long time ago, Mark. I really couldn't tell you. If Diana were here, she'd explain half of this P.T.S.D. thing. It has to do with the blocking of certain memories. So, there's pieces that..."

"Pieces that you don't remember because of stress, like a Vietnam veteran."

"Yeah, plus it was about twenty years ago. What's up?"

"Well, this might sound like a shot in the dark but it says that this judge, from Marquette has been on the bench for five terms. You don't think that it could possibly be the same one, do you?"

Dan's interest was piqued. "Let me see that."

Mark handed it over, pointing out the picture that was side-lined.

Dan looked it over and handed it back to Mark. "I wish I could answer that, but I can't tell."

"Answer this. Could it be?"

"Mark, I don't remember. What do you think is at the house?"

"Well, let's think about Dad for a moment. Not only was he a doctor, he was a pilot. Do you remember how he was being sued all of the time?"

"Of course," Dan said, pulling a California glide at a stop sign in North Lake.

"He saved everything. He had to because he never knew what or when he had to use something in court. Hell, I save everything regarding my license just to make sure it's safe in case something legal comes along."

"What are you getting at?"

"Remember when we put the Hot Wheels Flip-outs in the basement and we got the model airplane?"

"Yeah?"

"Well, the basement's full of records," Mark said. "There were boxes and boxes of them. It's a chronological history of his life. He didn't throw a thing away because he never knew when shit would come back at him."

"I still don't see where this is leading..."

"What if this judge in the paper is the same one that nailed you?"

Dan thought of Diana's comment before he had walked into the sanitarium. Something about shooting the judge who was indirectly responsible for where they were. "Yeah?"

"Do you think that he was paid off?"

"I'm not sure. Like I said, we were young. But, he's not going to have a diary down there that says he paid off the judge?" Dan said.

"No, but I'll bet that there are such things as financial records. If we find anything with his name on it, the judge's name, we can pinpoint this guy."

"I still don't see how that's going to help us."

Mark was getting excited. "Listen to me, Dan. We've got no one in our corner. If we can nail the judge like he nailed you, he owes us one, a huge one. Wouldn't things have a better chance of working out with a judge on our side? A judge who wants to protect a future political career?"

Dan pondered the issue. "It's weak."

"Weak or not, it's the only chance that you have!"

Dan thought about it over the next hour of driving. The closer he got to Marquette, the more afraid he became of turning himself in. Mark's idea was beginning to look more attractive by the minute. Even if it was a shot in the dark, it delayed his walking into the police station, if only by an hour or so.

He watched his speed as he went through Negaunee and Ishpeming, noting the increase of traffic, hence the increased visibility of the police department. His heart lurched when they went past the Michigan State Police building, near the airport. Fortunately, they didn't see one car. His nervousness increased for every mile closer to Marquette.

In the distance, he saw the steeples of St. Peter's Cathedral as it rose up in the distance off to their left. Dan pushed thoughts away of a priest he once knew.

Once they hit Shiras Hills, Dan thought he should park the car on Brule Road, before it intersected Allouez, where it would draw little attention. Mark added that they should cut through a trail into Farmer's Field and enter the house from the rear.

Before they got out, Dan looked at Mark. "I really hope that you're right."

"Me, too," Mark said.

The two of them got out of the car and made their way between two houses, quickly finding a well-worn trail to Farmer's Field. They headed to the old trail that led to the rear of the house. It was long and overgrown by brush. As they pushed their way through the trees, brambles threatened to tear their clothes and slowed their progress. They disturbed the hoards of Noseeums, which attacked them in swarms.

Finally, they broke through the trees. Police ribbon still surrounded the house, although the tapes were layered in fine dust, leaving them limp. They ran up the steps to the bay window in front, where Dan had seen the drape blowing out the day he found his mother's body. A chunk of plywood replaced what was once cardboard.

Dan pulled a Marlboro edition Swiss Army knife out of his pocket and proceeded to pry at the nails. With Mark's help, he pulled it off.

They stepped inside a musty home. It was still in disarray but it had been picked over for evidence, trails carved through the debris. Both brothers were as silent as the empty residence. A sickeningly sweet smell still tinged the air, although it was nowhere near as powerful as the fateful afternoon when Dan had found his surprise.

Strings of cobwebs criss-crossed the darkened chandeliers. A coating of dust covered the floor of the foyer, where the kitchen branched off to their right and the bedrooms faced above them off the landing, while the steps below pointed to the basement. Here and there, a creak sounded in the house, making them jump.

"Shall we?" Mark whispered, leading them to the basement.

Dan followed, resisting the urge to look behind him.

In the basement, Mark risked turning on the lights, knowing that since it was mid-afternoon, it was highly unlikely that anyone would notice from the street. He made his way to the corner where they had put the Hot Wheels in the ceiling above. He began picking up box after box of files, wiping the coating of dust from the top one of each stack.

He made a stack for Dan to look through and a stack for himself. Faded Magic Marker outlined the contents of each box. Whether there were tax records, appropriately marked with the years in chronological order, or whether there were medical records, marked in the same fashion, they painstakingly went through each box.

In the last box that Dan was looking through, excitement ripped through his veins. It was titled, barely readable, "Receipts, '76". He could hardly contain himself as he went through receipts for every purchase his father made that year, the year that the whole shithouse went up in flames.

Mark was looking over his shoulder as he went through the last one.

Dan stood up, stretching his back, tired from crouching. "Well, that's it," he said.

"I was sure..." Mark said, faltering.

Dan looked at Mark, a glint in his eye. "We haven't found any personal financial records," he said.

"Well, I did, sort of. Unfortunately, they're all from his office."

"Yes, exactly. But, I haven't found one checkbook nor have I found a savings book. If he saved all of this, wouldn't it stand to reason that he'd save his cancelled checks?" Dan asked.

"You would think so," Mark said quietly.

Dan started pacing. "We've got to think here. This is the only possible place that he would keep everything. If he..."

"Dan! Think about it! He wouldn't have wanted his kids nosing into his private stuff. He wouldn't keep that stuff where we could get to it, would he?"

Without answering, Dan stopped and turned around. They looked at each other, reading each other's mind.

Simultaneously, they said, "The study!"

It was everything they could do to keep from creating a ruckus as they ran upstairs, toward the family room, taking a quick left into the study. Mark pulled the heavy drapes closed while Dan turned on the lamp sitting on the large mahogany desk. From floor to ceiling, books adorned the walls, some literature but more being medical books such as Gray's Anatomy, American Book of Dentistry, and volumes upon volumes of, The American Medical Association's Annual Report. Intermingled with the books, gleaming jaws, in various arrays of construction, grinned at them silently.

"Somebody's broken into the drawers," Dan said, pointing out the splintered fragments.

"The police, no doubt," Mark commented.

Dan pulled two drawers out, heavily laden with bound supplies, and handed them to Mark. Meanwhile, Dan went through the other drawers. It was strange to be digging through years of times past, knowing their father was probably turning over in his grave at the thought.

"Look at this," Mark said, handing Dan a savings book from the First National Bank. "Isn't this a lot of money to move into a checking account, all at once?"

Dan looked it over. It was dated, July 12, 1976. It appeared that their father had transferred $25,000 from his savings account to his checking account. He handed it back. "It doesn't prove anything. There are any numbers of reasons that he could have transferred money. Consider the maintenance on the house, fuel or insurance for the airplane and, don't forget, he had his own practice, too. We need something more concrete."

"Like what?" Mark asked.

"Well, a name would be nice. Put it aside and let's keep digging," Dan said.

In the bottom drawer, Dan found boxes of cancelled checks dated in annual periods from 1971 - 1980. He pulled out the box that was marked from 1976, all from his personal account. He separated those checks from July of that year and went through them one by one. By the time he had reached the end of the month, he had nothing that looked suspicious.

"Dammit," Dan said.

"Nothing?" Mark questioned.

"A big, fat zero," Dan responded. "The only thing that indicates anything, like the fact that we're in the right time zone, is that he did pay out some healthy attorney's fees. It appears that I cost him some money."

"Oh, I know you did," Mark said. "And he wasn't happy about it. Hey, look at this."

Mark handed over an appointment book from 1976. Again, it appeared that it was his personal book and had little to do with the running of his office. In that month, it seemed that their father had seven appointments with lawyers, abruptly stopping on July 13. On the thirteenth, a notation marked an appearance at M.C.C. at 9:00 AM.

"M.C.C.?" Dan questioned.

"Oh, sure," Mark said. "Does Marquette County Courthouse fit?"

"Well, I'll be," Dan said. It was strange to think of that fateful day and where everything had turned since. The pages were yellowed and dried, time having taken its toll. He quickly looked back on July 12 and found his appointment with The First National Bank of Marquette, the day that he had transferred the twenty-five grand. Dan closed the book and put it with the savings account book.

Suddenly, both of them froze at the sound of knocking.

The two brothers looked at each other, afraid to move.

The knocking happened again, yet, this time, it had a hollow and resonant sound to it. They stared at each other, wondering why it sounded strange. When it happened again, they both sighed in relief.

"It's a woodpecker, banging on the fireplace outlet on the roof," Dan said, as it tapped again, doing a bird song of its own.

"Scared the bejesus out of me," Mark commented, resuming his work.

Dan found a number of manila envelopes behind the checks. Upon opening them, he discovered that they were monthly billings from the bank, notating check fees and an account of transactions. He scrutinized it carefully, finding the transfer of July 12. It, too, he placed in the pile that was deemed important.

"What do we have there?" Mark asked, picking it up.

"What we've got is nothing," Dan said. "Maybe this is all a figment of our imagination. It's possible, I suppose, that the lawyers pulled some sort of plea bargain ahead of time," he said, standing up.

For a moment, he felt like throwing a childhood tantrum. It was Friday, at four o'clock and it looked as if their efforts had been futile, again. Dan couldn't hold himself back as he slammed his fist against the wall.

Mark looked up, curious, and then went back to the billing that he was looking at.

Dan rubbed his hand, embarrassed at his little outburst.

"Hey, look at this," Mark said, walking over to Dan.

"What about it?" Dan asked, taking the sheet of paper from him.

"Doesn't something look strange to you on here?"

Dan looked at the twenty-five grand and at all the other financial notations.

"Like I said, Mark, the transfer doesn't prove anything."

"Oh, yeah?" he said, pointing to the charges at the base of the sheet.

"Since when is a person charged for moving money from one account to another?"

Dan looked at what he was pointing out, seeing a twenty-five dollar charge. "Hmm. Maybe it's a mistake," he said.

"A mistake? Since when did Dad let anyone overcharge him for anything? They watched every dime!"

"So, I still don't see what you're getting at."

"Think, Dan. Think! Why would anyone be charged for transferring money?"

"Well, they wouldn't."

"Unless?" Mark pushed.

"Unless..." Dan said, letting the word fade off.

"Where did you get the billing from?" Mark asked, driving to a point.

Dan reached down and got the envelopes where the billing had come from. He handed the package to Mark, who proceeded to slide the pile out.

"As far as I can see," Dan began slowly, "the only way that a bank could charge you for transferring money is if you transferred your money to another city."

"Or?" Mark prodded, delving through the paperwork.

"Well, if you transferred it to another bank..."

Mark stood up, his eyes gleaming, and handed Dan another sheet of paper.

Dan took it and looked at it. It was a copy of a transfer of twenty-five grand. "We already saw this," Dan remarked.

"Did we?" Mark said.

"Well, yeah."

"Look at the account numbers," Mark said.

Dan did, and then he saw what Mark might have been driving at. "Wait a second. This shows The First National Bank and The First of America Bank. I didn't know that Dad had two banks."

Mark looked at him, a serious tone in his voice, like an arrow hitting the centermost point of an archery board. "He didn't."

Dan held the paper, staring at it, waiting for the answer to jump out at him. He looked at the account numbers and then at the notation above, reading, "THE FOLLOWING WIRE WAS DEDUCTED FROM YOUR ACCOUNT TODAY."

"Is it ringing any bells?" Mark asked.

"Are you thinking that this went to someone else's account?"

"What do you think?"

Suddenly, the significance of the transaction grew. "Holy shit," Dan said quietly. "We don't have a name on here, though."

"Yeah, but whose account do you think that could have gone into?"

"It wouldn't happen to be the judge's, would it? Like the judge in the paper..."

"There's only one way to find out," Mark said.

Hesitantly, Dan walked over to the telephone. He picked up the receiver, thankful that there was still a dial tone. From information, he obtained the number to The First of America Bank. He wrote the number down and had to dial the number twice, his fingers were trembling so badly.

"Good afternoon," Dan said to the lady on the other end. "I hope that I'm not calling too late. Is there any way that I can get my account balance, for my checking account?"

Mark watched his brother, carefully.

"I realize that it's late, ma'am. But, we're going on vacation and it would be greatly appreciated. Is this Shirley?" he asked, making a name so that he could get a real name.

Dan didn't take his eyes off of his brother, remaining stoic and calm. "Oh, Caroline! Yes, this is Judge Paul Ferguson," remembering the name from the newspaper, "My account number is 4-5-7-0-0-0-9-3-1-3-4-6-8-8-3. Thank you, dear."

Both brothers waited for what seemed an eternity.

"Thank you very much, Caroline. Have a good holiday, would you? Thank you, again." Dan said, hanging up the phone. He looked at Mark, his face void of emotion.

"Well?" Mark asked.

"It seems that Judge Paul Ferguson has $121, 000 in his account at this very moment."

Mark smiled. "Bingo."

They had their name...

<u>43</u>

RIPPLE

To say that they were pissed wouldn't begin to cover the broad range of emotions that each brother felt. If the judge's decision had been different twenty years ago, neither of them would have been in the boat they were in. If the judge had rendered the decision that Danny had deserved, maybe their mother wouldn't have been murdered. Louise might never have been confined to a sanitarium. That, alone, glared at them from the dark corners of injustice.

It didn't take long for them to decide what to do.

The decision to use side streets was influenced by two factors, the first being that they were probably less likely to be spotted by the police. The second was that it was Friday afternoon of a holiday weekend and the last thing they needed to do was to get caught in a traffic snarl, even if it was Marquette. The clock had run down to forty minutes, so all risks had to be minimized.

They took Brule Road to Joliet and then took a right on Division Street, past the rock quarry where they used to play

Tarzan, swinging blindly from a rope and into the frigid green waters. They went past King's Korner, where Mark was so fond of shoplifting and took a right by the sister convenience store, Cal's. On Champion Street, they got stuck behind a school bus. Both brothers looked at their watches in frustration. Thirty minutes left.

They shook the bus when they neared St. Peter's Grade School. The steeples of the church signaled that the courthouse was only a block away. Dan ignored the thought that the police station was across from the church. It would be the highest risk they had taken that day, aside from passing the home of the Michigan State Police. Out of the pan and into the fire, he thought nearing the police department. They took a right on Baraga and the red stone courthouse came into view.

Dan's stomach jumped as if squirrels were doing laps inside of him.

Rushes of adrenaline coursed through his body as he pulled into a parking space in front of the building. Neither Dan nor Mark thought it important to drop money into the parking meter. They had only one thing on their minds and that was to rectify a mistake made years ago. With twenty minutes to go, they ran up the steps. They had no sooner gotten to the doors, when Dan turned around to see a police car slowing down behind their Marquis. He pulled the doors open and dashed inside, Mark at his heels.

The sounds of their shoes echoed eerily off the waxed, tiled floors as they made their way to the courthouse directory. Quickly, Dan scanned the list of courtrooms and their corresponding judges. Upon seeing Judge P. Ferguson's name, it was everything that he could do from breaking into a run.

"You've got all the evidence, right?" he said to Mark.

"Right here," Mark said, holding up everything from their father's savings transfer to the wire transfer.

"If that doesn't convince him," Dan said as they ran up the steps.

When they got to the courtroom doors, Dan looked at Mark. He wanted to say something to him, like what a great brother he was or thanks for the support but their eyes connected and nothing needed to be said. The only thing that they could feel was that it was now or never. He took a deep breath and pulled the oak door open, his last thought being that he hoped they weren't too late. If they were, he didn't relish the thought of hiding out for another three days, especially with Diana serving his time.

The first thing they noticed, upon entering, was that the courtroom had just been dismissed for the day. People were getting up from their seats, as lawyers closed their briefcases and justice employees packed up their various details. Quickly, they looked toward the bench. It was vacant, not a surprise since it was almost ten minutes to five.

Not to be discouraged, they marched their way to the judge's chambers.

"Can I help you?" a court reporter asked them.

"No, thank you," Dan said, pushing the door open.

"You can't go in there!" she said with consternation in her voice.

Mark boldly walked in behind Dan.

Judge Ferguson looked up in surprise as he was removing his robes.

"What's going on here?"

"Your Honor!" the court reporter broke in behind them. "I didn't allow these gentlemen in. I'll have an officer remove them right away! If I could..."

The judge interrupted her. "No, Lindy, it's okay," he said with a raise of his hand.

"Are you sure?"

"Thank you, Lindy. That'll be all," he said, ending their conversation.

Dan and Mark looked at each, relieved that they had gotten that far.

"Now, what's with all the commotion?" the judge asked.

Dan closed the door behind the exiting reporter. He turned around, looking at the Judge. "Well, actually, I doubt that you'll remember me. My name's Dan Wilcox."

The judge looked at him, recognition slowly coming over his face. "Was your father Dr. Wilcox, the surgeon?"

"Yes, sir," Dan said.

"I knew your father very well. I was sorry to hear of his passing."

"I bet," Mark said, barely under his breath.

"So, you must remember who I am," Dan said.

Judge Ferguson appeared to think about it for a moment, taking a seat behind his desk. He leaned back as the squeak of leather took his weight.

"It's been a long time. Weren't you in front of me for truancy or something of that nature?"

"Truancy?" Dan questioned, almost mocking him. "Hardly. You had me put away in a juvenile delinquency home for perjury."

"You can't expect me to remember every case that I've heard. Is there a point here?"

Mark spoke up. "You're damn right there's a point! Tell me, your Honor, how many cases have you decided after being paid off?"

The judge sat straight up in his seat. "I don't know what you're talking about! How dare you walk into my office and start throwing accusations around? I am a respected man in this city and I will not tolerate such behavior!"

It was Dan's turn to drive in the nail. He took the evidence from Mark, separating the wire transfer and placing it on his desk. "Why don't you explain a wire transfer of twenty-five thousand dollars and then we'll talk about respect!"

The judge looked at it and then back up at Dan. "This proves absolutely nothing. You will please leave my chambers or I will be forced to have you bodily carried out."

"Not until you explain the money," Dan said firmly.

The judge stared at him. "The money? Your father and I were associates. We had business dealings that are none of your business. Don't you forget that you were a truant and a problem child! I did only what I had to do. You were the one who walked into this office and lied."

"So, you do remember me!" Dan said.

"Get out of my chambers!" the judge said, picking up the phone.

"Please, your Honor! I need your help. All I'm asking is that you listen to my side of the story. We can fix this!"

With the phone in mid-air, the judge looked at Dan. "Is that what this is all about? Are you trying to bribe me?"

"No, Your Honor. I'm asking for help. My mother was murdered and I had nothing to do with it. The police are after me, a good friend of mine is in jail and all of this is a misunderstanding that began the moment that you said I was lying, the moment that you took that money from my father!" Dan said vehemently, pointing toward the record of the transfer.

"I know exactly who you are!" the judge suddenly said, recognizing his unexpected guest. He pressed a number on the telephone. "Lindy! Send two officers in here immediately!"

Dan looked at Mark, panic in his eyes. Everything had backfired and the corner they were in had closed around them. "You son of a bitch!" Dan said, immediately regretting his outburst.

"Let's go, Dan," Mark, turning around toward the door.

"You will pay for what you've done, Your Honor!" Dan spat, having no idea how he would enact the vengeance.

"Turn yourself in Mr. Wilcox!" the judge said.

Mark suddenly ran back into the office, scaring the daylights out of the judge. He reached on his desk and picked up the transfer. Before turning on his heel, he held it up in front of the Judge's face. "You will pay dearly, sir!"

As fast as the two brothers appeared, they were out the door. Neither one knew where they were running except for the fact that they had to get out of the building. They ran back down the steps as fast as they could go, not caring who they bumped into as long as it wasn't the police. If they could make it to the car, they could get out of town before the police caught up with them.

It didn't help that the police station was only a block away. The moment that they broke through the doors to the outside courthouse steps, cars were appearing from seemingly everywhere. Tires squealed and sirens were blaring with doors being opened before the cars were barely stopped.

The Marquis, their path to freedom, seemed miles away. Unfortunately, the police car that they had seen earlier had blocked the path behind it.

Dan looked behind him and to either side. As the seconds passed, bewildered spectators watched. It was as if he was the deer in front of the headlights of a truck, frozen and with nowhere to turn. Officers scrambled up the steps, pulled guns from their holsters, some of them on one knee, and aimed at their target.

"Freeze, asshole!" one of the officers screamed at Dan.

Dan raised his hands in the air along with his brother. He looked at Mark.

"I'm sorry!"

All Mark was able to manage to say was, "Holy fuck!"

A green sedan came screeching down Baraga and pulled to a stop in front of the growing commotion.

Detective Robinson hopped out of the car and ran up the steps to Dan and Mark, who were trapped. His handcuffs were ready and waiting, glinting in the late afternoon sun.

"I've been looking a long time for you, boy!" he said while grabbing Dan's arms. Guns were pointed and faces were grim.

To Dan, it was his worst nightmare come true. He gritted his teeth as Robinson roughly pushed him to the ground, pressing his knee into the small of his back. Robinson patted him down, searching for a weapon. Finding nothing, he squeezed a pair of handcuffs around his wrists.

Another officer grabbed Mark and shoved him to the ground, also. Robinson, with his grip firm on Dan, pulled him back to his feet as hoards of media vehicles began appearing, reporters coming out of the woodwork like a nest of carpenter ants scared up while doing the lawn.

Robinson milked the moment for everything it was worth, delaying the reading of Dan's rights until cameras were up and running. His face, looked like a man who had just run an Olympic marathon, tired but proud. He led Dan by his wrists to the green sedan, reporters firing questions behind him.

"I will give a statement in one hour's time," he said, shuffling the reporters off. "I'll meet you at the station after I have the accused out of harm's way. Thank you!"

The other officers flanked Robinson, placing their guns back in their holsters. Robinson looked toward the officer who was hauling Mark toward a police car. "Let him go!" he ordered.

The officer looked at Robinson. "But isn't he a suspect, also?" he questioned.

"I've got who I want," Robinson said with a tug of Dan's wrists. "We've got nothing on him. Let him go!" he repeated. "We're not about to risk a bad arrest."

The officer unlocked Mark's handcuffs as Robinson opened the rear door of his sedan and pushed Dan inside. He walked around to the front of his car and hopped in, nodding toward the reporters. He started the car and crept forward, forcing the reporters, their cameras running, to step aside.

As Robinson drove away, Mark saw the look in Dan's eyes, bewildered and confused. Only an hour before, the two of them had been in their parents' home, searching for a way to prevent what had just happened. Unfortunately, their plan hadn't worked, and they were left in the same situation as twenty years before. The system had become an enemy, leaving Dan frail and defenseless. The big boss man had his prize just as he had it years before and Mark was pissed.

Just then, as the reporters were beginning to disperse, he looked up the courthouse steps to see Judge Ferguson walking down, a briefcase swinging in his hand at his side. The Judge looked toward the throng of reporters and then directly into Mark's eyes.

Quickly, the judge looked away.

In that second, Mark figured out what had to be done. All the doors had been closed except one. They weren't kids anymore. They weren't defenseless and they didn't have to worry about getting the shit kicked out of them. Somebody had to know what had happened. Somebody had to right the wrongs that had been done to them. Mark had to do what Dan had done many years earlier as *the protector.* This time, the responsibility was on the younger brother's shoulders. If there were consequences, then so be it. But this time, it would be done right. This time, they would be heard.

Mark raised his hand and pointed at the judge. He called out to him.

"Judge Ferguson! They have the wrong man in jail, don't they?"

The judge looked toward him and then quickly looked away, quickening his step.

Mark held up the stack of papers in his hand, stepping forward. "Your Honor! Twenty-five thousand dollars! Was it worth it?!"

Suddenly, cameras were raised, some pointing toward Mark while others focused on the judge.

"Answer me, your Honor!"

He stopped and looked at Mark, his eyes squinting in the afternoon sun. "I have no comment," he said quickly, resuming his step, avoiding the cameras.

The cameras panned toward Mark who was still holding the damning evidence. As the judge hurried across the street, Mark began speaking, slow and sure in his words. The retribution would be simple and sweet. His only regret was that Dan wasn't there to watch it. But, he knew in his heart that Dan would have done the very same thing just as he had on countless occasions before, as kids. Whether it was the sweeping of glasses to the floor in an effort to save Louise or whether it was picking up Mark at the church to bring him home, it had been the effort that had counted. In a role reversal, Mark assumed the role as *the protector*.

"Let me tell you a story..." he said.

For the first time, somebody listened. The words were eaten alive by Hard Copy, The Mining Journal, WJMN-TV 3, and a host of other hungry media personnel.

As Mark talked, he became more confident by the moment. Questions were asked and Mark answered them as honestly as he could. In the back of his mind, he thought of the words of one of Dan's favorite songs, *Ripple,* and he sent the waves to the listening ears. "*Ripple in still water, when there is no pebble tossed, nor wind to blow. You who choose to lead must follow but if you fall, you fall alone.*"

He tossed something a lot larger than a pebble at the glass house.

One reporter after another dashed up the steps around Mark. Cameras rolled and pens scribbled furiously. Mark was amazed how easily the words flowed out of his mouth; the story of wrongdoing unleashed itself like a Doberman free from its chain.

The pens really began scribbling when they heard a story of a judge, a judge who had wronged an innocent boy named Danny.

But, as Mark spoke, two people were in jail, a killer was walking free and a judge was looking forward to taking his family to the house in the Cape for a much needed family vacation.

44

A TOUCH OF GREY

"Look, Diana. I'm sorry. There's nothing that can be done until Tuesday. It's a holiday weekend and everyone's on vacation. Trust me, I'm doing the best that I can."

"I know, Clinton."

"You sound as if you don't believe me."

"It's difficult, that's all," Diana said dejectedly. She looked behind her at the female guard who was watching her carefully in the cement walled room where they allowed her to use the phone. She picked at the peeling paint absentmindedly.

"Have they been treating you alright?"

"As well as can be expected," Diana said. "They've got me in a suicide watch cell. Thankfully, I've got no cellmates."

"What do you mean suicide watch?"

"One of the guards told me that since I'm a celebrity, they didn't want to risk putting me in with the general population, that's all. It's not so bad. I just wish I didn't have to stay here until Tuesday."

Clinton sighed on the other end of the phone. "At least you're safe and that's what counts. I've been worried sick about you. Also, your patients have been asking a lot of questions. It's been all I can do to keep things in order. I'm supposed to be retired, remember?"

"I remember, Clinton. There's no need to keep reminding me," Diana said as she leaned against the cool cement wall. This was her second phone call with him in as many days and it appeared that she would be spending Labor Day incarcerated, a thought that she didn't relish.

"You've got yourself in a fine mess this time. Didn't I warn you about this?"

"Please, Clinton, you promised to stop scolding me yesterday. I've got enough on my mind without your treating me like I was..."

"A bad girl," Clinton interjected. "Well, it's not easy on this end, either. By the way, I checked into the Louise Wilcox situation as you asked me to."

"Did you find anything?"

"It's a dead end for the moment. About the only way that I could see her is through a court order, which is just about impossible to get because of the holiday. We're going to have to wait until Tuesday unless I can get something to break. Are you positive that it was she who committed the murder?"

"That's just it, Clinton, I'm not positive. As I told you, I was arrested just before I was to meet her for the first time. If there was any way that you could speak with her..." she said, her voice trailing off.

"Diana, nothing can be done for the moment. Listen, I'll get by to see you during visiting hours tomorrow. In the meantime, take a pause and get your thoughts together. Judging from the news, you've had a harrowing couple of weeks," Clinton said, his tone soft.

"The news?"

"Oh, you haven't heard, have you?"

Diana looked back at the guard who had taken a seat, seeing that Diana wasn't much of a threat. "I'm in jail, Clinton," she said, stating the obvious.

"Well, the lid has blown sky high. It seems that when your partner in crime was arrested, his brother blew off some steam with the press in a pretty dramatic way. They've run with a story that condemns a judge for ignoring child abuse charges by Dan while also focusing on the two of you as fugitives. I can't go anywhere without hearing someone's opinion or another," he said.

"Really," Diana said, thinking about Mark.

"Anyway, the brother has opened a can of worms. So, who knows?

Maybe that'll be good for you in the long run."

"I hope so," Diana said.

The guard walked up and tapped Diana on the shoulder, pointing to her watch.

"Look, Clinton, I have to go. See what you can do about Louise. If there's any chance..."

"I know, Diana. I'll see what I can do. Just don't get your hopes up too much. Beyond that..."

"Thank you, Clinton. I owe you one," Diana said.

"You owe me more than one," Clinton said chuckling. "Try to relax and I'll see you tomorrow."

Diana set the receiver on the cradle. She was walked back to her solitary cell. As soon as the door slid shut, she sat on the bed and put her head in her hands.

She knew she should have been grateful that she hadn't been hurt while on the run. But now, she felt helpless. Her fate and Dan's rested in the hands of powers greater than the two of them. In that moment, she understood what it must have been like when Dan was, as a boy, sent to the juvenile delinquency home. It seemed futile to believe in a system that was contaminated with lies and injustice.

Strangely, the experience of being imprisoned was not entirely unpleasant. There was a certain amount of relief, as if the beast that you had been running from in a nightmare turned out to be nothing more than a slightly over- aggressive Collie. The guards were just people doing their jobs with regular hours and a nice handful of benefits. Their eyes showed that Diana had reached a celebrity status, causing them to take a little extra care in handling her.

Jail also gave her plenty of time to think. She thought about the past two weeks and realized that she had changed. It was as if some screw inside her had been twisted a notch, ironically, giving her a better grasp of reality, of people. She remembered a time when she looked at a Deadhead as some sort of miscreant and drug user, the name in and of itself like when Dan's father called someone a *Yooper,* its connotation almost dirty when vocalized. Instead, she had seen people who cared about each other in a way that surpassed the usual way of being. Whether it was a friendly handshake, like she had enjoyed by the hundreds at Maggie's Farm, or whether it was putting yourself on the line for someone else, as Derry had done for Dan, a silver thread kept everyone bonded. It wasn't the music, even though it enhanced the experience, but rather an idea. The idea of taking care of your neighbor as you would yourself. That was a value that had been reinserted inside her. The world wasn't as dark as it once seemed, even after the betrayal of her husband.

Then, she thought of the kiss at Maggie's Farm. She knew that she cared about Dan deeply but she also didn't want to lie to herself. Was it him or was it the moment? She hadn't dared to tell Clinton about it. She questioned that feeling, also. Was she afraid he would bring her to her senses? Well, she would tell him one day, but for now she chose to keep it to herself, until she could figure out where her heart stood.

The worst part of the ordeal for her was calling Clinton. For a moment, before she picked up the telephone, she felt ashamed of what she had done and felt she had to face a reprimand from her father. But, much to her surprise, Clinton understood. He promised that he'd find her legal counsel which, unfortunately, couldn't be handled until Labor Day passed. If she had been put away in Detroit, she might have been out the very evening that she was locked up. But, Clinton said, it was a damn small town and it would have taken an act of God for anyone to get off their asses and lend a hand. The overpaid judges were on holiday and there was nothing anyone could do to interrupt them.

So, Diana settled into the routine of being a prisoner. Breakfast was served at precisely seven in the morning, a tin tray of two eggs and bacon with a matching tin cup of coffee, no sugar or cream offered. Lunch was served at noon and dinner was served at five. The guards came by in the afternoon so that she could exercise for one hour in the caged, cement-floored yard. She walked alone and in silence, under the watchful eyes of two guards, who kindly explained that they didn't want her mixing with the other inmates for fear that they wouldn't take a liking to a famous doctor being in their midst.

Once she was escorted back to her cell, a trusty came by with a cart of books. Out of politeness, she took a finger worn copy of *The Celestine Prophecy*. She made an attempt at reading but found that she couldn't focus long enough for any of the stories to make sense. At nine o'clock, they turned the radio on for the inmates, obviously meaning to keep them quiet. Unfortunately, a news clip came on about the arrest of Dan Wilcox, leaving her restless and unable to sleep the rest of the night. Nightmares of unseen enemies seemed to pepper her dreams, leaving her dazed when breakfast was served the next morning.

At about eleven o'clock or so, she heard the jangling of a guard's keys coming closer to her cell. She sat up from her bed when she heard a key entering her lock. The door slid its way open with a resonant slam, jarring her senses. She expected to see Clinton. Instead, she was surprised to see the face of a man who had the uncanny ability to show up at the most unexpected times. To say that she was displeased would greatly understate what she felt.

"How have they been treating you?" he asked.

"As well as can be expected," Diana answered coldly.

"You're upset."

"Gee, Detective, that's quite a deduction. Might I ask what you're doing here? Or, are you here to taunt me?" she asked sarcastically.

Robinson shifted uncomfortably. He looked at the guard watching them behind him. "Everything's fine here. I'll call you when I need you."

The guard disappeared.

"Do you mind if I take a seat?" he asked, sitting down at the metal picnic style table in the middle of the cell.

Diana motioned indifference.

Robinson cleared his throat. He set a folded sheet of paper on the table, pushing it toward the prisoner.

Diana picked it up and read it. "A release form?"

"Only for the day and only under my custody. Are you interested?"

She looked at him cautiously. "I don't understand."

Robinson ran his fingers through his hair and took a deep breath. "I'm not quite sure where to start. I thought that I had this case locked up with an airtight seal. I still believe, as a matter of fact, with a reasonable amount of certainty, that I have the guilty party behind bars."

"You're referring to Daniel Wilcox."

"Yes," he said.

"Then, what are you doing here?"

"I have a shadow of a doubt."

"Isn't that for a jury to decide?"

Robinson shifted his weight and looked her directly in the eye. "Look, I was comfortable with the arrests of both of you until I saw the papers this morning. Now, what's interesting is that the papers don't focus on you or Mr. Wilcox but rather on a judge. It would appear that there's going to be some public outcry over a case he handled some twenty years ago. Some pretty strong proof has gotten into the media's hands that the judge was paid off by Dr. Wilcox."

"I'm not sure what you're talking about," Diana said. "Remember, I've been cut off from society?" she reminded him.

Robinson quickly told of Mark and his excursion with *Hard Copy.* Most of the newspapers in the area printed the story and talk was spreading about corruption within the Marquette County Judicial system. "Of course, any ancillary department is naturally going to be looked at. Which means, someone's going to come knocking on my door. As far as this judge is concerned, any political aspirations he might have are now in the wind. The way I see it, he's going to be out of a job in a week's time."

"I still don't see how this has anything to do with me or Daniel's capture."

"Well, I'm reading all this, knowing that you can't believe every word that the press prints, but there was one thing that kept creeping up in the back of my mind," Robinson said, his brow furrowed.

"Which is what?" she asked, getting tired of the rhetoric but interested in hearing about a judge who deserved worse than he was getting.

"Well, what's a high-falutin psychiatrist doing going on the run with a murderer?"

"Haven't we been there before?"

"We certainly have. So, within my realm of possibilities, I got to thinking about something and it all comes down to one word: *Unless...*"

"Unless what?"

"Unless he's innocent."

"Isn't that what I was trying to tell you?" Diana asked.

"Doctor, listen to me. I've explained what the State's evidence is against this man and, you have to admit, it looks solid," he said, pulling out his bottle of Excedrin. He dropped two pills in his mouth and chewed on them thoughtfully. "Anyway, I finished my breakfast and I decided to take a jaunt down to my office. I was thinking that I would clean up some details. Once I got in the office and got settled, I still had this nagging question in the back of my mind. Why did this lady, with the professional stature that she's got, drop everything to leave with this guy? Further, what the hell were they doing going into a place that they knew that I would be watching? Are they stupid?"

In the background, Diana could hear the trusty's and guards distributing lunch, with the rolling of carts and the tinkle of cheap silverware. "We needed to see Louise," she said.

"Exactly. So, I flipped through my paperwork and I realized that this girl was in line to receive a substantial sum of money. Mind you, I'm only playing with this thought. Remember, I've met her and she's in a sanitarium. Which means she has an alibi. But, I decided to run her name through the computer, specifically for records through the Secretary of State's office," Robinson said. He took a deep breath, obviously disturbed. "I didn't like what I found."

Diana sat forward, curious. "What?"

"A driver's license," he said, his voice solid.

"What?"

"Exactly, a driver's license. So, I called Dr. Margaret Fishman at the hospital..."

"The administrator," Diana said, remembering the lady from only two days before.

"That's right. We had a long talk. She knew nothing about a driver's license. You see, they would be opening themselves up to some pretty hefty liabilities if they were to sponsor patients in that realm. I mean, can you imagine a looney-tunes driver hitting someone else while they're in the care of a sanitarium?"

"Detective, you need to watch your references toward patients. I don't appreciate the terminology," Diana said.

"I'm sorry. I have a loose tongue at times," Robinson said. Then, he slid a manila folder toward Diana.

"What's this?" she asked.

"Open it."

Diana opened the file. Inside, yellowed and frayed pictures were paper- clipped to a stack of papers. Although the pictures appeared to be old, the images were clear. "Where did you get this?" she asked.

"I've got a friend who works in Marquette County records. She remembered the case. It took her an hour of digging through some ancient files in the basement of the courthouse. After the publicity and my finding the license of the sister, I figured it was worth digging into. Obviously, the file was altered..."

Diana looked through each picture from Social Services, slowly and carefully. She didn't have to be told that they were pictures of a battered Danny Wilcox. She could almost feel the fear he must have felt when the pictures were taken, as if he couldn't believe he was in such a position. She closed the file slowly, wanting to forget the black and blue images, the red dots on his head from having his hair pulled and the cut on his face from his mother's wedding ring.

"I also checked into the furloughs on Louise, as you had mentioned."

"And?"

"There's validity to what you told me."

"So, what do you want from me?"

"I'm not saying that anyone is off the hook. As frightening as those pictures are, it may hurt Mr. Wilcox in the long run. Any prosecutor can see a motive for murder. But, with the furloughs and the driver's license of the sister, it bears looking into." Robinson slid the release form toward her. "I did a lot of work to get you out of here for the day. Suffice to say that I have a judge out there who owes me one. I need you to talk to her. I'm giving you a chance to sell me."

In any other case, Diana might have laughed at him. "Why me?"

"You're the only game in town. I also spoke with a guy named Clinton, who called me yesterday. Let's just say that he convinced me to speak with you. I don't normally listen to idle threats but with the political heat..." Robinson added.

Diana smiled inside, knowing that Clinton had gone to bat for her, without mincing any words.

"Doctor," Robinson continued, "I'm giving you a chance to clear things up. If we can get a confession out of her..."

Diana cut him off. "A confession? It wouldn't do you any good because it would be coerced. That would hardly stand up in a court of law."

"Don't you think that I know that? To say that this case is unique is an understatement. I'll worry about that when we get there. What's important is that we get down to the heart of the issue. I may seem like a bad guy but I'm doing my job. Now, if you like, I could turn my head and pretend that I know nothing about this driver's license," he said, running his hand through his hair. "I've seen a lot of shit on the streets. Maybe it's made me think the worst of people at times. I can't help it. But, nobody will ever be able to say that I didn't do my job to the best of my abilities. Further, I would like to, for once, see justice handled properly. It starts with me and I need your help. If nothing comes of it, then at least we can say that we tried," he said, looking at her straight in the eye.

In that moment, Diana saw him as more decent down deep that he had behaved toward Dan and her. She also couldn't ignore his logic. After all, it had been the culmination of her trip with Dan.

"So, Doctor?"

"I can't make any guarantee's," Diana said.

"I'm not asking for any."

"I'm not wearing handcuffs," she said, determination in her voice.

"Then, don't run."

"You'll treat me like a professional?"

"That's what I need, your expertise."

"You'll avoid any slang terms?"

"Slang terms?" he questioned.

"Well, yes, Detective. For example, referring to patients as "looney - tunes"?

"I began my career as a street cop. It happens once in awhile," he defended.

"I expect us to stay on the up and up. No slang terms," she said firmly.

"All right! All right! No slang terms," he agreed quickly. "Look, I'm sorry about your arrest and how I acted. But, again, I was just doing my job. I capture killers, okay? You repair the mistakes of parents. Either way, you're going to be hardened into believing the worst in people. Can we start over?"

Diana knew about believing the worst in people. All she had to do was think about Dan as a boy or herself with her uncle and she knew the worst.

Or, all she had to do was open the file on Danny and look at the pictures, a thought that made her stomach turn.

Then again, as she agreed to go to Houghton with Robinson, she wondered if she really did understand the worst in people. Then, in the back of her mind, she thought of a line from a song she had heard but couldn't remember where she had heard it: *"If the thunder don't get you, then the lightning will."*

Half an hour later, Diana was walking out of jail into the cool mid- afternoon sun with Robinson at her side. She inhaled the fresh air deeply, enjoying the freedom but knowing that it would be short-lived. Then, she thought of something that had been bothering her during her incarceration. "Detective, I have a question for you," she said as he was reaching in his pocket for the car keys to the green sedan.

"I'm all ears."

"Well, remember when you caught up with us in Houghton?"

"Yeah?"

"How did you figure out that we were coming into the airport? Was it the flight plan?"

He stopped in tracks and looked at her, a light smile crossing his face. "The flight plan? Actually, it was nothing as complicated as that."

"Well, then how?"

"It was quite academic, if you want to know the truth. Mr. Wilcox's brother had left a message on his answering machine. I have to admit that we were stumped, at first." He jangled the keys as he enclosed them within his fist, holding out the door lock key. "I held onto that message for days, turning it over and over in my head. I happened to leave it out on the kitchen table one night after work. My son picked it up. He's all American, you know." Robinson said proudly. "He's a Grateful Dead fan. The music doesn't appeal to me much, though. Anyway, it took him about forty-five minutes to unravel the songs and, well, knowing that Louise was in Houghton..." he said, his voice trailing off. He started walking toward the car and inserted the key into the lock and then opened the door for Diana.

Before getting into the car, she looked at Robinson. "You make it sound so simple."

"Doctor, there are no coincidences in life."

Diana smiled as she got into the car, knowing where she had heard that before.

As Robinson walked around the back of the car, her smile disappeared as she thought of the situation they were getting ready to face. A pang of nervousness shot through her stomach. On one hand, if they got the answers that they were looking for, it would all be over. But, there was no arguing that it might very well be the most difficult mountain they were to climb.

For the first time, without the frightful rhetoric of Dan's stories, she was going to meet Louise in person. Had the bolt of lightning hit her as hard as it had hit everyone else in the family?

The moment of truth was at hand and she prayed that blood wouldn't be dripping from its gleaming teeth.

45

VICTIM OR THE CRIME

"May I ask you something, Doctor?"

"Of course, Louise. What is it?"

"If I pass all of these tests, will I be going home?"

Diana looked across the boardroom table at Louise. She rubbed her eyes. In the corners, artificial flowers and plants adorned the room, giving the false illusion of comfort and warmth, stained by the fluorescent light overhead. Stacks of paper from Louise's file were set around her in a semi-circle, piled chronologically. She set her pen down, thinking carefully before she spoke. The one thing that she didn't want to do was to deceive her, excepting anything about the murder itself. "The tests aren't about passing or failing, Louise. Have you ever visited a doctor for a health check-up?"

Louise played absentmindedly with her long, dark hair. "Um, well, they come to us every few months."

"They weigh you and check your blood pressure. Am I correct?"

"Oh, yes, Doctor. I don't like when they do the blood pressure, though. I don't like things that squeeze around my arms. It makes me nervous."

"It shouldn't make you nervous," Diana said, carefully jotting a note in the margin. "When they do a check-up, it's for your health. It's to make sure that there aren't any problems. If there is a problem, it can be caught immediately. These tests that you've been taking for the last two hours are very much like a check-up."

Louise appeared to ponder it for a moment. Hesitantly, her eyes glancing around the room, she approached a question. "Am I okay?"

"That's what I'm here to find out. Does it bother you?"

"Well, I get scared sometimes."

"What are you scared of?"

"A lot of things," she answered, looking down toward her partially completed Thematic Apperception Test.

"What kind of things?" Diana asked.

Then, the tape player shut off, signifying the end of another Maxell tape. Diana quickly replaced the tape with the new one and resumed recording. She looked toward Louise who was back to filling out her test. "Louise? What kind of things?" she asked, resuming their conversation.

Louise looked up, a blank stare in her eyes. "I don't remember," she said timidly.

Diana made another note in her book, a confirmation of A.D.D. (Attention Deficit Disorder), a disorder marked by a person forgetting what they're doing upon the interruption of a sound. This had been the fifth time in two hours that they had to start a conversation over because of a noise. In one instance, Dr. Fishman had tapped on the door to give Diana some supplies that she had requested. In another, a car had honked outside, bringing them back to square one.

"We were talking about things that scare you," Diana reminded her. "What kinds of things scare you?"

"Well, I don't like the Fourth of July very much."

"Why is that?" Diana asked patiently.

"I get confused when the fireworks go off. The noises make me jump."

"Hmm. What else scares you?"

Louise thought for a moment and then looked up, her eyes bright. "Well, if I had to stay here and I couldn't go home."

"Where's home?" Diana asked.

"In Marquette."

"When was the last time that you were there?"

Louise's brow furrowed in concentration, searching for the answer. "I think it was Christmas."

Diana looked through the file. "Christmas? This past year?"

"Oh, yes," Louise said.

In actuality, according to the notes, she hadn't been home to visit in over three years. Correspondingly, there were no records of anybody having visited Louise in over six years, Diana noted.

"Did you enjoy yourself?" Diana asked.

"I did, Doctor."

"You can call me, Diana. Okay?"

"Yes, Diana. It's a pretty name."

"Thank you," Diana said. The more that she looked into the situation, the more her doubts grew about Louise being capable of murder. There was a sweetness and innocence within her countenance that seemed to defy the very possibility. She had been wrong before but, in this case... "Now, let's get back to Christmas. Did you get a lot of gifts?"

"Um, I think so."

"What did you get?"

Louise looked away, her eyes turning red while a flush ran over her face.

"What is it, Louise? What's wrong?"

A tear slid down her cheek, reflecting the white light. She began wringing her hands. "I don't remember," she said. "Does that mean that I'm failing?"

In that moment, something twisted in Diana's heart. If the situation weren't as serious as it was, she might very well have given up for the day. Unfortunately, she didn't have an office to go to or a home. Outside, waiting impatiently was Robinson. Diana sighed. She got up and walked over to Louise and squeezed her shoulders. "Would you like to take a break?"

"Yes, Doctor," she said, wiping her face quickly.

"Okay, Louise. Come back here in ten or fifteen minutes. Why don't you get something to drink?"

"Okay," she said. "Can I get you something, too?"

"Sure," Diana said.

Louise faltered for a moment.

"What is it?" Diana asked.

"Well, could you tell me how long that I'll be taking tests today?"

"I would say we have another two hours. Don't worry. It'll go by quickly," Diana said gently.

"I don't mind taking tests," Louise said. "If I have to take one hundred tests so that I can go home and see my mom and dad, then I'll do it. I wanted to know so that I could tell Cassidy when we're seeing each other tonight."

At first, Diana almost missed it. Louise was turning to walk out the door when Diana stopped her. "Louise?"

"Yes?"

"Who is Cassidy?"

Louise put her hand to her mouth. "Oh, no..."

"Louise? What is it?"

"Please don't tell anybody, Doctor. Please?"

"I don't understand," Diana said. "Who's Cassidy?"

"He'll be mad with me. I promised that I wouldn't say anything," Louise said, her voice fearful.

Diana walked up to her. "I'm not here to hurt you. Do understand that?"

Louise's eyes fell to the floor. "I think so."

"Can you tell me who Cassidy is?" Diana asked again softly.

Louise looked up and then turned slightly, her hand on the door. She turned the handle. "Can I still take my break?"

"Yes, Louise. Will you answer the question first?"

"He's my, um..." she said, stalling.

Diana kept her voice calm knowing that the odds of her receding inside herself at any given moment were high, especially when she remembered some of Dan's recollections when they were children. "Please?"

Louise opened the door and then turned toward Diana. "He's my boyfriend," she said quickly, walking out.

Diana stood there a moment, realizing the possible magnitude of what Louise had just told her. It was the first breakthrough that she had in the last two hours. She walked over and turned the tape player off. Then, she rewound it for a few seconds and played it back. The information was saved clearly on the tape.

Robinson walked into the office hurriedly. "You're not done for the day, are you?"

"No," Diana said. "We're just taking a little break. Here, listen to this," she said, pressing the 'play' button.

Robinson listened and caught it immediately. "A boyfriend?"

"It would appear that way."

"Let's get her back in here immediately!" Robinson said.

"Detective, please! She needs time to take a break and so do I," Diana said.

"Doctor, might I mention that time is something that we don't have. Once the judicial process starts rolling, the harder it becomes to reverse it. Need I remind you that this is a murder investigation?"

"I understand that, Detective. I don't expect you to understand my job but we agreed that you would trust my expertise in this matter. It does us no good to push her," Diana said firmly.

"Why don't you hypnotize her and get it over with?"

Diana sighed with exasperation. "Because I don't believe in hypnotism. If the mind isn't ready to re-live the experience, the results can be catastrophic. We need to get our information out of her naturally. There's no other way."

"Dammit!" Robinson muttered. "You do your job and I'll do mine. I'm finding the boyfriend. That's my job."

Diana knew there was no way that she could stop him. She picked up the phone and called Dr. Fishman's office. "Would you mind meeting me in the boardroom?" she asked.

Moments later, Dr. Margaret Fishman walked in. "What can I help you with?"

"You didn't mention that Louise had a boyfriend," Robinson said, accusation in his voice.

"I don't know what you're talking about," she answered.

Robinson looked toward Diana. "His name is Casey."

"No, it's Cassidy," Diana corrected. "Listen, this is a somewhat touchy situation. Louise divulged it accidentally. Do you know anything about him? Is he a patient here? Is he a visitor? I didn't see any records of anyone visiting her."

Dr. Fishman took her glasses off. "To be honest, I don't know anything about him. I'll be glad to talk to some of the therapists but..."

"But what?" Robinson asked.

"Well, with this being Labor Day weekend, much of the staff takes their vacation time to be with their families. I would have a better chance of speaking with the right parties next week, after Tuesday," she added.

"I thought you took care of your patients here. How can you not know about a boyfriend?" Robinson queried.

"Detective," she said firmly. "Do you know how many patients we handle here? We do our best to monitor them but there are times that we can't know every single detail about their lives. Louise is a long term patient so we give her a little more freedom. She's shown improvement and our goal is not to incarcerate but rather to provide therapy so they may move on to lives of their own. If she has a boyfriend, as long as it isn't an employee and it isn't detrimental to her mental health, I see no harm in it. Now if..." she said, stopping in mid-sentence.

"What is it?" Diana asked.

"What did you say his name was?"

"Cassidy," Robinson piped in.

"Would you give me a moment? I'd like to run to my office. That name seems familiar," she said.

"Sure," Robinson said, glancing at his watch.

While Dr. Fishman walked out, Robinson pulled up a chair. "Have a seat," he said to Diana.

She took a chair and sat down while Robinson sat across the table from her.

"If you were to make an educated guess, based on the last two hours, are we barking up the wrong tree?" Robinson asked.

"I don't know," Diana answered thoughtfully. "I need more time with her. She's suffering from the same disorder as Dan, her brother. I feel that Post Traumatic Stress Disorder has marred her memory. Further, it's complicated by an Attention Deficit Disorder," which she briefly explained. "But, if you're asking if she had the intelligence to do it...?"

"I am," Robinson said.

Diana looked at her stacks of paper. "Is it possible that it was an accident?"

"You haven't seen the murder site," Robinson said. "Not only was it brutal, with the victim wearing a knife like a piece of jewelry, the whole house was destroyed as if it was covered up to make it look like a robbery attempt gone foul. So, no, I don't think it was an accident."

Diana chewed on her fingernail, a habit she had dropped years before.

"What is it, Doctor?"

"It doesn't make sense. Usually, I'm pretty intuitive about things like this. I have a difficult time in believing it was she. If the violence was as it was..."

"It was," Robinson said.

"Then, I need more time."

"Something that we're running out of quickly, Doctor. I suppose that I need not mention that your career as a psychiatrist is over in Marquette, if we keep you in jail. In a small town, memories are long," he said.

"I'm doing the best I can," Diana said, knowing that Robinson was right.

Dr. Fishman walked in holding a print-out in her hand. "I thought I had heard the name before," she said, handing the paper to Robinson. "His name is Cassidy Jones. He was hired about nine years ago. His records show him to be a good employee. About two years ago, he was even given an employee of the month award," she said, concerned.

Robinson looked at the paper. "A janitor?"

"Well, yes," the Doctor answered. "He's on our janitorial staff. I know of him but with a hospital of this size..."

"We need to talk to him," Robinson said.

"He's on the way down as we speak," Dr. Fishman said. "He just came on shift. Look I'm very sorry about this. Not only do we frown on staff consorting with patients, we will terminate them once we get wind of it. It isn't healthy."

A moment later, Louise walked in, two Cokes in hand.

Diana looked toward Robinson and Dr. Fishman. "Hello, Louise. Look, we have a little meeting going on. Would you mind waiting outside for a few minutes until we finish?"

"Uh, sure," she said, looking at Robinson.

Behind her, a young man walked up and then turned around and began walking the other way, hurriedly. Robinson jumped up and dashed past Louise.

"Wait a minute, son," he said, halting the young man in his tracks. "We need to have a word with you. Will you come with me?" Robinson asked, leading him lightly by the elbow back into the boardroom.

As they walked past Louise, he avoided her eyes.

Louise looked at Robinson, Dr. Fishman and then toward Diana. "I don't understand," she said.

"It's okay, Louise," Diana said, hardly believing her own words. "We'll be out in just a few minutes."

Louise looked at the two Cokes in her hand. She took one of them and set it on the table, hard. The sound just about made everyone jump. "I'll be outside," she said, throwing Diana a look of contempt.

"What's going on?" Cassidy asked nervously.

Robinson closed the door behind him and motioned Cassidy toward a chair.

The room settled into silence as Cassidy nervously sat down. By the color of his skin, Diana thought he was Hispanic or Puerto Rican. He was small with a wiry frame, his wavy hair a dark, ebony black. She guessed his age to be in the late twenties or early thirties. He looked up at everyone and then back toward the floor. "I didn't do anything," he said.

"We didn't say you did," Robinson said, taking a chair and inverting it between his legs so that he could lean on its back. "How long have you been dating Louise?"

"I don't know what you're talking about," he said quickly.

"Look, son, don't lie to us. Louise told us all about it."

"Isn't she a mental patient?" he answered. "You believe her more than me?"

"Cut the shit, boy," Robinson said. He looked toward Diana, as if he was apologizing for swearing in front of the ladies. "How long have you been dating Louise?"

"Like I said, I don't know where you heard this and I don't know what you're talking about," he said, glancing furtively around the room. "It's against hospital rules, you know? We aren't allowed to be with the slow people."

"Yeah? Let's say that I bring Louise in here and we'll get her opinion."

"Do what you want."

"You don't want me to do that," Robinson said, sliding his chair forward. "I'm going to have take you in for being accessory to murder."

"What? Are you a cop?"

Robinson pulled out his wallet and showed him the badge.

Cassidy appeared to turn a lighter shade of gray as he handed the badge back to the Detective. "Murder? What are you talking about? I'm a damn janitor. I don't know nothing about any murder!"

"Then, start talking. Otherwise, you're going to jail!"

He looked toward Dr. Fishman.

Diana spoke up. "Dr. Fishman. If he were to tell us the truth about the relationship with Louise, is it necessary that he be terminated?"

"Like I said, hospital policy is very clear on this issue."

Cassidy looked at the administrator. "Please, Doctor. I didn't mean nothin' by it. She hasn't got anybody. Nobody's been in to visit her in as long as I remember and I've worked here almost ten years. This job is all I got!"

Dr. Fishman sighed deeply. "I don't know," she said.

Robinson looked at Cassidy. "Let's say that we start with the truth. You be honest with me and then I'll talk to the administrator here. I can't make any promises but I'll do my best. Is that a deal? It's the best that we can offer. Otherwise..." he said with an upraised finger.

"Alright," Cassidy relented. "But I don't know nothing about any murder!"

"Tell us about Louise. How did you meet her?"

He fidgeted with his hands for a moment and glanced at the people in the room. "I started noticing her about eight years ago. I'd be cleaning the recreation room and I'd see her sitting by herself, you know? But, I was new here. Well, one day, I walked in and she was crying. Look, I know the rules but I couldn't just leave her there. I was thinking that it wouldn't do no harm, you know? I walked up and sat with her. She was really upset and I think it was Christmas week. She was saying that she was going to die here, alone..."

"Go on," Robinson said.

Nervously, Cassidy started talking again, looking down. "So, I put my arm around her and held her. We must've sat like that for an hour. Well, she calmed down and I actually got her to smile a little. I couldn't stop thinking about her, you know? It wasn't like I was after nothin'. I just felt sorry for her. So, along comes Christmas and I got her a little gift. It was one of them crystal roses. She got to cryin' again except she was cryin' happy. After that, we just hung together once in awhile. She treasured that rose like I treasure my car. I was kind of responsible to that, you know?"

"What kind of car do you have?" Robinson asked, glancing through his notes.

"It's a 1969 Lincoln Mark III. I restored it myself," he said proudly.

"Uh-huh," Robinson said. "Did you sleep with her?"

Diana shot him a look but kept her mouth shut.

"No, sir! We figured that she had enough problems without that happening. Besides, where would I do that without getting caught? It ain't like I can take her to my place! Besides, I can't lose my job. It's hard enough gettin' by without being in the unemployment line, too!"

"So, why did you stay with her?" Robinson asked.

"At first, I felt sorry for her. After a couple of years went by, well, I got to thinking."

"About?"

Cassidy looked toward Dr. Fishman. "I mean no offense, ma'am."

"It's okay," she said softly. "Just tell the Detective the truth."

"Well, it didn't seem like no one was helping her none. So, I started bringing her books. But, she wasn't too good at that. I understand 'cause I ain't much of the book type, neither. But, see, we were friends now. It made me sick to think that she was going to be here forever. So, I started teaching her things. Like, how to cook, stuff like that. If she was ever going to get out of this place, she had to know normal stuff. The pills weren't helping her none, either."

The room fell silent for a moment as Robinson searched for another question. "Cassidy, when you mentioned that you were teaching her things, did you teach her how to drive?"

Cassidy looked up proudly. "How did you know that?"

"Well, she has a driver's license."

"It took a long time, too," he said. "It took her almost two years to learn. See, she wanted to go home to her parents. I told her she was wasting her time seeing them. If they never visited her none, then what's she want to go see them for? But, she said it was all on account that she was bad when she was younger and they didn't believe in her, anymore. She thought that if she could drive, they'd be all proud and everything would be like before. So, who am I to argue with that?"

"How did you get the license?" Robinson prodded.

"Through a lot of work. One time, she banged up my right front end by hitting the curb. It cost me about three weeks of overtime to fix it. Anyways, every week, she gets a day where she gets to go to town. So, I went with her to the Secretary of State's office and she took a test for her Learner's Permit. After thirty days, she applied for the driving part. She failed twice before getting it," he said smiling.

"So, she drove to her parents' home with you?"

"Oh, no, sir. Not with me. Matter of fact, I'm not sure that she ever got there," he said, faltering.

"Why do you say that?" Robinson asked, leaning forward.

"Well, it gets kind of confusing here. See, she wanted to do this by herself. I told her it was my car and I didn't want nothin' happening to it. Then, I got to thinkin' that, well, why not? If I believed in her enough to take the driver's test, then I should believe in her all the way. But, I ain't sure what happened. See, she gets memory problems once in awhile..."

Robinson looked toward Diana.

"The P.T.S.D. with A.D.D.," Diana said.

"What do you think happened?" Robinson asked.

Cassidy wiped the brow of his forehead. "See, we did two practice trips. It's awful hard for her to drive, sometimes. You can't have the radio on or she gets lost. Then, she isn't too good with maps. It takes like two hours to get there. Well, the night before, I made a map for her, nice and big. I had all the stop signs and street lights on it with every turn marked by a landmark. But..."

"But what, son?"

"It was strange because all the gas was gone but she couldn't remember if she made it. This was only about a month ago. Every time I ask about it, she gets all frustrated. So, I was thinking that she never made it and she was, like, embarrassed to tell me. The only thing is, I'm wondering. I was walking by her flex exercise class and she was telling a story that kind of scared me."

Robinson looked up. "Flex exercise class?"

"Yes, Detective," Dr. Fishman interjected. "When we have group therapy sessions, we prefer to stay away from medical jargon. So, one of the exercises, we refer to it as Flex Therapy. It allows our students to learn by telling stories. They can pick anything they want. The point is to get them to inter-relate concepts in their minds. They each get a turn to stand up in front of other patients. It builds self-confidence," she explained.

"What was her story about?" Robinson asked, directing his attention toward Cassidy.

"I only caught a piece of it."

"You're doing fine, son."

"Well, it was something about being called a looney-bird and then it was, like, violent."

Diana looked up from her notes, her attention caught by the term. Her stomach lurched, thinking of Dan.

"How was it violent?" Robinson pushed.

"I don't remember," he said.

"Oh, come on!" Robinson said, standing up and walking over to Cassidy. "You were doing great. Don't give up on me now!"

"I'm not, sir!" Cassidy defended. "It was, like, a split second that I heard it. I didn't think about it until later. She wouldn't hurt a thing. I figured that it was a fantasy. They're just stories and it ain't my business. I'm telling you the truth!"

Robinson directed his attention toward Dr. Fishman. "Do you keep records of this Flex Therapy thing?"

"No, Detective. It's all fantasy. We don't have the manpower to write everything down. They're only stories, so..." she said with her voice trailing off.

"Diana?" he asked.

"Oh, no, did I get her into trouble?" Cassidy asked with concern.

"No, Cassidy, it's fine. Hold on one second. Diana? Any opinions?"

She looked at the Detective, thinking. "We might have something here. I can't be sure but..."

"But what?" he asked.

"I need some time with Louise. There's a direction that we could head, I think," she said, biting her nail. "If we're to do this, I need your full cooperation."

"Well, let's bring her in here!" he said quickly.

"I do it... done."

"What? In a court of law, that does me no good whatsoever! If I'm going to get a conviction on this case..."

Diana stood up from her chair and walked over to Robinson while everyone else in the room watched. "You promised me your full cooperation. I can guarantee you that, with all of these people present, she will fall into her shell. She has a problem with those in authority. It has to do with her past. The best that I can give you is a tape," she said, pointing toward the tape recorder in the center of the table. "I am not an officer of the law nor am I a lawyer. I'm a doctor and this is what I do. The number one priority is her health. You don't understand how delicate this is."

Robinson, obviously perturbed, stepped back.

"I'm on your side," Diana said.

"You don't understand the law," Robinson said. "This case will go out the window..."

"But, Detective," Diana said pointedly, "Whether you like it or not, justice has already gone out the window. There are two innocent people in jail. Let's focus on the truth and we'll worry about justice, later. Isn't that what we agreed on?"

"It stinks," he said.

"The truth," Diana said firmly. "We'll be lucky to get that."

Dr. Fishman spoke up. "If it's any help, what she's saying is true. Louise is as delicate as they come. A long term patient like this has little chance of recovery as it is."

Cassidy spoke up. "I don't know what I said but, please don't hurt her. She's a good girl with a good heart. I know that isn't much nowadays but she deserves a chance."

"Okay, okay!" Robinson said, backing down. "I don't like it but if that's how it has to be..."

"Thank you," Diana said. "If you all don't mind, I have a lot of work to do."

"Hey, am I gettin' fired?" Cassidy asked, nervousness in his voice.

Dr. Fishman looked at him. "We will take this matter under advisement."

"Doctor," Diana said. "They love each other. I think that he's been good for her. I understand hospital policy and, in any other case..."

"Besides," Robinson interjected, "we may still need him this afternoon. If we can come to a resolution on this case, he was a great help. I, for one, see no harm done."

Dr. Fishman put her glasses back on. "Make sure that you keep yourself available for the Detective. You have a certain amount of tenure here that is admirable. But," she said with an upraised finger, "keep this quiet and maybe it can be overlooked."

Needing no prodding, Cassidy hurried out.

"Thank you, Doctor," Diana said.

"I'll be in my office if you need anything," she said.

"And I'll be waiting outside," Robinson said to Diana.

"Thank you, Detective. Will you send Louise in?"

"Sure," he said. In the doorway, Robinson stopped and turned around, clearing his throat. "It would appear that nothing is as it seems. Who's the detective now?" he said, stepping out.

Diana found the energy to smile.

She had just pressed the 'record' button on the tape player when Louise walked in, shutting the door behind her. Diana looked up. "Are you angry with me?"

Louise sat down in a chair and played with her hair.

"Louise?"

"I heard you," she said quietly.

"You're angry with me, aren't you?"

"A little," she said.

"Why are you angry?"

"Because I let it slip out," she said, her head down. "I always let things slip out and other people get into trouble because of me. He told me that if it came out, he would be leaving. People are always leaving me."

"Like your mother and your father?" Diana asked.

"I was bad. But, I'm getting better. Maybe I'll be going home, soon," she said, perking up a little. "But, then I'll be leaving Cassidy, won't I?"

"Maybe," Diana said.

"I don't want to do that."

"Why not?"

"Because I'll miss him like my brothers. They left and it still hurts sometimes. Like, especially late at night, when I get pictures."

"Pictures? Do you mean dreams?"

"Yes, like dreams, I guess. They're like stories in my head."

"Do you like stories?"

"Oh, yes, Doctor. I like stories a lot," she said, smiling.

"Would you like to tell me a story?"

She pondered the question for a moment. "I like to watch stories on television. I watch stories every night for two hours. There are short ones like Hawaii Five-0 and Starsky and Hutch. My favorite long one is Forrest Gump."

"Do you know what Flex Therapy is?"

"Oh, yes. Flex class. I like it a lot. Sometimes, those stories make me laugh."

"Would you like to tell me a story from Flex class?"

"Hmm. I don't remember any. It's easier to watch, first. Then, I'll get a story to tell," she said confidently.

Diana knew that she could hardly bring in a class full of students to get her started. But, she also had a deep suspicion where to trigger her. She had built to the moment and she had waited. She remembered Dan on the road and the visions of his re-surfaced memories. All she had to do was to place the key into the lock and turn it.

The tape ran silently in the background.

Diana sat forward in her chair, looking straight at Louise. "I want you to tell me a story about a blackbird," she said.

"A blackbird?" Louise questioned. "I don't know any blackbird stories."

"Hmm. Well, then, could you tell me a story about a looney-bird?"

Louise appeared to have stopped breathing for a moment, looking straight ahead, unblinking.

Diana waited patiently.

"Yes, I think I could tell you a story about a looney-bird. I don't like the looney-bird story, though."

"Please?"

A tear rolled out of her eye while the tape ran, sounding like the soft patter of rain on a cool, fall day.

And *the beast* screamed while the looney-bird sang a song of death...

46

CASSIDY

"Louise, you gotta pay attention when I'm talkin' to you. This is important stuff," Cassidy said as he walked around to the trunk of the Lincoln.

"I am, Cassidy."

"Well, you never know. You gotta plan on the worst. Come here and look at the things that I've set up for you."

Louise walked to the back of the car while Cassidy showed her the things that she might need, in the event of an emergency.

"Now, right back here, behind the spare, you got your jumper cables. You remember what to use them for, right?"

"Yes," Louise said. "If I leave the radio on or the headlights on, the car won't start. If it doesn't start, I get somebody to help me connect the cables. Positive is positive."

"That's right. Don't get no woman to help you. Get a man. If it's a stranger, you're better off with a man 'cause he's gonna know cars better. You got that?"

"We've done this many times, Cassidy. I'll remember."

"Now, here's a couple milk jugs of water for the radiator," he pointed out. "What are you going to remember?"

"Um, I have to watch the needle in front, the one on the left of the steering wheel. If it gets near the red part, I have to stop and let the car rest. Then, with a towel, I have to open the cap and pour water in," Louise said carefully.

"Good, Louise. It's gonna be hot so don't go forgettin' yourself. You watch that needle. Ain't no way I'm gonna be able to come pick you up. You don't want to get stranded somewhere. That's how bad shit happens."

"Okay," Louise said.

"There's spare towels back here, too. Don't you worry none 'bout getting them dirty. That's what they're here for. And I don't want no grease gettin' on the seat covers. You got that? They cost me about twenty hours of work a piece."

"I'll take care of your car, Cassidy. I promise! I did the driver's test well, didn't I?"

Cassidy wiped his brow, looking toward the late-morning sun. "It's gonna be hot today. Sorry about the air conditionin'. I don't know what's wrong with the damn thing. I put a piece of tape over the button so's you wouldn't hit it by accident. It's nothin' personal, just happened that way. You keep the windows down, you should be cool enough."

He shut the trunk and walked toward the driver's side of the car and opened the door. "I got you set up with sodas on ice. And, here is the best part," he said proudly, pulling out a map. He looked up to see Louise still standing at the rear of the car. "Hey, you gotta pay attention, Louise! Now, get up here."

"Sorry, Cassidy. I was just thinking," she said, walking up behind him.

"About what?"

"Oh, about Momma and Daddy and how happy they're going to be to see me.

"Yeah? Well, if you ain't paying attention, ain't nobody gonna be happy. Take a good look at this map. You only got eight hours before you have to be back here. Hospital's gonna think you're in town and they's gonna get awful suspicious if you don't get back in time. Besides, I'd lose my job, sure as shit, and we don't need that, do we?"

"Uh-huh," Louise said. "If you lost your job, I'd lose my only friend."

"Hey," Cassidy said, taking her hand. "Aren't I your boyfriend?"

Louise smiled and kissed him on his cheek. "Of course."

He let go of her hand and picked up the map. "Now, you know how to read it, right?"

"Yes. Those marks mean that it's a stop light and those marks mean that it's a stop sign," she said, pointing to each. "Those numbers there are the roads that I'm on and those big numbers mean that I put my speed on the big needle in front of the steering wheel. It's easy," Louise said.

"It should be easy," Cassidy commented. "I even got the landmarks where you gotta make your turn. I spent my whole day off yesterday drivin' up there. So, where you see this statue," he pointed, "that's where you turn left. If that statue ain't there, you stop and ask somebody, okay?"

"Don't worry. I know what I'm doing," she said confidently.

"Yeah? That's what you said when you messed up my alignment hittin' that curb."

"I told you I was sorry," she said, a wounded look in her eyes.

"Yeah, baby, I know. But you can't make no mistakes. You make a mistake, we find ourselves a whole shitload of trouble that we don't need."

"You sound like you don't trust me."

"Aw, I trust you or I wouldn't be givin' you my pride and joy. I still don't know why you're wastin' your time seein' them, though. If my parents left me in that damn hospital and can't find no time to visit, I don't see why you wanna bother with 'em. I figure they's a write-off, ya know?"

"But, it was an accident. They wanted me to learn to be good. You just see, they're going to love me again. And, then," she said, looking into his eyes, "I'll get to introduce you to them. If we ever got married..."

Cassidy reached in and opened the glove compartment, pulling out a stack of papers. "Well, don't you be talkin' about gettin' married 'til you get through this trip, okay? Now, look here. If the police pulls you over, you make sure you show them this paperwork. If they ask about insurance, you just tell them you forgot the paperwork, okay? I ain't got the money to afford it but they don't need to know that. That's why you gotta be careful about hittin' curbs and other cars. You pay attention when you're driving. Remember, don't be playin' the radio unless you're stopped somewhere. You don't wanna get yourself all confused, like you do. Okay?"

"No radio," Louise said dutifully.

Cassidy put the papers back into the glove compartment. "I guess that's it," he said.

"I guess so," Louise commented.

Cassidy took his watch off and placed it on her arm, fastening the strap. "Remember, you have 'til six o'clock to be here at the hospital, okay? No mistakes!"

"No mistakes," Louise said.

He put his hands on her shoulders. "Most of all, you remember that I'm proud of you. If we ever get through all this shit, maybe we *can* get married one day. I'd be the proudest guy in the world."

Louise smiled and kissed him on the lips. "Thank you, Cassidy. I'll be careful. I promise."

"Well, time's a wastin'. You better get going."

Louise got into the car and put her seatbelt on. She put the map next to her so that she could clearly see Cassidy's notes. Next, she pulled out a Coke and put it in the holder that he had set up for her. Quickly, she checked the controls on the panel and then made sure that the car was in 'Park' before starting it, her foot pressed on the brake.

Cassidy shut the door softly. "Be safe now. I'll see you tonight, right?"

"Good-bye Cassidy," she said, carefully turning the key in the ignition.

Everything seemed to be in order as she put the car into 'Drive', keeping her foot firmly on the brake. She looked up to see Cassidy looking worried, as if it was the last time that he might see her or his car. She smiled nervously, taking her foot off the brake and pressing the pedal on the right side. The car pulled forward slowly as she came to the driveway exit. Quickly, she pressed the left pedal at the stop sign, jolting her forward. She checked the street in both directions and then checked her mirrors, getting a final look from Cassidy in the rear-view mirror. Hesitantly, she waved, returning her hands to the ten o'clock and two o'clock positions. After two cars passed in front of her, she pulled out onto 5th Street, bumping off the curb on her right. Her soda splashed as she accelerated down the street.

Two blocks in front of her, she saw a red light. She glanced at the map next to her. She was supposed to make a right turn at the light, where the gas station had a picture of the cartoon character, Joe Camel. Just to be safe, she turned on the turn signal early. That street would take her to the Houghton- Hancock Bridge, headed south.

As she approached the light, it turned green. She knew that meant that she could go forward. Just in case, she slowed almost to a stop before turning, making sure that no one was coming through the light and no one was walking across the street. She didn't want to imagine what it would be like if she ever hit somebody. She remembered Cassidy's warning when she was getting ready for the driver's test. "You gotta remember that this car's a weapon. It's big and it ain't gonna be forgiving to you if you hit someone. They's gonna die sure as I'm gonna be tore up over you for dentin' my car. Babe, it ain't no lie."

She drove over the bridge, afraid to look down at the dark blue waters of the river. The height made her nervous. Her mind wandered to the thought of falling when she remembered that she had to concentrate. There was a left turn coming up. Carefully, after checking her mirrors for other cars around her, she moved over one lane. The car arched into the turn, its springs squeaking. Cassidy told her to ignore those noises. "You just pretend they ain't there!"

Once she had executed making the turn, she risked picking up the Coke to take a sip, keeping her eyes peeled on the road. The liquid washed down her throat, refreshing her. She glanced at the map and saw the yellow letters that told her to watch the big needle. She was going to be going fast at fifty-five miles per hour. As the car picked up speed, her hair started flying in all directions. She had forgotten to use a rubber band to tie it off. Suddenly, she couldn't see with it streaming in her face, scaring the daylights out of her. She tried to hold it back. Then, she remembered that she could roll up the window on her left side.

After the window was rolled up, she tried to enjoy the drive. Unfortunately, her stomach was dancing in nervous jitters. She wasn't sure if it was because she was scared of driving. Cassidy had told her not to be scared of it. "If you're scared, you're gonna crash, for sure." She didn't want that. Part of her kept thinking about Momma and Daddy. They were going to be proud of her. She would be driving up in a nice, big Lincoln and they would know that she was all right. If they liked her enough, maybe she could come home, again. Only this time, it would be for good.

She wondered what they would think of Cassidy. He was nice and he would treat them as nice as he treated her. Then, her brow furrowed. If she went home, she wouldn't get to see Cassidy, anymore. Well, maybe he could come and live with them in Marquette. He got along with everybody.

Suddenly, a huge noise made her jump out of her skin. She gripped the steering wheel, which started feeling wobbly. She looked in her mirrors and all she could see was a flat white wall behind her. What was that, she thought as panic caused her heart to race. She stared at the white-striped lines in front of her, remembering Cassidy's words of caution, "You gotta make sure that line's on one side or the other. If it's going in the middle, you're gonna crash, for sure! Make up your mind!"

What had Cassidy told her about two-lane highways? She had to stay between the lines! But, it was in the middle and she didn't want to crash. There was a wall behind her, making that noise again! What side? What side? Relax, she thought quickly. Make the line on the left! No! Make it on the right! She looked in her mirror on her side and yanked the wheel sharply to the left.

The car fishtailed and then caught traction as she saw the white line move to the right.

Moments later, the wall went by, a Red Owl symbol grinning as it went past. It was a big truck. She saw the driver put his hand out the window, the bad finger was upraised.

Once the truck was gone, she decided that she had to stop for a moment. Her heart wouldn't stop pounding in her chest. She wasn't going to make it! She forgot where she was on the map. Oh, no! She turned on her left turn signal and pushed the pedal on the left. The car slowed to a stop as she ran over the gravel.

She stepped out of the car, inhaling the fresh air as if it were the last breath that she'd ever take. Gradually, her breathing returned to normal. She sat in the front seat and stared at the map. Relax! She couldn't be lost already, could she?

She looked around her quickly. She saw a roadside park on the opposite side of the road. She looked back at the map and it made sense. She was supposed to make a left turn soon. She would be alright!

She took a couple of breaths, refastened her seatbelt and followed through with the ritual of starting the car and pulling back out onto the highway. Of course, she always checked her mirrors. Her stomach danced with excitement. After she had made the turn, the rest was easy. All she had to look for was the airport and the Michigan State Police building and then she would be close to home.

An hour and a half later, she saw the airport followed by the police station shortly thereafter. She was going to make it! Momma and Daddy were going to be proud of her. They would see what she had done!

She ran into a problem trying to decipher Cassidy's map. What were those boxes on the map? She couldn't remember what he had told her! He said it was important that she didn't forget! She almost pulled over when she saw a trailer park. That was it! Too bad that she missed the right turn.

When she saw King's Korner, she managed to pull in and turn around. A minute later, she was going up the steep road of Joliet. She made a right on Brule, recognizing her neighborhood. She knew right where she was! It was Allouez! She had made it! When she got to the driveway, though, she got scared. It was steep and narrow and the Lincoln looked too big for it. She couldn't risk crashing the car, not after she had gotten so far! She did the best she could by parking on the side of the road, just past the house. She didn't mind walking up the driveway. Momma and Daddy would still be proud of her, wouldn't they?

She walked up the steps toward the brass embossed black doors. It seemed like a long time since she had seen them last. As a matter of fact, normally, she would have walked through the garage door and into the laundry room, removing her shoes before going upstairs. But, she wasn't sure that was okay. If they were still mad at her, she would have to get permission to go inside. So, she figured it best to go to the front door and knock.

A thought crossed her mind as the doors loomed in front of her. What if they weren't home? Her plan would fall apart. She looked at her watch. If they weren't home, she would wait one hour on the porch steps. If they didn't show up by then, she would have to go back. She couldn't risk getting into trouble at her other home. Even worse, Cassidy would be angry with her because he had trusted her.

She knew very well what would happen if you broke someone's trust. Danny had done it a long time ago when she had slipped on their secret. She knew that the punishment would haunt the stories in her head for a long time to come.

Hesitantly, she knocked on the door. Butterflies moved in her stomach like the fish in the aquarium in the recreation room. Hearing no answer, she knocked again, a little louder this time.

She was just about to knock again when she heard the sound of the deadbolt as it turned.

Her heart lurched. Would it be Momma or Daddy? Or, would it be both of them? It seemed like forever before the door opened. She moved herself in front of the peephole so that they would know who it was.

Suddenly, the door opened, revealing Momma. "Can I help you?" she asked.

Louise looked at her. She looked different. Her hair seemed to be turning white. Had it been that long? She took a deep breath before she spoke, standing taller. "Hello, Momma," she said.

Momma stared at her for a few seconds without saying anything. Recognition flashed across her face.

Louise couldn't help herself. She stepped forward, over the threshold and threw herself into her mother's arms. "It's so good to see you!"

Momma fell slightly backwards with the weight of Louise, momentarily disoriented.

Louise felt something odd, something that she hadn't felt in a long time. It was as if Momma was peeling her away from her.

"What in God's name are you doing here?!"

"I came to see you," Louise said excitedly.

"You what? "

"I wanted to make you proud of me! I'm going to be better now. You'll see. We're going to be a family, again," she said with a smile.

Momma looked at her in the darkened foyer, her face stoic. "I can't believe this. How did you get here?"

"I drove here, Momma. Do you want to see my car?"

Momma looked at her with eyes as small as a bird's. "Why aren't you at the hospital? That's where we put you and that's where you were meant to stay!"

Louise didn't understand for a moment. Stay? Wasn't she supposed to be getting better so that she could come home again? "But, Momma, I thought that..."

"You thought what? You're a Goddamned looney-bird! You can't think! You can't even function, you nincompoop!" Momma said, storming off toward the kitchen.

Louise hurriedly followed her, seeing the rays of the afternoon sun grazing the linoleum floor of the kitchen.

Everything was starting to get confused. She passed the railing that led upstairs. It was all too familiar.

She remembered the sound of glasses crashing to the floor. It was something about the foyer, jarring a dust covered memory.

"Momma, I don't understand!"

"I'm calling the hospital. Maybe they can explain why you're not there! If your father were around, he'd have them sued!"

Louise stepped into the kitchen to see Momma rifling through a telephone book. "Please, Momma. Don't call them!" she said, thinking of Cassidy and how much trouble he would get in.

Suddenly, the doorbell rang. Momma looked up from what she was doing. It was as if time had come to a screeching halt with the two of them staring at each other, wondering about the doorbell.

The doorbell rang again.

Momma looked at Louise, hissing, "Don't you dare say a word! Do you understand me? You are to stay put until I come back. Is that clear?"

"Yes, Momma," Louise said.

Momma stormed out of the kitchen, leaving Louise standing near the telephone. She looked at the phone cord. Now was her chance. If the telephone wasn't working, Momma wouldn't be able to call the hospital. She would never forgive herself if Cassidy lost his job on account of her. She heard the front door open.

There were voices, soft at first. Then, they grew louder, more direct. Two people were fighting. Momma was yelling at her visitor!

Louise had to act quickly. She needed something to cut the wires of the telephone. She looked toward the center of the kitchen and saw a knife sitting on a cutting board on the counter-top where they used to eat their meals. Quickly, without glancing toward the foyer, she walked over and got the knife. She hurried back toward the telephone.

Suddenly, the front door slammed, echoing throughout the foyer. Louise looked up with trembling hands. She turned around just in time to see Momma come storming back into the kitchen.

"Go back to where you belong, you looney-bird! Go! I thought I had gotten rid of you!" she screamed at her.

Louise stepped back, afraid as she had been many a time before. She was confused and messed up. She didn't do anything wrong. She hadn't cut the phone cord, yet. Why was Momma so mad?

"Get out of my sight before I call the police! You damn looney-bird!" Momma screamed at her.

Louise's back was against the wall. She started crying. The noises, they turned everything around. "Momma, listen to me..." she begged, her hand raised.

Momma stopped in her tracks. "What are you doing?! Get out!" she screamed at the top of her lungs. Then, she saw the knife in Louise's hand. "Oh, you want to fight? "

Louise didn't have time to react as Momma's hand lashed out. Both of them struggled and Momma's head lolled sideways, the knife glinting in the sun. Red liquid surged out of the wound. *Oh my God BLOOD!*

It was all wrong! She didn't mean to do it! It was an accident, Daddy! I'm sorry...I'm sorry...I'm sorry...

Louise fell back on her butt, pressing her head between her legs, trying to close the dreams out. They wouldn't go away.

She didn't know how long that she had sat there. The sun had changed, growing dimmer as it fell over the window sill, orange rays washing the floor.

As she stood up, she saw the other man. What was another man doing here? Where had he come from? Who was he? What If Daddy saw him in the house?

Cassidy hadn't warned her about this!

Louise carefully stepped over her sleeping mother and touched the face of the man. He looked familiar. There was something about his face. But, his hair was long with a rubber band in it. He must have taken a long drive, too.

Danny oh Danny oh Danny oh Danny!

He groaned and somehow, it brought her to her senses.

She tried to shake him awake. "Danny? "

No answer.

Carefully, Louise felt his pockets for a wallet. He was sleeping but sort of awake, a groan emanating from deep inside of him. She opened the wallet, confirming her worst nightmare. She started sniveling uncontrollably, as if she had the unshakable hiccups.

She looked at her watch. Her heart jumped again. She had to go back to the hospital. She had to. But, she couldn't move. She kept thinking of the blood and the screams. Then, she remembered the sound of glasses crashing to the floor. Over and over again, it turned in her head as she tried to block a recurring vision of her mother standing on her chest in the hallway.

Answer me! Answer me! Answer me!

It wouldn't go away. She had to make it go away! The car! She had to get the car back or Cassidy would be gone!

Louise stepped out of the kitchen and walked into the living room, a deafening sound of silence was screaming in her ears. It had to stop!

Her arms reached behind a large curio cabinet and pulled. At first, it was unyielding. Then, it tipped forward. She pulled harder as adrenaline moved through her veins. Suddenly, it had a power of its own as it fell to the soft, white carpet. The resounding crash sounded like the glasses flying to the floor of many years earlier.

The daydreams were going away!

Glasses crunched under her feet as she grabbed the other curio cabinet using a greater strength to pull it down. She saw the black ebony table and picked it up, dashing it to the ground. The sounds made the dreams disappear.

And the beast screamed to an audience of the dead...

Louise dashed from one room to another, crashing and breaking everything upstairs in the bedrooms to downstairs in the living room. She walked by the study with her head pounding. Gleaming jaws grinned from the shelves. She didn't like skeletons. No, she didn't like skeletons at all! She passed the room as she thought of Danny. He had saved her many times, hadn't he?

She passed the basement without a glance. She remembered staying down there when Danny was babysitting. She didn't like the basement at all. Besides, she had a bigger problem.

If Daddy came home and found Danny there, he would be in trouble. It was Louise's fault this time. Daddy was a doctor. He could fix Momma. But, if he found Danny there...

Louise ran outside and down the steps. There was another car there! She stopped and stared at it. Slowly, she walked up to the driver's side and looked inside. No one was in there. Was it Danny's car?

She opened the door and looked inside, pushing a tape off the seat. She reached into the glove compartment, remembering where Cassidy had told her where the important paperwork was. She looked at the address on the registration. She had seen the road, Lakeshore Drive! She held the paper and ran down the driveway toward her car, looking for her map.

She looked at it for five minutes before she realized that Lakeshore Drive was just past the neighborhood across the street. If she could get Danny back there, then Daddy wouldn't be upset at him!

Before Louise went into the house, she put his registration back into the glove box. She had to hurry, she thought, glancing at her watch.

She walked into the kitchen, carefully avoiding Momma. Daddy would be home soon. He would help. He wouldn't help Danny, though, would he? Oh no, Daddy would be very upset with him.

Louise separated Danny's body from his mother's and pulled him toward the foyer, careful not to drag his legs through the puddle. He had grown and he was heavy. She panted heavily as she pulled him by the shoulders and out the front door.

She sat on the steps, leaving him to rest. She wanted to cry but she couldn't. She wasn't sure *why* she wanted to cry, anymore. She took a few deep breaths as the birds sang their songs in the woods next to the house.

Half an hour later, she had her map and Danny inside his car. She would have to take him home so that he would be safe. She wasn't sure if she could do it. But, she had no other choice. His head leaned against the window in the passenger's seat. He was sleeping, wasn't he?

Because when Daddy came home, he would surely be mad. He might even kill them.

***

"Because the looney-bird had to fly him home so that he'd be safe. She reached into his pocket and found his keys. She didn't think that she'd be able to get him up the steps. She was so scared. He made noises and he had blood on him. But, if he took a nap, then he'd be okay, wouldn't he? Tell me that he'll be okay, won't you?" Louise said as trembles of fear ran through her.

Diana stood up quickly and walked over to Louise, putting her arms around her.

"It's the looney-bird and she won't get better, will she? Will she?" Louise cried.

"Shhh," Diana said, calming her and stroking her hair. "Shhh. It's going to be okay, Louise. Everything is going to be okay. It's over..."

"Is it?" she asked, her tears soaking through Diana's chest.

"Yes, Louise. It is," Diana said, squeezing her close.

"The looney-bird had to run back to her car. She couldn't fly, anymore. She was scared. She thought she was going to get lost in Cassidy's car. She thought Cassidy would leave her, too. But, he didn't! He didn't! Nobody notices the looney-bird. So, it's okay, right?"

There was a light tapping on the door. Diana looked up to see Detective Robinson, tired and weary. She pressed her finger to her lips as she held Louise close, motioning silence.

Robinson nodded.

Diana pointed toward the tape recorder at the center of table, telling him to shut it off.

He picked up the player and pressed 'Stop'.

"Give us a few minutes, will you?" she said quietly.

"Sure," he answered walking back toward the door, the player in hand.

"Oh, Detective?"

"Yeah?" he said, pausing.

"After you listen to the tape, you tell me..."

"Tell you what?" he asked.

She looked him the eye, unyielding in her strength. "The victim or the crime."

47

TERRAPIN STATION

"But, Your Honor, the tape that the State has submitted is evidence of a coerced confession! Also, I'm finding that my client is incompetent to stand trial because she doesn't understand the nature and gravity of the offense," the Defense Attorney said adamantly.

"Whoa, Counselor," Judge Quinn said, removing his glasses and leaning forward on the bench. "How many things do you want to hit me with at once? I understand the publicity in this case but I will not tolerate this courtroom being made a mockery of. So, in that respect, I'm going to exercise my authority. This charade has gone on long enough!" he said, irritated. He took a deep breath and placed his glasses on, moving piles of paperwork in front of him. He looked at the attorney as if he were a student studying for the bar exam. "Do you understand the concept of *Sua Sponte?*"

"Well, yes, Your Honor," he said, stalling for time with a quick glance at his opened briefcase.

"Counselor?"

He took a quick drink of water, and then stood his ground. "If I recall, it means, 'The Court, on its own motion'."

"Correct," Judge Quinn said. "You're mixing apples and donuts. You have two issues present. The issue is not whether we have a coerced confession but rather that the defendant is incompetent to stand trial. In that, there is no reason to waste the court's precious time by making a determination on the evidence. So, the court, on its own motion, will schedule a competency hearing for the defendant. Is that acceptable to the State?"

"Yes, Your Honor," the Prosecuting Attorney said, standing up.

"Very good," he said, moving through his file. He put his glasses back on, leaving them on the end of his nose. He twisted his Cross pen and made a notation. "The hearing to make a determination of competency will be on November 25, 1996," he said with a tap of his gavel.

He looked down toward the two attorneys. "Now, how does the State stand with respect to the charges brought up against Daniel Wilcox?"

Dan looked at the cuffs around his wrists. This was the moment of truth. Diana and Detective Robinson had assured him that everything would work out. He tried to believe their words of encouragement. But, deep inside, he would believe it if he saw it. He knew the system and he knew that it could go in any direction. When his name was mentioned, his stomach jumped. Instead of looking toward the Judge, he looked down at his hands, as if he were waiting for a lazy lightning bolt to strike. He held his breath.

"The State is comfortable with having all charges dropped. The evidence doesn't support detaining him any longer. Further, his cooperation with the State was responsible for bringing this case to a resolution," the Prosecutor said, with a glance toward Dan.

"Let the records show that all charges are being dropped against said defendant, Daniel Wilcox," Judge Quinn said, holding the gavel in his hands. He nodded toward the bailiff, who walked over to Dan.

Dan let out a long sigh of relief, hardly believing his ears. His handcuffs were removed while the courtroom waited for the gavel to fall.

"Daniel Wilcox, will you please stand up?" the Judge asked him.

Dan looked around nervously, wondering what was next. He stood up and faced the judge.

Judge Quinn rested his gavel down. "If I may, Mr. Wilcox, I would like the records to show that The Court extends its apologies for any injustices that have been committed in the past. It would appear that an ex-colleague of mine was responsible for a great injustice. As you know, this case, in connection with a case from some twenty years ago, has received a lot of media attention. I, for one, take the media's rendition of facts with a grain of salt. But, my interpretation of the facts, based on the account of the recently unseated Judge P. Ferguson, has led me to believe that without the first injustice, we wouldn't be here today," he said calmly. "If I could personally go back and change the past, I would. But, I can't. The best I can do, in the name of The Court, is to say, I'm sorry."

"Thank you, Your Honor," Dan said shyly.

"Let's hope that we have all learned something today," Judge Quinn said with a firm rap of the gavel. "The Court will take a fifteen minute recess."

Suddenly, people were standing up and patting Dan on the back. His attorney shook his hand aggressively.

But, Dan's mind wasn't there. He was pleased with the moment but he was quickly trying to look toward the other side. A throng of people blocked his way. He tried to move ahead, step by step.

Mark appeared with a smile on his face. "You're free, Dan. How does it feel?"

Dan hugged his brother. "How the hell did we get out of this mess?" he asked in disbelief.

"A little faith goes a long way," Mark said.

Over Mark's shoulder, Dan saw the lady who had carried the ball over the goal line. She smiled back at him. Dan pulled himself away from his brother telling him to wait right there. "We still have something to do."

"I'm not going anywhere," Mark said.

Dan walked to Diana. He looked at her as if she were some great warrior who had slain the dragon. Without saying anything, they drifted into each other's arms, squeezing each other tightly. People bumped and moved around them with occasional pats on the back of congratulations. Dan savored the moment.

"Everything's going to be okay," she said.

His eyes felt ready to flood but he held it back. "This time, I think so."

Diana pulled herself lightly away from him. "Look, there was something that I wanted to say to you. Do you remember Maggie's Farm?"

"How could I forget?" he said warmly. Then, he shifted his weight uncomfortably. "Jail gave me a lot of time to think. I'm not sure that this is the right time to start anything up. I mean, I couldn't have gotten this far without you. But, circumstances were different. It's one thing to live in the moment..."

Diana leaned up and kissed him softly on the cheek. "I'll hold the memory dear to my heart. If I didn't have the legalities of my divorce, then it might be different. We need to get some balance back in our lives. You have to admit, that was a long, strange trip its been."

"I know," Dan said. "Besides, I think I have a book to write."

"A long awaited Rusty Wallace novel?" she asked.

"No," Dan said. "Not exactly. I might do something a little different this time."

"Well, whatever you do, I'm sure that it'll be the best," Diana said.

"No more pseudonyms," Dan said. "I like myself as an author with my name."

Dan felt a tapping on his shoulder. He looked behind him to see none other than Detective Robinson. At first, his heart lurched, trained to run from the cops.

Robinson held his hand out. Dan squeezed it firmly.

"I hope things work out for you," he said.

"Likewise," Dan answered.

"Look, I'd like to apologize for what I did to you about your father. The cemetery?" Robinson added.

"It's water under the bridge, Detective," Dan said, releasing his hand.

"Listen, I have one question for you."

"Yeah?"

"Why did you think I did it?" he asked.

The Detective looked at him and then reached into his pocket for his bottle of Excedrin and then, changed his mind. Instead, he scratched his head. "Among other things, you ran," the Detective answered. "Maybe, next time, you'll let justice run its own course."

"I promise you, Detective, there won't be a next time. As they say, that's it for the other one."

Diana jumped in. "Where's your brother?"

"Right over there," Dan said, with a quick wave toward Mark.

"Well, you have a have a lot of catching up to do. Good luck to you, Mr.

Wilcox," Robinson said, stepping away.

Dan smiled. A job is a job. You gotta pay the rent and do the best you can. Maybe cops weren't so bad, after all.

Mark walked up and joined them.

"I'm nervous," Dan said.

"Don't be, Dan. She wants to see the both of you," Diana said, leading them toward the front of the courtroom.

"What's going to happen to her?" Dan asked.

"In a case like this," Diana said, "everything depends upon the competency hearing. Remember, it was an accident, too. Of course, I've been asked, along with a number of other doctors at the hospital, to render an opinion. I'll be recommending therapy for up to three years. It's best for her. Don't worry, she'll be well taken care of," Diana said with a squeeze of his hand.

Suddenly, a camera was in their face. "I'm from Hard Copy, Mr. Wilcox. We're offering you five thousand dollars for an exclusive on you. What do you say?"

Dan looked toward Mark and Diana and then back toward the reporter. "Five grand? My agent said that you offered to do this story for twenty-five grand?"

"Yeah? Well, it's different now. You were on the run, then. It'll still make a great story!"

"Take the camera away. I think this is our story now," he said with a wink toward Mark.

Mark returned a shit-eating grin.

"But..."

"Excuse me," Dan said as they pushed their way forward.

Dan and Mark saw her standing there, looking lost and somewhat confused. She looked nothing like they had remembered yet she was as familiar as rain on a steaming, hot summer day. She carried the same look that she had before Momma caught her in the laundry room, before the swinging of a Spray and Wash aerosol can. The brothers were wondering what to do next. Would she be angry? Would she be resentful over ten lost years? Would she remember?

People were running about and it appeared that she was waiting for someone. She happened to turn, seeing Diana first.

"Diana!" she said happily.

Diana took her hand and led her forward. "Louise, these are your two brothers, Dan and Mark."

For a moment, it looked as if Louise didn't recognize them. Then, her features changed. She grabbed Mark, who was closest. "Oh Mark, you're safe! You look good!" she said, squeezing him as hard as she could.

Mark was at a loss for words, holding her tightly. They held each other as if they were the last two people in the world.

Louise looked up from his neck, seeing Dan. "Danny?"

In that second, Dan saw the woman in his resurging memories. It *was* her! He tried not to think about a knife, glinting in the afternoon sun. He also pushed away the memories of standing in a kitchen, waiting by a phone while Louise screamed in terror twenty years ago. Instead, he let the new feelings come in, one by one. New memories would be created as the old ones washed away. Life was about moving ahead. Mistakes were made but disappeared with forgiveness. Anger was replaced with a smile deep inside his heart.

As they walked up and held each other, tears flowed. Only this time they were different.

For the first time in their lives, they cried as if life had been born.

EPILOGUE

THROWING STONES

"Come on, Mark. Hurry it up, will you?" Dan called upstairs, his voice echoing in the foyer.

"I'm almost done!" Mark said.

"Well, it's clean already, okay! We've got some things to do before we take off. I'd like to leave this year some time," Dan said.

Mark came down the spiral stairway with a garbage bag in his hands. "I know, I'm detailed. But, the buyers paid over a million for the place. It ought to be spotless."

"Yeah, I know. Is that everything?"

"Yep," Mark answered.

"Good."

The two of them walked out to the front porch and then down the steps toward the garage. Both of them looked around for anything they might have left. Dan pulled out the remnant of a rotting stake, left there from a year before. Mark picked up an errant piece of paper and shoved it in his trash bag. They walked into the garage and pulled out the trash cans, wheeling them down the driveway. It was the last load from the last two months of cleaning.

They parked the cans and took a deep breath.

"Well, that's it," Mark said.

Dan kicked at the loose pebbles at the bottom of the driveway, remembering a night from a long time ago.

"You're not going to get sentimental on me, are you?" Mark asked.

"No more sentimental than I was at your wedding," Dan said, remembering Mark's marriage to Carrie, four months earlier. "I was just thinking; that's all."

"Well, stop thinking, will you? You've got a new book on the shelves and I'm off for two weeks. It took an act of God to convince Carrie that this was important," Mark said, tossing a small stone across the street. "I've killed one week working my butt off. So, how about we get on with the vacation?"

"Good idea," Dan said with a sigh, as he looked up the long, winding driveway of the house. It struck him that it looked like the corpse of *the beast,* empty and powerless.

"Come on, let's go. Didn't you say that we had a lot of stops to make?"

Dan checked his Marlboro Edition Swiss Army watch. He couldn't believe that it was three o'clock already. "Yeah, you're right. We have to stop at the real estate office so we can give the agent the key and pick up the check."

They walked up the driveway, leaning slightly into the incline.

"Does it ever bother you, Mark?" Dan asked, musing.

"I told you to stop thinking." Mark responded.

Dan stopped and walked up to a tree. It was just one of a virtual forest that had grown to surround the house. Squirrels danced in the leaves, scurrying and rustling, doing their business while birds chirped their language above, filling the air. The cool breeze was as fresh as the waters of Lake Superior. He could feel the toughened grain of the birch tree with the peeling, paper feathers.

Mark stopped and watched him, placing his hands in his pockets. He took a deep breath, taking in the freshness of the air, knowing that it would be one of the last on that forbidden driveway. The same driveway that had the heating coils in it so the snow would melt as it landed. As far as he was concerned, he would have enjoyed shoveling the driveway with his father. Well, when his father was in a *good* mood.

"It bothers you, too. Doesn't it?" Dan asked, feeling the silence.

"Sometimes," Mark said, looking at the sun through the trees. "You know what bothers me most?"

"What?"

"Remember that time that I spilled all my papers at the bottom of the driveway? It was the middle of winter. I was trying to get out of here as fast as I could and I messed it up. And he got me, anyway," Mark said, touching a long, lost world. "But how many neighbors knew about it?"

Dan thought about it for a moment. "I suppose we all have things that we want to protect," he said.

"Yeah," he said. "But sometimes I can't believe that we were put on this earth just to collect a bunch of toys. This house isn't what it's all about, is it?" he asked, waving his hand at the expansiveness of it.

Dan didn't answer. The ghost would always be there. The questions would always surface. But, in the end, it would disappear like the smell of an expensive cigar long after the person had left the room. It was time to continue the journey, the discoveries and the smiles.

The two brothers took a deep breath and started walking back up the driveway.

"We have to whip to the bank so I can get that money into Louise's account," Dan said, returning to the business at hand. "I guess Cassidy is pretty excited about getting his auto body shop going."

"Can you believe that in one year we're going to have a new brother-in- law? It's like the beginning of a new family," Mark said. He paused and then spoke carefully. "Carrie's hinting about kids..."

"I think you'd make a great father."

"It makes me nervous. I don't want to make any mistakes," Mark mused.

"Nobody's perfect, Mark," Dan commented. "So, you make a couple of mistakes. Learn from them and move on. You balance the good with the bad and you pray that the good wins in the end."

They came around the bend in front of the garage where Rose was sitting.

"Don't let me forget to stop at Valvoline. I want to make sure that Rose gets an oil change."

"I still don't understand why you call her Rose," Mark said. "She's about as red as a Radio Flyer wagon."

They walked around the VW bus while Dan slid the side door open.

"Haven't you figured it out? She's called Rose because of the song."

"What song?"

"You've got it on about fifty tapes, Mark. You don't listen to them or what? Does *Ramble On, Rose* ring any bells?"

Mark looked at him, standing toward the back of the bus. "I like the new sticker," he said in reference to where the FUKENGRUVEN sticker had been on Blossom. Now, it said, "Smile. Smile, Smile..."

"I found that a couple days after I bought this bus. It goes with the rest of the stickers quite well, I think. I wish you could have met her."

"Who?" Mark asked.

"Blossom," Dan said with a smile. "She wasn't as pretty as Rose but if her road wear could talk, it could have sang a symphony of experiences. Well, she's packed and ready to go. Shall we lock the house for the final time?"

"Let's get it over with."

They walked up the steps and stood in front of the brass-embossed, black doors. Dan searched his pocket for the key and handed it to his brother.

"You do the honors."

Mark took the key and placed it into the lock. He stopped, after turning it half way and looked at Dan. "We forgot something."

"What?"

Mark turned the key the other way and opened the door, stepping inside.

Curiously, Dan followed him through the foyer and down the steps toward the basement.

"You're going to have to hold me up," Mark said. "There isn't any furniture to stand on."

"No problem," Dan said.

Mark stepped into his folded hands and reached the tiles on the ceiling.

"Hurry it up, will you?" Dan said, grunting with his weight.

"I am! I am! Hold your horses!"

Dan could hear Mark searching as flecks of dust fell on his head. He strained as he supported Mark.

"I got 'em!" Mark said, triumphant. He jumped down and held his prizes for Dan to see. "Which Hot Wheels Flip-out do you want?"

"This one," Dan said, choosing the red '67 Camaro.

"Cool," Mark said, holding the black State Police car. "Now we can go."

Both of them ran up the stairs with one final look at the empty house. Mark pulled out the key as Dan pulled the door closed.

"Hey, Dan. Any final words of wisdom before I lock it?"

Dan thought about it a second. "Yeah."

"Keep it short."

"Okay. It's just a *Box of Rain.*"

"Good words," Mark said as he twisted the key into the lock. He pulled it out and handed it to Dan, who shoved it in his pocket.

They walked out to Rose, whose bright red color all but blinded them in the sun. Dan hopped in the driver's seat and started her up. She purred like a cat in front of a fireplace. He pulled out his cigarettes and pressed the lighter in while Mark slid her side door closed.

"Dammit!" Dan said, irritated. "I thought this thing was completely restored. Derry told me it was in perfect condition."

"What is it?" Mark asked.

"She's just like Blossom. The lighter doesn't work."

"Yeah? Well, at least this one doesn't have a radiator," Mark commented.

Dan smiled as he put her into gear and drove her down the driveway with a, Soldier's Field, Chicago, July 9, 1995, tape in the deck. Strains of *When I Paint My Masterpiece* tickled their ears, reminiscent of days of old but still as fresh as the day it was performed.

They dropped the key off at the real estate office in exchange for the check on the house. Before leaving, Dan reminded the agent that Cassidy would be by to look at the new house for Louise later that week.

Next, they stopped at the jeweler's and Dan picked up the package that he'd been waiting for. He was pleased with the jeweler's work. He hoped that she would like it. There was just one question he had for her and maybe, just maybe, it would do the trick.

After that, came the bank and the oil change for Rose. It was almost four o'clock before they were finished.

"Where do you want to stop next?" Mark asked.

"Well," Dan said, glancing at his watch. "I guess we'd save a little time by going to Diana's office first. The second stop is a little out of the way and I'd like to make it there before they close."

They drove down Washington Boulevard and found a place to park for Rose. The man in the Cadillac next to them shot the brothers a dirty look.

"Do you want to come up?" Dan asked.

"Nah," he answered. "I think you should enjoy this one. But, please, make it quick. We're on vacation, finally!"

"Back in five!" Dan said, shutting her door.

He walked into Diana's office a minute later, his two packages in hand. Diana happened to be in the reception area with an older gentleman. "I hope I'm not coming at a bad time," he said.

"No, no," Diana said with a smile. She walked up and hugged him. "It's always good to see you. Meet my mentor and friend, Clinton."

Clinton extended his hand. "It's a pleasure to finally meet you."

Dan shook his hand warmly. "No, the pleasure's all mine. I thought you were retired."

Clinton chuckled. "Yeah, me, too."

"We're partners, Dan. It just kind of happened. Remember when we were on our little trip?"

"Of course."

"Well, as would be expected, all my patients took a liking to him. It didn't make sense for it to be any other way," she said, glancing at Clinton.

"Besides," Clinton interjected, "The wife got used to me being out of the house. Said something like, she would need my services if I stayed retired any longer."

Dan handed the first wrapped package to Diana.

She looked at him with questions in her eyes. "What's this?"

"Just a little something," he said. "For all the work you've done with Louise; especially, for arranging her private care. I think that she and Cassidy are going to be very happy and that would never have happened without you."

Diana tore the wrapping off the small gift and opened the lid. Inside, she pulled out a gold necklace with a gold embossed medallion on it. "It's beautiful..."

"I had it made for you. You don't have to wear it if you don't want to," he said. "It's the Yin and Yang symbol. It means..."

"I remember, Dan. It means balance. Good and evil, black and white, work and pleasure and so on..." she said, placing it over her neck.

"You'd make a good Deadhead, Althea."

Diana smiled, remembering another world.

"And, I have one more thing," he said as he handed her the second package. "It's a copy of a book that I thought you might like to read."

Diana looked at the title, wondering. *Secret Life of a Juror: Voir Dire - The Domestic Violence Query* stared back at her, authored by Dan Wilcox. Ironic, she thought.

"Do you mind if I ask you a question?" Dan asked, a little nervously.

"Sure. Anything," she answered.

"Would you ever consider having a cup of coffee, sometime?"

"She'd like that a lot, Dan. Trust me, it's a little inside information,"

Clinton piped in. "Sorry! I talk a lot!" he said, toward Diana.

"Clinton, please," Diana said.

"Well?" Dan prodded.

Diana felt her medallion while the weight of the book settled in her hands. How long ago was Maggie's Farm? She looked at Dan, admiring his resilience. She took a deep breath. "Sure."

Dan looked at Clinton and then back at Diana. "Good! I'll call you when we get back. You never know, do you?"

"No, you don't," Diana said, flashing a smile, thinking of a kiss from a time of a long, strange trip.

Dan left as quickly as he had arrived. It was a good day.

Five minutes later, Dan and Mark ran into a flower shop and picked up a dozen roses. Then, they headed toward Presque Isle, turning on Wright Street. Dan parked Rose and the two brothers hopped out relieved that it closed at five o'clock instead of four o'clock. Now, it looked like they'd have everything done before their vacation.

"I hope it came out looking nice," Dan commented.

"Me, too," Mark said.

They walked into the cemetery as the sun played over the whitened stones. As usual, a cool breeze blew through the trees and whisked their hair.

When they reached the plots, neither boy said a word. Dan looked at the stone and placed the roses on the ground in front of it. His fingers felt along the words of the engraving on their mother's tombstone.

Mark put a hand on his shoulder. "It looks good," he said.

"The words speak for themselves," Dan commented.

Even though the dates and their mother's name was on there, that wasn't what they were looking at. The two brothers stepped back, as if to check the perfection of the etching.

'Such a long, long time to be gone and a short time to be there', by Robert Hunter.

The roses sat in the sun while the two boys walked away to take their vacation. Momma and Daddy slept quietly.

"Hey, can I drive, for once?" Mark asked.

Dan held the keys in his hand, remembering a scrap he had with Diana a long time ago, something about channel-surfing and the Grateful Dead tapes.

He looked at his brother and tossed him the keys. "When I drive, I get my choice of music, okay?"

"What are you worried about?" Mark said as he caught them. "I think our tastes are pretty similar, aren't they?"

"I suppose. And, no speeding! This isn't an airplane. You've got to handle her delicately."

"I don't tell you how to write so don't tell me how to fly," he said, checking underneath Rose for any possible oil leaks.

Dan stopped at the door, admiring her. "Hold on a second," he said.

"What is it?" Mark asked.

"There's something wrong," he said as he walked around the bus, inspecting her. "I feel like we're forgetting something."

"What could be wrong with her? She's in perfect condition," Mark said as he followed him to the back of the bus.

Stickers of every sort adorned the rear of Rose, looking very much like the Blossom of old. Instead, a new sticker held the throne: EVERYTHING I LEARNED ABOUT LIFE, I LEARNED ON THE BACK OF A VOLKSWAGEN BUS.

Dan scratched at his chin.

"What is it?" Mark asked.

"We're missing something or we're forgetting something."

Mark studied it for a minute and then walked toward the driver's side of the bus. A moment later, he walked up and handed Dan something. "It must have dropped out of your knapsack when I flew in to pick you and Diana up in Alabama. Is that what we're missing?"

Dan smiled, holding the tin plate, remembering a getaway from the law after the fire from Blossom's fiery demise "You can keep it. I have a new one. Do you got a screwdriver handy?"

Mark pulled out a Swiss Army knife and handed it to Dan.

Dan busied himself by screwing the new license plate, after taking off the temporary paper license. As he twisted the screws, he thought of Diana and a moment they shared, wondering.

The two brothers stepped back, admiring Rose's new namesake, fitting on her as well as it did on Blossom except this time, it read: "RATDOG".

"It's still missing something, though," Dan said.

Mark looked at it. "It's obvious."

"What?"

"Road wear," he said, walking toward the driver's side of Rose.

It made sense, Dan thought. "Precisely."

"You want to drive to California, see what's on the open road? I've got a week to kill."

"I thought you'd never ask."

The two of them hopped in the bus, with Mark behind the wheel. He started Rose and searched around for a tape. Finding one, he dropped it in.

He pulled out of the cemetery with his fingers tapping on the steering wheel while Mickey and Billy banged on the drums and Phil cranked out his bass, while Vince danced on the keyboards, Jerry performed magic with his guitar and Bob belted out the words to *Throwing Stones: And the politicians throwing stones So the kids they dance and shake their bones 'Cause it's all too clear we're on our own.*

Dan looked at his watch. It was shortly before five o'clock. He couldn't believe that they had to run the clock, again. "Dammit!" he said.

"What now?" Mark asked. "We're on vacation, aren't we?"

"We have to make one more stop and we don't have much time."

"I don't know what you're talking about."

"The license plate. We have to whip by the Secretary of State's Office before they close. The registration?"

Mark looked at his brother and smiled. "Alright," he said, accelerating. "I still hate rushing the clock, though. Can we take a vacation sometime this year?"

"Will you just shut up and get us there?" Dan asked. He watched the wrought iron gates of the cemetery disappear out of sight while Rose increased in speed, determined to beat the clock.

Maybe fear is the harbinger of strength, Dan thought. He was grateful that they were alive.

Fare you well, fare you well

I love you more than words can tell

Listen to the river sing sweet songs

To rock my soul

Goodnight, Jerry Garcia and Robert Hunter

The End

NATIONAL CHILD ABUSE HOTLINE:

1-800-4-A-CHILD (1 800-422-4453)

RECOMMEND THESE BOOKS:

A BOX OF RAIN:

COLLECTED LYRICS OF ROBERT HUNTER

(Copyright by Robert Hunter: Viking Penguin 1990)

DEADBASE:

THE COMPLETE GUIDE TO GRATEFUL DEAD SONG LISTS

BY

JOHN W. SCOTT, MIKE DOLGUSHKIN, STU NIXON

(Copyright 1993)

SEARCHING FOR THE SOUND:

MY LIFE WITH THE GRATEFUL DEAD

BY

PHIL LESH

(Copyright 2005)

DISCOGRAPHY

Grateful Dead: Jerry Garcia, Robert Weir, Phil Lesh, Mickey Hart, William Kreutzmann, Ron McKernan, Brent Mydland, Bruce Hornsby, Donna Jean Godchaux, Keith Godchaux, Vince Welnick, Tom Constanten, John Perry Barlow

(Paperback 6x9, 681 Pages)

ALTHEA by Hunter/Garcia 1979 *Go To Heaven* Ice Nine Publishing/Warner Chappell Music, Inc Pg. 491

BALLAD OF A THIN MAN by Bob Dylan 1965 *Highway 61 Revisited* Columbia Records Pg. 28, 35

BEAT IT ON DOWN THE LINE by Jesse Fuller 1967 *Beat It On Down the Line* RCA Studio A Pg. 473

BELIEVE IT OR NOT by Hunter/Garcia 1999 *So Many Roads (1965 – 1995)* Rhino Records/Arista Records Pg. 246

BERTHA by Jerry Garcia/ Robert Hunter 1970 *American Beauty* Ice Nine Publishing/Wally Heider Studio/Warner Bros. Pg. 493

BOX OF RAIN by Robert Hunter/Phil Lesh 1970 *American Beauty* Ice Nine Publishing/Wally Heider Studios/Warner Bros. Pg.90, 664

BRIDGE OVER TROUBLED WATER by Simon & Garfunkel 1970 *Bridge Over Trouble Water* Columbia Records Pg. 237

BROKE-DOWN PALACE by Jerry Garcia/Robert Hunter 1970 *American Beauty* Ice Nine Publishing/Warner Bros. Pg. 465

BUILT TO LAST by Robert Hunter 1989 *Built to Last* Ice Nine Publishing/Arista Records Pg. 322, 337, 343

CANDYMAN by Garcia/Hunter 1970 *American Beauty* Ice Nine Publishing/Universal Publishing Group/Warner Chappell Music, Inc. Pg. 335

CASEY JONES by Jerry Garcia/Robert Hunter 1970 *Workingman's Dead* Ice Nine Publishing/Pacific High Recording/Universal Music Publishing Group/Warner Chappell Music, Inc. Pg. 264

CASSIDY by Robert Weir/John Barlow 1981 *Reckoning* Ice Nine Publishing/Arista Records Pg. 632

CHILDREN'S LAMENT by Robert Hunter 1974 *Tales of the Rum Runners* Ice Nine Publishing/Round Records Pg. 74

CHINA CAT SUNFLOWER by Garcia/Hunter 1969 *Aoxomoxoa* Ice Nine Publishing/Pacific Recording/Warner Bros. Pg. 212

CRAZY FINGERS by Garcia/Hunter 1975 *Blues of Allah* Ice Nine Publishing/Rhino Entertainment Pg. 394

CRY DOWN THE YEARS by Robert Hunter 1987 *Liberty* Relix Records/Ice Nine Publishing Pg. 168

DARK STAR by Garcia/Hunter/Hart/Kruetzmann/Lesh/Weir/McKernan 1969 *Live Dead* Ice Nine Publishing/Universal Music Pub./Warner Chappell Music. Inc. Pg. 438, 464

DAYS BETWEEN by Garcia/Hunter 1993 *So Many Roads* Arista Records/Rhino Record Pg. 62

DEAL by Garcia/Hunter 1972 *Garcia* Ice Nine Publishing/Warner Bros. Pg. 206